ONCE UPON A CRIME

ONCE UPON A CRIME

Once Upon A Crime Trilogy: Book One

NOLON KING

Chapter One

YEARS earlier
  Outside the cabin
  Mission Station, Pennsylvania

THE COKE OVENS called to him. A battery of twenty-five of them, parallel to the train tracks, cut into the earth. He'd been obsessed with them for years. How he longed to step inside, explore their lengths. Despite what Mother said, he didn't think they were dangerous. He dreamed they were portals to a magical land, like Narnia. A place full of wonder and whimsy. Full of creatures who would love him. Protect him.

Sacrifice for him.

The Pevensie kids had a wardrobe. Perhaps he had the coke ovens.

The pull toward them — toward escape — was powerful.

Mother was more powerful.

She forbade him to go near them. And he would not cross her. Didn't dare consider it.

Father once told him the openings reminded him of mouths — gaping maws, waiting to devour disobedient children who got too close.

But most of the time, Father said they made him think of Hansel and Gretel and the oven in the woods.

Lord, how he hated that story. Which was probably why Father told it so often.

He suspected Mother had told Father to say those things. Father did everything Mother said. And nothing else.

Father obeyed, as a dutiful husband did. As a dutiful son should, too.

Now, at last, he'd found a way to escape Mother without breaking her rules.

He stood on the tracks, the breeze rustling his hair as it blew through the trees, his feet vibrating with the force of the train chugging toward him. The ovens now looked less like tunnels to freedom and more like the holes on a flute, just waiting for the wind to pick up and play a dirge in his honor, harmonizing with the shrill whistle of the engine hurtling his way.

Escape. It was so close now. Just a few moments more. He'd never get to learn the secrets of the ovens, but he'd be free. And his unsatisfied curiosity was a small price to pay for liberation.

The wheels beat a frenetic, staccato rhythm.

So close.

The whistle shrieked a panicked alarm.

Any second.

The *click-clack, click-clack, click-clack* turned into an ear-splitting squeal.

He closed his eyes and smiled. No brakes could stop

the train fast enough at this point. Escape was imminent. Inevitable.

Inviting.

His pulse raced, not from fear but from anticipation.

Talons dug into his forearms.

His heart, along with his hopes, plummeted.

He looked back and up into Mother's face, her usually pale complexion flush with fury, her sharp features slanted with the effort of savage strength.

She yanked him off the metal rails. Jerked him clear of the speeding locomotive.

The screeching gave way to the rhythmic *click-clack* again as the cars rumbled past with a gust of hot air and an angry warning blast.

He'd been inches from freedom. It might never get so close again.

As he sprawled on the ground at her feet, she loomed over him, chest heaving from exertion and rage, eyes narrowed in accusation and bright with insanity. "What were you thinking, boy? Were you not told to stay away from the tracks?"

Mother had forbidden him to *cross* the tracks and ordered him not to *play* on the tracks. But she'd never said he couldn't *touch* them, and he certainly wasn't *playing*. Pointing out such a distinction, however, would only make his punishment harsher. So, he said nothing.

"I asked you a question." She hauled him up by the front of his shirt, held him nose-to-nose with her, so his feet dangled above the ground.

"I'm sorry, Mother."

"I'll ask again. What. Were. You. Thinking?"

"I made a wish … " But finishing that sentence would be worse than explaining he hadn't technically broken her rules.

She set him down. Slowly. Deliberately.

He'd rather she'd dropped him.

Mother straightened his clothes. She licked her thumb to smooth down an errant strand of his long hair, then wiped what he assumed was a smudge off his cheek.

He struggled not to flinch from her ministrations, gross though they were.

"You know Mother loves you."

"Yes, ma'am."

"And I only do what I do to protect you from the dangers of the world."

"Yes, ma'am."

"How do good parents show their love?"

"By setting rigid boundaries and stringently enforcing the rules."

She scowled.

"Ma'am."

A thin smile crossed her face, turning her expression from psychotic to merely severe. "Then you know what to do, yes?"

He swallowed past a lump in his throat. Nodded when he couldn't find his voice.

"Tell me."

Tears welled in his eyes, but he willed them not to fall. To show weakness at this point would only make things worse. "Go inside." His words were soft, tremulous. When she scowled, he lifted his chin and summoned the strength to speak with conviction. "Retrieve your switch from the wall." She hung it there as a deterrent, though seeing it daily didn't keep him from breaking her litany of rules. What he'd done today was proof of that.

But he dare not tell her that, either.

"Then?" she prompted.

"Take off my clothes. Bend over, hold my ankles. Wait for my punishment."

"Very good. Afterward, if you don't cry, I'll read you a story. I think 'The Fisherman and His Wife' is appropriate for this situation since you spent the morning *wishing* for things" — she spat the word — "when I've already given you more than you need. Now, run along. And tell your father to join you. He needs to learn to be disciplined, principled. Vigilant. When I tell him to watch you, I expect him to do so. Diligently."

"Yes, ma'am."

"Go on. I will be in shortly."

She might follow him immediately; she might make him wait — naked and nervous — for hours. He never knew what she would do.

And the unknowing, the dread? That was sport to her, part of the punishment. The way she toyed with his mind and trifled with his emotions was worse than the beatings, worse than the humiliation.

Well, maybe not worse. But at least as bad.

At last, she'd won. His spirit was broken. His will, crushed.

Despite the dread gnawing his guts, he didn't dawdle. He ran off to find his father, praying the search would be short and simple.

The longer it took him to comply with Mother's orders, the worse he'd have to endure.

Chapter Two

CHELSEA PULLED a long blonde hair off her lapel, wiped damp palms on her pants, then took a deep breath. She'd been walking in the same door for more than six years, but today was different. No uniform this time. No silver shield.

She fingered the gold badge clipped onto her belt and smiled.

Goodbye, Officer Sullivan. Hello, *Detective* Sullivan — first female to make the grade in Zone Four. Dad would be—

Nope. Not going there. Today was too big a day.

A quick tip of her head left then right yielded a *pop, pop* in her neck, releasing some of the tension she was holding. Captain Davenport said she'd be meeting her new partner first thing this morning. She dearly hoped to be paired with someone like Charlie Paxton or Norm Anderson … a kind, experienced detective. Compassionate, patient. Someone with a keen eye, a couple decades of experience, and infinite wisdom he'd be happy to pass down.

"You just going to stare at it all day, Sullivan?" Delfino

approached her, cup of coffee in one hand and glazed donut in the other. "In or out, I don't care, but open the door for me, would ya?"

"If I'm going to be your doorman, you could have at least brought me a danish." She swung the door wide and gestured for him to proceed.

"Got to earn it, Chels. It's your first day. You should be buying for us." He headed for his desk without waiting for her reply.

Just as well. She didn't have a comeback, anyway. Even though she'd known these guys for years, she'd never been "one of the boys" and hadn't developed the ease of banter so many of the uniforms had with them. He'd referred to the detectives as "us" while excluding her from the club. Well, she was a detective now, too, and it was time they all came to terms with that. It wasn't totally his fault, though. She needed to do more to foster those relationships. Maybe she'd bake cookies and bring them in tomorrow.

Sure. Look like the new girl who's trying too hard. And *baking*, for Pete's sake. How Stepford could she be?

She sighed and headed for Davenport's office. The door was closed. Smoothing back a few stray strands of hair, she briefly rethought the wisdom of a ponytail. Reached for the band to release it. Decided to leave it in and lowered her hand. This was ridiculous. Shaking her head at herself, she rapped three smart knocks on the window.

"Come in." Davenport's gruff voice didn't even sound muffled through the glass.

Chelsea took one last deep breath, swung open the door, then stepped inside. She tried to hide her disappointment that her partner wasn't already there. But maybe it was better that she arrived first. Wouldn't want him to think she was tardy.

Her thoughts pinged back and forth so fast, she was getting motion sick.

Crazy. She was being totally nuts. Nerves were pointless. Irrational. She'd earned her spot, same as the rest of them had.

She forced a smile on her face, affecting an expression of composure she didn't feel. When she spoke, her tone was soft, measured. "Good morning, Captain."

"Take a seat, Sullivan."

Chelsea slipped into the chair across from him.

His phone rang. He held up one finger to her while grabbing the receiver with his other hand.

As he barked orders at someone — somebody who had clearly done something wrong, poor thing — she glanced around the room. If possible, it was even messier in there since she'd last been summoned to his office. Her fingers itched to straighten his papers, dust his shelves, organize his books. File the stack of folders threatening to topple over and scatter across his scarred linoleum floor.

The resounding *ding* of a handset slamming onto a phone base cut off her thoughts.

The captain's eyebrows were drawn down in severe slants, and his face was turning an alarming shade of red.

"Everything okay, sir?"

He waved his hand. His forehead smoothed, and his coloring returned to normal. Ish. "I wanted to officially introduce you to your new partner."

She looked over her shoulder.

"He's not here yet, Sullivan." He rolled his eyes.

"Want to give me a hint, then?"

The corners of his lips quirked. "I'm glad to have you on the squad, Detective. Your calm demeanor is going to be good for all of us."

Calm demeanor? If he only knew. She hid her manic nerves behind a smile.

Davenport leaned back in his chair. "Have you heard of Jim McPherson? Detective in Zone Two?"

Who hadn't? The guy was a legend. Highest cases-closed ranking in the city. And several colorful stories about the ways he arrested some of his more nefarious collars. He was a maverick. A bit on the wild side for her taste, but his numbers couldn't be argued with. "I believe so, yes."

"Well, then the introduction can be quick."

"He's Zone Two."

"Yeah. I just said that."

She shook her head. "I'm sorry. I don't understand. Are you transferring me? Already?"

"McPherson is transferring here. And I'm pairing him with you."

"Why in God's name would he want to transfer from Downtown to College Row?"

Davenport's eyebrows arched.

Chelsea cleared her throat. "What I meant was, he'd already made a name for himself in Zone Two. Why would he transfer to Four? Or any other zone?"

"Why don't you ask him yourself?" Davenport looked over her head. "Come on in, Jim."

She turned and followed the captain's gaze. So much for a kind, wise, near-to-retirement detective as a partner. The man strutting through the door was in his prime. He wore a roguish demeanor like a coat, and attitude rolled off him in palpable waves. On many men, the bravado and swagger would be affectations to hide insecurities. But his reputation proved otherwise. His long legs could quickly eat the distance in a street race, and his broad shoulders and bulging biceps indicated a strong fighter. He was supposed to be off-the-charts smart, too.

Keywords there had to be *supposed to be*. No one was a complete package. Had to be something wrong with him.

He sported a wicked grin and a sparkle in his eyes that would have most women turning to goo.

But she wasn't most women.

She extended her hand. "Detective Chelsea Sullivan."

Even though she was seated, his gaze raked over her — head to toe and back again. She bristled under the scrutiny. Absolutely hated when men did that. To her or any other woman. Couldn't imagine disliking anyone more upon first meeting.

Then he spoke.

"Sullivan, huh?" McPherson took her hand. His grip was warm, firm.

The shake felt far more intimate than a colleague's touch should be. She yanked her hand free.

He cocked an eyebrow. "Knew a Lieutenant Cormac Sullivan."

She gritted her teeth against the reminder. Despite all her efforts to make her own name for herself, people were always going to think of her as Sully's daughter.

Then they'd wonder if her apple fell far from his tree.

"We called him Sully. Hell of a lot easier than Cormac. Easier than Chelsea, too. Mind if I call you Sully?"

"Not if you don't mind being ignored."

His grin widened.

"Running a bit late today, Jim," Davenport said.

Took McPherson a second or two to turn his gaze from Chelsea to the captain, but when he did, his sneer became more of a smile. "The older I get, the harder it is to get out of bed. Particularly when there's a naked woman in it."

Chelsea clenched her teeth. And her fists. And pretty much every other body part.

"Old?" Davenport shook his hand and gestured to the chair beside Chelsea. "You're still a young buck."

McPherson folded himself into the seat next to her, scooting the chair a bit closer in an almost imperceptible move.

What was he up to? That was her personal space, darn it. And she couldn't shift away without it being noticeable. Was it a test? If she moved, she failed? If she stayed, her observational skills were subpar?

Or she was overreacting to a simple chair scoot. Could have been an accident.

Seriously, she needed to get a grip.

Her nostrils flared as she vented a breath through them. Probably looked like a snorting horse. Not that she cared what she looked like to him. She fought to control her breathing.

Did he have to look so smug? Why couldn't she have been paired with Charlie or Norm?

How long did a detective have to wait before requesting a new partner?

The captain was talking — she didn't know for how long or about what — but the mention of her name pulled her back to the conversation. And before she could figure out what she'd missed, his phone rang.

Again, he held up his finger to pause the discussion while he took the call. "Davenport."

She glanced at McPherson out of the corner of her eye. He rested his ankle on his knee, sprawled in his chair, and idly tapped his fingers on his knee.

Talk about an annoying habit.

Chelsea racked her brain for something witty or intelligent to say while they waited, but nothing came to mind. Well, if he could stand the awkward silence, so could she.

At least until she pled her case to the captain and got a new partner.

Davenport hung up the phone. "Looks like this meet-and-greet is over. You'll have to get to know each other on the fly. You've got your first case. And it's a doozie."

JIM DIDN'T NEED a cup of coffee, a bathroom break, or any other stall tactic before hitting the road, but his new partner had requested one. Gentleman that he was, he didn't refuse her. Didn't even comment.

Jury was still out on whether them teaming up was going to work, though.

He was an excellent judge of character. First impressions of merely a few seconds were usually enough for him to make up his mind about someone.

That's what perplexed him about Sullivan. He couldn't get a read on her.

Seemed smart, diligent. Almost *too* good.

The kind of detective who would make a difference in the community.

Then again, that was exactly the reputation her father'd had, once upon a time. Could be a like-father/like-daughter situation. This might all be a ruse.

If the scuttlebutt about Sully's indiscretions were true.

He had no reason to believe they weren't. And, based on personal experience, every reason.

Jim zipped up, walked to the sink. Washed his hands. Though he tipped his head toward the soap dispenser like it was the most fascinating invention on the planet, he kept an eye on the mirror, clocked the three cops who ambled into the room.

Three cops talking a little too loudly about a situation they had no knowledge of.

"Rumor has it he's an addict. When he was undercover with Vice, got in too deep. Became reality for him."

Clearly, they hadn't done their homework. Jim had never worked Vice, never been undercover.

"I heard he's rich."

Did he? Jim pumped the soap dispenser a tad too hard.

"His family made their money in the seventies by selling weapons to the Vietcong. Been supplying one group of bad guys after the next ever since. Sonny Boy here has an arrangement with the *capobanda* downtown. Been stealing seized weapons and putting them back on the streets."

Vietcong? Sonny Boy? He scrubbed his hands nearly raw before he rinsed off the suds.

"People been saying you killed your partner."

The third moron didn't even bother talking *about* him. Said it right to his face. Well, to his back.

Not much difference when it came down to it. The guy wanted to engage, so he'd engage.

He ripped a stream of paper towels from the dispenser. As he dried his hands, he turned to face his accusers. Looked down at them as they shuffled out of his reach.

Okay. Face-to-face made a little difference.

Jim made a show of looking right and left. Then he stared down the middle stooge. "I don't see anyone else in here, so I assume you're talking to me."

No reply.

"Something you need to get off your chest?"

One of them scooted toward the door. Another took a step back. But the moron between them stood his ground. Took a modicum of courage to do that. Or a whole lot of stupid. Either way, Jim ignored the other two and focused on him. "Well?"

The uni cleared his throat. "Just that we don't want any dirty cops in our house."

"And I'm to infer you mean me?"

"I don't know what you infer—"

Jim was pretty sure the guy didn't know what that meant.

"—but I'm not afraid to say it flat-out. We heard you're on the take. Betrayed your partner. This isn't Downtown. This is College Row. Just a bunch of good kids from nice families, working hard to better themselves."

He was clearly out of touch with campus life.

"Keep your extracurricular activities away from those kids. Don't tarnish the badge or the brotherhood, and we won't have to mess you up. Got that?"

"Little man, you've got a lot to learn." He bumped the guy's elbow on his way to the door.

When thick fingers wrapped around his wrist, Jim stopped. Turned. Looked down at them then up into the guy's face.

"I'm not done talking to you, McPherson."

He slowly pried the man's stubby mitt from his forearm. "Yeah, you are. *Brother.*"

The other two cops slid out of his way as he strode to the door. As he left the room, the loudmouth called after him, "This isn't over!"

Jim had a feeling that was true.

Chapter Three

CHELSEA SCOWLED out the passenger-side window of their unmarked SUV. McPherson had insisted on driving. Which, if she wasn't in a foul mood, she'd admit she preferred. Steel City traffic was dreadful at a good time of day, let alone during rush hour. And they'd caught the tail end of the morning gridlock.

No, it didn't bother her that he was driving. It bothered her that he just assumed he would. It was never a discussion. Either he thought he was her superior — and even though he had more years on her, they were the same rank, thank you very much — or he thought all men were.

Neither option sat well with her.

He hit a button on the center console and started fiddling with menu options.

She crossed her arms and huffed. "Could you please focus on the road?"

"I can multitask, you know." Another few buttons, then country music blared from the speakers. "Besides, we're in bumper to bumper. I'm not even moving."

Chelsea leaned over to turn down the volume. "We're on our way to a murder scene."

McPherson's forehead wrinkled. "Yeah. So?"

"So, don't you think music is inappropriate?"

"We're not at the scene yet. It's not like I'm line dancing over a corpse."

"Thank God for that. But we should be preparing, not listening to 'The Thunder Rolls.'"

"It's a country playlist. I didn't specifically choose this. Besides, I didn't figure you for a rap fan."

"Is that all you have? Songs about murder?"

"Not all rap is about murder. And there's no proof this song is, either."

"It most definitely is. In concert, Brooks plays a final verse where the wife gets her pistol. Even ends the song with the sound of a gunshot."

"And you wouldn't know that if you weren't a country music fan. Seen him in concert?"

This was *not* the way she wanted them to get to know each other. "Could you please turn that off?"

"Don't suppose you'd want to listen to rock?"

She glared at him.

"Fine." He turned off the music. Traffic began the slow crawl forward. "So, what do you think we're going to find? Strangulation? Stabbing? Poison?"

"Men don't typically use poison. That's primarily a woman's weapon. So, unless she was in a homosexual relationship, that likely won't be the cause of death."

"And what page of the manual was that on?"

Her cheeks burned. "I didn't learn that in the academy. Or in college."

"First-hand knowledge, then?"

"Can you please just stop? A woman is dead. Show some respect."

"How am I disrespecting her? She's not even here. And I was talking about you."

Chelsea cracked her neck again. She definitely needed a new partner.

"Why so tense, Sully?"

She clenched her teeth. "Do. Not. Call. Me. That."

"Touchy." He glanced at her. "Is it because it's your … never mind."

If he so much as mentioned her time of the month, she'd punch him.

They finally made it to the intersection, and McPherson turned down Fifth Avenue. A few silent blocks later, they were parked in front of an old stone apartment building equidistant from Steel City University and Alcoa College. Twenty or so college-aged people milled about on the sidewalk and in the lobby, many in tears or hugging each other. Or both.

"Looks like the tenants are mostly college kids," he said.

She bit back a sarcastic retort. "Let's go see what we've got."

"Scan the crowd on the way in. Killers often linger to admire their work." McPherson led them, somehow making his slow pace look casual.

There were too many people for her to commit any of the faces to memory. None stood out as looking more energized than the others. She kept her head on a swivel as she followed her partner.

The officer at the door let Jim in but stopped her.

Chelsea got a tingle flashing her gold detective's badge for the first time, followed immediately by shame. How could she be so selfishly prideful when there was an innocent life cut short in the same building?

She found McPherson by the elevator. At least he waited for her.

"What took you so long?"

Scratch that. Too bad he waited for her. She'd have preferred the time apart. Instead, she found herself pressed against him in a rickety elevator. "Would you please move over? You're in my personal space."

"Sorry. I thought more people were getting on." He stepped a few inches to the right.

"You have a problem with boundaries."

"Funny. I'd have said that about you."

Chelsea glared at him, but he didn't have the courtesy to notice. He just looked straight ahead. And she silently seethed.

The bell dinged, the doors slid open, then they stepped out into a cocoon of beige — carpet, baseboards, walls, ceilings. Everything had a bland, depressing tinge. What a sad place to live.

Sadder place to die. Not that there was a happy place.

Noise from the crime scene reverberated down the unadorned hallway, but she couldn't see the room yet. Chelsea turned left toward the victim's apartment, McPherson right at her elbow. She stopped, stared at him. Stepped away. "Like I said. Boundaries. Internal and external."

"If you mean I'm candid, and like the company of women, I don't consider either of those things an issue."

"That's not what I meant." Well, it wasn't entirely.

"Then, by all means, enlighten me. You clearly have something on your mind. Let me have it, then we can move on." He leaned against the wall and waited, an expectant look on his face.

His calm demeanor only made her angrier. "Since we met, you've dismissed me based on my gender, behaved inappropriately in the vehicle, and implied I'm hormonally-compromised because of—" Her cheeks heated, and she hated herself for it. Chelsea cleared her throat then lowered her voice. "You insinuated it was my time of the month." She continued in a conversational register again. "All this among various other less-offensive yet still annoying behaviors. And we've known each other for less than thirty minutes! How am I supposed to work with such an arrogant, selfish misogynist?"

McPherson tucked his hands in his pockets and crossed one foot over the other. His posture was relaxed, but she glimpsed something much harder in his eyes. "One, I don't have a problem with women. I fucking *adore* them. Two, there's nothing wrong with listening to music in the car. Sorry, you don't share my taste in tunes, but the selection was innocent. And three, I don't know what hormonally-compromised comment you think I was about to say, but I haven't so much as thought anything of the sort, let alone stopped myself from blurting it out. Don't put words in my mouth. Detective."

Aside from the sarcastic emphasis on her title, he sure put her in her place. Maybe she'd read him wrong. An apology was on the tip of her tongue when she remembered their conversation in the car. "You almost had me. Almost. But you did nearly say it. You stopped yourself, but the implication was there."

McPherson shrugged. "I give up. How did I imply something I didn't mean?"

"You told me I was touchy, then you said, 'Is it because it's your … never mind.' You were going to ask if it was my time of the month. Something you'd never ask a male colleague." Vindicated, she squared her shoulders and lifted her chin.

Shaking his head, he pushed off the wall. "No. I was

going to ask whether it was because your father went by that nickname, and you didn't want the comparison, but I thought maybe we didn't know each other well enough for me to pry into your family baggage." He strode down the corridor then rounded the corner without looking back.

His proclamation deflated her. She'd been so sure he thought little of her. Of women in general. But instead of calling him out for insulting her, she'd insulted him. And embarrassed herself.

Crappy start as a detective, all things considered.

Chelsea chased him down the hall, but she didn't have a chance to straighten things out with him. After being forced to flash her badge — again, which was much less gratifying the second time — she took booties and gloves from her pocket, slipped them on, then joined her partner inside.

And her first day went from crappy to downright crestfallen.

The girl — and legal adult or not, she was just a girl — had been stripped naked and posed on her bed. She lay on her back with her eyes closed and hands clasped together, resting on her navel. The expression on her face was almost peaceful.

It was the creepiest thing Chelsea had ever seen.

A chill raced through her. It was a fifty-fifty guess as to whether it was from the look on the victim's face or from the frigid air blowing through the open window. "Who leaves a window open in February?"

"That's the first thing you noticed?" McPherson asked.

"No. But it's awfully cold in here. Can't we close it?"

"Not until MCU is done processing the scene. Anything could be relevant. Even an open window."

Steel City PD's Mobile Crime Unit was one of the best in the country. Didn't mean they were fast, though. If anything, their thoroughness made them slower. The crime scene investigators didn't miss anything, and such detailed analysis took time.

Chelsea pulled her blazer tighter across her midsection, trying to ignore the brisk wind. And the occasional snow flurry that breached the screen. She stepped closer to the bed then peered over the ME's shoulder. A thick, silken cord was wrapped around the girl's neck. "What an unusual rope."

The medical examiner checked the liver temp. Then he stood aside to offer Chelsea more room. "Look again."

She bent down and stared at it. It wasn't a twisted cord. It was a braid. The color and texture matched the vic's hair precisely. And based on the hack-job Chelsea had originally thought was a choppy, tousled cut — a college girl's trendy alternative to super-long locks — the killer had cut it from her head.

Chelsea stood and looked around the room. Photos of the girl with friends or family dotted the walls — and her hair was down to her waist in every one of them. Another chill ran through her. This was familiar. All too familiar. And all too disturbing.

The murder reminded her way too much of Grimm's fairy tales. Her father had delighted in reading them to her when she was young. Maybe other little girls had enjoyed the watered-down modern versions turned into multi-million-dollar franchises. She probably would have, too, if that's what she'd been exposed to. But her father had an ancient tome, a prized possession, of the original versions of the stories. His mother had read it to him when he was a boy, and her mother had read it to her. It went back generations. And that edition was rife with blood and violence and death.

This young girl had long, blonde hair reminiscent of Rapunzel.

In the original Brothers Grimm version, the princess hadn't been strangled with her own braid. She had been imprisoned and abandoned in the forest, left alone to bear and raise twins on her own. Eventually, she and her beloved were reunited, but only after years of misery.

And that was one of the happier tales.

"Are you all right, miss?"

Chelsea turned her attention to the medical examiner. He was studying her, concern evident on his face. She glanced around the room. McPherson was in a deep discussion with one of the MCU techs. If he knew she was upset, he didn't show it.

"I'm fine, thanks." She smiled at the ME, though she suspected it didn't reach her eyes. It definitely didn't reach her voice.

"Crime scenes can be upsetting. Especially for new detectives. Am I correct in assuming you're new? I don't recall seeing you before."

"Not new to Steel City PD. I am a new detective, though."

"I see." He nodded. "Well, the adjustment from first responder to active investigator can be daunting."

"It's not that. It's fine. I mean … Obviously, this isn't fine. It's tragic. But it wasn't the scene or the victim that disturbed me."

"Oh? Can I be of any help?"

His eyes were a soft brown, and he looked genuinely interested. Meanwhile, her partner had forgotten she was even in the room. Still, she wasn't one to share personal problems, especially with strangers. Even astute ones. "I was just distracted by something unrelated. But thank you, uh … "

"Fletcher. Scott Fletcher. I'm the medical examiner. But you already know that." He chuckled and extended his hand.

She stared down at it. Even with her gloves on, she didn't want to touch him knowing where his hand had been. Looking up at him, she raised her eyebrows.

"Oh. Sorry!" He pulled off his gloves, looked at his bare hand. Glanced at her gloved one. "Actually, this probably isn't much better."

She smiled. "How about a raincheck until we both wash up?"

"You've got a deal."

"So, what can you tell me about the vic?"

He took a deep breath and looked down at the dead girl. His look was compassionate, almost reverent — something unheard of in crime scene analysis. People didn't last long if they let their emotions get the better of them.

His empathy touched her. "Seems it gets to the experienced as well as the new."

Dr. Fletcher nodded and gave her a soft smile. Then he cleared his throat. "Liver temp and lividity suggest she's been dead for about six hours."

"That puts the time of death around two-thirty. Not many witnesses around at that hour of the night."

"No. Not usually. Maybe when they canvass, they'll find someone who closed down a bar and was walking home. Or maybe someone up late studying."

"Cause of death?"

"Well, I'll have to do an autopsy to be sure, but I'm guessing strangulation."

"But she looks so peaceful. Strangulation takes time. She should look worn out from the struggle. Or terrified of her fate."

"Like I said, I'll know more after the autopsy."

"And did she just lie there and let her killer cut her hair?"

"You're going to make an excellent detective. You ask the right questions. That shows a keen, agile mind. Coupled with compassion? You're one in a million, detective."

Her cheeks burned. Maybe her partner didn't appreciate her, but someone did. "Thanks, Dr. Fletcher."

He smiled. "Call me Scott."

"Okay. Scott."

He raised his eyebrows. "And you are?"

"Oh, I'm sorry. Chelsea Sullivan."

"Nice to officially meet you, Chelsea." His smile was warm, sincere.

She smiled back even as her gaze traveled to McPherson again. Cocky jerk. Then she met Scott's gaze. "Thanks for your help, Scott. Any idea when you'll be finished with the autopsy?"

"I need to get her back to the morgue. Assuming none of the techs have received bodies ahead of this one, I'll need two to four hours, then I can have a preliminary assessment. It could take twenty-four hours or more to have the final report."

Chelsea took a card out of her pocket. "Please let me know as soon as you have anything."

"Will do." After offering one last smile, he turned away and started giving orders for the transportation of the victim.

At least he'd get to leave soon. A niggling feeling in the pit of Chelsea's stomach told her she'd probably be there a while.

Chapter Four

Jim jotted down the information the MCU tech gave him, though he knew he'd remember it. The girl gave him her number, too. He also wrote that down but doubted he'd ever call. Not in a social manner, anyway. She was cute and smart but a little young for his taste.

Or he was getting old.

He sighed to himself. It was probably a little of both.

Chelsea finished flirting with the ME then made her way over to him. Had to give her credit, she was exceptionally careful with where she put her feet, and even when her balance was compromised, she didn't touch anything — even with her gloves on.

Given the look on her face, she was miffed. Again. Wonder what egregious insult he'd committed this time. He hadn't even been near her.

"McPherson?"

"Sullivan." He didn't look up.

"I was talking with the ME."

"Is that what you kids are calling it these days?"

"What?"

He met her gaze, then rolled his eyes. "Come on, Chelsea. You don't think he was being so nice because he's a genuinely kind man, do you?"

"I don't know what you're talking about." She tugged her jacket down. Looked at her hands and wrinkled her nose. Glanced back toward the ME. "He seems like a sweet man."

"I can't tell if you're naive or trying to get a rise out of me."

"I beg your pardon?"

"Fine, naive." He sighed. "The coroner may or may not be a nice guy, but the only reason he went out of his way for you was because he's interested. In *your* body, not the vic's."

"You're crass."

"And you're clueless."

She stepped closer. "And what about you and the hotsy-totsy tech you've been flirting with?"

Huh. He hadn't thought she'd noticed. Couldn't help but smirk at how wrong she'd gotten the situation, though.

She sighed. "So, what is it?"

"What is what?"

"Either you're holding a grudge after our earlier exchange, or you simply don't work well with others."

"Excuse me?"

"I get it. Some people prefer to work alone on-scene. But we're supposed to be a team, and you're not communicating with me. As far as I can tell, you forgot I was even here."

"Oh, I was well aware you were here. As were most of the men in the room."

"What's that supposed to mean?"

Was she really that blind? When she entered the room, everyone stopped and took notice. And it wasn't because she was the new girl in the department. Jim shook his head. "While you were flirting with Dr. Death, I was doing our job. Girl's name is Brianna Lawson. She was a senior at Steel City U. Studying to be a special needs teacher. Fluent in ASL. Set to graduate in May with high honors. GPA was a three-point-nine, and unless she blew this semester, she would have been sitting damn near the top of her class."

"Fluent in sign language? Was she deaf?"

"No. Don't know if any of her family or friends were, either."

"That's an impressive record."

He nodded.

"She's what? Twenty-one, twenty-two?"

"Twenty-two."

Chelsea shook her head. "So tragic. Her life was just beginning."

Warning bells clanged in his head. "No. Her life began twenty-two years ago. Don't romanticize it."

"Romanticize it? What about this could possibly be considered romantic?"

"Is her death tragic? Yes. Did she have a full life ahead of her? Perhaps. But are you going to be of any use to her if you're waxing poetic about her being too young to have her life cut short in such a vile way? Absolutely not. You need to learn to compartmentalize this shit. Lock the sad stuff away. Get justice for the victims but still manage to enjoy your own life. You can't take on all that suffering. It'll consume you if you don't learn to shove it in a box and seal it tight." He would know.

"There's nothing wrong with showing some compassion. Some empathy."

"Save it for family and friends. You chose the wrong job if you intend to wallow in tragedy."

Chelsea studied him for a long time, her expression unreadable. He braced for a tirade, but none came. Instead, she sighed, and her body deflated a little. "I don't like it, but you're right. It rankles a bit, though. I've always been sensitive to other people's feelings. It's second nature to me. It's one of the reasons I became a cop — I want to help."

McPherson frowned at her. "We are here to help. We just don't want to end up needing help when the dust settles."

"I think there's room for some empathy."

And he thought he'd had her convinced. "Why don't you go see what Dr. Death has found out?"

"YOU NEED to stop calling him that." Chelsea glanced over her shoulder to see if the ME heard him.

Scott was escorting the gurney holding the body bag into the hallway. He looked her way, waved, then walked out the door.

At least some men could be considerate. Chivalry wasn't dead, after all.

Chelsea turned back to her partner, who was scowling at her. Or at Scott. Maybe the entire room in general. She didn't know him well enough to read his moods and expressions.

With a little luck, maybe she never would. She wasn't too deep into this case yet. There was still time to ask for a different partner, a different case.

Oh, who was she kidding? She was already hooked. Brianna Lawson might have lived twenty-two years, but that wasn't nearly long enough. And Chelsea was going to see to it that the killer paid for her murder.

After that, though, she was requesting Charlie. Or Norm. Even Delfino. Anyone else had to be better than McPherson.

Maybe she was being too picky, too demanding. Dad always said she was high maintenance. Fussy.

Dad. Just thinking about him brought back memories of that darn book. The faded gold letters on the scuffed leather cover. The musty smell of the thick ivory parchment. The ornate gothic font on the story title pages. The graphic drawings of maimings and impalings. Her thoughts took a dark turn, and the apartment faded away.

Chelsea was a little girl again. Rain streamed down the windowpane, drops pelting the glass. The occasional flash of lightning illuminated her bedroom, stretching doll shadows into spectral phantoms. She huddled under her blankets, cowering when thunder shook the house on its foundation.

Her door flew open, coinciding with a *boom*. A monster loomed in the darkness of the hallway, poised to enter.

She shrieked. Covered her face with her pillow. Trembled until her teeth chattered.

Footsteps thudded across the hardwood floor, one step for every four beats of her racing heart.

They grew silent when the intruder reached the rug under her bed.

He was close enough to touch her. To bite her. To suck out her soul.

Chelsea squeezed her eyelids shut, pulled her bedding tighter around her.

Then her quilt was ripped from her grip.

Another scream escaped her, more shrill than the last. It echoed through the room, bounced back to her to mingle with her desperate gasps and sobs. She barely recognized her own voice.

"Chelsea. That's enough."

The words were growled. The tone was low, harsh.

Frightening.

But not unfamiliar.

Her father.

She opened one eye and squinted up at him.

He towered over her, still clad in the dark pants and shirt that made up his work uniform. His silver badge gleamed on his chest while the rest of him blended into the dim room.

No daughter of Cormac Sullivan was allowed a soft lamp or night light. She was expected to be brave, to face her unreasonable fears.

Chelsea scooted up and leaned against her headboard. She opened her eyes wide, trying to make out details in the darkness. The storm raged on, lightning creating a strobe effect in her room, making Dad's movements choppy and adding to the disturbing distortions and charged atmosphere. Her mattress sagged when he sat beside her, toppling her toward him. Finally, she was able to get a decent look at his features. His shoulders sagged, and he had bags under his eyes. He looked weary. Dejected.

Beaten.

She wanted to ask what was wrong, but another crash of thunder made her yelp instead.

Dad clicked on the bedside lamp. The soft glow illuminated him but didn't reach much farther into the shadows.

He looked even worse than she initially thought. His hair dripped, his clothes sodden. Her sheets dampened where he sat.

But his eyes … They haunted her. The pain in their depths. The agony. Desperation and fury.

A fire that promised retribution.

She pulled her thin sheet up to her chin.

"Settle down." Dad reached for a book — *the* book — and opened it to a story in the middle.

The left-hand page sported a picture of a crumbling tower rising from the center of a garden overgrown with weeds and choked off by thorns. The colors were muted. Inky blues, fathomless blacks. Forest greens and bloody reds. The only spot of brightness, of hope, was a swirl of gold hanging from a lone window at the top of the spire.

"Not 'Rapunzel,' Dad. Please."

"Every story I choose, you say the same thing."

"But it's scary."

"Life is scary, Chelsea. This is just a story, and stories can't hurt you. It's time you learn the difference."

To her, there was no difference. Fiction or reality, scary was scary.

"Chelsea!"

That wasn't her dad's voice. She blinked, looked around. The room was a bedroom, but not hers. It was well lit, not dark, and snow rather than rain fell outside.

McPherson snapped his fingers in front of her face. "Earth to Chelsea."

"Sorry. I was lost in thought."

"What about? Did you see something?"

Yeah, she saw too much. Nothing relevant to the case, though.

Well, almost nothing.

"What do you know about fairy tales, McPherson?"

"Now's hardly the time or place for a princess fantasy."

Her cheeks heated. "Can you please put aside the attitude for a minute and consider my theory with professional courtesy?"

"Oh, you have a theory now?"

She sighed.

He waved his hand for her to continue.

"Fairy tales. You've heard of Rapunzel, right?"

"Of course."

"Doesn't this remind you of her?"

"It will probably come as no surprise to you that princess stories aren't my forte, but if I recall correctly, Rapunzel escaped. No one strangled her with her hair. Or anything else."

"True." Her resolve deflated a bit. "But that long blonde braid is reminiscent of the story."

"She's just as much Goldilocks as she is Rapunzel. Maybe more so. Didn't the bears kill her when they found her in the cub's bed?"

Chelsea sighed. "No. She ran away and never went back. And in the original version, it was an old woman, not a young girl. People know the sanitized cartoon rewrites, not the authentic stories, which were much darker."

He shrugged. "You'd know better than I would. Either way, a girl dead in a bed is more Goldilocks than Rapunzel."

"How do you figure? Goldilocks didn't die."

"She was never heard from again, though. Was she? Bears probably ate her."

"And didn't leave a drop of blood behind as evidence?"

"Did they have crime scene investigators back then?"

"You're impossible. I'm trying to discuss a serious theory, not fictional forensics."

"And I'm telling you there's no connection to fairy tales here. Rapunzel, Goldilocks, Mother Goose. Doesn't matter."

"Mother Goose was nursery rhymes, not fairy tales."

"Sullivan, we've got a dead college student here. There's not a bigger picture. No theme or message. It's a murder. A not-so-common one, sure. But it's not based on children's stories."

She hoped he was right. But the niggling feeling in her gut said he wasn't.

CHELSEA TOSSED her keys on the console in her tiny entryway. Most of the snow on her shoulders had melted during the walk through the lobby and the ride up the elevator, but her coat was still damp, so she hung it carefully on the hook to dry. After kicking off her boots, she headed straight for the kitchen.

A filet of salmon was thawed in the refrigerator, but making dinner was the last thing on her mind. Her gaze flitted to her liquor cabinet, but she wouldn't give in to the urge. Had to be better than that. Above reproach.

Only kept the stuff on hand for guests, anyway. Unless wine for cooking counted. But marsala didn't strike her as a nerve-calmer.

She only allowed herself one vice, one no one could think less of her for. And if ever she needed it, now was the time.

Instead of grabbing the half-empty bottle of wine, she opened the freezer for a carton of spumoni ice cream. Only three containers left after she finished this one. And no doubt about it — she was finishing this carton tonight. Had to add ice cream to her shopping list.

After grabbing a spoon from the drawer, she took a huge bite. Flavors of pistachio, cherry, and chocolate burst on her tongue. She'd barely swallowed when a pain stabbed her behind the eyes. Brain freeze, but totally worth it.

Chelsea left the container on her counter to soften

while she got ready for bed. A quick, steaming shower thawed her chilled bones, relaxed her tight muscles. She donned flannel pajama pants and a baggy sweatshirt, then ran a wide-toothed comb through the tangles. Usually, she straightened her long, thick hair by blow-drying it, but the spumoni beckoned. So, she merely tousled the damp tresses with her fingers. Once dry, her locks would fall in soft waves halfway down her back. But the ubiquitous February snowflakes would turn it into a frizzy mess. She'd solve the problem tomorrow by pulling it into a bun, twist, or braid.

Braid.

The memory of Brianna Lawson's dead, strangled body slammed into her, followed by drawings from her father's book. The images swirled into one horrific, demented vision until tears rolled down Chelsea's face.

She closed her eyes against the onslaught. Rocked back and forth on her bed until her thoughts cleared, her heart rate calmed, her breathing slowed. Maybe McPherson was right — she needed to find a way to remain detached if she wanted to stay sane.

Could always ask Dad how he did it. He never showed any emotions. No tender ones, anyway.

After sliding her feet into fuzzy slippers, she padded to the kitchen. The ice cream had softened to the perfect consistency. She grabbed the container and her spoon, then headed to the living room to watch a *Bones* rerun.

Chelsea hugged the carton to her chest, using it as both a balm and a shield. Thirty seconds into the program, she realized a murder mystery was the last thing she wanted to watch and changed the channel. HGTV seemed like a safe choice. *Stone House Revival* was on, a show she first watched because it was set in Pennsylvania. After one episode, she'd been hooked. Watching the host return homes to their traditional glory evoked warm images of a simpler life.

But tonight, the stone walls and rough-hewn beams conjured images of fairy-tale cottages.

She turned on SyFy. Didn't matter what they were airing — nothing scientific or futuristic could possibly remind her of the case. Except, of course, the movie *Hansel and Gretel: Witch Hunters*.

What were the odds?

Chelsea checked the local sports channel. They were broadcasting the hockey game. Dad would definitely be watching. Would he answer if she called? Probably not. He hated to be interrupted during sporting events, especially when the hockey was on. When a bunch of guys were pummeling each other on the ice, he wasn't likely to give her good advice about how to be less invested in her victim. Didn't know what she'd say to him, anyway.

The safest bet was music, so she flipped through the selection provided by the cable company. She was tempted to put on the country station just to see if fate was teasing her and Garth Brooks was on. If she heard "The Thunder Rolls," though, she knew she'd freak out. She settled for soothing classical music while she ate her way to an empty carton of ice cream.

But not even Vivaldi could calm her thoughts.

Chelsea switched off the television then went to the kitchen to dispose of the container and wash her spoon. With no satisfactory way to spend the rest of her evening, she went to bed.

As she lay in the darkness, she couldn't escape the events of the day. Why had Davenport paired her with Jerk-Wad Jim? Why had someone cut short the life of such a promising young woman? Why did she *know* with every fiber of her being, the murder had something to do with fairy tales?

And worst of all, why couldn't she put aside the thought that she — a young woman with a bright future — fit the profile of the killer's victim?

Chapter Five

EARLY MORNING

Outside Brianna Lawson's apartment building
Neighborhood of Oakbridge in Steel City, Pennsylvania

HE BLENDED into the crowd seamlessly. Mother had taught him to be seen and not heard. To survive her, he'd taught himself to not even be seen.

Now, as an adult — as an upholder of virtue — that lesson served him well.

Angry clouds in various shades of desperation and despair roiled across the sky, shrouding the morning hour in shadow so dark, it hinted of twilight. Fat flakes of snow glittered in the beams of street lamps the way dust motes danced in the sunlight. They caught in the pillow-messed tresses of the co-eds on the sidewalk clung to the tips of their long, lush lashes.

Winter wenches. Frost nymphs.

At least they were honest about who they were. Those who lied deserved the harshest punishments. Mother taught him that. Two wrongs did not make a right. She'd beaten even his smallest trespasses out of him until he was a paragon of virtue. If he ever even thought about a misdeed or vice, he need only think of the criss-crossed scars his buttocks bore from years under her switch.

Bad enough to commit a transgression. Compounding it with dishonesty showed weakness of character. The world didn't need people void of honor.

People like Brianna Lawson.

Now she was gone, and there was one less degenerate to contend with.

Morally-bankrupt college students congregated in intimate clusters. Young sylphs hid a multitude of sins beneath long woolen coats, flesh spilling out of bra cups and bared above low-slung, obscenely-tight pants. The second those jackets were shed, men of all ages would be tempted by their not-so-subtle offerings — dewy skin pebbling from the frigid air, ample breasts jiggling with every shiver.

Harlots, the lot of them.

All but one.

Older than the college girls yet still young enough to be unspoiled. And her bearing suggested she was still wholesome and pure — hair pulled back in a simple style, face free of garish cosmetics, no visible piercings or tattoos, clothes stylish yet conservative.

She had better still be wholesome and pure. He'd hate to have to judge her.

Electric rage sizzled through him at the thought of her allowing a man to defile her.

Mother taught him to hide his fury, temper his passions.

He counted to ten. Took a few deep breaths, in through his nose, out through his mouth, the warm vapor misting in the bitter air then wafting away with the arctic wind.

Some of the girls nearby wailed, their false anguish tinny and grating to his ears.

But not his princess. She'd been composed. Compassionate, yet restrained.

He couldn't wait to see her again. To be in the presence of someone worthy of his time and company.

But today was not about his longings. Today was about justice. It was about standing vigil in the aftermath. He considered Brianna Lawson — who she'd had the potential to be and who she'd regrettably become. The responsibility had fallen to him to be judge and jury. The verdict had been swift, the sentence absolute.

It had also fallen to him to be her executioner.

Her corpse was now bagged and tagged and ready to be loaded into the coroner's van. His work was now done. Had been for a few hours before the police had even called. And he'd waited in the cold, wondered when his message would be found.

He'd carried out his duties expeditiously, dispassionately. Resolutely. Had even left a warning to all willing to heed it. But how many would?

The frigid air chilled him to his core. Still, he stood there, watching. Waiting. Knowing he would not get the credit for administering justice where no one else could.

Dreading his evening, when he would have to discipline himself for breaking the law when good boys always upheld it.

He thought of Mother's switch, now hanging on his own wall. Thought of standing naked in his living room and meting out his punishment. Unable to properly whip his own backside, he would have to flog himself where he could reach, much as Mother had when she'd caught him fondling himself those many years ago.

The one and only time he'd committed that transgression. Never made that mistake again. She'd seen to it. Now, he was perpetually flaccid. And grateful to Mother for taking away that temptation.

One less sentence he'd need to carry out.

Thinking about his last task of the evening, he shivered. And it wasn't from the cold.

Chapter Six

Jim sat at his desk across from Sullivan, both of them poring over the evidence they'd gathered so far. It was snowing, typical for a winter morning in the city. As a general rule, his former partners didn't seem to have a problem with the cold. But Chelsea seemed to be having an issue. She kept shivering and occasionally rubbed her hands together or blew on them. Her hair was pulled back — which had to leave her ears cold — and some strands around her face had fallen free and were tickling her nose. She'd swiped at them a few times, wrinkled her nose, squinted her eyes. Even batted at them like she'd walked through a spider's web.

It was both annoying and adorable.

He turned back to his work when she made some sort of surprised noise.

"What'd you find, Sullivan?"

Her brow wrinkled as she stared at him like he'd sprouted a second head. "I didn't find anything."

"Then what was that?"

"What was what?"

"That noise."

"What noise?"

"Sounded like a squeak."

She wiggled in her chair, the ancient supports groaning in reply. "This?"

"No. It was more—"

Chelsea closed her eyes, scrunched her face, and tucked her head into the crook of her arm. She made that noise again.

"What the fuck was that?"

She opened her eyes and sniffled. "What?"

"That mini convulsion you just had accompanied by the squeak."

"It was a sneeze. Perhaps you've heard of them?"

"That wasn't a sneeze. Sneezes sound like *ah-choo*, not … whatever the hell that was."

"Maybe you sound like a trumpeting elephant when you sneeze, but I'm a lady. My sneezes are dainty."

"Dainty? No. Your whole body spasmed. Keep holding that pressure in, and your brain's liable to explode."

"Thank you, Dr. Sinus, for your expert opinion. Can we get back to the case now?"

"Speaking of doctors, let's go see your boyfriend. His preliminary report should be done by now. Thought we'd have had it before leaving yesterday."

"He said there might have been bodies brought in before Brianna Lawson. Autopsies must be first come, first served. And he's not my boyfriend."

"He still may not have done the autopsy yet. But he should have sent us preliminary observations."

"I'm sure something came up."

"Whatever. Come on." He headed for the door.

She darted after him.

"You ever been down here before?"

"No."

"I'll show you the way."

"How do you know where it is?"

"Uniforms seldom need to go to a morgue, but detectives often do. You didn't learn that when you studied for the test?"

"Of course I did." She huffed.

He took a small amount of pleasure in her being out of breath, but he slowed down for her.

"I just meant, you're new to this precinct. I'm surprised you already know where *our* ME's office is."

"Work enough cases in this city, you'll end up in all the station houses and all the morgues at some point." And how he wished that wasn't true.

Jim waited for her at the door. Her pace slowed on the last flight of stairs, then she stumbled to a stop in front of him.

"What?"

Her eyes were wide, her face pale. She shook her head. "Just … my overactive imagination. It's nothing."

"You're white as a sheet. It's something."

"I'm fine." She went to step around him.

He blocked the door. "I'm your partner. If there's an issue, you need to tell me."

A mutinous expression marred her soft features before she shrugged and rolled her eyes. "Fine. If you must know, I didn't sleep well last night. Which tends to make my thoughts run wild. My mind was conjuring images of candlelit dungeons and shadowed mausoleums, which I know is ridiculous, really, given we're in a justice building in the middle of a metropolitan area. But I hear 'morgue,' and I can't help but think of every horror movie I've ever seen."

"And do you watch a lot of horror movies?"

"No. I hate them."

She must have become a cop to honor her father because she certainly didn't fit the mold of most — or any — cops he knew. A quip was on the tip of his tongue, but he couldn't bring himself to tease her when she was so obviously nervous.

"Maybe you should watch a few episodes of *Castle*. Ours isn't much different than that one."

Her eyebrows shot up. "I love that show."

"Then this shouldn't surprise you. Morgues aren't dungeons, even though ours is also below ground. You'll see. Come on."

The Medical Examiner's suite took up the entire basement. And it looked nothing like a dungeon. The doors from the stairwell opened to a well-lit vestibule of sorts, decorated with plants, contemporary art, and modern furniture. The place was far more modern than the rest of the building. It looked like any high-end business lobby.

Didn't smell like it, though. The scent of acrid disinfectant permeated the air.

Jim hoped it didn't bother Sullivan too much. Also hoped she didn't consider what the disinfectant was being used on. Or why.

A middle-aged woman sat behind a sleek desk, and she offered a cautious smile as they approached. "Good morning. May I help you?"

He glanced at her desk. The surface was tidy. The personal effects consisted of her teacup, a few potted plants, and three framed photos of cats. Her left hand bore no sign of a ring. And she worked in an office that saw more dead people than living. Either she was painfully introverted, or she'd thrive under some genuine attention. Odds were, she'd come alive with a little friendly banter.

Jim offered a flirtatious smile and leaned on the desk to

speak with her, eye-to-eye. "Well, I just bet you can." He made a show of looking at her nameplate. "Janice."

Her cheeks pinked, and she batted her eyelashes.

He called it right. Donned the role of charming rogue as easily as he shrugged on a jacket.

"My partner and I," he tipped his head toward Chelsea without breaking eye contact with his new friend, "need to talk to the ME."

"He's getting ready for court."

"It'll only take a minute. Mind if we just go back? We'll be quick."

Janice bit her lip, then she smiled. "Sure. Through these doors, then turn right. His office is at the end of the hall."

"See that? I was right. You were a big help." He winked, stood, then headed for the door. "Coming, Sullivan?"

"Thanks," Chelsea said to the woman as she hurried to join him in the corridor.

Jim blinked a few times. The bleach smell was more pronounced there, and his eyes began to burn.

Sullivan rubbed hers.

When the doors closed behind them, she rounded on him. Her eyes narrowed, but they were red and glassy and didn't look nearly as intimidating as she probably hoped. "What is the matter with you?"

What had he done this time? He started down the hall. "What do you mean?"

She scurried to keep up with his long strides. "Do you seriously look at every woman like she's a piece of meat?"

Hard to say whether she was jealous or just contrary, but he didn't feel like bantering with her. When he spoke, he struggled to keep the sharpness out of his tone. "I consider women to be a lot of things, but I can't say 'brisket' has ever come to mind."

"Come on. You were flirting with her."

"So?"

"So, isn't she a little old for you?"

"What do you care? Jealous?"

Chelsea sputtered, but no actual words came out of her mouth.

He chuckled. "I turned on the charm to get us through the door. We wouldn't have gotten in otherwise. Receptionists are there to run interference."

"Uh, no. They're there to *receive* people. Says so in the name."

"Oh, yeah, they receive people all right. So their bosses don't have to."

"Scott's a medical examiner, not a politician. He has no reason to avoid us. Or anyone else."

"Is that what *Scott* is?"

She frowned.

"You're right, Chels." Now he didn't care if his exasperation showed. "I'm sure he's never incredibly busy and must love interruptions. So unlike every other person on this planet."

"Do you have to walk so darn fast?"

He glanced over his shoulder. She was practically jogging to keep pace with his long strides. Kinda wanted to break into a jog, but instead, he slowed for her. Again.

"Regardless of what *Dr. Fletcher* is doing, you shouldn't have teased the receptionist like that. Women don't like to be used. It's debasing."

"I didn't use her. I was cordial. Probably made her day."

"You're so full of yourself."

"It's not arrogance. It's a fact. Everyone else probably

barges in, demands something from her, then leaves again without a thank you or even a smile. A cordial manner and a few polite words cost me nothing and her?" He shrugged. "Trust me, she appreciated the effort."

"You're — never mind."

"What? Go ahead. Don't hold back."

"Several words come to mind."

"Each more vile than the last, I'm sure."

She scowled. "I was taught not to speak unless I had something nice to say. And right now, nothing nice comes to mind."

He grinned. "I'll take that as a compliment."

"How can that possibly be a compliment?"

Far easier to play it off than let her know she was getting under his skin. So, he didn't answer.

They reached the last door in the hallway. He knocked, opened the door. Entered without waiting for an invitation.

From the corner of his eye, he watched her bristle. She berated him under her breath, muttering something he couldn't quite make out about his lack of manners.

The ME sat behind an uncluttered desk, putting a single folder into a sleek leather briefcase. His bookcase was filled with tomes, organized by color, then height. No knickknacks filled the shelves, no photos covered any of the surfaces. Seemed the clean, methodical career necessities translated to his office space preferences.

Something wrong with a guy who lived like he was in basic training. Probably lose his mind if a paperclip was out of place.

"No need to knock, Detective. Please, come in."

But Jim was already inside. Sullivan scurried after him.

"Oh, Chelsea. How nice to see you. I'm sorry, but I can't chat right now. I need to be in court in thirty-three minutes."

Jim tried not to roll his eyes at his precision.

She smiled. "We won't be long, Scott."

"Thought we'd have had your preliminary report last night," Jim said. "When we still didn't have it this morning, I figured I'd check and see what the delay was."

"It's done. I completed it yesterday at thirteen minutes to four. Mason should have emailed it to you before clocking out."

"Mason?" Chelsea asked.

"One of my technicians." Scott picked up his phone and pressed a few buttons. When he spoke, his voice came through the speakers in the ceiling. "Mason, please report to my office." He replaced the receiver on the cradle, then he looked at her. "Should be here in a few seconds."

The words weren't out of his mouth when a knock sounded. "Hey, Dr. Fletcher. What do you need?"

"Was there a problem with the preliminary report on Brianna Lawson? The detectives never received it."

"I sent it before I left last night. Copied you on it, Doc." Mason looked at the detectives. "Did you check your spam folder?"

Chelsea shook her head.

Jim nodded. "Not there."

Fletcher turned to his laptop. His fingers danced over the keys. "It's not in my inbox, either."

"Huh. Wonder what happened." Mason shrugged. "Doesn't matter, I guess. I'll go resend it." He jogged down the hall.

"Sorry about that," Fletcher said.

"Mind giving us a quick rundown?" Jim asked.

He glanced at his watch. "I'm down to twenty-eight minutes. Could we do this when I return?"

"If you have a lead, I'd rather do it now."

"Then perhaps you'd care to walk with me?" He gestured toward the hallway.

The trio exited the office. Fletcher closed his door. While he was locking it, Mason burst out of another room down the corridor.

"I just sent it. It was in my 'drafts' folder instead of my sent items. Sorry about that. Must have forgotten to hit the 'send' button before I shut the system down."

"No worries," Chelsea said.

The ME smiled at her, then he looked at Mason. "Thank you. I have to leave now. I expect to be back before noon."

"I'll hold down the fort, Doc." Mason went back into his office.

The rest of them walked toward reception.

"So, the lowdown?" Jim said.

Fletcher sighed. "As you'll see in the report, there was no sign of sexual assault."

"Thank God." Sullivan vented a relieved breath.

"There was also no sign of struggle. I found an anomaly in her blood work. At the risk of making an assumption, I suspect she was poisoned before she was strangled. I sent a sample to the lab for a full tox screen. Until that comes back, I can't tell you for certain what kind of chemical was used. Only that one was. If I knew precisely what to look for, I'd have an answer faster, but I can't narrow things further at this time."

"No DNA under her fingernails?" Jim asked.

"No. I told you, there was no sign of struggle. We did, however, find a hair that wasn't hers. It has the follicle attached, but there's no match in the database. If you get the lab a sample to compare it to, though, you might get lucky."

"So, we're right back where we started," Sullivan said. "A hint of Rapunzel and no leads."

Jim sighed and rolled his eyes. "We've been through this. That's not how Rapunzel died. You're making something out of nothing."

"Rapunzel?" Fletcher's eyebrows arched. "That's a fascinating angle."

"You know, she was imprisoned in Gothel's garden."

Who the hell was Gothel? Not that he cared.

"Do you think that's significant?" the ME asked.

"Maybe the poison is something found in a garden."

Jim scoffed. "Or maybe the killer is just a sick fuck with a fetish for long blonde hair."

Fletcher paused mid-stride and glared at him. "A little decorum, please, Detective. And perhaps you'd like to reward out-of-the-box thinking instead of dismissing it out of hand." He turned away from Jim and smiled at Sullivan. Then they reached the vestibule. He turned to his receptionist. "I should be back around noon, Janice."

"See you then, Doctor."

Chelsea waved at her.

"Until next time, Janice," Jim said.

Her giggles faded as they walked up to the ground floor.

Fletcher turned to Sullivan in the lobby. "I'm sorry I can't stay and talk further, but I'm due in court. Would you care to meet for lunch?"

Jim, standing behind Dr. Death, smirked at her.

"I don't know what I'll be doing then. Stop at my desk or give me a call when you get back."

"Happy to."

"Good luck in court."

"It's not about luck." He patted his briefcase then walked away.

Jim scoffed. "And you want to lecture me about flirting with people to get what I want?"

"Are you kidding me? I was only being nice. You, on the other hand—"

"Potato, po-tah-to. Looks like we're not as different as you'd like to believe." He headed toward their desks.

"Can we just get back to the task at hand?"

"Sure. Let me pull up the report from my email."

Sullivan sat at her desk then started clacking at her keyboard, presumably to read the email for herself.

As promised, it was waiting for them. And after a quick scan, Jim realized it offered no new information to add to what Fletcher already told them.

"Maybe you were onto something in the elevator yesterday," he said.

"You're going to have to be more specific."

"Poison. It's a woman's choice. Could be Lawson was killed by a girlfriend. A rival of some sort."

"Because women are catty and couldn't possibly work through their differences. We're naturally vindictive and would resort to murder to get our way."

"Go like this." He brushed off his shoulder.

She looked at her shoulder and frowned. "I don't see anything." But she repeated the gesture. "Did I get it?"

"I don't know. How heavy was that chip? Does it feel like it's gone?"

Sullivan glared at him. "I don't have a chip on my shoulder."

"Could have fooled me."

After a deep breath, she spoke through clenched teeth. "Fine. Let's consider a female unsub."

"Nah. Feels like a guy to me."

She closed her eyes.

He swore he could hear her counting to ten.

"Maybe we should spitball some theories," she said. "Anything, no matter how outlandish."

Didn't take Sherlock-level deductive reasoning to know she was going to pitch her Rapunzel idea again. Before they dove down that rabbit hole, he decided to try a different angle.

"You know, maybe it's a cult thing." Jim slid his laptop aside, so his view across their desks was unblocked.

"A cult-thing? How do you mean?"

"I don't know. This isn't your run-of-the-mill murder. Could be some kind of murder/suicide pact."

"Well, she's the murder. Where's the suicide?"

"What makes you so sure she's the murder? She might be the suicide."

"How do you figure?" Sullivan closed her laptop. "She was poisoned and choked."

"Maybe she took a drug, so she didn't feel her death."

"That doesn't explain how she ended up strangled."

"Was she strangled? Or did it just look that way? Until we get the full ME's report, we can't know for sure. Maybe the cult leader told her to stage her death that way."

"I can't believe you're more willing to run with this theory than mine."

He laughed. "What's more likely? A weird cult-thing or a fairy-tale-themed murder that doesn't even follow the plot of the story?"

"Scott likes my theory."

"Scott likes *you*. Big difference."

"Well, even if my theory doesn't pan out, I think it's more likely to be a weird murder than a cult-mandated suicide."

"Maybe."

"You're so smart? Explain the hair, then."

Jim shrugged. "I can't. Not yet. But you can't explain why Naked Rapunzel was strangled with her hair, either."

"Why'd you have to call her that?"

"Because she was *naked*. Another detail different from the fairy-tale version. And I'm pretty sure that's a big piece of the puzzle."

"Let's say you're right. Cult members are brainwashed. That's sad in and of itself before you even factor the murder into it. Can't you be a little less crass? She's someone's daughter. Someone's friend. People are mourning her."

"Wow. You're gullible, rookie."

"I'm not a rookie!" She sat back in her chair. "And gullible about what?"

He chuckled. "A cult pact? Murder/suicide? Come on. I was screwing with you. That theory is as outrageous as your fairy-tale idea. New detectives always want to think they stumbled onto some mastermind serial killer. That almost never happens. This is just your run-of-the-mill murder. Nothing special about it."

"There's nothing run-of-the-mill about murder. And this *is* special. They all are. Do you think her parents are going to shrug this off? It's deeply personal to them."

"Yeah. To them. But not to you. Or it shouldn't be. You better grow a thicker skin, Sullivan. And fast. Or you're not going to make it in this business." Jim stood up, stormed out.

It pissed him off, but he wanted to protect her. He didn't really want her to lose her compassion, her innocence. Wearing her heart on her sleeve wasn't good for her. Wasn't good for the case.

But damn it, he liked her and didn't want to see her hardened into a female version of him.

Chapter Seven

CHELSEA SAT BACK and rubbed her eyes. She'd been going over notes for far too long. The words had begun to swirl together.

"We're not going to get any further with our info from the crime scene and the ME's report," McPherson said. "I think it's time we start interviews."

"Works for me. Where do you want to start?"

"Oh. Maybe we should do it after lunch, instead."

Chelsea followed his gaze across the room. Scott had come in the door and was walking toward her. She turned back to McPherson. "No. That's all right. The job comes first."

"My, my. So professional all of a sudden."

"All of a sudden? When have I been anything other than professional?" How was she ever going to get through this case with such a horrible man as her partner?

"You really want me to answer that? I have a list."

She scowled.

Scott waved as he weaved through the congestion of sprawling detectives and cluttered office furniture.

When he reached her, he perched on the corner of her desk. "Hi."

Her cheeks warmed. "Hi." She took her coat from the back of her chair.

"I'd like to hope you're putting on a jacket so we can go out, but I have a feeling that isn't the case."

"I'm sorry, Scott. Raincheck? We were just about to conduct some interviews."

"Of course we can go another time. Your work ethic is one of the things I admire about you."

McPherson's back was turned, but she watched his shoulders shake and knew he was laughing at her. She turned her attention to Scott. "Thank you. That's very kind. Maybe when we've wrapped up the case, I'll have more free time."

"There's always another case, Chelsea. If you wait for a crime-free day, you'll be waiting forever. You have to learn to make the time. But today, duty calls. I hope you have a productive afternoon." He tipped an imaginary cap to her before leaving.

"Let's go." McPherson snatched a set of keys off of his desk then started toward the back door.

"How about I drive?"

"Why?"

So she could be in control for once. "Leaves you free to man the radio." Wow, was she lame.

"Fine. Grab your keys."

Chelsea searched her desk, but she couldn't find them. "Sullivan?"

"I can't find my keys."

"Then I guess I'm driving."

"But I always put them on my desk."

"Well, not this time. Get a move on."

Chelsea dug in her coat pocket. There was a hole in

the lining. Stupid keys probably fell out. The darn things could be anywhere, and there wasn't time to look for them. She hurried after him.

He smirked when she caught up, but he didn't say anything.

"What, no snarky comment?"

"About what? Me driving?"

"No. I meant about Scott."

"Ah." His lips quirked again.

"I saw you laughing, McPherson."

"At Dr. Death?"

"Would you stop calling him that?"

"Look, Chels, if stuffy and posh is what does it for you, who am I to comment? Or laugh at you. As long as you're happy."

"You're infuriating."

"I've been called worse."

Of that, she had no doubt.

Neither spoke in the car. His playlist was set to classic rock, and Chelsea actually appreciated the pounding beat. In no time, they pulled up to Brianna Lawson's building.

When they reached her apartment, they found her door ajar.

McPherson drew his gun, gestured at her to do the same.

They crept along the adjacent wall, taking the best angle at viewing the room.

Soft sobs sounded inside.

Chelsea started to lower her gun, but McPherson shook his head. She held it up again.

He counted to three by bobbing his head, then he burst inside, Chelsea on his heels.

"Freeze!" he yelled.

Three girls seated together on the sofa shrieked and clutched each other.

"Who else is here?" McPherson demanded.

The girls' screams quieted to wails and sobs.

He sighed. "Watch them." Then he left to clear the rest of the apartment.

"Girls. Girls!" Chelsea gave them all a careful look. Didn't see any weapons, not that a glance from across the room could definitively clear them. She took the calculated risk and returned her gun to her holster.

They continued crying but calmed slightly.

Chelsea raised her hands. "All right, ladies. Time to settle down. We need some answers."

"To … to … to what question?" one of them managed.

"For starters, to what you're doing here."

McPherson burst back into the room. "All clear." Then his brows drew down. "Where's your weapon, Sullivan?"

"In my holster. I was trying to get them to talk."

He shook his head. Then he gestured with his gun for them to stand. "Get up."

The girls scrambled to their feet.

"Pat them down."

"They're just kids, McPherson."

"Frisk. Them." His gun was still trained on the girls, whose sobs were coming louder and faster.

Chelsea hesitated. He was just following procedure, but instead of diffusing the situation, his actions were causing it to escalate. And he wouldn't back down. Finally, she approached the girls with cautious, deliberate steps. "Any of you carrying a weapon? Knife? Gun?"

They all shook their heads.

"I'm going to frisk you now, just to confirm you're telling the truth. It won't take long."

"Hurry up, Sullivan."

Three quick pat-downs and her suspicions were confirmed. The girls were clean.

Only after she gave the all-clear sign did McPherson return his weapon to his holster.

"Okay, ladies," she said. "You can sit."

They collapsed together onto the sofa.

"Who are you?" McPherson asked.

The one in the middle spoke. "I'm Danica Freeman." She pointed to her left. "This is Cara Holt."

"And I'm Heidi Baumgarten," the girl on the right said. "We're Brianna's sorority sisters."

Cara sniffled. "Well, we were."

Danica sobbed and swiped at her eyes.

"What are you doing here?" McPherson asked.

"We just wanted to be close to her," Heidi said.

Cara held up a tiny stuffed animal. "And take something to remember her by."

"Did you somehow miss seeing the sticker on the door? The yellow police tape?" He crossed his arms.

Who would have thought it? Jim McPherson finally met a woman — a trio of women — he didn't flirt with.

"Of course we did," Danica said. "We had to cut the sticker to get in."

"It was supposed to keep you out."

"Plastic tape and a sticker?" She snorted.

He exhaled slowly through pursed lips. "Not physically. They're warnings for you not to cross. We can arrest you for this violation."

Three sets of wide eyes peered up at him.

"We aren't going to arrest you," Chelsea said.

"Speak for yourself," he muttered.

"You said you were sorority sisters?" she asked.

They all nodded. Heidi added, "Gamma Tau."

"Isn't that a philanthropic sorority?"

"We're all supposed to do community outreach," Cara said. "Our big focus is kids in hospitals."

"Brianna loved the work," Danica added. "She made trips to Children's Hospital at least once a week. Sometimes more."

"She was studying to be a special needs teacher," Heidi said. "Our sophomore year, one of the kids at the hospital was deaf. Brianna decided to learn ASL so she could talk to her." She sniffled. "That was just the kind of person she was."

"Why didn't she live at the sorority house?" McPherson asked. "Did she have a boyfriend who liked to stay over? Was she a partier?"

Danica scoffed. "Bree? No way. I never saw her take a drink. Ever. She didn't go to frat parties, didn't go to bars. Didn't even go on many dates."

"Junior year, there was a rumor floating around that she was gay," Heidi said. "Shortly after that, she started dating Simon. But it didn't last."

"Simon who?" Chelsea asked.

"Simon Kinsey. A chem major at SCU."

"Who initiated the break-up?" McPherson asked.

"She did," Danica said.

"And how'd Simon take it?"

"He tried to get her back for the better part of a year," Cara said. "But she wasn't interested."

"Why'd she break it off?" Chelsea asked.

"I don't know," Cara said. "Maybe she *was* gay."

Heidi shook her head. "I don't think so."

Chelsea looked at him. "Does it really matter?"

"If she was gay?" McPherson said. "No. But her reason for breaking up with Simon might."

"Sorry." Danica shrugged. "I just don't know."

McPherson pulled out a business card then dropped it

on the table. "If you think of anything that might be relevant, anything at all, call me."

"Time to go." Chelsea gestured for them to stand.

Cara chewed her lip and looked around the room. "What?"

"We just wanted some quiet time here. It's like she's not really gone, and she'll be walking in any minute with stuff to make salad. She made the best chopped salad."

McPherson shook his head. He strode to the door and opened it for them. "This is an active crime scene. You can't stay."

The girls filed out, one at a time, each taking a last glance over her shoulder before leaving the room.

Once they were gone, he scoffed and shook his head. "Kids today. The future is screwed. How hard is it to make a salad?"

"They're just nervous babbling. And they're sad."

"They shouldn't have been here."

"But they weren't wrong." Chelsea looked around the room. "You can still kind of feel Brianna here."

"Come on, Sullivan. You didn't even know her."

"No, but … I don't know. It's like there's still a presence."

"Yeah. The lingering aura of evil. As soon as we catch the SOB that did this and her family clears out the apartment, this place will feel like any other beige, boring home. Now, let's go."

"What's our next move?"

"Finding Simon Kinsey. Chemists are experts in poisons. And an ex-boyfriend has a motive. Right now, he's my number one suspect." When they reached the hallway, he pulled the door closed. Then he sealed the entrance with another CRIME SCENE: DO NOT ENTER sticker. "But we're stopping for lunch first. I'm starving."

On the ride down the elevator, Chelsea looked up at him. "The sorority girls were quite lovely."

"I suppose."

"You didn't notice? I thought you appreciated all women."

"Women, yes. Jailbait? No."

"They're in their twenties. Early twenties, but still legal."

"I like my ladies to have a little more experience and a lot less drama. Girls in their twenties are the opposite of that."

Chelsea shrugged. She was twenty-nine and proud to say she was drama-free, thank you very much.

Except where he was concerned.

The second this case was over, she was requesting a new partner.

JIM ASKED Sullivan where she wanted to go, but she wouldn't pick. Typical. Since it was his choice, he drove to Willow Street. He found a meter that still had some time left on it but fed it for an additional thirty minutes. Then he led her to Mamani's, one of his favorite places to eat, and occasionally, shop for a gift for his mother.

She looked up at the sign. "I've never been here before. What kind of food do they serve?"

"Peruvian."

"Is that like Mexican?"

He chuckled. "Don't let my mother hear you say that."

Her eyebrows arched. "You're part Peruvian? With a name like McPherson?"

Jim nodded. "One quarter on my mom's side. And no, the food is different from Mexican. But you'll like it."

"It's not too spicy, is it?"

"It's delicious. Go into it with an open mind. Or should I just go through a drive-thru somewhere?"

"I have an open mind, thank you very much. And no, this will be fine. I'm sure there's something on the menu that will appeal to me."

Jim held his tongue as he held the door for her. Unless she had a teenager's palate and lived on ramen, chicken tenders, and pizza, she'd find more than one appealing "something" on the menu.

They sat at a table for two near a rack of Peruvian textiles for sale. She reached out and ran her fingers over a blanket. "This is beautiful. And so soft."

"It's alpaca."

Sullivan pulled away as though she'd been burned.

"They're not killed for their hides, Sullivan. They're shorn. No alpacas were harmed in the making of that blanket."

She touched it tentatively, then rubbed it almost reverently. A smile softened her expression, made her look almost sweet. He considered how she'd react if he said so and almost laughed aloud.

A menu slid onto the table in front of him. "Jim! So glad to see you. And you brought a friend."

He knew the voice — and the passive-aggressive tone — without looking up. "Chelsea, this is Alessa."

Sullivan stared at him before looking up at the waitress. "Hello."

"I'll get you water and give you a few minutes to look at the menu. Though I'm sure I already know what Jim wants." Alessa squeezed his shoulder as she walked toward the kitchen.

"Girlfriend? Former girlfriend? Friend with benefits?"

"It's not what you think."

If he'd known Alessa had switched from the dinner shift to the lunch shift, he never would have chosen Mamani's. This meant he should expect a call from his mother tonight. Couldn't wait.

"Jilted lover?"

"Look at your menu."

Jim didn't have to open his. He always ordered the *lomo saltado* — either the meal or the sandwich. After Sullivan made her selection, he'd decide which.

"This *ají de gallina* ... is that good?"

"It's all good. But yes, theirs is particularly tasty. Only my grandmother made it better. But don't tell my mom hers isn't at the top of my list."

Alessa returned to the table and laughed. "Your friend may keep your secret, but I won't."

Of course, she wouldn't.

She placed their waters in front of them.

"The menu said you don't always have that," Sullivan said. "Did the chef make it today?"

"Sorry, no."

"Okay. What do you recommend?"

"Since we don't have the chicken stew, how do you feel about a turkey sandwich?"

"Is it very spicy?"

"No. It's very ... tame. Should suit you nicely."

"Sounds good."

Alessa's jealousy was manifesting in ugly ways. And poor Sullivan didn't seem to notice, so she wasn't even defending herself.

Or maybe she did and simply didn't see the need to.

"One *pavo*," Alessa said as she wrote. "Your usual beef stir fry, Jim?"

"Make it the sandwich, not the dinner."

"Comin' right up." She scooped their menus off the table, then started writing their ticket as she walked away.

"Your usual? You must come here often."

"Apparently too often," he mumbled. "Just have to be careful about who's working."

"So, how do you know her?"

"If I recall, you were supposed to go to lunch with Dr. Death. Why don't you call him and have him meet you here?"

"Would you please stop calling him that?"

"Why?"

"Because it's rude. He's an accomplished man who—"

"You don't know he's accomplished. Maybe he had to work with dead people because he's no good with the living."

"I'm sure his bedside manner is just fine."

"And I'm sure you'll find out soon enough."

She huffed. "Why do you have to be so crass?"

"Honey, you're a cop. If you haven't heard worse on patrol, you must have been paired with a priest. Uniforms aren't known for their discretion. Or their charm-school vocabulary."

"Oh, I'm aware. I've heard quite a lot already." Her voice was quiet, her words measured. She sipped her water and avoided his gaze.

He supposed it was only a matter of time until they had to discuss it.

"Do you want the truth, or do you believe the rumor?"

Sullivan toyed with her napkin. "I'd like the truth, of course, even though I'm afraid of it. He's my father. I don't believe he's capable of what they say. But what if I'm wrong? What if he … did what they've accused him of?"

Jim had been certain she'd been talking about the

rumors concerning him, but she was thinking of her father. He'd read her wrong. Again. So, he softened his expression. And his attitude. "You know him better than anyone. If you don't believe the gossip, you're probably right not to."

"And if I'm not?"

"You'd be surprised how much it means to have even one person believe you when you're falsely accused. Until you have proof to the contrary, I think you should keep supporting your dad. I'm sure he appreciates it."

"He doesn't appreciate anything. He never even talked to me about it, so he can't know my thoughts on the matter."

"Maybe he didn't bring it up because he didn't want to see a flicker of doubt on your face."

"Because he's guilty." She glared across the table, but there was only pain in her eyes.

"No. Because he's innocent and needs to at least pretend you're on his side."

"You don't know what it's like to have a cloud like this follow you around."

Was it possible she hadn't heard the rumors? Hadn't already judged him?

Then that meant she disliked him because of *him* and not because of who she thought he was.

Maybe he was the one with the chip on his shoulder.

"You'd be surprised, Sullivan."

"You know what's the worst? People believe blood's thicker than water. They assume I'll be like my biological family instead of my professional one."

"So, prove them wrong."

"That's one of the many reasons I became a cop. To clear my family name."

"Admirable." Foolish. Good way to get herself killed if her motivations were really distractions.

"That's the thing, though. It's not a matter of biology."

"Of course it's not."

She sighed. "What do you think is more important — nature or nurture?"

"What?"

"You know, the old philosophical debate. Nature or nurture. Genetics or grooming? DNA or developmental experiences?"

"I don't know. I never gave it much thought."

"Well, think about it now."

It seemed important to her, probably because she didn't want people to associate her with her father, so he chose the answer that he suspected would ease her concerns. "We aren't responsible for the sins of our fathers, Sullivan. I mean, I inherited some of my parents' traits — some good, some less than desirable. But I think who I am is more because of how they raised me than because of any biological marker."

She slowly vented a breath he hadn't noticed her holding and shook her head. "That's the thing. I was raised by Cormac Sullivan. Groomed to be a mini-Sully. I can't claim any of his biology. Or Mom's. They couldn't have kids and adopted me. I don't know a thing about my birth family. All I am is because of who he made me to be. So, what if he did the things he's accused of? And what if he made me in his image?"

Jim couldn't have played that one more wrong. Time for damage control. "Okay, Sullivan. What if you are all nurture and no nature? Didn't you spend time with your mother, too? Isn't she as responsible as your father for who you became?"

Sullivan toyed with her napkin. "I hadn't thought of it like that."

He'd heard Sully's wife left him after his fall from

grace. Whether Cormac Sullivan was guilty or not, it seemed his wife had unwavering moral fiber. That had to count for something. And it was good his partner was beginning to consider that fact.

Alessa brought their sandwiches. She stood a little too close to him and leaned over a little too far as she placed his meal in front of him. For some reason, she walked around the table before heading to the kitchen. Probably so he noticed the extra sway she put in her hips.

Sullivan's cheeks flushed, and she looked away.

His phone rang. He looked at the caller ID. Mom. Wow, Alessa wasted no time at all in sending word through the grapevine. Jim thought about ignoring it but instead decided to get it out of the way. "I need to take this."

She nodded.

He answered the call as he rose. Didn't even get to say hello before the questions started.

Sullivan glared at him as he walked out of earshot, though for the life of him, he couldn't figure out why.

Chapter Eight

CHELSEA GOT Simon's schedule and contact information from a quick call to Steel City University's Dean of Admissions. Based on the time of day, he was supposed to be working on a project for his advisor, so she and McPherson headed for his science lab.

It was only a few blocks from Brianna's apartment.

McPherson was uncharacteristically quiet, and the perpetual grin he wore was nowhere to be seen. Chelsea thought his silence would make him more tolerable, but she actually found it made her uncomfortable. Just not enough to ask him about his mood shift.

Simon's lab was at the Perry Institute, an iconic building in the Oakbridge section of Steel City. The wide stairs and massive columns proclaimed its significance amid other historical sites and contemporary steel-and-glass structures. Chelsea had always loved the simple, elegant facade and was excited to finally see the inside.

To say it didn't disappoint was an understatement. The lobby boasted towering rectangular columns spanning soaring walls. Coffered ceilings and inlaid marble floors added a look of elegance, while potted plants and cushy sofas softened the look. Sunlight shining through windows decorated with sculptured iron gridwork cast an intricate shadow pattern on the tiles.

After they crossed the lobby, McPherson turned to her. "I'm taking the lead on this, got it?"

"Because you did so well with the sorority sisters?"

"I was going to wait until later to address this, but if you want to do it now, we'll do it now. You were reckless back at Lawson's apartment. Not only were you a danger to yourself, you endangered me. You were alone in the room. No backup, three potential suspects. And what did you do? You voluntarily disarmed. What the hell were you thinking? You could have gotten us both killed. Never put your gun away before a suspect is cleared. Never. Got it?"

"What was I thinking? I was using my instincts, which is what good detectives are trained to do. And every fiber of my being told me those girls weren't dangerous. They were frightened and grieving."

"But you didn't know that, Sullivan. You suspected it. Big difference. You're too new to the job to have instincts yet."

"And your experience worked so well? Please. If I hadn't been there, the situation would have escalated. Someone could have gotten hurt. Or worse."

His face turned red, and he glowered at her. "Never, and I mean never, speak so glibly about a cop shooting a civilian. Me or any other brother in blue."

She took a step back. "I didn't mean to imply —"

"I know damn well what you meant."

Chelsea took a deep breath. "You want to take the lead with Simon? Fine. But if I think you're going down the wrong path like with the sorority sisters, I'm stepping in. Got that?"

His eyes narrowed. "I don't take orders from you."

"Nor I, you."

McPherson's jaw clenched. He opened his mouth as if to say something but closed it before speaking.

She wanted to tell him to say what he was thinking but thought better of it. They had a job to do, and fighting with each other wouldn't get it done. Pretty sure she didn't want to hear it, anyway.

They stopped in front of Kinsey's lab and found the door ajar. Jim knocked. When no one answered, he stepped inside. Without a warrant.

Hopefully, that didn't come back to bite them.

Chelsea followed him, an admonishment on the tip of her tongue, but what she saw stole her words. And her breath. The facade and the common areas of the building were traditionally elegant, but the lab was impressive. State-of-the-art. She didn't know what all the bells and whistles were, but she could tell the equipment was new, expensive, and required a clinically-pristine environment — which it had. The room was austere, spotless. Almost sterile.

And completely empty.

She turned to McPherson. "Coincidence that a person of interest in our murder investigation is MIA?"

"Nothing's a coincidence."

They started poking around the room, leafing through folders and studying chemicals in the storage cabinet. The sound of the door opening caught Chelsea's attention, and she turned around.

A man wearing a lab coat entered the room. Tissues were balled in his fists, and his red-rimmed eyes grew wide. "Who are you? What do you want? You shouldn't be in here."

McPherson walked over to him. "Door was open."

"I guess now I know better. Figured I'd only be gone a minute, but …" He shrugged.

"Are you Simon Kinsey?"

"Who's asking?"

"I'm Detective McPherson." He pulled his jacket aside to show off the shield clipped to his belt. "This is my partner, Detective Sullivan. We need to ask Mr. Kinsey a few questions."

"I'm Simon Kinsey." His words warbled with a slight tremor. "What's this regarding?"

Chelsea stepped forward. "We understand you had a relationship with Brianna Lawson."

McPherson shot her a look, but she didn't care. It was her case, too, and it was a free country. She was allowed to speak.

"Yeah, she's my ex." He sobbed, and his voice broke. "I mean, she was my ex."

"I take it, despite your breakup, you aren't over her."

"Over her? I don't know how anyone could get over her. She's perfect. At least, she was."

Uh-oh. This guy had definite attachment issues.

McPherson took a step closer. "Why did you break up?"

He shrugged. "She said she didn't want to get serious. Wanted to focus on school, then her career. I told her there was room for me in her life, too. Told her all work and no play was no kind of life at all. But she was adamant. Felt like there was more to it, but she wouldn't talk about it. Said her mind was made up."

"More to it, how?"

"Brianna was honest to a fault. The few times she lied, it was obvious. She couldn't do it. No poker face at all."

"If she was 'honest to a fault,'" McPherson said, "she wouldn't have lied for you to see she sucked at it."

Kinsey shook his head. "Maybe 'lying' is the wrong word. I'm talking about fibs. To make people feel good. Like telling someone their shirt is nice or their haircut is flattering, or their pants don't make them look fat. She couldn't even pull off a disingenuous compliment for the sake of someone's feelings. *That's* why I know there was more to our breakup. I just never found out what."

Chelsea studied him, looking for any signs of deception. So far, she found none. "Had she moved on? Was she dating anyone new?"

"Dating anyone? Are you kidding? She barely left her apartment. Other than school, work, and volunteering, that is."

"What did she do for fun?"

"She was a sci-fi geek. I think she knew every line of dialogue in every version of *Star Trek*. She watched all the comic-cons on YouTube. The few times she celebrated Halloween, she dressed as a cosplay character. Brianna was a little nerdy, but that only made me love her more."

"She have any problems with friends? Classmates?"

"No. Everyone loved her. And she loved everyone. Her greatest goal in life was to help people."

McPherson crossed his arms over his chest and leaned against the table. "Where were you on the night she got killed?"

"Here. In the lab." He shrugged. "These days, I'm almost always in the lab. I can get you my ID card time-stamp. There's probably camera footage, too."

Chelsea nodded. "We'll want both, please."

"Never mind. We'll get it ourselves." McPherson took a card from his pocket, then handed it to Simon. "If you think of anything else, give me a call. In the meantime, don't plan on leaving town. We may have follow-up questions for you."

Simon dabbed at his eyes again as he tucked the card into his lab coat pocket. "I'm not going anywhere. Besides, I have nothing to hide."

"Are you sure she didn't have any enemies?" Chelsea asked. "A rival in her major, maybe? Someone who might have wanted to hurt her?"

"I'm telling you, no. It was impossible to dislike her. That's why this was so shocking."

McPherson walked to the door. "Thanks for your time. We'll be in touch."

Simon nodded then walked toward a cabinet at the back of the room. His shoulders were shaking, and he sniffled a few times.

Chelsea followed McPherson into the hall. When they were out of earshot of the lab, she said, "What do you think?"

"My gut tells me he didn't do it. Doesn't mean we don't follow up, though. We need to talk to building security, get the camera footage, and scan codes."

"I don't think he did it, either. But I feel bad for the guy. He clearly loved her. And he's grieving."

"She broke up with him, Sullivan. They weren't a couple."

"Doesn't mean he didn't love her."

"There's that bleeding heart again. I'm telling you, if you don't shut down your emotions, this job is going to eat you alive."

She sighed and chose to ignore his comment. Apparently, it had become his mantra. "Let's stop at the security office and see if they can give us the information we need."

"Then we'll talk to her parents."

The head of security was efficient, quickly providing them with recordings of all foot traffic and printouts of all the ID card scans in and out of the building and Simon's lab. Never even asked for a warrant.

Simon hadn't lied about the night of Brianna's murder. He walked into the building at six-thirty that evening, then entered his third-floor lab five minutes later. Only left the room twice — once for a trip to the vending machines and the other time for a quick visit to the restroom. Didn't leave the building until eight the next morning. Unless he sprouted wings or learned how to teleport, he wasn't their man.

Half an hour later, they arrived at Brianna's parents' home. Luckily, they lived in Riverside, just a short drive from the Perry Institute.

Chelsea rang the doorbell. Her stomach flopped, and she wiped her damp palms on the gloves in her pockets. Of all the duties she had as a detective, talking to grieving family members was the hardest. At least she didn't have to break the news to them.

Mrs. Lawson opened the door. She looked like an older version of her daughter, but with bags under her bloodshot eyes. She had crumpled tissues tucked into the cuff of her sweater and a damp one in her hand. "May I help you?"

"Good afternoon, ma'am. I'm Detective McPherson, and this is Detective Sullivan. We're sorry to disturb you, but if you're up to it, we'd like to ask you a few questions about your daughter."

A tear trickled down her cheek. She nodded and opened the door wide. "Please, come in." They followed her to the living room, where she gestured to the sofa. "Have a seat."

"Is Mr. Lawson home?" McPherson asked.

She shook her head. "He went into the office." Another tear ran down her face, and she swiped it away. "The police can't tell us when they will release my baby, so we don't know how long this nightmare will continue. Kevin is going to take an extended leave of absence. He just has a few things to take care of today before he can stay home."

McPherson nodded. "The sooner we solve this case, the sooner we can release your daughter to you."

She covered her face with her hands. Her words were muffled and broken by sobs. "We just want to bury our little girl."

This was what Chelsea had dreaded. Her heart broke for the poor woman. And even with all the power of the Steel City PD behind her, there was absolutely nothing she could do to ease this poor woman's pain. She felt useless, so she let McPherson handle the interview.

He got Mrs. Lawson to open up about her daughter's life. Everything she said confirmed what they had learned from the sorority sisters and Simon. Brianna was shy, quiet. Compassionate, philanthropic. Not very social but incredibly bright. She'd had a promising future ahead of her.

They asked to see her room, despite her no longer living there full-time. Found nothing other than stuffed animals, books, and a few family photographs. No indication of enemies, a stalker, a cult, or criminal relationships that could have turned bad.

McPherson offered their condolences, which was good, as Chelsea didn't know if she could talk without her voice breaking. Before walking out the door, he handed Mrs. Lawson his card and promised to keep her apprised of any developments in the case. They said their goodbyes then returned to the car.

As he drove back to the station, Chelsea rounded on him. "You know we can't discuss ongoing investigations. Why would you tell her you'd be in touch?"

"She needed some reassurance that we were doing

everything we could. I don't intend to reveal any unpublished evidence, but I don't mind visiting her once in a while. Setting her mind at ease."

"You're unbelievable. She's a married woman, McPherson. And a grieving mother. The last thing she needs is a dog like you sniffing after her."

"So now I can't even try to do a little something nice for a grieving lady?"

"If I thought for one second you had her best interests at heart, I wouldn't have said a word. But I think you're more interested in getting into her pants than you are consoling her."

"She's married, Sullivan, but she's alone. Her husband isn't even there. A little extra attention was good for her."

"Like I said, if you genuinely felt that way, I wouldn't have said a word. But something tells me her well-being isn't your concern."

His jaw ticked. "Don't pretend you know anything about me, Sullivan. Because you don't. And you haven't made an effort to break the ice."

"Oh, and you've been so inquisitive with respect to my life. You haven't tried to get to know me, either."

"I don't have to. I already know everything about you."

"What?"

"Cormac Sullivan's daughter. Top of your class at the academy. First female detective in Zone Four. Tenderhearted. Foolhardy. Need me to go on?"

"How'd you know all that? I mean, about my history."

"I did my homework. That's what good detectives do."

They pulled into the parking lot behind the station. Chelsea got out, slammed the door, then stormed toward the building.

McPherson's long gait ate up the distance between

them in a few seconds. Without a word, he brushed past her as he strode into the precinct.

She glowered after him. Maybe she didn't know him well, but she'd seen enough to know he was a manwhore. And that kind of reprehensible behavior was inexcusable, especially when he turned his attention toward emotionally compromised, married women.

Besides, he didn't know her as well as he thought.

Chapter Nine

JIM DIDN'T KNOW where his partner had gone, nor did he care. He sat on his squeaky chair at his battered desk, pretending to work while feeling completely unable to focus. It wasn't like him to lose his cool so fast with a female. Or a coworker. Or especially with a female coworker. But then he thought about the assholes in the locker room.

Maybe that's what had his boxers in a wad. He still wasn't sure where he stood with Sullivan or anyone in Zone Four, other than the captain. And Jim wasn't even one hundred percent sure about Davenport. If he wanted to settle in at his new job, he would have to be the one to make the effort. Much as it rankled him.

On the other hand, did he really need friends on the force? Professional courtesy might be enough. Not that he even had that at the moment.

Sullivan walked in, her pace a little too brisk for someone who'd gotten over being angry. Even so, she had a smile plastered on her face. Disingenuous, as it didn't come close to reaching her eyes, but he'd give her props for trying.

She went to her desk, took her seat. Fired up her computer. After only a few anemic taps at her keyboard, she tilted her head to look past her screen at him. "Do we need to talk?"

"About what?"

"About us. Our relationship."

"Thought you had a problem with me and my relationships."

She took a deep breath then vented it slowly. "Our working relationship. Our partnership."

Jim should have taken the olive branch, leafless though it was, but it felt more like a club. And she was beating him with it. He leaned closer, pitched his voice lower. "Our partnership? Why? Don't you plan on asking Davenport for a replacement?"

Sullivan gasped.

A bitter chuckle escaped him. "Wondering how I know?"

She nodded.

But he merely shrugged. "Forget it. Let's get to work."

"I can't help feeling like we're not on equal footing."

"Because we're not."

"No. I don't mean professionally."

He raised his eyebrows.

"What I mean is—" But she squeezed the bridge of her nose instead of finishing her thought.

"Well?"

She looked at him. "I know you have more experience than I do. Obviously. So, I didn't mean equal footing at work. I'm talking about … about the things you know. I feel like you've read a full dossier on me, and I barely know your name. How is that?"

"It's called detective work, Sullivan."

"What do you mean?"

It was his turn to sigh. "I may not be much older than you, but I've been around the block a hell of a lot more. No way was I making this move without knowing what I was getting into. So, I did a little digging."

"On me?"

"No. On the Queen of England. I heard she was looking for something to do in her spare time."

She scooted her chair over to glare at him without obstructions in her way.

"What do you want me to tell you, Sullivan? I'm sorry? Because I'm not. If I can't trust my partner, I can't work with my partner. And that's a lesson you'd benefit from learning sooner rather than later."

"So, you trust me?"

The vulnerability in her voice softened his stony heart. A bit. He inched his chair to his right, then hunched over to use his screen as a shield. "Enough to work with you." He kept the *for now* to himself.

Sullivan rolled her chair behind her workstation. When she spoke, all traces of emotion — anger, resentment, relief — were gone from her voice. "Okay. Now what?"

"We need to review all our notes. Again. What do we know so far?"

She picked up the case file, then shook her head.

"What?"

"Nothing. Found my keys. They were right there, under the folder. Don't know how I missed them before." She slipped them into her pants pocket. "Okay. The evidence. With respect to Brianna, she was poisoned, strangled. Posed naked on her bed. No sign of forced entry, although her window was open."

"But it wasn't a ground-floor apartment. And the

screen was still in the window. I doubt the killer got in that way."

"I agree. Must've come in the front door. And she must have known him or her."

"Or at least felt comfortable enough to open the door to this particular stranger when he knocked."

Chelsea grabbed a pen then began twirling it through her fingers. "We need to think about a profile. She wasn't sexually assaulted, so why pose her naked?"

"Maybe the killer liked how her body reacted to the cold air."

"Of course, your thoughts would go there."

"It's a possibility. Why else leave the window open?"

"If she was alive, she wouldn't have lain still for him. And someone would have heard her screaming."

"Uniforms canvassed. No one heard anything."

She sighed. "Well, if she was dead before he opened the window, the air wouldn't have mattered."

"We'll circle back to the window." He sipped from his coffee cup, then winced. "Ugh. Old."

"It's been there all morning. Forget that's not a Thermos?"

Okay. Don't bite on that. Get back to business. "Why the braid?"

"The braid says Rapunzel to me."

Now, he sighed. "Not this again. Come on, Sullivan. Rapunzel wasn't strangled. And I'm pretty sure no fairy-tale princesses are ever naked in the stories."

Sullivan frowned. "Is it always about nude women to you?"

"In case you didn't notice, our vic was found without clothes."

"Fine. Whatever. You're a choirboy."

"I didn't say that." He grinned.

She rolled her eyes. "I'm waiting for a better theory than Rapunzel. And I'm pretty sure you don't have one."

"I already floated a cult theory."

Sullivan tossed the pen on her desk. "One you teased me with. I mean something credible. Convince me it's not Rapunzel."

"Okay. We need to look at the jealous ex-boyfriend."

"He didn't do it."

"How can you be so sure?"

She shrugged. "Just a gut feeling, but I know you don't place much stock in my instincts."

"Don't start, Sullivan. We're getting along." Kind of. "No point making waves now."

She nodded. "You're right. Sorry. But I stand by what I said. Instinct can't be enough. We need evidence. And the camerawork and timestamps at Perry Institute suggest it wasn't him."

Jim looked through a few files on his desk. "Agreed. Although it's possible someone that smart could circumvent the scan codes."

"And the cameras?"

"I would think so."

"That doesn't seem likely to me."

"We've only talked to three of her sorority sisters. Even if they aren't suspects, there's a whole house to look into. Could be a vindictive sister."

"The three we talked to would have told us if there was bad blood between Brianna and someone else."

"Okay. Maybe it was a former or wannabe-girlfriend of Simon's who is jealous of his devotion to her."

"So, where does that leave us?"

"With a lot of suspects and no real leads."

Sullivan sat back in her chair and sighed. "Not the sorority sisters, not the ex. Unlikely it's family. She didn't appear to have any enemies. Could be a hidden jealousy that festered. Any other theories?"

"As clean-cut as she appeared to be, I doubt she was in the trade. Probably no angry pimp or jealous Johns to be on the lookout for."

"Does your mind always go to sex?"

"Sex is a big motivator. We have to consider it, regardless of my interests. Or yours."

"You mean my lack thereof?"

And there it was again. Her assumptions — her misguided assumptions. "I didn't say that. Stop putting words in my mouth."

She stared at him for a long moment, then she seemed to deflate. "You're right. I know you're right. Both about you and especially as it pertains to Brianna Lawson. The girl is — was — as innocent as they come."

Jim tapped his fingers on his desk. He considered continuing to defend his honor, but there was no point fanning the embers when the flames of her ire were almost out. "My guess is, it's someone she met online. Someone into cosplay. All those costumes and fantasies could make for some sick shit."

"So stereotypical. Just because people are into something you consider geeky doesn't mean it's dangerous."

"Why must you be contrary about everything?"

"Because you aren't always right!"

He glowered at her.

"Consider me your devil's advocate." Her words weren't much friendlier, but her demeanor was softer.

"Consider this, Sullivan. Online relationships and fantasies are dangerous. The anonymity the Internet provides gives people a sense of bravado they otherwise wouldn't have. And what you call innocent cosplay costumes can quickly veer into obsessive role-play games.

It's possible Miss Lawson wasn't as pure as people thought."

"I see what you're saying, but I don't buy it. She wasn't a partier. Wasn't into wild things. I think you're barking up the wrong tree."

"Okay. Could be a stalker. She never filed a police report about one, but we should probably check with campus police. Maybe they have information we don't."

"That's a good idea. Can it wait until tomorrow? It's late, and I'm beat."

He glanced at his watch. "Well past dinner. Sorry. Lost track of time. We'll pick this up in the morning. Have a nice night, Sullivan."

"You, too." Chelsea took the coat from the back of her chair. "McPherson?"

"Yeah?"

"You think this is a one-time thing?"

"They usually are."

"The posing, the braid … It feels ritualistic. I hate to say it — hate to even think it — but I think this is only the beginning."

"You're letting it get to you. Go home. Take the night off. After a good night's sleep, you'll have a clear head and fresh eyes. Don't even think about it until tomorrow."

"Actually, it's Friday. We're supposed to be off tomorrow."

"Huh. You're right. Even better."

"Shouldn't we come in anyway? We're in the middle of a case."

"We'll always be in the middle of a case. Usually more than one. Enjoy the downtime. I'll see you Monday."

"Aren't you leaving?"

"As soon as I place a call to campus security. We can explore her sorority relationships next week."

"All right. Good night, then." She gave a half-wave as she headed to the door.

Jim couldn't wait to call it a day, either, but he needed to place the call before the weekend. Campus security would need time to go through their records, and notifying them now should give them enough time to have their findings ready by Monday morning.

THE WHOLE WAY HOME, Chelsea's spine tingled. She kept looking over her shoulder, convinced someone was following her. Watching her.

Stalking her.

But she never saw a soul. No one suspicious, anyway. When she reached her apartment building, she ran in the door then up the stairs. If someone was watching her, they'd be denied the opportunity of seeing what floor the elevator stopped on. And since no one followed her into the stairwell, she felt confident her apartment number, if not her apartment building, was still confidential.

Even after a hot shower and a bowl of spumoni, she still couldn't shake the feeling. "Come on, Chels. Get a grip. You're letting the case get to you."

Dad got that way a few times. He'd come home with a far-away look in his eyes, unable to focus on simple conversations or family events. And when she joined the police academy, he told her that at least once in a cop's life, a case would get under his skin.

Just her luck. It was her first case as a detective that got under hers.

She tried to follow McPherson's advice and put the case out of mind, but she couldn't. As soon her dad entered her thoughts, fairy tales followed.

"Darn it all, anyway."

Chelsea set aside her ice cream, then walked to her bookshelf. There it was, stuffed in the bottom corner. The world's worst childhood memento.

Dad's old Brothers Grimm fairy tale book.

She took it back to the sofa with her. In no time, she had it open to the Rapunzel story. The picture was even more vivid than she remembered. Creepier, too. And even though she knew it was a bad idea, she read the darn thing. Every last word.

When she was finished, she slammed the book shut. Couldn't return it to the shelf fast enough.

McPherson might be right about her needing a clear head and fresh eyes in the morning, but no way was it going to happen now.

After Chelsea crawled into bed, she lay there, wide awake, thoughts of thorny vines and choking braids haunting her until the soft light of dawn crept through her window.

Chapter Ten

Chelsea slept much of Saturday away, exhausted from her sleepless night. Before her sleep schedule got too messed up, she set her alarm to get up for church Sunday morning.

Afterward, as always, she bought donuts at Dad's favorite bakery, then went to visit him.

When she knocked, he didn't answer. But she could hear the TV, so she tried the knob. Open. What kind of cop — former or active — didn't lock his door? His carelessness irritated her, and she stormed into his living room, where she found him engrossed in a hockey game. "Dad. Your door was unlocked."

A Seal scored. He raised his fisted hands and cheered.

Did he even realize she was in the room?

Chelsea opened one of the bags the bakery had given her, removed two paper plates and a handful of napkins. Then she opened another bag to get each of them a donut. She handed him a napkin and one of the dishes — vanilla creme, his favorite.

"Thanks, kiddo."

Okay. He wasn't surprised to see her. That meant he knew she had come in and had chosen to ignore her. Probably the better of the two options. She sighed. "How's it going, Dad?"

"Did you see that slap shot? Hardest in the league, I'll wager."

She hated Sunday afternoon games. Finding something to discuss with her father was difficult enough without struggling to capture his attention first. "You didn't ask me about my first week as detective."

He took a bite of his donut and grunted something at her with a full mouth.

"Davenport assigned me a new guy for my partner. Jim McPherson from Zone Two. Just transferred to College Row. Do you know him?"

Another grunt.

"We caught an interesting case. A sorority girl was strangled with a long blonde braid. Her own hair."

Dad looked at her. Put his plate down, wiped his fingers on his pants. "Long blonde hair? Like Rapunzel?"

Sometimes great minds — or obsessive ones — did think alike. "It's far too early to tell if this is a fairy-tale-inspired murder."

His eyes seemed alert for the first time in weeks. He leaned toward her, almost vibrating from the excitement. "Tell me the facts."

"You know I can't do that."

"Then why'd you even bring it up?" He sat back, a scowl on his face.

"It's my first week, Dad. My first case. I thought you'd be interested."

"I was. Then you went and shut me out of it." He turned his attention back to the television, tossed a pillow at the screen. "The hell it was a high stick!"

Chelsea rose, grabbed both their plates, then retreated to the kitchen. She was going to put them in the trash can, but it was already overflowing with an assortment of pizza boxes and frozen food trays. She gagged when the odor wafted to her, and her eyes watered. After wiping the tears away, she scanned the rest of the room. The sink and counters were littered with unrinsed dishes and cups, crusty pots and pans. The collection reeked, and spots of mold were beginning to grow.

When she was a kid, Mom and Dad split the household chores. He washed the cars, mowed the lawn. Mom cooked and cleaned, did the laundry. After their divorce, Mom moved to California, and Dad took an apartment in the city. He had a lot less to maintain but still couldn't be bothered doing any of the domestic tasks. She did it for him when she lived there, but she moved out a while ago. And keeping up with his mess on Sundays was becoming more and more difficult, especially when she missed a week or two picking up extra shifts. Clutter littered his rooms. The carpet needed vacuuming, the linoleum needed scrubbing. Everything was covered with a thick layer of dust or grime, and dirty clothes were everywhere.

The kitchen repulsed her.

It would be so easy to walk away, but she just couldn't do it. So, she gathered his laundry, threw a load in the washer, rolled up her sleeves, then got to work on the dishes. While she scoured, she thought about the turn Dad's life had taken. A questionable bust had led to an IA investigation, where they dug into rumors of his being on the take. When allegations of police brutality surfaced, he was forced into an early retirement. Shortly after that, Mom filed for divorce.

Dad had been a decorated officer, a legend in the department. Then things went so wrong so fast. Through it all, he maintained he was innocent. But his resolve wasn't enough to save his career.

Since then, he'd grown listless. He barely went out, and she didn't think he ever spoke to anyone but her. Maybe an infrequent phone call with his old partner, who had also moved to California. If it wasn't for Chelsea's weekly visits, he would be completely cut off from society. And if she was worried before, now she was a wreck. His moods were erratic, going from sad to indifferent to angry in a matter of seconds. It had been months since she'd seen even a glimmer of something positive in him — until she mentioned her case. But she couldn't reveal more to him.

If anything, he was worse once she shut him out. And that was on her.

She continued scrubbing and polishing until the kitchen gleamed. When she was done, she started the next load of laundry. There wasn't time to give the furniture a proper cleaning, but she quickly hit the surfaces with his feather duster and straightened the piles of papers and magazines he'd accumulated. After that, she ran the vacuum. The apartment was far from pristine, but it was better than before.

The dryer buzzed. She folded his clothes. The washer still had twenty minutes on it, but she couldn't wait that long. So, she headed back to the living room.

It was the second intermission, yet she still didn't have her father's attention.

Chelsea doubted he'd even noticed her efforts. "I have to go now, Dad. You need anything else before I leave?"

He dismissed her with a halfhearted wave.

"All right, well, I'm going to be busy with my case this week. Probably won't have a chance to visit again until next Sunday."

Dad spun away from the TV.

It was hard to get excited about his attention. The sportscasters had cut to a commercial, and unless it was about beer or another game, those rarely caught his interest.

"You know, if you need a consultant on your case, I'm happy to pitch in."

How she wished he could. But with the blemish on his record, his involvement wouldn't be welcomed by the captain.

"I really think you need to pursue the Rapunzel-angle. There's something there."

She took a deep breath. It was nice to see him animated, so she gave a little. "I think you might be right. I even re-read the story. It still creeps me out."

Dad shook his head. "For the love of Pete, Chelsea. You're almost thirty. Don't you think it's time you put that childish nonsense behind you? Stories can't hurt you —"

"But people can," she finished for him. "I know." She kissed his cheek. "If you need something, call me."

"And if you need my help, call me." He turned back to the television. The commercial was over, and so was the intermission. The referee dropped the puck, and Dad was immediately immersed in the game.

"There's a load of clothes in the wash, Dad. Make sure you put them in the dryer — and turn the dryer on — or they'll get moldy."

He didn't answer.

Chelsea left without another word. Why did she even bother? He didn't seem to care if she visited or not. Unless her feet sprouted ice skates, she'd never get his attention.

Well, maybe if she talked more about the case. And *that* wasn't going to happen.

She went to the grocery store, grumbling the whole way. After filling the cart with a few things she needed, she grabbed a week's worth of frozen dinners for her father, then returned to his apartment.

As expected, he'd ignored the buzzer on the washer. He was still in his recliner, watching the post-game report. She put away the groceries. Put his clothes in the dryer, too.

He didn't seem to notice she'd returned, and when she left, neither said goodbye.

JIM TURNED off the hockey game. Seals had won, which made his day. Wasn't much else to get excited about on a snowy Sunday afternoon.

He'd spent Friday night at an obnoxiously loud club with an obnoxiously shallow woman. It was a kindness to call her dance moves obscene. Didn't take him long to lose interest and leave the floor. And it didn't take ten seconds after that for other guys' interest in her to skyrocket. As he was walking out the door, he glanced back to find a dozen men surrounding her. The way she was grinding would have made Patrick Swayze and Jennifer Gray look like prudes.

Never understood Roger Murtaugh more. Jim *was* getting too old for this shit.

Couldn't think of a Saturday when he'd been so happy to wake up alone in his own bed. He'd spent most of the day looking into cults and serial killers. By the time his eyes were crossing, he hadn't come up with a single concrete theory. Hell, he hadn't even stumbled onto a loosely formed one.

Now, it was closer to Sunday night than Sunday afternoon, and all he'd done was make a tasty pot of chili and down a couple beers to celebrate the Seals' victory.

Jim glanced at his laptop. He didn't want to be one of those cops who lived his cases, but he couldn't get Brianna Lawson out of his mind. Or her poor mother. Much as he chastised Sullivan for being too emotional, he had to admit his own issues. This one was getting to him, too.

He got himself another beer and a second bowl of chili, then he opened his laptop.

Campus security hadn't sent the report yet. Couldn't say that surprised him.

Obituary had run yesterday. A quick scan revealed no new details. Couldn't say that surprised him, either.

His cult hypothesis was a joke when he'd said it. And despite checking into those fringe groups — both locally and nationwide — nothing popped.

That left him with no leads. And one theory. One ridiculous, long-shot theory.

Rolling his eyes at himself, he did a search for Rapunzel. He knew fairy tales were popular among certain groups, but he never expected the sixty-eight million entries that came up. His vision glazed over before he clicked the first link.

Wasn't gonna happen.

Jim finished his late lunch/early dinner, then cleaned the kitchen. The whole time, he turned over all the evidence. Or lack thereof. His resistance to the fairy-tale angle built with every second that passed, but he had no other strings to pull. When the dishes were put away, and the counters were gleaming, he glanced at his laptop again.

With a sigh, he walked into the living room. Plopped on the couch. Opened his browser. Typed "Rapunzel" in the search box.

Just before hitting enter, he had an idea. One that embarrassed him, as he should have thought of it days ago. But all of his work time — and much of his free time —

had been spent going over statements of witnesses, interviews with loved ones, reports from the ME, and even a
few outlandish theories.

Brianna Lawson may have been an introvert, but he'd
bet his next paycheck she was on social media. Double that
he'd find a clue there.

And a few minutes later, he wished he'd had Vegas
odds on that as he placed a call.

WHEN CHELSEA ARRIVED at work on Monday morning,
McPherson was already there. The last thing she felt like
doing was bickering, so she forced a bright smile and
greeted him with a cheerful hello.

He nodded his greeting then gestured to her desk.
"First week on the job, and you're already getting mail
here."

"Nope. It's *your* first week here. It was *my* first week as
detective, but I've been in this precinct for years."

McPherson shrugged. "Regardless, someone sent you a
package."

She tucked her gloves into her pocket, hung her coat
over her chair, then rubbed her chilled hands together.
"Well, this is a pleasant surprise. I love presents."

"All women do."

Chelsea ignored him.

"Who's it from?"

"I don't know." She grabbed her scissors, then cut
through the tape. When she folded back the flaps, she
found a card sitting on top of folded tissue paper. The
paper was a thick, ivory parchment, and the words "Miss
Chelsea" were written on it in tidy calligraphy.

She opened it, then read it aloud. "You seemed to

enjoy Rapunzel, so this might be of interest to you, too. I think you'll like it."

"What the hell is that supposed to mean?" McPherson asked. "Are you talking to people about your theories?"

A pang of guilt stabbed her. Dad was the only one she said anything to, and even then, it wasn't much. "Of course not. We can't discuss ongoing investigations."

"Then what's that all about?"

"I have no idea."

"And it's not signed?"

She flipped the card over, but the back side was blank. "No."

"Wait!" McPherson nodded toward the box.

But Chelsea unfolded the parchment. Inside the box was a red velvet cap trimmed with an intricate gold brocade. The style was vintage, something decades — if not centuries — old, but the material was obviously new. And expensive. She pulled it out. Held it up for him to see.

"You don't even have gloves on."

Chelsea dropped it on her desk. "I didn't think of that."

"It could have been an explosive. Or anthrax. Or anything."

"It wasn't!" She could hear the hysteria in her voice, so she knew Jim had to notice it.

"Okay. Calm down. You're all right."

Of course, he heard it. But she wasn't all right.

"So, What the hell is it?"

Her hands shook. She hid them in her pockets. "A cap."

"I can see that. What's it for?"

A chill raced through her body. The hair on the back of her neck stood on end. "Little Red Riding Hood."

He shook his head and scoffed. "Hood, Sullivan. The word is *hood*, not *cap*."

But she ignored him. He could think whatever he liked, but she knew the truth.

The cap was from Brianna's killer. Her murder did have to do with fairy tales.

And the evil SOB was just getting started.

Chapter Eleven

CHELSEA SAT BACK in her chair and stared at the red cap on her desk. Goosebumps sprouted on her arms, and her hands grew even colder. The card mentioned Rapunzel. It had to be from the killer.

McPherson was right. It was little red riding *hood*, not little red riding *cap*. Still, she knew with every fiber of her being, this "gift" had to do with fairy tales.

But which one?

She looked across the desk at her partner. "What do you think about this?"

"I think it's a little old-fashioned, but in the right role-play setting, you'd look cute in it. Especially in a tiny little dress."

"What's the matter with you? I'm being serious."

"So am I." He gave her a lascivious grin.

This was too dire a situation to allow his one-track mind to derail her train of thought. Chelsea closed her eyes, took a deep breath, opened them, then met his gaze. "Really. What do you think this means?"

"What does it mean? It means you said something to

someone you shouldn't have, and it's coming back to bite you."

"But I didn't." She'd only briefly mentioned it to her father, and he never left his apartment or talked to anyone, so it couldn't be him breaking her confidence or messing with her. Besides, for all his tough love, he'd never try to scare her like that. Would he? No. Force her to listen to creepy stories, sure. But send anonymous packages with references to murders? That was beyond even his idea of teaching hard lessons. At least, she hoped that was the case. "This has to have come from the killer."

"It's a hoax, Sullivan."

"I don't think so."

"Then what's the alternative? Some sicko out there is playing with you?"

Sure felt like it. But not some random psychopath. It had to be Brianna Lawson's killer. If it was, that meant he knew she was on the case and had figured out his MO.

And he knew where to find her.

The only saving grace so far was that the package came to the precinct and not her home.

A tingle crawled up her spine. She'd talked herself out of believing someone had watched her on Friday night. But perhaps her instincts had been spot-on.

No. She wasn't going down that road. Not yet.

She looked at McPherson. "Okay. Let's say you're right. Who sent this? And why?"

"The 'why' is easy. Someone knows you're a new detective, which makes you easy prey for pranks. The 'who' is a bit more tricky. If it was intended as a good-natured joke, I'd say it's somebody giving you an inappropriate welcome to the ranks. If it was meant more maliciously, it's someone who thinks you jumped the line when you got promoted."

"Gee, McPherson. If I didn't know better, I would say you just described yourself."

"I've been a detective for years. Why would I be jealous of your promotion?"

"I meant the good-natured part. But maybe that doesn't quite suit you after all."

He sipped his coffee, stared at her over the rim of the cup. Didn't say a word.

"What's the matter? Does it surprise you to learn I don't find you and your actions amiable?"

McPherson put down his drink. He leaned forward, resting his elbows on his desk. "I'm going to pretend you're a little emotional right now because this package scared you. So I'll let that comment slide. But if we're going to continue being partners, you're going to have to stop insulting me. Otherwise, we will have a problem. And I doubt you'll like the solution."

Chelsea swallowed. He had a hard edge she feared she'd never get used to. And hopefully, she'd never have to. She lifted her chin and squared her shoulders, feigning a strength she didn't feel. "I'm not trying to insult you. I was actually looking forward to a close relationship with my partner. But you're abrasive, arrogant, and impossible to get to know. You tell me not to let my feelings influence my actions. What about you? You seem to take exception to everything I say."

"Did it ever occur to you that everything you say is either a complaint or a commiseration?" McPherson rolled back his chair then pushed to his feet. "Maybe you would see my better side if I ever got to see yours." He tossed his cup in his trashcan as he walked away.

Chelsea stared at his broad shoulders as he retreated. The way he carried himself, his irritation radiated off him in waves. And she was the one who made him feel that way. Certainly hadn't meant to. Maybe he was right. She could be nicer, more tolerant. And if she was, his better side might, in fact, show.

Oh, who was she kidding? He was the abrasive one. He was the one who was impossible to read. He was the one who had an open-door policy in his bedroom and made sure she knew it. Which was hardly workplace chit-chat. Why couldn't he keep his comments — those kinds of comments — to himself?

A better question was, why did she care?

Didn't matter. At the moment, he was gone, and she had a red velvet clue in her hands. Now that she'd calmed, Chelsea set the cap aside then turned to her computer. After opening her browser, she began searching for literary references to the cap.

She started with fairy tales but didn't find anything. Moved on to historical works like *Robin Hood*, *Ivanhoe*, and *The Three Musketeers*. Nothing popped. Then she checked romantic classics. *Wuthering Heights*, *Madame Bovary*, anything and everything by Jane Austen and the Brontë sisters. Still didn't discover anything useful.

It had been over an hour, and she had nothing more to go on than when she started. McPherson still hadn't returned, and she was out of ideas.

With no partner to bounce ideas off of and no leads from her search, she decided to process the cap as evidence. Of course, her prints would be all over the mate-rial, the card, and even the box and tissue. Rookie mistake. But after forensics ruled her out, maybe they'd find some-thing. She donned gloves to prevent further contamination, collected everything, then headed for the lab.

Chelsea stopped mid-stride when she walked in the door.

McPherson was there.

"What are you doing here?"

He looked up at her. "Going over evidence. What's it look like I'm doing?"

She shrugged. "You disappeared. Didn't say where you are going, didn't come back. I had no idea what you were doing."

"Maybe we could both do a better job of communicating with each other."

Wasn't much in the way of a peace offering, but it was more than she expected. So, she nodded.

He tipped his chin toward the bundle in her hands. "Bring those for processing?"

"Yeah. Even if it's not from the killer, it's somehow connected to this case. Maybe the lab can find something."

"Good idea."

Rather decent of him not to berate her for contaminating the evidence in the first place. But now, they were working with a false, awkwardly polite demeanor toward each other. All things considered, she'd rather he be ribald and rough — a fact that surprised her. There had to be a happy medium.

They'd get there. Just not now. Or she'd get a new partner, and it wouldn't matter.

After Chelsea dealt with the lab tech, she turned to McPherson. "Now what? The sorority?"

He opened the door and gestured for her to precede him into the hallway. "Later. Since we're here, we might as well check with the ME again."

ON THEIR WAY from the lab to the ME's office, Jim struggled with the awkward silence. He considered about seventy-eight different topics of conversation, then discarded every one of them as either too personal or too lame. Finally, he settled on work chat.

"I found something over the weekend."

"Lob an easy one like that over the plate, and you shouldn't be surprised if I hit it out of the park."

"What?"

"Just saying that sentence was too easy to follow with an insult."

He hadn't figured her for someone who enjoyed sarcastic banter, especially when she was clearly upset. But he also wasn't about to let her get one up on him. "Give it your best shot, Sullivan."

"Too late. The moment's gone."

"You had nothing."

"Fine. You found a modicum of civility and compassion."

"Weak."

"A legal doc telling you you're a dad and owe child support."

"Please." Though his stomach flopped a bit at that one.

"A rash" — she pointed at his crotch — "down there."

"Now you're just embarrassing yourself."

She rolled her eyes, but her cheeks pinked. "Whatever. What did you find?"

Back to business. Okay. He could work with that. "What's the first place we should have looked?"

"Family. Friends. Boyfriend. Classmates. We talked to all of them."

Jim shook his head. "She's young, Sullivan. These kids live online. We should have checked her social media accounts."

"Of course." She slapped her forehead and muttered, "Rookie mistake."

He stopped walking and waited for her to do the same.

When she turned and looked at him, he said, "Did you just slap your forehead? Like a 1970's sitcom character?"

This time, she rubbed it. "You're giving me a headache."

"It probably hurts from smacking yourself."

They started walking again. She lowered her hand and looked at him. "What did you find out on her social media account?"

"Nothing."

And it was her turn to stop. "You really are giving me a headache. What is the point of all this?"

"You don't get it. I found *nothing*. It was typical social media. Actually, typical adult social media."

Sullivan shook her head. "If you're trying to lead me somewhere, stop slow walking and get to the point. I don't understand what you're trying to tell me."

"College kids post seven million selfies. Pics of parties and events. The occasional political or activist statement to make themselves look woke, right?"

"Don't say 'woke.' You sound ridiculous."

"But you agree that's what should have been on her streams?"

"Yeah. So?"

"So, hers was more like an adult's feeds. Pics of coffee, salads. The occasional recipe or joke. Animal photos. Some charity events. Each with a dozen likes or less, maybe a comment here or there. What she didn't have were pics of parties, friends, selfies. Her accounts looked like my mom's accounts."

"Your mom is on social media? That's so cute."

"Everyone's mom is on social media. Focus."

"Fine. Brianna Lawson didn't use social media the right way. According to your opinions of kids her age. What of it?"

"Her last post didn't match." Jim leaned against the wall, fished his phone from his pocket, then pulled up their vic's LiveLyfe account. "She posted a video and a series of pics of her with Simon. They'd just done a fun run and were celebrating at a park." He showed her the top pic — girlfriend and boyfriend, arms around each other, each holding up a beer.

Sullivan stood beside him to look at the screen. She played the video then started scrolling. "She got over a hundred likes. And a ton of comments. All favorable."

"Which shows she was popular and had a lot of friends. They just didn't usually have anything to say about videos of fainting goats or pictures of wheatgrass smoothies."

"I still don't know what you're getting at."

He scrolled back up through the comments until the first picture was visible. "Look what she's wearing — spandex leggings, a sports bra, and an unzipped jacket."

"Pretty much the standard uniform for any college-aged jogger."

"It's noticeably cold out."

Sullivan scowled at him. "I take it you don't mean because of the earmuffs and steam coming from their breath."

"Stop looking at me like I'm some kind of perv."

She raised her eyebrows.

"Look at the date. It was the last post she ever made, it differs from the wholesome image she usually portrays, and it was right before she broke up with Simon, which is odd, as they look very happy there."

"He said it wasn't that she didn't like him. She just wanted to focus on her studies."

"And you believe that? Look at her, Sullivan." He scrolled to a picture where the two were kissing. Then to another right after the kiss, where they're staring into each other's eyes. "These kids aren't just smitten. They're love-struck. A girl doesn't look at a guy like this one day then break up with him the next."

"So, your big discovery last night was an anomaly in her posting right before the breakup?"

"No. The anomaly made me wonder *why* the breakup followed. And why her posts stopped. So, I called the techs and asked if they'd had any luck with her phone or computer."

"I'm assuming they did, or we wouldn't be having this conversation. What did they find?"

"Brianna Lawson received an email right after her last post went live, no signature. The sender used a burner account and a VPN. Techs couldn't trace the IP address, but they did recover the message."

"And what did it say?"

He opened the email the tech had sent him then turned his phone so she could read the screen. It included the link to her LiveLyfe post and a brief message.

I had such high hopes for you, Brianna. You kept to yourself, you were chaste. Like a princess in a tower. Protected. Virtuous.

But you're a whore, just like all the others. Drinking alcohol, wearing slutty clothes, kissing in public.

You're a disappointment. A disgrace.

Naughty girls deserve to be punished. And as your parents didn't raise you right, the duty falls to me.

I'm coming for you.

Chapter Twelve

"SEE?" Chelsea said. "I was right!"

"About what?" He pocketed his phone and started walking again.

She chased after him. "Rapunzel."

McPherson shook his head. "Now I'm the one who doesn't follow."

"This message proves the fairy tale angle. A princess in a tower. That's who Rapunzel was."

He sighed as he opened the door to the stairwell, then he ushered her through. "I'm pretty sure he was just making a point. Practically painted a picture of a fair maiden in a chastity belt."

"Why won't you even consider what I'm telling you?"

"All rookies like to think they're going to land, and *solve*, a big case. But that just doesn't happen. This is a run-of-the-mill murder. Well, maybe not run-of-the-mill, as the MO was weird, but you see a lot of weird shit in this job. It doesn't mean there's a fairy-tale motif. And it doesn't make our unsub a serial killer. It's just one in a number of weird-ass murders."

"But—"

"Give it a rest for now, huh?"

They'd reached the ME's suite. Chelsea was steaming, but it wasn't the receptionist's fault. She swallowed her ire, plastered a bright smile on her face, and offered a cheerful greeting as she approached the desk. "Hi, Janice."

The receptionist smiled at McPherson like Chelsea wasn't even there. "Nice to see you again. Are you here to see Dr. Fletcher? He's in the middle of an autopsy right now."

"We just have a few quick questions," he said. "Is it okay if we go back?"

"If it doesn't bother you, I don't think he'll mind. He and Mason should be wrapping up soon, anyway."

"Thanks." Chelsea waved, knowing the receptionist's gaze was on her partner, then she and McPherson headed down the corridor. "Pretty sure she'd have given you the keys to the kingdom if you'd asked for them."

"This is one kingdom I wouldn't want to rule. Ever attended an autopsy before?"

"No, but I've seen plenty of dead bodies in the field." They stopped in front of the autopsy room door. A whirring noise sounded from inside. "Can't be much different." She grabbed the handle.

McPherson said, "Wait!"

But he was too late.

Chelsea flung the door open then stepped inside. Immediately, her eyes watered, and her gag reflex kicked in. The stench was overpowering. She'd been to crime scenes where bodies had been decomposing for days, sometimes weeks. Those odors clung to hair and clothing and were impossible to ignore.

This was so much worse.

The fetor was a palpable cloud that enveloped and

choked her. The coppery scent of blood was faint under the more dominant, vile funk of intestinal tissue and human waste. A rank, acrid miasma covered all of it — a sour combination of bile, formaldehyde, and chemical disinfectant — while a cloyingly sweet smell tickled her nose and coated the back of her throat. She bent over the trashcan by the door and retched.

While her head was over the bin, McPherson reached down and offered her a tissue and a surgical mask. Chelsea dabbed at her lips with the first then covered her face with the second, but even that buffer didn't stop the assault on her senses. Nor did breathing through her mouth. The stench ran over her tongue, and she gagged on the taste.

"You can wait outside if you want." McPherson's voice was soft, soothing.

She both appreciated and resented his concern.

"Just part of the job. I'm okay." But she still took a moment to try and settle her stomach.

After she composed herself, she turned toward the table. A bloated body lay on it, arms and face patchy and blue. The torso was cut open, skin pulled back like pages of a book, rib cage and sternum removed and set aside. The cavity was empty — the cadaver's internal organs lay in hermetically-sealed bags a few feet away next to the bones.

Scott turned off a saw, and the room was cloaked in thunderous silence. He pulled the cap of the skull free with a squelching *pop* that echoed in the quiet room.

Chelsea's stomach roiled again, and she turned away. Her gaze landed on Mason, who was donning a pale glove over a blue latex one.

When he began touching an ink pad, she stole another glance at the cadaver — the flesh had been stripped off its hand.

The technician had slipped the corpse's skin over his fingers to take prints.

She yanked off the mask, wheeled toward the trash can. Vomited again, then darted out of the room.

Her head spun in one direction while her stomach rolled in another. Horror-induced vertigo had her sliding down the wall then sitting with her head between her legs, gasping for breath.

A warm hand rubbed circles on her back. Imagining Mason's hand made her gag again, but thankfully, she had nothing more to expel and didn't soil her clothes. When she was finally settled enough to look up, she found McPherson beside her, comforting her.

"Sorry about this," she managed. "I wasn't expecting … that."

"I tried to warn you."

He had. But she'd been too stubborn and in too much of a rush to take heed. She had thought he was making it into a bigger deal than what it was.

Boy, had she been wrong.

"I'm sorry I didn't listen."

"I bet you are." He stopped rubbing her back and reached down to her.

She slipped her palm into his and allowed him to pull her to her feet. The room rocked, then her vision steadied. "Thanks."

"Don't mention it. That's what partners are for."

Mason stepped into the hallway, followed by Scott. He glanced at their joined hands.

A pang of guilt stabbed her. She released her grip on McPherson then smoothed her clothes and hair.

"Are you all right?" Scott asked.

"Yes, thanks. I'm really sorry about that. McPherson tried to warn me, but I thought I could handle it."

"It gets easier with time." He smiled at her and rubbed her arm.

She recoiled from his touch even though he'd removed his gloves. But that wasn't the problem.

Blood and viscera had spattered the gowns of both him and Mason, neither of whom seemed to notice or care. Chelsea, however, had noticed. And she did care.

Of course, they had masks and visors, aprons and gloves to protect them. Layers and layers between the dead and the living. Besides, they were used to it.

Chelsea had no protection, no experience with the procedure. And no interest in obtaining either.

Scott withdrew his hand. "My apologies. I seem to always be infringing on your personal space when you'd rather I be scrubbing my hands raw."

"Not raw." Her voice still sounded weak.

He managed a rueful chuckle. "I'm assuming you didn't come down here to watch an autopsy."

She shook her head.

"We wondered if you had anything more than your preliminary findings," McPherson said.

"No. The pathology report won't be in until this afternoon at the earliest. More likely tomorrow. Tissue analysis of the brain will be next week, maybe the week after."

"So long?" Chelsea asked.

Mason laughed. "You're one of those people."

"What people?"

"The ones who think TV crime shows are accurate."

"No, I'm not." Well, maybe she was. TV cops got results a lot faster than she did, which was contributing to her expectations. And frustrations. But she'd learned in college what realistic timeframes were for autopsy results.

Didn't mean she had to like it.

"Could you just notify us the second you have anything?" McPherson asked.

"Of course," Scott said.

"Will do," Mason added. "But it might be a while. Doc's going to be short-handed for a bit. I'm going on vacation. One of my old frat buddies is getting married."

Chelsea so didn't care. She just wanted to get out of there.

"Got it. Thanks." McPherson turned to her. "Let's get out of their way so they can get back to work."

Gladly. She gave the two men a quick smile and wave, then she followed her partner down the hall.

"Wait a second!" Scott called. He loped toward her.

Chelsea stopped where she stood, but McPherson drifted a few steps away before leaning against the wall to wait for her.

Again Scott reached for her, but this time he realized he was covered with bodily fluids and pulled back. "Sorry. Doesn't even faze me anymore, so I tend to forget."

"That's okay. So, did you remember something about the case?"

"No." He cleared his throat. "I have a personal question if you don't mind."

"I don't mind. What's up?"

"Do you like plays?"

That wasn't the question she was expecting, and she wasn't prepared to answer him. "I'm sorry?"

"Plays. You know. *Hamlet. Arsenic and Old Lace. Uncle Harry*. Live performances that aren't musicals."

"Oh. Plays. Yes, of course. Why do you ask?"

"I happen to belong to a community theater troupe. We're putting on Eugene O'Neill's *Mourning Becomes Electra*, and it's our opening night. I thought perhaps you'd like to attend. Afterward, we could go out. It's always nice to celebrate a good open. Or bemoan a bad one."

So far today, she'd received a veiled threat from a killer and gotten sick from an autopsy. And it wasn't even lunch yet. All she wanted to do was go home and huddle on the sofa with a tub of spumoni and the remote control. Her refusal was on the tip of her tongue when she stopped. When was the last time she'd been on a date? When was the last time she'd gone out with friends? It wasn't healthy for a young woman to do nothing but work and eat ice cream. And he was handsome, educated, mannerly — unlike some people she knew.

Chelsea glanced at her partner then back to Scott.

Bones reruns would have to wait.

"I'm sure it will be a celebration. And I'd love to. Thanks, Scott."

"Great. I have to be at the theater early, so I'll leave your ticket at Will Call. If that's okay?"

"It's fine."

"Wonderful. We're performing at the Lumina. Show starts at eight."

"I'll be there. See you tonight."

"Looking forward to it." He headed back down the hall.

"Break a leg!" she called after him.

He turned toward her. After a brief pause, he waved, then he went back inside his chamber of horrors.

Chelsea had watched him until he was out of sight. Still, she didn't turn around. She knew what expression her partner would be sporting and had no desire to see it.

McPherson cleared his throat.

Her shoulders slumped, and she hung her head.

"So, you're going out with Dr. Death tonight."

She spun around and walked right past him, trying to

avoid the discussion. Didn't stop her from seeing the sneer on his face.

Just like she expected.

His long legs made short work of the distance between them. "Do you think it's an omen that he invited you to a tragedy?"

"What?" They'd reached the lobby. Janice wasn't at her desk, so it saved Chelsea the embarrassment of being blatantly ignored. She started stomping up the steps.

"Omen. Tragedy." He took the stairs two at a time but slowed his pace to stay even with her. "O'Neill's play."

"What do you know about O'Neill's work?"

"I read."

She stumbled.

He grasped her elbow, keeping her from taking a header on the landing. "Does it really shock you that much?"

"That you read? No. I just figured you more for a *Hustler* fan than classic literature."

McPherson scowled and flung her arm away from him. He jogged the rest of the way up the stairs.

Chelsea caught up to him at his desk. "I'm sorry. I was just teasing."

"Mm-hmm." His jaw was set. And ticking.

"No, really. Let me make it up to you."

He looked up at her. "How?"

"Come with me tonight."

"And be the third wheel? No way."

"It's not a date. Scott won't even be with me."

"It's definitely a date. He's taking you out afterward."

She sighed. "Then come for the first part, so I don't have to be there alone."

"Sullivan, he's only leaving you one ticket. You're probably going to be in the first row. I'd have to pay my own way and end up in the cheap seats, so you'd be alone, anyway."

"Then I'll go ask him for two tickets." She spun toward the stairs.

He caught her elbow again. "Whoa. Save yourself the effort. I'm not interested."

"But I feel bad."

"And your idea of making it up to me is to force me to go to Dr. Death's show?"

"Would you please stop calling him that?"

"No."

Chelsea rolled her eyes. "So, will you come? I'll buy you dinner first. Anywhere you want to go. Part apology, part peace offering."

"Anywhere?"

"Yes."

"Even Mount Williamson? Cristoffs?"

Of course, he'd pick a premier gourmet restaurant on the other side of the river. Neither her schedule nor her bank account could handle it, but if that's what it took to gel their relationship, she'd do it. "If that's what you want."

He laughed. "Lighten up, Sully."

She winced at her father's nickname.

"I was only kidding. I'd be happy with a sandwich at Ficca's Cucina."

Thank God. The deli was a favorite of hers. It was also on the right side of the river and far more affordable.

"But you don't owe me a meal."

Chelsea shrugged. "I offered."

"I respectfully decline. Besides, I was just stringing you along. Wanted to see how you'd react. You don't owe me an apology, and even if you did, I'm not available. I have a date."

Why didn't that surprise her?

Chapter Thirteen

CHELSEA SPENT the afternoon going over the evidence again. She and McPherson had come to an unspoken truce, which made the working environment far more tolerable.

Too bad it was no more productive.

Their shift ended at three. Chelsea still couldn't get the cap out of her mind, but talking to McPherson about it was pointless, as he didn't subscribe to her theory. Still, she knew she was missing something but couldn't figure out what. As she put on her coat, she decided to stop and visit her father on her way home from work. She parted ways with her partner in the parking lot, then headed out.

All the talk about Ficca's Cucina had her craving their famous cheesesteak — the number two seller on their menu. She always laughed at that joke. It was their best-selling sandwich, hands down. But Steel City residents loved their beer, apparently even more than food, and the ice-cold brew came in at number one on their list.

Chelsea didn't drink, although she still found it funny.

Her stomach growled, and she headed to the Warehouse District for two number-twos, topped with fries, coleslaw, and tomato slices. No beer for Dad, although he'd want it. And probably complain about not having it. Instead, she asked for two sodas. When the order was ready, she headed for Dad's apartment.

His door was unlocked again. For a guy who didn't leave his recliner, the door was always unlatched, which was especially odd for a former cop.

"Dad!"

No answer. Not surprising. He was probably engrossed in the television.

She closed the door behind her. The house smelled faintly of dirty socks. After the autopsy, she didn't think she could tolerate another vile odor. This was about as much unpleasantness she could handle. At least she'd knocked back the musty, mildewy smell when she'd cleaned over the weekend. Wouldn't have been able to stand that today.

Chelsea made her way to the living room. Dad was seated right where she expected, glued to a hockey game.

"I brought dinner." She shook the takeout bag.

He didn't even blink.

She went to the kitchen to plate the food and tried to ignore the new collection of dirty dishes in the sink. Couldn't. After she unloaded and loaded the dishwasher, she took their sandwiches and soft drinks back to the living room.

Dad hadn't moved.

"I brought dinner. Sandwiches from Ficca's."

He leaned to the side to look past her.

She slammed his dish on the coffee table, then plopped down on the sofa. "Isn't it early for a hockey game?"

"Game comes on at seven."

"What are you watching now?"

"Rerun of the 2017 Stanley Cup championship game."

"You already know who won. You saw the game live when it aired."

"Saw it at least thirty times since, too. Hell of a team. Hell of a series."

Hell of a game.

"Hell of a game."

Chelsea rolled her eyes. "You taking your medicine, Dad?"

He grunted.

It was supposed to sound like a "yes," but she recognized it for the "no" it was. She excused herself then went to his bathroom. No point in locking the door, as he wouldn't leave the television long enough to check on her. If he even noticed she was gone, which he probably wouldn't.

Nor would he care when she found proof of her assumptions.

She opened his medicine cabinet, looked at the bottles. The fill dates were three weeks earlier, and every bottle was full.

Darn it all, anyway.

Chelsea palmed his required dosage then stormed back to the living room. "What are you thinking? You haven't taken a single pill. That stuff is expensive. You can't afford to throw money down the drain like that. But more importantly, you *need* it."

He shrugged. "Not down the drain. Still in the bottle."

"Depression is serious, Dad."

"As a heart attack. Want me to take pills for that, too?"

She took a deep breath and struggled not to scream at him. Instead, she spoke softly. "Dad. You have to take your pills. The medicine needs to build up in your system. You can't miss one day, let alone one month. Besides, going off cold turkey is really dangerous."

"I've been off for weeks. Nothing happened."

Yeah, by the grace of God. She needed to pay closer attention to him, or she'd have to place him in an assisted living home — something he'd hate. And neither of them could afford. Not even if they combined their money.

"Goal!" He pumped his fist in the air.

She sighed. Picked up his cola. Handed it to him.

He glanced at it. "Rather have a beer."

"You can't drink on your meds."

"I'm not on any meds."

At least he wasn't lying. She took his hand, forced his fist open, then dropped the pills into his palm.

He started to tip his fingers toward the floor.

"So help me, God, if you don't take those right now, I'll have you committed."

"You don't have the authority."

That was another thing she needed to do — get her Dad to give her the rights to make decisions for him regarding his medical care. "I'm a cop. If I tell the hospital I think you're a danger to yourself and others, they'll put you in the psych ward for evaluation. No hockey in there, Dad."

He glowered at her. "You wouldn't."

"I would." In truth, she didn't know if she had the strength of will to do that to him. Not at this point, anyway.

Dad popped the pills in his mouth then downed them with a sip of his drink. "Didn't know you had the stones, Toots."

As long as he thought it, she'd run with it. "Eat your dinner."

They munched on their sandwiches in silence.

"How's the case going?"

Chelsea was so surprised when he initiated a conversation, she choked on the bread. After coughing, she sipped her drink. Her eyes had watered, and she dabbed at the tears with her napkin. "Actually, something strange happened today."

"Oh?"

"Someone sent me a red velvet cap and a note referring to Rapunzel."

"Not Rapunzel. Little Red Riding Hood."

"No, Dad. Not a hood. A cap."

"Little Red."

She shook her head. Why didn't he get it? Was his mind going, too? "You're not listening to me. I didn't get a hood. I got a little red velvet hat."

He took a huge bite of his sandwich, then answered, spitting crumbs as he spoke. "Thf soignal stry thiz clld *Lillel Rod Cop*."

"What?"

Dad swallowed, sipped his drink, then cleared his throat. "I said, the original story is called *Little Red Cap*."

"It is?"

"You really don't remember these stories from your childhood? Read the book I gave you. It's a first edition. The original versions, before all the feel-good changes that softened them up. The little girl didn't wear a hooded cloak. It was a little velvet cap made by her grandmother."

She should feel vindicated that her original theory was correct, but instead, she was chilled to her core.

There was a killer out there — one as obsessed with the original Grimm's tales as her father.

And she had caught his attention.

JIM GLANCED at his watch for probably the twentieth time. Maybe more. He'd lost track after looking five times in five minutes.

Served him right. He'd scheduled this date, so it wasn't technically a lie when he told his mother he couldn't go out with Alessa because he was seeing someone else. He looked at Patty across the table. She was still talking about herself.

And as he was "seeing" her as she did so, he hadn't officially lied to his mother.

Semantics, to be sure. But good enough to assuage any guilt he might be feeling. Besides, spending time with Patty was penance enough for any sins he committed.

She broke a breadstick in half then swiped one end through the sauce in her otherwise empty plate as she pointed at him with the other. "I mean, I'm not wrong, am I?"

He had no idea what she was talking about. "No. Not at all."

"I didn't think so." Patty took a bite of the sauce-soaked bread then continued with her story. A few crumbs sprayed from her mouth as she did, though she didn't seem to notice. Or care if she did.

Jim sipped his water and wished, for about the hundredth time, he'd ordered something stronger.

"I mean, I'm the eldest granddaughter. I spent more time in the kitchen with my grandmother than my sister or any of our cousins. Sure, I don't really like to cook, but why shouldn't I get her recipes?"

"Can't you guys digitize them, so everyone has a copy?"

"But if everyone has access to them, they're not special anymore."

Of course, she was more concerned with getting something for herself than she was with being fair to her family.

"I think family recipes should belong to, you know, the family."

Her eyes narrowed. "I thought you agreed with me."

"I agree that you should get something that means something to you and reminds you of your grandmother, but it doesn't have to mean you don't share. That's your legacy."

"That's right. It's *my* legacy. They can find their own way to immortalize themselves."

"How are you immortalizing yourself with your grand-mother's recipes?"

"Because they're fucking delicious. I could make a fortune if I opened a restaurant."

"But you said you don't like to cook."

"I'd hire someone to do that."

"So, you'd share your family recipes with strangers but not your family?"

"They're welcome to work for me. Geez. You act like you don't get me at all."

He didn't. "Sorry. I didn't understand your plan."

"Obviously. Now, what was I saying? Oh, right. Recipes."

Jim tuned out again. It felt like his brain was bleeding from the effort of dealing with her. After he took her home, he was blocking her number.

"So, then my grandmother … "

Grandmother. Every time she'd said that word this evening, something niggled in the back of his brain. Grandmother. Grandmother. Grandmother.

Why did it matter? What did it mean?

He heard a racket outside and glanced out the window. A group of high school kids were somehow engaged in a snowball fight as they walked down the sidewalk together. It was like today's youth had no idea how to play outside.

Snowball fights required distance, a bunker, a pre-made surplus of projectiles, and deadly aim. This gaggle of morons was pretty much just flinging loose handfuls of snow at each other.

A girl in a red knit cap shrieked as a boy in a Woodland Falls varsity jacket shoved snow down her neck.

Woodland Falls.

The Woodland Falls Wolverines.

Wolverines. Wolves.

Red cap. Grandmother.

Fine. A wolverine wasn't a wolf, and a cap wasn't a hood. But as soon as he made those mental connections, that itch in his brain stopped itching.

Much as he hated to admit it, Sullivan might be onto something. And she might be in danger.

Chapter Fourteen

When Chelsea reached her car, she pushed the "unlock" button on her key fob. Didn't hear the *click* of the lock disengaging, though. Just a hollow *whiff*. Must have hit the wrong button.

Tried it again. Same result.

She stepped up to the door. Idiot. She'd been so distracted, she hadn't locked it. Lucky for her, no one had taken anything. Not even the six quarters she'd dropped into the cupholder.

It was freezing, so she climbed inside. She called McPherson as she turned her key, then cranked the heater to high. The call bounced to the hands-free system. One ring sounded through her car's speakers before Jim answered.

"What?"

Talk about phone etiquette. "Hi. It's Chelsea Sullivan."

"I'm aware."

Right. Caller ID. "I just got back from a visit with—" Well, she didn't think that one through. She couldn't let him know she'd talked about the case with her dad.

"With who?"

"With a friend of mine. Known him for as long as I can remember. We go way back."

"Is there a point to this story?"

"Of course. See, he's an expert in literature. Specifically the Brothers Grimm version of fairy tales."

"A guy?"

"Yes." She sighed.

"What's your point?"

"I'm pretty sure he just confirmed my theory."

"What theory?"

A soft giggle sounded through the hands-free system.

"What was that?"

"You mean Rapunzel, Sullivan?"

"I mean the killer's obsession with fairy tales."

"You should let this go."

She was about to go off on him, but something in his tone stopped her. For the first time, she didn't hear exasperation. She heard … concern. "My source said the original title of *Little Red Riding Hood* was *Little Red Cap*. It was about a little girl who fell prey to a wolf in the woods when she was on her way to see her sick grandmother. The girl wore a red velvet cap."

Another giggle. Louder. Longer.

McPherson groaned. "Sullivan, we're off duty."

"But—"

"But, nothing. You have plans tonight, remember?"

"I don't *have* to go to the play. If you think we can run down this lead, I can come in."

"Personally, I don't know why you accepted Dr. Death's invitation to begin with. Go, don't go. Doesn't matter to me. But there's no lead to run down, so let it go. And let me go. I'm. On. A. Date."

That explained the giggles. "Oh. Sorry. I forgot."

Wasn't it a little early for the giggling and groaning part of the evening? And why the heck was he answering the phone in the middle of that, anyway?

"Good night, Sullivan."

The call ended. The second Jim's voice wasn't coming through her speakers, her radio blasted through the car — the fading refrain as Bruce Springsteen's "Glory Days" ended. Then the announcer launched into his station identification spiel. "WPRT The Parrot. Home of Steel City's Classic Hits."

Classic hits. She was born in the eighties, for Pete's sake. The last year of the decade, but still. Didn't seem right that eighties music played on the "classic hits" station.

Her brow furrowed. The classic hits station?

She'd been listening to 106.1 on the way to her Dad's.

Chelsea shook her head. Must have changed the station when fumbled with the temperature controls.

The fact that she'd found her car unlocked niggled in the back of her brain.

But without a key, the station couldn't be changed. Right?

No. She was just being paranoid. Time to put it all out of her mind.

She had a date to get ready for.

CHELSEA FOUND a ticket waiting for her at Will Call, just as Scott had promised. And, as McPherson had predicted, it was for the front row.

She made her way to her seat as the lights were dimming. Perfect timing.

It was too dark to read her program, and she hadn't

asked Scott his role, so she sat back to watch, excited to discover who he was playing.

What if he wasn't any good?

Her stomach made a tiny flop — nothing like earlier, just a hint of nerves. She didn't want to lie to him. But if he tanked? How could she tell him the truth?

Why had she agreed to this?

The curtain rose. An actor stepped onto the stage.

Nothing she could do now. Sure, she could pretend to be called away for work. But then she'd have to dash up the aisle, disrupting the audience and possibly the actors.

No, she'd have to stay.

So she sat back, settled in, and hoped Scott's performance was stellar.

Two hours later, she breathed a sigh of relief — the performance was even better than she hoped.

Unfortunately, Scott wasn't in it. At least, not that she'd noticed. He may have been one of the extras who blended into the background, but she'd tried to pick him out and never saw him.

The cast took its final bows, then the curtain closed, and the house lights came up. The audience filtered toward the exit, but Chelsea didn't move. She and Scott hadn't discussed a meeting place, so she's stayed in her seat, figuring he would know where to look for her.

If he was even there. She was really starting to wonder.

The theater was nearly empty when Scott stepped onto the stage. When he saw her, his eyes lit up. He jumped to the floor, took her hands, then pulled her to her feet. "I'm so glad you came. What did you think?"

"The performance was wonderful." She bit her lip, afraid to say more.

His face clouded, and his smile disappeared. "What's wrong?"

"I really wanted to discuss your performance with you, but I'm sorry. I couldn't find you."

A sharp blast of laughter burst from him. "My apologies. I guess I should've told you. I'm not an actor. I'm in charge of wardrobe and makeup. Would it surprise you to know that the actor who plays Ezra is actually younger than the actress who plays Lavinia?"

What a relief. She was starting to question her powers of observation — not a good thing for a detective. "You're kidding?"

He beamed.

"Well, I can honestly say you did a stellar job. I loved the costumes, and I would have never guessed Lavinia was the same generation as Ezra, let alone older."

"Then I shall consider my work a rousing success."

"As you should."

"Are you still up for a drink and a bite to eat?"

"I'm not really into the bar scene."

"I see."

She shook her head. "That wasn't me declining your offer. I just don't drink alcohol. But we should celebrate tonight. Pick a place. Anywhere you want. I can teetotal with the best of them."

"How about DiAntonio's?"

That was at least a mile and a half away. She'd hoped to pop in somewhere close by, then head home and go to bed. A nighttime hike through frozen city streets didn't appeal to her in the slightest. But he was so excited. How could she refuse? "Sure."

"We could go somewhere else if you'd rather."

"Nope. This is your night. DiAntonio's it is."

"Their food is delicious. Have you ever been there?"

"Sunday brunch once."

"Only once? You didn't like it. We can go somewhere else."

"No. This is fine. I loved it. Really. I just haven't had the chance to return. This is the perfect opportunity."

"They make a honey chestnut cappuccino that's worth the walk."

The walk? This was turning into an all-night affair. But she affected an agreeable smile. "As long as I can get mine decaf. I don't want to be up all night."

He offered his elbow. "Shall we?"

Chelsea slipped her arm through his, then he led her outside. The sky glittered with stars, more than were typically seen in the city. But with no cloud cover, the universe came closer.

No cloud cover also meant the temperature plummeted. She shivered and looped her scarf around her neck again.

"I'm sorry. I don't know if my body temperature naturally runs high or if I'm just used to the cold from the autopsy room, but this weather never bothers me. I forget other people hate it. If you're too chilly, we could take a taxi or a FASTr."

"If we wait for a ride, I'll turn into a popsicle. A brisk walk should warm me right up."

Scott looked up and down the street. There was almost no traffic — definitely no cabs. "I'm sorry. I'm always so keyed up after a performance. I tend to walk or burn off the energy in other ways. But you've had a full day at work. You probably don't feel like a stroll. Especially in this weather."

"It's fine, Scott. Stop worrying about my energy or my comfort, or my cuisine preferences. This is a big night for you. Let's just go celebrate."

Two new men in her life. One tried too hard to please her. The other seemed to go out of his way to annoy her.

Where was the middle ground? She needed that Goldilocks-zone.

Just the thought of the fairy tale made a shiver run through her.

Scott's eyebrows arched. "You're shivering."

"I'm *fine*."

"If you're sure." Then he picked up the pace slightly.

Her toes felt like they were going to snap off, but at least she managed to keep her teeth from chattering.

As they walked, he started humming.

"Is that 'All I Ask of You' from *Phantom*?"

"Oh, yes. Sorry."

"Stop apologizing!"

"Sorry."

She shook her head.

He chuckled. "I often hum. Music soothes me. Not that I find your company difficult. I'm—"

"Don't say 'sorry.'"

"On a performance high." He smiled at her.

"I loved *Phantom of the Opera*. In fact, that's the last performance I saw in person." He didn't need to know she was a child at the time. "Afterward, I bought the CD." Well, her mother bought it for her. "I think I listened to it for a year straight. I still play it now and again. I have the soundtrack in my playlist, but I'm still partial to the Steel City performers rather than Andrew Lloyd Webber's original release, and I can't find it online to download."

"Where did you see it? Here? Toronto? New York?"

"Here. I know we didn't have Michael Crawford, but I can't imagine even he was as good as our phantom. Can't remember the guy's name, though." Her brain was probably frozen.

"I agree. The Steel City production starred Franc D'Ambrosio. He blew me away. Did you know he was the actor who played Michael Corleone's adult son in *The Godfather Part III*?"

She shook her head. "I didn't realize."

"His voice is amazing."

"It is. But you have a lovely voice, too. You should perform."

"No. The stage isn't for me."

"It's too bad. I could listen to you all night."

He looked at her, a small smile on his lips. "If you played the CD so much, you must know the songs."

"Every word."

"Sing with me."

"What? My singing is limited to showers. It's definitely not street-worthy."

"No one will hear you. I've never seen so few people out at night."

Because it was thirty below. "I don't know …"

"Come on. It's a duet. Don't leave me hanging."

Before she could argue, he launched into "All I Ask of You." His voice was strong, rich. When he reached the part where Christine sang, he nudged her. She stalled, but then she started. Quietly at first, with a tremolo to her words — part nerves, part cold. But then she got caught up in the passion of the music and the beauty of the lyrics, and by the end, she was belting out the number at the top of her lungs.

When they finished, she was breathless. "Well, if the streets weren't empty before, I cleared them out."

"Don't be silly. You have the voice of an angel."

The parallel between his words to her and the Phantom's to Christine was a little too close for comfort. She cleared her throat and searched for a way to change the subject. "So, tell me about your theater group."

He told her stories about the actors in his company, their current director … even an off-color tale about their prop master, though his tone reflected disdain more than humor.

She didn't know if she should chuckle or not, so she changed the subject. "I have to ask, Scott. Why don't you act? Your passion for the theater is evident."

"I don't like the spotlight. If I made a mistake, I'd… I couldn't handle it."

Chelsea understood. She had some type-A tendencies, too. "You could try for a role like the Phantom. Wear a mask."

"Masks. We all wear them in some form. I don't care to don another."

"Sorry?"

He shook his head. "I don't think even a mask would be enough of a buffer for me."

"You're a talented makeup artist. Change your appearance. Use a stage name. Then if you did make a mistake, no one would know it was you."

"I'd still know."

"Mistakes are inevitable. Even Broadway stars flub their lines now and then. In fact, Hugh Jackman wet himself on stage trying to hit a high note."

"You're joking?"

"No. He admitted it in an interview."

"Now I'm really not taking the stage."

She laughed. "What about directing?"

Scott stopped walking, unlinked their arms. He stepped back and stared at her. "Chelsea, I have a full-time job plus what I do at the theater company. That's more than enough responsibility on my shoulders. Are you embarrassed to be out with a lowly makeup artist?"

"Oh, Scott. No! I'm sorry if you took this the wrong way. You know so much about the theater, and you're so passionate about it. I just know an audience would enjoy your work — on stage or directing the action."

He sighed. "No, I'm sorry. I didn't mean to get so upset. Like I said, I have a lot of pent-up energy after a show. My emotions are all over the place."

"So, decaf for you, too?"

"Maybe we should do this another night."

That was her out. She could go home, go to bed. Start fresh another time.

But it was his opening night, and instead of celebrating with him, she'd hurt his feelings. She had to make it right. "Come on. We're almost there. DiAntonio's is half a block away. One cup of coffee. Even better, chamomile tea. It'll help you sleep."

Chelsea really thought he was going to decline.

But then he smiled. "One quick cup. It's been a long day for both of us."

Couldn't argue with that. She linked her arm through his again, and they picked up the pace. A few minutes later, she was thawing out across the table from him, cradling her teacup to warm her hands. "So, did you have any other family or friends there tonight?"

He shook his head. "Most of my friends are in the theater."

"We should have invited them along."

Scott gave her a funny look but didn't say anything.

"What about your family?"

"I don't have any."

"I'm sorry."

"My dad died when I was in high school. My mother and I …" He shrugged. "We had a complicated relationship, but she was …" He sighed. "I loved her. She died a few months ago."

"Oh, Scott! I'm so sorry."

"Thank you."

"No brothers or sisters?"

"None to speak of."

"I understand. Family relationships can be difficult. I don't have any siblings, either, and my mom lives on the other side of the country."

"Oh? What part?"

"California. Napa Valley."

"Ah, wine country. Lovely. I just visited California, myself."

"Business or pleasure?"

"There was a coroner's convention in Las Vegas. Gambling isn't really my scene. I needed to wind down afterward, so I took a drive to Los Angeles. Tried to steep myself in the show business culture."

"Did you enjoy it?"

"Not in the slightest. But I squeezed in a family visit, so it all turned out okay in the end."

She frowned. "I thought you didn't have family?"

"No immediate family left. I visited my cousin."

"Oh. Well, that's nice." They fell into an awkward silence, but she couldn't think of a thing to say.

Luckily, Scott picked up the slack. "So, your mother's out west. What about your father?"

"Things with him are difficult."

"He used to work for the force, right?"

Seemed she couldn't get away from Dad's reputation. Even on a date. If this was, in fact, a date. "A long time ago."

Scott nodded. Then he raised his cup. "To forging newer, better relationships."

Chelsea tapped hers against his, then drank half the tea in a few gulps. It was time to go home.

"About today."

She dabbed the corners of her mouth with a napkin. "What about it?"

"I'm sorry about what happened in the autopsy room."

Her cheeks burned. "That's on me. I should have listened to McPherson. He tried to warn me."

"Your face was green. I felt terrible."

"Green? Too bad. That's not a great color on me."

He chuckled. "Don't worry about that. You're always a vision. How's the case going?"

"Slow. We have a few leads to run down, but I'm not optimistic."

"Do you need a sounding board? I'm told I'm a great listener."

"That's sweet of you to offer, Scott. But right now, I'm exhausted. I don't want to go over the case. I just want to go to bed and put this day behind me."

"And here I am, keeping you out late."

"It was my pleasure. But I really have to go."

Her car was back near the theater. He walked her there, their pace faster than earlier. She hoped it wasn't because he was tired of her and wanted to get away. He was sweet, cultured, caring. A little too apologetic, but in an endearing way. Chelsea liked him and wouldn't mind going out with him again. Preferably earlier or on her day off.

Whether the evening was a flop or success, though, she was glad to go home. She could barely keep her eyes open. Would be nice if he mentioned doing this again, though.

To give him the chance, she hovered by her door.

He glanced at his watch. "You're right. It is late. You better go."

And yet, she got the feeling he was the one who wanted to go their separate ways. "Okay. Well, thanks, Scott." And still, she waited.

"See you at work." He kissed her hand then opened the car door for her.

After she crawled in, she looked up to say goodnight.

But he was already walking away.

Chelsea sighed and shut her door. She was exhausted, and bed sounded great. Best not to dwell on where things went off the rails with Scott.

She turned the ignition. Music blared from her speakers, this time of her own doing. But it reminded her of that strange thing with the radio earlier, which got her thinking about the case again.

And the whole way home, she couldn't get fairy tales out of her mind.

Chapter Fifteen

JIM TOSSED AND TURNED, unable to sleep. He seldom had woman problems, but tonight was an exception to the rule. Then again, so were the women giving him problems.

Alessa was jealous, and green was a color she didn't wear well. She didn't know he and Sullivan were just partners — not even friends — nor did she care. Because she wasn't over him, any woman in his life was competition, and she fought dirty.

Calling his mother was about the dirtiest punch she could have thrown.

Mom wasn't one to keep her opinions to herself. She'd had plenty to say about his dating choices and his life choices, many of which were also low blows.

He hadn't been interested in a word of it at the time. And after a miserable dinner with Patty — during which he'd have knocked himself out if he could have — he'd been even less interested.

Yet his mother's opinions weighed heavily on him in the middle of the night when he had no one to take his mind off things.

Guilt was the loudest of emotions at three a.m.

And it wasn't just guilt over Alessa and Mom and even Patty. He was nursing some serious conscience pangs about how he'd treated Sullivan. She was like a gnat. An innocent, optimistic, altruistic gnat, but a pest all the same. No matter how many times he swiped at her, she was still there. Still working hard. Still insisting her theory had merit.

As much as he'd tried to keep her at arm's length, she'd managed to squeeze past his defenses. He was starting to see merit in her work. And danger in her future.

He'd started putting all the pieces together and didn't like the picture they made.

After he'd left the restaurant, he'd hurried home to do some research. The first version of Little Red Riding Hood wasn't a hood. It was a cap. Someone knew about her theory and knew how to reach her.

If she wasn't talking outside the station — and a rule-follower like her wouldn't discuss the case with her friends, not in any detail that jeopardized what the department was doing, anyway — that meant the cap wasn't an in-house prank.

Which meant it could only have been sent by the killer.

And *that* meant all kinds of terrible things.

Jim crawled out of bed, then padded to the kitchen to make a pot of coffee. If he wasn't going to get any sleep, he might as well make good use of the time.

He was just taking his first sip when his phone rang.

CHELSEA PULLED on a long-sleeved sweatshirt with an embroidered duck face on it and stepped into yellow, orange, and pink plaid flannel pajama bottoms. She crawled into bed, but her eyes were wide open and her thoughts cyclonic. So, she got up.

After a quick trip to the kitchen, she plopped on her sofa, where she nestled under a fleece throw with a container of ice cream in one hand and a spoon in the other.

The remote control was in reach, but she didn't bother turning on the television.

She spent a few minutes analyzing the details of her date — if it even was a date. Heck, she wasn't even sure what to call it. It certainly had its ups and downs. She'd started the day vomiting in front of him and ended it with an awkward conversation and a brusque goodbye. But the part in the middle was good. Mostly. And he'd kissed her hand. But he didn't say anything about calling or doing it again.

If women were from Venus, men weren't from Mars — they hailed from outside the Milky Way.

Usually, spumoni could make anything better, but no amount of chocolate, cherry, and pistachio could help her make sense of the male species. Or her innate ability to constantly say or do the wrong thing in front of them.

Her hand paused halfway to her mouth as a horrible thought struck her — she was going to grow up to be a crazy old lady with a hundred cats, hunched in a creaky rocking chair on a dilapidated porch, cackling at the frightened children who were double-dog dared to open her gate.

Crazy old lady.

A moment later, she was slammed with fairy-tale images. The hag offering Snow White an apple. The crone knocking on the prince's door and cursing him to look like the Beast. The forest-dwelling witch who lived in a house of sweets and baked children in her oven.

Chelsea jolted, dropped her spoon. A marbled puddle in shades of brown, pink, and green spread across her blanket then seeped into the fuzzy threads of the fleece.

Crones and caps. Plaits and packages.

Didn't matter that Jim didn't believe her. She knew it was true. There was a fairy-tale killer out there. One who was invested in her involvement.

One who planned on striking again.

She carried her snack and her throw into the kitchen. After putting the ice cream in the freezer, she put dish detergent on the muddied stain she'd made then scrubbed until her muscles burned.

Cinderella

Dressed in yella

Went upstairs

To kiss her fella

A *thunk* in the living room made her jump.

Her gun was in her bedroom.

She dropped the blanket, took a chef's knife from the block on her counter, then tiptoed out of the kitchen, blade poised to strike.

But no one was there.

Chelsea checked her door. Knob and deadbolt were locked. None of the windows were open or broken. Bathroom, closets, under the bed … no intruders.

As she padded back to her kitchen, she caught a glimpse of her remote control on the floor in the living room. The thunk. It had fallen.

Why would it have fallen without being bumped?

Right. Because random items resting on curved furniture arms never lost a battle with the forces of gravity.

Chelsea placed the remote in the middle of her coffee

table, then she returned the knife to the kitchen. She poured more detergent on the stain then left it until the morning. After one more round of checking door and window locks — all secure — she went to bed.

And kept her gun under the pillow.

Adrenaline and sugar had her too wired to sleep, so she reviewed the facts of the case. They either had too many suspects or too few. Some had no motives. Others had motives and alibis. She was left with a slew of facts that didn't seem to go together.

Why the open window if that wasn't the place of entry?

Why strip the victim if the crime wasn't sexual?

Why the fairy-tale reference if the cause of death didn't coincide with the story?

Why had she been sent the cap, which she was convinced was a clue to the next murder? Why her and not McPherson or Davenport? Was it because, like Dad said, she was overly emotional and easy to rattle? Was it as her partner implied — she was too empathetic and reached for too many straws? Was the killer playing games with her because she was weak?

And most troubling of all, would she be able to figure out what all this meant before the unsub struck again?

Did he want her to stop him? Would he be angry if she didn't?

Despite the disturbing thoughts, her eyelids grew heavy, and soon she drifted into a restless sleep.

Ping!

She snatched her gun from under the pillow as she bolted upright. Hadn't she just fallen asleep? Couldn't be her alarm already.

The numbers on her clock were too bright in the darkness — 3:18. She'd been asleep for hours.

A quick glance around the room showed no one was there. Nothing was out of place.

But her cell phone screen was glowing. She'd received a text. The message faded before she could read it.

Who'd contact her in the middle of the night?

Chelsea reached for her cell, turned it on.

The text was from McPherson.

We caught another one.

Chapter Sixteen

JIM'S PHONE rang seconds after he'd sent the text. Didn't even have to look at caller ID to know it would be his partner. He held his cell to his ear. "Hey."

Sullivan sounded way too alert for the middle of the night. "What's going on? Aren't there other detectives on duty?"

"I didn't feel like getting up, either." Which was a lie, as he'd already been up. Hadn't felt like leaving the house, though, so that was close enough. "Now I'm out here in the cold."

"Out here, where? And why were we called instead of the on-duty detectives?"

"I'm in the middle of Emerson Park."

"The park is closed for the night."

"If you were a killer, would you choose a highly-traveled, open area in the middle of the day for a body dump?"

"You have a point."

McPherson sighed. "We were called instead of the detectives on duty because it looks like you're right. We just might have a serial killer on our hands. There's a similarity between this body and Brianna Lawson."

"Another blonde braid? Or does this have to do with the red cap I received?"

He hated to even say it. "Red cap."

A rustle and a thump came through the phone, followed by a muffled *ooof*.

"You okay?"

"Stubbed my toe. I'm getting dressed. Where in Emerson Park are you? The place is huge."

"Head toward the center. Follow the lights. You can't miss us."

"I'll be there as soon as I can." Then she ended the call.

He wished she didn't have to be there at all. It wasn't a knight-in-shining-armor thing. Jim expected her to protect him as much as he wanted to protect her. That's what partners did. That's what all police did, and even though she was a new detective, he could tell she was good at her job. No, this wasn't about chivalry. It was about this case. And the killer being fixated on her.

It rankled that Sullivan had seen the fairy-tale connection before he did. But it flat-out frightened him that the unsub had *known* she'd seen it.

This guy was fixated on his partner.

Jim wanted to — no, he *needed* to — catch the creep before things went all kinds of wrong. Two vics were already two too many. He wouldn't let his partner become number three.

While he waited for her to show, he looked around the crime scene. Emerson Park spread over more than six hundred acres of Pennsylvania woodland. It was Steel City's largest park, and while it had a playground, tennis courts, baseball fields, a no-leash dog park, and the state's only public lawn bowling area, most of it was pristine nature. The park was known for its serpentine trails, steep slopes, and deep valleys. Countless species of animals made their home there, including bears, coyotes, bobcats, and snakes.

A howl echoed through the forest, setting his teeth on edge. Perfect fucking timing.

At least it wasn't a wolf. They didn't have those nearby.

Sullivan made it there in record time. Seemed she'd found him easily enough. He never doubted she would — the flashing lights of emergency vehicles and steady beams from cameramen easily cut through the stygian darkness of a forest night. They had been a beacon to him, and if he'd somehow missed them, the squawks of radios and cacophony of brusque voices would have guided his way.

The site had only gotten brighter and louder since he'd arrived, so of course, she had no trouble locating the scene.

She was slathering Carmex on her lips as she approached, and he was glad to see she'd been less concerned with a professional appearance and more concerned with warmth and comfort. She wore jeans, a turtleneck sweater, lined boots. No makeup. A fleece band did double duty, holding back her hair and covering her ears. Coat and scarf, glove on one hand. After she pocketed the lip balm, she slipped on the other for both warmth and evidence integrity.

Unfortunately, even though Chelsea's appearance was far different from the day they'd found Brianna Lawson, she was still very recognizable.

The killer would undoubtedly be able to pick her out in a crowd.

Jim scanned the faces of all the people milling about, but no one stood out to him. They were all first responders, all busy working. Maybe they'd be lucky, and the guy wouldn't have returned to get his kicks. Or luckier still, he would return and somehow reveal himself.

When Sullivan was about fifteen yards away, she tipped her head back the way she'd come. "We've got a bunch of looky-loos behind the trees."

He cursed under his breath and looked around for some uniforms. When he found two standing around with their thumbs up their asses, he stomped over to them. "Hey. We've got people sneaking past the tape. Go push them back. And get pictures of all the faces you can."

They hurried off as Sullivan reached him. She shook her head. "I wish I wasn't right. Never wished anything more."

"I know."

"It even looks like a fairy-tale setting here."

She wasn't wrong. The woodland park might be in the middle of a bustling metropolis, but because it spanned so many acres, it had the appearance of a dense fairy-tale forest.

And Little Red was dead.

A girl, roughly the same age as Brianna Lawson, lay in the middle of a path. She, too, had been stripped naked and posed as though she were sleeping — or in a coffin — fingers interlaced on her mid-section. A splotch of scarlet marred the pale flesh at her collarbone, and a darker puddle spread beneath her, staining the blanket of white a vivid crimson. The rest of her body was dusted with snowflakes, giving her a frosted, crystalline appearance.

But instead of a red cap on her head, she'd been fitted with a furry cowl, the face of a wolf above her own. Its nostrils were flared at the end of its snout, and its fangs were bared in a feral snarl.

Sullivan's teeth chattered.

A flash cut across the scene. A steady wash of light bathed the ground in front of them.

Jim looked over her shoulder and called to one of the uniforms. "Hey! Get the press out of here."

The officers started directing the news crews and reporters further from the scene, but the activity was a distant buzz in his head. His priority needed to be the victim, not the crowd, but even the frozen corpse was going to have to wait.

Sullivan looked shellshocked.

First, his priority had to be his partner.

He put his hands on her shoulders and bent to stand eye-to-eye with her, capturing her attention. Then he gave her a lopsided grin. "You look rough tonight. Were you otherwise engaged when I called? You hit it off with Dr. Death?"

But she didn't take the bait and ignored his crass remark. Her voice stayed soft, her eyes vacant. "He sent me a clue, Jim. He warned me, but I didn't stop him."

The smirk disappeared from his face. It was the first time she'd called him by his given name, and the import of that wasn't lost on him. She felt vulnerable. And he felt impotent to help her. He squeezed her shoulders then rubbed her arms. "Don't do this, Sullivan." He pulled her aside to make room as the ME hurried down the trail.

They'd called in Scott instead of the graveyard shift coroner. This was serious.

He didn't even look in their direction. Just bent down and began his examination.

"Hey," Jim whispered to her. "Look at me, Sullivan."

But she couldn't tear her attention from the poor girl.

"Chelsea." This time, his tone was much more commanding.

It did the trick. She looked at him. But then she looked at the vic again.

Jim chucked her under the chin and forced her to turn toward him. "This is not your fault."

"How can I think otherwise?"

"We didn't even know it was a serial killer then. In fact, we still don't."

"Come on. How can you still be questioning it?"

"What's the magic number, Sullivan?"

"I know what you're getting at. But you know that's just lip service."

The FBI refused to categorize a murderer as a serial killer until three killings were made over a month or more, each with downtime between. Cops knew after two — sometimes had a gut feeling after even one — but it took three to make it official.

"I asked you a question," Jim said.

"It's obviously the same guy. The same themes."

"The number?"

She sighed. "Three."

"That's right. And we've only got two."

"That we know of."

"I'll concede that point. Nothing else." But he knew she was right.

"Come on, McPherson. When we talked on the phone, you said we had a serial killer."

"No. I said it looked like we did."

She scowled at him.

"Chels, I'm not trying to be difficult here. I'm just trying to be objective. We can't jump to any conclusions."

"I'm not jumping to anything. But I saw this coming. I saw it as soon as I saw the plaited hair around Brianna Lawson's neck."

"That was definitely a stab in the dark. A gut feeling, nothing more."

Sullivan held up a finger as she yawned. "The scene said 'Rapunzel' to me."

"And this one is saying 'Little Red' to you?"

She nodded. "He wanted me to stop him."

"You don't know that."

"Then why send the cap?"

"To test you? To torment you? To distract you? Who knows?"

"Doesn't matter. I had a clue, but I couldn't stop him."

"You don't even know it's a man. What if it's one of the sorority sisters?"

"Was this girl poisoned, too? With all that blood, I assumed she'd had her throat slit."

"Not slit." Fletcher approached, pulling off a latex glove with a snap. He'd been close enough to hear at least the end of their conversation, and he jumped right in.

"What, then?" Jim asked.

"For lack of a better term, bitten."

"I'm sorry?" Sullivan covered her mouth and stifled another yawn.

"This woman has puncture wounds consistent with a large animal's teeth all around her neck, face, and head. One of the fangs — if they are fangs — got her carotid. That's how she bled out."

"Why aren't you confirming fangs at this point?" she asked.

"Because wild animals don't bite necks then, instead of eating their kill, strip and pose them. Furthermore, there's a dusting of snow on the ground. I didn't see any animal tracks. All signs point to …"

"To what?" McPherson asked.

Fletcher shrugged. "I don't know, exactly. To it not

being an animal so much as a crime staged to look like it was an animal. Well, not even that. Staged to make a statement."

"Any idea what kind of animal?" Sullivan asked through chattering teeth.

"Not without running conclusive tests, but I could venture a theory based on her headwear."

"A wolf." Her body began trembling. She tucked her hands into her pockets.

"That's my theory. I'm sure you already came to the same conclusion, though."

Jim shook his head. "This doesn't make any sense. We don't have wolves in Steel City."

"Well, not pure wolves, no," Fletcher said. "But there are coyote-wolf hybrids."

"Hybrids, Scott?" Sullivan asked. "People are cross-species breeding these things?"

He chuckled. "No. The animals handle the procreation part on their own."

"But if we don't have wolves, how do we have wolf-coyote mixes?"

"Because they're coming from areas where there are wolves."

"You're telling me they're migrating here?"

Fletcher nodded. "It makes sense. Think about it. Our woodlands have an overabundance of their preferred prey — rabbits, mice, rats. Of course, they'd come here. It's a veritable feast for them. Pretty sure the coyote population is bigger than the otters' now."

She cringed. "Otters are at least cute."

"Don't let appearances fool you. Otters can be ruthlessly mean. In fact—"

"I don't want to know. You'll ruin otters for me. And I

like to watch videos of them online. Did you know they like to slide down snowy hills like they're sledding?"

Jim rolled his eyes. "Can we get back to our vic?"

Her cheeks somehow managed to get redder. "Sorry."

The ME cleared his throat. "We'll know more after lab work and the autopsy. Care to observe?"

And just like that, the flush in her cheeks was gone, and her complexion took on a green-tinged pallor.

"The autopsy? I'll pass, thanks."

"I might stop by," Jim said. "When are you doing it?"

"Maybe around ten. I'd like to get some sleep first. Better to be alert, so I don't miss anything."

Funny. He looked completely alert now. And no bedhead, either. Didn't seem like he'd gone home with Sullivan. Bastard better not be two-timing his partner.

"I'll find something else to do," Sullivan said.

Jim skewered Dr. Death with a heated glare. He spoke through clenched teeth. "Ten, then."

"If you don't need anything else right now, I think I'll head home." Fletcher waved as he headed over to Mason. After giving a few orders for body transportation, he began the walk up the steep hill and blended into the darkness as soon as he cleared the halo of emergency lights.

Jim glowered at him the whole way.

But she didn't seem to notice. Her attention was back on the body. She stifled a yawn. "Sleep sounds like a great idea."

"Nothing more we can do here tonight. Go home, Sullivan. Looks like our work on this case just doubled."

He prayed it was only two times the work. But if they had a serial killer on their hands — and he knew they did — that meant it wouldn't be long until they found a third body murdered and staged as a Grimm story.

And he'd never forgive himself if it was his partner.

Chapter Seventeen

THE SCARIEST PART of getting home wasn't the walk through the dark woods. There were so many people milling about — EMTs, police officers, morgue technicians — that Chelsea felt safe.

It was walking from her parking garage to her apartment that freaked her out.

She was sure someone stood in the shadows, watching her. Assessing her. Plotting an attack on her. Sporadic traffic noise sounded like sinister whispers in the distance, and her own footsteps echoed through the parking structure, convincing her a stealthy figure stalked her.

Chelsea hurried to the elevator and stabbed the UP button. Again. And again. Her finger tapped a staccato beat on it.

Where was the darn thing?

When it finally arrived, she darted inside. Punched CLOSE and the button for her floor simultaneously until the elevator doors slid shut and the car started moving. When the panels opened to her hallway, she ran to her apartment. Almost dropped the keys three times as she fumbled with the locks. Finally flung her door wide, then dashed inside. Couldn't flip all the bolts and latches fast enough.

As she leaned against the door, she panted until her breathing regulated.

But her heart still raced. Hot sweat cooled on her brow. Her skin tingled.

Just because she hadn't seen someone follow her didn't mean she was in the clear. She felt someone's gaze on her even now.

Chelsea ran window to window, lowered the blinds, and drew the draperies. Still, she sensed a presence some-where. Watching. Waiting.

She hung her coat and scarf on the hook by the door but didn't take off her boots. If she had to run, she'd be ready.

Then she went to her bookshelf to dig out the book Dad had given her. Freaking fairy tales. Why? Why couldn't it have been nursery rhymes or Dr. Seuss? No. This sick psycho had to fixate on the Brothers Grimm.

But why choose her? Other detectives had higher profiles. This was her very first case.

Maybe that was the reason. Her inexperience and innocence would make her a fun pawn in his demented chess match.

Chelsea plopped on the couch. After setting her gun next to her on the table, she hefted the book onto her lap. It would be dawn in an hour. She should be sleeping. Or trying to sleep.

Not reading horror stories.

But she opened the book anyway. Flipped through the pages until she found the story.

Little Red Cap.

Her fingers traced over the flowing ribbons of the

bonnet. Almost looked like the strings transformed to trails of blood, dripping spatters across the dark forest floor.

Who drew this creepy stuff? Wasn't the story ominous enough? Did the graphic have to be as disturbing as the story?

The words jumped off the page. She wasn't far into the tale when she remembered how much she'd hated this story. Even more than Rapunzel.

The moral of the macabre fable was to beware of strangers, but all Chelsea took away from it was that the little girl's parents were horrible. Who would send a small child into the woods without a guardian? Without any means of defense? Without a weapon or a plan?

Chelsea's family, that's who. Metaphorically, anyway.

She thought about chucking the book across the room. Instead, she slammed it closed. Hoisted it. Lowered it again.

Her parents weren't as bad as Little Red's. But they hadn't exactly been sitcom-considerate, either.

Mom knew she didn't like the stories, but she didn't stop Dad from reading them.

Dad knew she hated them, but he insisted she learn her lessons from them.

Was that the key? Had the killer singled her out because she was like one or more of the fairy-tale princesses? Her parents had divorced years earlier, but Dad had never remarried. Chelsea didn't have an evil stepmother like Snow White did.

What she had were parents who had fallen on hard times. Like the parents in Hansel and Gretel.

But neither of those tales were associated with the current murders.

She, like Rapunzel, had a strict caregiver who didn't let

her socialize when she was young. But it was Gothel, not Rapunzel's father, who hid her away.

Like Little Red, Chelsea often failed to notice the bad side of people. Not a great attribute in a detective. But unlike Red, when faced with the evidence, she both saw and fought against the injustice. A great quality in a detective.

Maybe the killer was tormenting her because he wanted her to relate to the storybook characters. Wanted her to recognize her shortcomings then rise above the flaws.

But which character? Rapunzel? Red? One yet to be revealed? More than one?

The cursed book her father gave her had over two hundred stories in it. She'd never figure out how the killer perceived her weaknesses, let alone how she could overcome them.

And how did the killer come to target her in the first place? If she was a target.

Of course, she was a target. He'd sought her out by name.

Maybe she was reading too much into the cap. After all, if she was his mark, it would have been her lying naked in the park.

That thought made her shiver.

This was ridiculous. She needed to rest if she was going to get justice for Rapunzel and Red. Er, Brianna and … Huh. She didn't know the new vic's name. Had never even asked Jim a single question about her. Some detective she'd turned out to be.

Chelsea walked into her kitchen. She passed by the liquor cabinet. Ignored the freezer, too. Whiskey was for company. And ice cream was for better times. This situation called for something else.

She grabbed the bottle of marsala from the counter next to the stove. She'd made chicken a few weeks ago and hadn't finished it, nor had she made the recipe again. Marsala wasn't too bold. It had a sweet, fortified taste. Not too strong, even for a lightweight. Perfect for putting her to sleep. So she poured about an inch into a glass.

Did she shoot it or sip it? It was wine, so she should probably just sip it. But she wanted the fastest effect she could get.

"Bottoms up." She downed the contents in one big gulp.

Ran to her sink. It came right back up. As she ran the disposal, she gargled with milk. Apparently, cooking brought out the sweetness in the wine. The sip she'd just swallowed tasted like vinegar.

What a lightweight. What a sad, pathetic lightweight.

Chelsea hurried to the bathroom. Brushed her teeth then gargled with mouthwash. Twice. When she was done, she flopped onto her mattress. Didn't bother undressing. Didn't bother pulling down the covers. Didn't plug in her phone, set her alarm, or retrieve her gun from the living room.

It had all caught up to her, and she was too exhausted to do anything but sleep.

Chapter Eighteen

MIDDLE of the night
 Woodland clearing
 Emerson Park in Steel City, Pennsylvania

DESPITE THE FRIGID TEMPERATURES, he was hot. Rage did that to him. Mother had always told him she could see his anger in the flush of his skin and the heat of his eyes, and unfailingly, she'd punished him for it.

Anger was one of the seven deadly sins, and she'd been determined to beat it out of him.

God help him if his ire was directed at her. Expressed or not — and he knew better than to express it — the punishment was two-fold. First, for his fury. Second, for breaking the fourth commandment.

He secretly suspected Mother didn't care if he honored his father. But not honoring her was inexcusable. Unforgivable.

His body bore the scars to prove that.

Now, he stood at the top of the hill — cloaked in darkness, shrouded in righteous indignation — watching another pure soul succumb to the vile filth of modern society.

Detective Sullivan had not heeded his warning. He'd sensed her wavering, torn between innocence and corruption, and had tried desperately to save her.

Tried and failed.

She now stood a stone's throw from him, unconcerned with or unaware of his presence.

Unless she knew he was there and didn't care.

Perhaps her debauchery had escalated to the point that she didn't mind being watched.

Moreover, she might now be titillated by exhibitionism. Aroused at the thought of voyeurs watching her swoon in the embrace of that barbarian she called a partner.

It would seem they were now partners in the biblical sense of the word. And they flaunted it. Wanted everyone to see it, to know it. Their entwined bodies would be on every media report and in every news article by morning. And they'd revel in the reveal.

She would revel in it. Harlot. Whore.

Snowflakes fell in a gentle flurry, melting on his burning hands and face. Despite the cold, he was taken back to one summer, long ago, when the sun scorched the grass, the temperature rose to triple digits, and the humidity drove everyone mad. The water level of the river had dropped several inches, revealing tiny islands in the middle of its undulating path. Locals knew better than to sail their boats, though many people still paddled kayaks or canoes.

Mother forbade him to go in the water, even when it was low and the current was lazy. Swimsuits were immodest, revealed too much skin.

After his chores, he was permitted to play outside. He'd

hurried out of view of his home then ran for what felt like miles. He snuck to the water's edge, where he removed his shoes and socks. But wading in up to his ankles wasn't enough to cool himself off. Neither was bending over and letting the river flow through his fingers.

He climbed back onto the bank then rounded a thick pine. Took a careful look and a more careful listen. The air was still, as though even the wind was too hot to exert any effort. Birds were too tired to chirp, bees too burdened to buzz.

Confident he was alone, he stripped off all his clothes then slipped into the river, immersing up to his shoulders with a contented sigh. The ends of his hair got wet, but he was sure it would dry in the heat before he returned home. Or he could pass the dampness off as perspiration. It might very well be that very thing by then, anyway.

The receding water level had revealed a long-dead tree, and he hid behind its trunk, just in case Mother came looking for him.

She didn't. Nor did Father.

But someone came.

Too late to climb out without being seen, he heard splashing and laugher. He peeked around a gnarled limb.

Two teenagers, probably four or five years older than him, had rowed a raft to one of the tiny islands. The boy was begging, the girl making feeble protests that had no conviction behind them. Soon, they'd both stripped away their scanty garments to lay on the small sandbar, part in the water, part out. Limbs tangled in passion as moans tore from their lungs in frenzied ecstasy.

He'd never seen a naked girl before that day. Or even a naked boy. He had no full-length mirror at home to study his own body and only had a general idea of what the human physique might look like. Even when he and his father had to strip for their punishments, they were forbidden to make eye contact with each other.

Now, he had two real-life models to observe.

The differences between her soft curves and her partner's sculpted angles fascinated him. He looked down at his own pre-pubescent form, devoid of bulging muscles.

Devoid of bulging member.

Oh, he felt the stirrings inside him. The urge to touch, to taste. The desperate, gnawing desire to … to …

To do what? He didn't know. Mother had made certain of that years earlier. Now, he could only watch, fascinated with their erotic ardor and frustrated with his impotent response.

His face flushed with embarrassment though no one could see his inadequacies.

"Enjoying the show?" Her voice was soft. Low. Laced with disgust and flirting with malice.

Despite the heat of the day, his blood chilled. Goosebumps rose on his flesh. Any stirrings he might have felt shriveled and withered and wasted away.

He turned to find her in the shadow of a pine tree.

"I'm sorry, Mother."

"For what, I wonder. For disobeying me? For exposing yourself for the world to see? For watching those two debauched perverts fornicate in public, writhing in heat and enjoying the attention?"

"For all of it." And he meant it. But he was most sorry for getting caught because he knew what came next. Knew it. Loathed it. Feared it.

"Get out of the water."

"Turn around."

Her eyebrows arched. "Did you just give *me* an order?"

"I'm sorry, Mother. Would you please turn around? To protect my modesty?"

"Modesty?" She scoffed. "You weren't concerned about your modesty a moment ago. You will walk home unclothed."

"But … someone might see me!"

"Oh, people will see you. I'll make sure of that. You bring shame to our family. But you must learn your lesson."

"Mother, please. I beg of you."

"Get out of the water. Now."

Face flaming, he clambered onto the bank, doing his best to cover the useless organ dangling between his legs. Water sluiced down his pale, scrawny body in clear rivulets, the tears streaming from his eyes blending into their tiny trails.

"Your clothes."

Relief washed through him. He bent to retrieve them then started to get dressed.

"No."

Her chilling reprimand stopped him before he got one foot into his underwear.

"Are you simple, boy? I said you would walk home unclothed. Now, give me your garments. All of them."

"What?"

She held out her hand.

"But what will I wear?"

"You must be daft." She stepped closer then slapped his face, the impact stinging as much as his shame. "You will wear nothing."

He offered her the clothes, but she merely cocked a brow. After quickly folding them, he passed them to her.

"Clasp your hands above your head."

Eyes wide, mouth agape, he stared at her.

"Clasp. Your. Hands. Above. Your. Head."

He raised his arms, interlaced his fingers, then bent his

elbows until his palms cradled his neck like he was about to do sit-ups.

She looked at his penis and sneered.

His stomach flopped. His face heated more than the relentless sun beating down upon him.

Then she met his gaze. "You will not lower your hands until you reach our door. Now, walk home, slowly, sticking close to the river's edge, calling out in a loud voice that you are a depraved child who likes to watch sinners copulate."

"But there are people in houses all along the river, maybe even in their yards." They lived far enough into the woods that he didn't know any neighbors, but that hardly eased his humiliation. And that didn't fix the worst of his problems. He glanced toward the water, but the foliage was blocking his view of the teenagers on the island. Unfortunately, he could still hear them, so he knew they were still there. "And the couple in the river!"

"That's the point, isn't it? They deserve the courtesy of knowing you watched them. It's anyone's guess whether they'll mind, of course. But however they respond, whatever they do to you, you've earned it."

"Mother, please don't make me do this."

She merely pointed.

He swallowed. Took a few steps. Managed to croak a few hoarse words past the lump in his throat before she stopped him.

"I said to call out in a loud voice. I can barely hear you, so I know they can't."

Pebbles and twigs dug into the soles of his feet with every step. The sun burned on his fair flesh. Tears stung his eyes, making it almost impossible to see. But he managed to choke out the words as he walked. "I'm a depraved child who likes to watch sinners copulate!" He stepped out from behind the pine, in clear view of the water. Of the island. Of the fornicating couple. "I'm a depraved—"

The girl shrieked. The boy yelled.

He heard frantic activity in the river but couldn't make out anything definitive through the watery haze clouding his vision.

The first contact rendered him speechless — an explosion of pain centered on his cheekbone then radiating across his face. He cried out, but his assailant's cries were louder, every punch punctuated by a staccato burst of words. Questions and insults snarled between blows of unbridled fury. Nose, ribs, stomach, legs … no part of his body was spared the assault. A kick to his testicles brought him to his knees.

Then it was over.

He fell to his side, curled into a fetal ball, vomited. Tears and blood and snot mixed with dirt and effluvium and grass until he was all cried out. It may have been seconds, may have been hours. It felt like forever, but he had no way to mark the passage of time. All he knew were the pain and the shame and the fear of more to come.

A shadow fell over him, and he squinted up into the severe face of his mother. "Get up."

He struggled to his knees, then his feet. But through it all, he never lowered his arms. Because he hadn't reached their door. Because she'd forbidden him.

As he took his first labored step toward his house, he sucked in a painful, wheezing breath. Then he yelled as loud as he could past swollen, bloody lips, "I am a depraved child who likes to watch sinners copulate!" He continued his proclamation the whole way home. Neighborhood laughter rang in his ears long after the people were a distant memory.

Now, he whispered the phrase again as he touched his

face, mildly surprised to find it cold and uninjured. His breath evaporated into the frigid air, and his gaze settled on Detective Sullivan.

He very much did not want to watch her copulate with her partner. And he was going to make sure it didn't happen.

Or he would punish her if it did.

Chapter Nineteen

Jim glanced at the clock on his screen as Sullivan stumbled in. If he'd checked it once, he'd checked it twenty times. Another ten minutes, and he would have called to check on her. Or driven to her fucking apartment and kicked in the door if he had to.

She didn't stop at her desk or greet anyone. Instead, she hurried to the coffee station, poured some of the precinct's signature sludge into a chipped mug, then shuffled to her desk.

Her damp hair was in a messy bun. She had no makeup on her face and wore the same clothes she'd had on the night before.

"Nice of you to join us, even if you look like shit."

"Thanks. So kind of you to notice." Chelsea raised the mug to her lips and glared at him over its rim. When she took a sip, she jerked. Coffee sloshed onto her hand and jacket. Tears welled in her eyes. She sputtered, coughed. Gasped for air.

McPherson laughed. "Man, you are having a rough day."

She dropped into her chair. "Do you have to enjoy it so much?"

"Who says I'm enjoying it?"

"Your laughter speaks volumes."

"My, my." He smirked. "Someone is touchy today."

"I'm not touchy. I forgot to set my alarm and overslept. Had to take a fast shower that didn't quite wake me, so I didn't have time to do anything with my hair."

"Didn't have time to choose a clean outfit, either?"

"These clothes are clean."

"They look like you slept in them."

She sighed. "No donuts or anything by the coffee. You wouldn't happen to have a protein bar or something, would you? I missed breakfast."

"Seems this case is getting to you."

"Burning my mouth on hot coffee and missing a meal has nothing to do with the case."

"It's more than that. Look at you — no makeup, bags under your eyes, running late. My guess is you didn't sleep. Tells me you're letting the case get to you. What'd I tell you about keeping an objective distance?"

"Shows what you know. I slept like a log. Too well, in fact, as I slept in. Which we already established, Mr. Detective Who Misses Nothing. My objectivity is just fine, thank you. I'm sick and tired of everyone thinking that because I'm a woman, I'm too emotional to handle this case."

Jim had been half-teasing, half-testing her to this point. But now, he was concerned. He narrowed his eyes and studied her. "Everyone, who?"

Her breath caught. She blinked then stared at him in a doe-in-headlights, hand-in-the-cookie-jar kind of way. Then she recovered. Her face became a mask, her voice grew frosty. "It's a turn of phrase. I mean you. Besides, your ego is so big, it's like dealing with three people."

He easily caught the lie but chose not to call her on it. "See? Touchy. Emotional."

She sighed. "Emotional or not, you forget. I was *right*. I knew Brianna Lawson's case was related to fairy tales before you. Or anyone else. Even after I got the cap, you discounted my theory."

"Touché. Maybe you have a knack for investigation, after all."

Her jaw dropped. She sat there, silent, just looking at him.

It was the closest he'd come to giving her a compliment, and she clearly didn't know what to make of it.

Jim didn't know what to make of it, either. So, he slipped back into jackass mode as he pushed away from his desk. "I'd ask if you want a replacement cup of coffee, but you can't seem to handle it."

"I still have some in my cup, thank you very much. Besides, I handle it just fine. This and anything else that comes my way."

"Maybe you can, Sullivan. Maybe you can." He headed for the coffee station as she unwrapped her scarf and took off her coat. She was just about to sit when he returned with his Thermos. "Should've told you to stay dressed. We're heading out."

"Where are we going?"

"The vic's apartment. Her ID came in overnight."

"Who was she?"

"Mariah Jones. Lived in Riverside. Worked as a physical therapist for St. Grace Hospital."

Chelsea blew on her coffee then took a cautious sip. At least she didn't choke on it this time.

"Want to pour that in a to-go cup?"

She shook her head, downed it, winced, then grabbed her coat.

He held the door for her. She bundled up on the way to his car.

It was a short drive to Mariah Jones's home — a one-bedroom apartment on Walnut Street, one of only a few with a designated parking lot, which meant higher rent. McPherson tracked down the building manager, who let them into her unit.

The warmth from the coffee didn't stay with Jim. Entering the dead girl's apartment chilled him to his core, not that he'd ever show it. All his years, all his cases, and he still was affected by the senseless tragedy of murder. He could only imagine how Sullivan was faring.

But now wasn't the time to ask. They had work to do.

It was small but clean. Pristine, even. Furniture was dusted, hardwood floors gleamed. No clutter, nothing out of place.

They each took a separate room. Sullivan chose the bedroom, so he headed to the kitchen. The dishes were all washed and put away. The counters and stovetop were clean. The refrigerator was stuffed full of fresh produce, coconut water, and kombucha. He called out the contents as he discovered them. Looked like the girl was a health nut and a clean freak.

Seemed she may have had a touch of OCD, too. A color-coded wall calendar hung near the archway, every work schedule, and appointment written in tidy block letters.

"Well, look at that."

He jolted at the sound of Sullivan's voice in his ear. Had never even heard her step up behind him.

She smirked but — wisely — chose not to mention it. "Take a look at this calendar."

"Disturbing, right? Who has the time for such nonsense?"

Sullivan rolled her eyes. "One, it's not nonsense. It's good organization. And two, did you notice the green entries?"

Jim leaned closer and peered at the calendar. "She had a second job."

"Yeah, as a masseuse. Stands to reason. Rent on a place like this isn't cheap, even if it is small. But a masseuse? Doesn't quite fit the good-girl vibe I first got."

"Not all massages conclude with happy endings."

"You would know."

His eyebrows arched. He'd clearly somehow given her an unfair impression of his social life. But what he found even more surprising was that it bothered him.

She sighed. "I'm not suggesting they do. But Mariah Jones reminds me a lot of Brianna Lawson. Good girl. Clean, wholesome living. Then we discover she had a second job at a massage parlor. What if the killer is taking exception to an activity he believes deviates from their pure personas?"

"Not a bad theory. But if that's the case, what was Brianna's impure activity?"

"Well, we've got that picture of her in revealing clothes when she was with her boyfriend and drinking."

"One picture, one time."

"It could be enough. It's proof she's not the good girl she looked like. Got that email after it calling her out. No … threatening her. Feels like we're on the right track."

"It's not about what you feel, Sullivan. It's about what you know."

"Yeah, that's what you said when I first had my Rapunzel theory. And look who was right."

"I'm not discounting it outright. It's certainly an angle worth exploring. But it's not evidence."

"The email is evidence."

"But that's all we've got. And only to Brianna. We have no correlating evidence suggesting the killer knew Mariah worked as a masseuse. Even if he did know, I'm sure she wasn't giving happy endings, so it doesn't fit the profile."

"Unless the killer is assuming the happy ending part."

"It's not *evidence*, Sullivan. If we can't make a case, we can't make an arrest. There's still a lot to do here, even if you're right."

She scowled, and her nostrils flared, but she remained silent. Brooding but silent.

Jim wouldn't blow off her theories outright anymore. She'd proven knowledgeable, and her instincts had been spot-on so far. But she had to learn the difference between supposition and proof, and they didn't have anything more than a hunch at the moment.

If they worked together instead of at cross-purposes, they just might find the evidence they needed before another victim fell. He had a big ego — and he wasn't afraid to admit it — but he also knew when to drop his ideas in favor of better ones. Sullivan was onto something. Had been since the beginning. With her instincts and his experience, they stood a good chance of stopping this psycho before he struck again. And he'd do almost anything to make that happen.

He studied the calendar again. "Did you look at the purple entries?"

She scanned the notes. "Every Sunday at the assisted living center over on Donovan Street. That's not far from here."

"Guess we found our next lead."

Sullivan took her phone from her pocket, snapped a picture of the calendar, then headed for the door. "You drive. I'll call and get MCU to process the apartment."

He snorted.

"What?"

"Of course I'm driving. Like it even needed to be said."

She rolled her eyes and walked into the hallway.

~

THEY WAITED for what felt like forever for the volunteer coordinator to meet them in the lobby. Jim hid his impatience by sitting and leafing through a home improvement magazine.

Sullivan paced.

"You're going to wear a groove in their floor. Relax. And if you can't, act like you've done this before."

"I'm not nervous. And I've interviewed people before, thank you very much."

"Then what's your problem?"

"I'm starting to get a bad feeling about this."

"About an assisted living facility?"

"Are you always this dense? Or are you just screwing with me?"

He grinned. Getting her riled up was a lot more fun than reading about ways to unclog pipes without chemicals.

She took a deep breath. "About this case."

"Your feelings got worse in the last five minutes?"

A woman stepped into the lobby before Sullivan could respond. She wore yoga pants, a hoodie partially unzipped to reveal a tank underneath, and sneakers. Her hair was in a ponytail.

"Hi. I'm Laura Vitale, the activities director." She shook their hands. "I was told you wanted to speak with me. Are you considering placing a loved one here? I'm happy to discuss our programs. Also, we have some lovely brochures, and I can give you a tour."

Jim moved his jacket out of the way so she could see his shield. "No, thank you. That isn't why we are here. I'm Detective McPherson, and this is my partner Detective Sullivan. We'd like to ask you a few questions."

"Detectives?" Her face paled. "What's this regarding?"

Sullivan stepped forward. "It's all right. You're not in any trouble. This is regarding one of your volunteers. Mariah Jones."

"Mariah? Is she in trouble?"

"Does she have a history of problem behavior?" Jim asked.

Her eyes widened. "Mariah? Oh, no. Never. I couldn't ask for a better volunteer. In fact, if we had the funds, I'd hire her in a heartbeat. Not that she'd accept. She says she only comes here because she enjoys helping out. I've even offered her money out of petty cash before, but she never took it. Not even once."

He looked past her into the hallway. "Would it be possible for us to talk to some of the residents?"

"I suppose." She turned and followed his gaze. "I just finished a sit-and-be-fit session with some of our more active residents. That's what delayed me. But many of them lingered afterward. My staff brings juice and cookies at the end."

"Cookies?" Sullivan said. "After exercising?"

"It's just a little nibble. And everything in moderation, right?"

"Right." Jim smiled at her.

Sullivan rolled her eyes at him.

"I have to ask you not to say or do anything that might upset our residents. It's not good for them, and once they get worked up, they're difficult to settle again."

"We'll do our best." He gestured to the door. "Lead the way."

She started toward the hallway, then stopped. Turned toward them. "You said Mariah isn't in trouble."

Jim sighed. This was always the worst part. He'd hoped to avoid it, as the woman wasn't family and didn't necessarily need a notification, but it was going to be on the news soon, anyway. If it wasn't already. He shook his head and said, "She's not."

"Then, if I might ask, what's this all about?"

When he didn't answer right away, Sullivan took a deep breath. "I'm sorry, Miss Vitale. Mariah is dead."

"Dead?" She grasped the door, clutched it with both hands. "Mariah? No. No! She was just here."

"Maybe you should sit for a moment." Jim took her by the elbow, then guided her to the chair he'd vacated.

She dropped into it. Her eyes glistened with unshed tears. "If you're here, that means … that means it wasn't an accident. Something bad happened to her."

Sullivan looked at him.

He couldn't even muster half a smile.

The woman looked up. "What happened?"

"We're looking into it, ma'am," he said.

She used her cuff to mop her tears. "How can I help? Other than taking you to the residents, I mean. Or maybe I shouldn't. This will be so upsetting for them."

"What else can you tell us about Mariah?" Sullivan asked.

"She was wonderful with the residents. Not only did she provide her services free of charge, she was so polite. So cordial. And she really cared, you know?" She dabbed her eyes again. "Mariah would hear about the birth of a grandchild one week, then ask to see photos when she visited the following week. She paid attention to everything they said. A lot of volunteers can't do that. They don't have it in them. It takes a special heart to work with the elderly. But she had a knack for it. Was genuinely kind. Our residents really seemed to matter to her." Then she broke down, sobbing freely into her sleeves.

Jim patted her back. "Perhaps we can return tomorrow. After you've had a chance to process this and prepare your residents."

She nodded, then rose and ran from the lobby without another word.

Sullivan sighed. "I feel like I've been through the wringer. And it's not even lunch yet."

He held the door for her.

Seemed the temperature had dropped ten degrees since they'd gone inside. He tucked his hands into his pockets. Sullivan wrapped another loop of her scarf around her head, this time covering her nose. Once seated in the car, she took off her gloves and held them over the vent.

McPherson let the car idle and turned toward her. "Thoughts?"

"You mean other than the sadness of it all?"

"I thought you were getting over your empathy problem." No point admitting he had one of his own since he knew how to compartmentalize it. It was a trick she'd need to learn fast, or she wouldn't make it a year.

She pulled her scarf off her face and sighed. "It's not a problem. I happen to consider it a strength. But more to the point, it is sad. That's not a feeling. That's a fact."

"Speaking of facts, let's go over them. What do we know so far?"

"Are you testing me? Or are we just spit-balling here?"

"Talk about sensitive."

Chelsea turned away from him and tried to adjust the heat, but it was already up as high as it went.

"Fine," McPherson said. "I'll start. Mariah's apartment was tidy. Practically austere. No drugs, alcohol, or cigarettes on the premises. No evidence of a gambling problem. Checkbook register had nothing but rent and utilities in it. No large deposits or withdrawals. There was nothing risqué or deviant in her bedroom, either — no lingerie, sex toys, porn. She didn't seem to have vices of any kind. Based on that and the contents of her kitchen, I'd say she was a wholesome girl who lived a clean life."

"Do you have to look so disappointed about not finding anything sex-related?"

"What?" Disappointed? If anything, he was impressed. Frustrated they didn't have more to go on, but he admired the girl for her choices.

Wasn't real thrilled with what his partner thought of him, though. But now wasn't the time to get into that.

"Never mind," Sullivan said. "I agree. She seemed like a good person. All that, plus her volunteer efforts, would make her an ideal target for our killer."

"Both Mariah Jones and Brianna Lawson were posed in a similar fashion. Naked, no signs of sexual assault."

Sullivan shivered and held her hands near the vent again. "Both murderers have a connection to fairy tales. Not word-for-word accurate, but symbolic."

"I wonder about the weather."

"What about it?"

"Jones was found outside. Lawson in her house, but with the window open. Maybe we need to consider the cold as a theme."

"Hmm. That's astute. Worth pursuing."

"Gee, thanks."

She rolled her eyes.

Jim hadn't been sure what the open window signified at Brianna Lawson's apartment, but if it was linked to the climate or the snow, that would give them another avenue to pursue.

"Why don't you look into the weather angle," Sullivan said, "and I'll look into whether Lawson or Jones deviated from their pure reputations in some way."

"Barking up the wrong tree, Sullivan." She probably wasn't, but he didn't want her going down that road, especially if they were doing the divide-and-conquer thing.

"You don't know that."

"My money's on this guy having a fetish for princesses. He's not looking for tarnished girls. He wants to do the defiling."

"But there's no evidence of sexual assault."

"He may not have raped them, but that doesn't mean he didn't get off on what he did."

The vents were blowing too hot, but his blood flowed icy and slow. Thinking about the murderer wanting to punish his victims was one thing. Thinking he targeted pure women then pleasured himself by stripping and killing them? That was quite another.

Especially because his partner was in the killer's orbit.

Sullivan stabbed at the heat controls and opened her coat. "Do you have to be so cavalier about it?"

"Told you, you've got to learn to detach. Makes it easier." He knocked her hand away from the console, put on a classic rock playlist, then put the car in gear. As he drove, he sang "Don't Fear the Reaper" at the top of his lungs.

She rolled her eyes then looked away.

Jim knew the song was bothering her, but he'd chosen it on purpose. Right now, the themes of death and eternal love would be eating at her. His hope was that she'd learn to lock that shit down, file it away. That was the only way she'd survive her vocation. It was the only way he survived his.

He didn't fear the reaper, not that he had a death wish. But he couldn't be a good cop if he wasn't willing to die for the cause.

Pretty sure his partner wasn't thinking about that, though. Her bleeding heart was focusing on the romance, the tragic loss of young innocents cut down in the prime of their lives before finding the kind of love Blue Oyster Cult sang about, the kind that transcended time and space and eternity.

Damn it. Now he was thinking about star-crossed lovers and tragic romances. About obsessive personalities and sick fantasies. About that damn red cap addressed to his partner.

Their unsub had set his sights on Sullivan. And Jim had no idea how to stop him.

Chapter Twenty

Chelsea and McPherson spent the next several days interviewing friends and family of Mariah Jones, talking to the residents at the assisted care facility, and poring over all of the evidence for both cases.

Despite their efforts, they had nothing more to go on.

In the evenings, she continued reading her father's fairy-tale book. No darn wonder she hadn't been sleeping. The stories still creeped her out and reading them right before bed guaranteed her restless nights.

Even McPherson seemed to be brushing up on the Brothers Grimm. He wasn't making any progress, either.

He walked into the station, dropped into his seat, then flung a piece of paper across their desks. "Check that out."

Chelsea grabbed the report. After a quick scan, she looked up at him. "Another hair? With the follicle?"

"Forensics found it inside the wolf cowl."

"That's not a coincidence. He's planting them for us to find. But why? He clearly knows we don't have his DNA on file. And when we do catch him, we can use the hairs to tie him to each murder he's committed. It's reckless."

"It's not reckless. It's arrogant. He's taunting us."

"That's foolish. He has to know we'll keep at it until we catch him."

"I didn't say it was smart. I said it was arrogant. He's trying to prove he's more intelligent than we are. Probably looking for publicity, too."

"Publicity? We haven't released anything to the press."

"And if we don't make progress soon, we'll have to. He's playing with us until he gets the notoriety he's seeking."

"That's his mistake. And that's how we'll get him."

"Jack the Ripper. Zodiac Killer. Freeway Phantom. The Doodler. I-70 Killer. Ring any bells?"

Some did. "What about them?'"

He shook his head. "Serial killers. All with fancy names and a place in the history books. Not one of them was caught. And some of them left clues. Our guy thinks he's in their league. Maybe better. Your confidence isn't enough to bring him down."

It was hard to hear a serial killer described as talented. Harder to know her own partner didn't think she was up to the challenge of catching him. "And what is? Your smug attitude and obsession with women?"

His gaze skewered her. "Despite what you think of me, I'm a damn good detective, more than up for the task. And I have every intention of bringing this sick bastard down. Soon. He doesn't think I'll get him. But I will."

"We, McPherson. We'll get him."

"That's what I said."

"No. You said I, not we. You aren't a solo act. I'm part of this team, whether you want me to be or not."

"There you are again, letting your emotions get the better of you."

"No, I'm just telling you not to shut me out. If anything, I have more invested than you do."

"And that's the problem," he muttered.

"What's that supposed to mean?"

He shook his head.

"You aren't cutting me out, Jim. I'm going to be there when we take this creep down."

McPherson didn't answer her. Instead, he pushed back from his desk so hard, his chair rolled across the floor. He strode to the coffee table.

Chelsea didn't sit there, either. She made a beeline for Davenport's office, then snapped, "Got a minute?"

The captain looked up at her, eyebrows arched. "Come in."

She entered his office and closed the door — a little more forcibly than she intended. "This'll only take a minute."

"Good, because that's all I've got. What's the problem?"

"How did you decide to team up McPherson and me?"

"It was pretty simple. He was a transfer, you were new. Both of you needed a partner." He shrugged.

"But why not give each of us an experienced partner? Charlie? Norm?"

"Why would I break up a successful partnership of several decades? Particularly when they're both looking at retirement in the next decade? It only made sense to team up the two youngsters and keep the veterans together."

"We're not youngsters. And I think we both would've benefited from partnering with experienced detectives."

"I did put you with an experienced detective. He's almost ten years your senior and has an impressive arrest record."

"That's not what I meant."

"Then what? Is there a problem with McPherson?"

"You tell me. Why did he transfer here from downtown? Our zone is a step down for him."

"Have you asked him?"

"No. I'm asking you. Is he reckless? Not good at what he does? Insubordinate?"

"I think his record speaks for itself."

"He sure seems to know a lot about serial killers."

"I would think that's to your benefit, given the case you caught."

"He's misogynistic."

"You think so? He's had nothing but positive things to say about you."

That stopped her rant cold. She blinked as she processed what he said, then she continued, her voice now soft. "He's talked to you about me? When? Why? What did he say?"

Davenport sighed. "Chelsea, he's your partner. If you want to know something about him, I suggest you ask him."

"But …"

"But, what?"

"Never mind." How could she be angry with McPherson for talking to the captain about her when she was doing the same thing behind his back? Especially when it sounded like he was complimentary. She hadn't been.

"If there's nothing else." Captain Davenport stood, walked to his coat tree, then retrieved his suit jacket. "I've got a meeting with the commissioner and the mayor. They're concerned about the Grimm Reaper—"

"Ugh. Is that what they're calling him?"

"Read the news, Sullivan. While you do that, I need to reassure the big wigs that my best people are on it and up to the task. Or should I give the case to someone else?"

"Of course not. Your best people are on it."

"Then unless there's something else I should know …"

"No, sir."

"Good. Now, is the report ready?"

"What report?"

"I emailed you and McPherson last night. I need the latest info for my meeting."

It must have come in after she left work last night, and she hadn't checked her email yet this morning. She'd have to pull her notes together. Fast. "I'll go print it out now."

"I'll come with you." He followed her out.

It was going to be difficult to assemble everything he needed right under his nose. He'd realize she was unprepared. And that she'd lied.

Chelsea didn't know what was worse.

She slipped into her chair and logged into her computer while Davenport stood behind her.

McPherson walked over, two cups in hand. "Morning, Captain. I was just getting us coffee. Would you like mine? I can go get another."

"No, thanks. I'm on my way out. Chelsea is printing the report I asked for."

He put the cups down on his desk. "Don't bother, Chels. I printed it earlier." McPherson grabbed a folder off his desk then handed it to Davenport.

The captain opened it and leafed through the pages. "Looks good. Should get them off my back for a while. Thanks, Jim."

"It was a team effort."

Davenport stared at Chelsea.

Her cheeks heated, and she looked away.

"Thank you, Sullivan." His comment was pointed. It was obvious he knew. "You and McPherson make a great team."

She nodded and mumbled something that didn't even make sense to her own ears.

The captain tapped the folder on her desk, then he strode out of the bullpen.

Chelsea looked up at her partner. "Why'd you cover for me?"

"I wasn't covering. You did the work."

"But I didn't even know he wanted a report. You took care of all of it."

"And I'm sure someday you'll handle something that I didn't get to. Partners have each other's backs. I've got yours. Do I have to worry you don't have mine?"

Her face flamed even hotter. She'd been on the verge of asking for another partner. Meanwhile, McPherson had taken care of her. Of them.

Chelsea shook her head. "No. You don't have to worry about me. I've got your back."

He nodded. "Good to know."

CHELSEA SQUIRMED IN HER SHOES. It was right before quitting time. But instead of leaving, she was on her way to the ME's office.

Her loyal and dedicated partner had suggested she check in with Scott and find out the results of the autopsy. Of course, he didn't have time to do it himself. He had a hot date.

But she owed him one for earlier.

So McPherson went to the parking lot while she walked downstairs, worrying about being alone with Scott. The two of them hadn't had a proper conversation since their awkward date after the play, and she didn't know what to expect when she saw him.

At least he was in his office and not the autopsy room.

He offered her a warm smile when he saw her. "Chelsea. It's so good to see you. It's been a while."

She shouldn't have been surprised at his cordiality. Sometimes they had awkward exchanges, but he was always the model of decorum. Relief washed over her as she walked to his desk. "Are you leaving? I know it's late."

"I always have time for you. What do you need?"

"The autopsy report. I know you had a backlog, but this case is really eating at me. Us." She sighed. "Me."

He gave her a soft smile. "We finished a couple of hours ago. Mason should be emailing you the initial findings. Or maybe he already has. But I have a copy." He took a folder off his desk and handed it to her. "In there, you'll find a printout of the DNA report. It's a ninety-nine percent match to the hair we recovered from Brianna Lawson, but we still don't have a sample of a suspect to compare it to. There's also an analysis of the wounds indicating teeth made them and are from the canine family. The punctures are too deep to be from a dog, though. The impressions we took indicate they are the length of wolf fangs. But without saliva, I can't confirm the species."

"Wait. How can there be no saliva in a bite?"

"I never said they were bites. I said I analyzed the wounds and the tooth impressions. Given the shape and the depth of the punctures, I'm confident they were made by wolf fangs. But like I said, without saliva, I can't confirm that. I can't even confirm it's a bite."

"If it's not a bite, though … Are you telling me the killer took the time to assemble a weapon designed to look like wolf teeth? That's how he punctured the vic's carotid?"

"I can't tell you what the killer did. I can only tell you what the body indicates. Evidence suggests the wounds were made by wolf fangs, but there is no saliva in the wounds. What you derive from that information is up to you."

She was having trouble wrapping her head around that one. Who would even think to do something like that? "Maybe McPherson will be able to make some sense of all this."

He snorted. As much as a culturally-refined man snorts, anyway.

Chelsea took a step closer, unsure if she was going to defend Jim or agree with Scott's clearly negative impression of her partner. "What?"

"I realize McPherson has a high close rate—"

"You do?"

"Of course. I know a lot of things, Chelsea. Knowledge is power. But I'm inclined to think he got as far as he did on charm and luck. That's not going to be enough on this one. You're the brains of the duo. If anyone can figure this out, it's you. In the short time we've known each other, you've really impressed me. I know you can do this."

She looked down as heat flooded her face. Maybe their date hadn't been as awkward as she'd thought. No man would heap such high praise on a woman he wasn't interested in, even if it was true. Not that she thought it was. As many issues as she had with McPherson, his intelligence wasn't one of them. Still, it was nice knowing someone, especially someone as bright as Scott, believed her to be a smart woman and a valuable member of the team.

He touched her arm. Bent so he could meet her gaze. "I mean it, Chelsea. I know you'll be the one to figure it out."

She shrugged. "I hope so. We're all a part of this — you, me, Jim. Working together, we have a good chance of getting this guy. I don't want him to be the one who haunts me."

"I don't follow. How will Jim haunt you?"

"No. Not Jim." Chelsea sighed. "Every detective has that one unsolved case that sticks with them forever. I'd hate to think my first case is the one. Especially when he's a serial killer. Who knows how many lives he'll take before it's over?"

"That sounds awfully negative."

She shrugged. "I'm just trying to be realistic. Do you know how many serial killers have never been caught?"

"No."

"Well, I don't either. But McPherson named quite a few, and I'm sure there are loads more. I can't let this guy be one of them."

"You won't. You're going to learn his identity, and before McPherson does. Or anyone else. This is your case, Chelsea. This is the one people will remember you for."

"I just hope we get him. I don't care who gets the credit."

"Regardless, I still think it will be you. And let me get you started."

"Okay …" What could he possibly do for her?

"As the ME, I can only present my findings. It's not my place to interpret the results. But this is a fact, so I'm comfortable sharing it. Wolves are not native to Western Pennsylvania."

"Yeah, I know."

"What's that tell you?"

"The killer is from a place where wolves roam free?"

"Possibly." He leaned against his desk. "Or he raises them himself."

"I didn't think it was legal to have wild animals as pets."

"It's not. Not in Pennsylvania. Which means you're looking at one of two places. The zoo and I'm pretty sure you'd have heard if they had a missing wolf. Or one whose teeth had been extracted."

"I haven't heard anything like that."

"Right. So consider the other option. It has to be someone who's raising exotic animals."

"But you just said that's illegal."

"It is. Which means if you look through arrest records for someone who's been caught with exotic animals, you'll have a lead. Or leads."

"Thanks. I gotta go!" She kissed him on the cheek then headed toward the hall.

"Chelsea, wait."

She stopped in the doorway and looked at him.

"Do you have plans this evening? I'd like to take you to dinner. I won't make you walk. I promise."

She smiled. "I'd love to go out again, Scott. But not tonight. As soon as I get a handle on this case, though, I'm all yours."

"There's always going to be a pressing case, Chelsea. You can't put your life on hold for work."

Now he sounded just like McPherson. "Sorry, Scott. I can't right now. I need Jim. Raincheck?"

His face darkened, but he smiled. "Definitely. You're worth the wait."

Chelsea sincerely hoped he meant it. She didn't want to blow her chance with him, but she couldn't split her focus right now.

Hopefully, they'd solve the case fast.

Chapter Twenty-One

Jim hadn't lied about having plans. He'd just lied about who they were with. His "date" was with his mother.

After that little stunt Alessa had pulled, he didn't have a choice. A little damage control was in order. Or a lot. It depended on how worked up Mom was.

He'd thought of everything. A public venue so she couldn't blow up at him. An early reservation so she still had time to do whatever she and Dad did on Friday nights. Her favorite Italian restaurant so she couldn't complain about the food. Might put her in a slightly better mood, too.

Yes, he was sure he'd thought of everything.

Until he arrived and saw he hadn't.

Mom must have called and changed their reservation from a party of two to a party of three. And she hadn't brought Dad with her.

Alessa had joined them.

Jim gave serious thought to turning and leaving, but that would only make things worse later. Still, he could use work as an excuse …

No, he needed to nip this in the bud. Make sure they both understood.

As he approached the table, both of them looked up and smiled. Mom tipped her head for him to press a kiss on her cheek, which he dutifully did.

Alessa did the same then gave a fake laugh when he ignored her.

"Oh, don't be rude, darling," Mom said.

Funny, he been as civil as he could manage. He pulled out the chair beside her.

She grabbed his hand. "I thought you'd sit across from me so I could see your handsome face."

More like she wanted him across from her so he'd be beside his not-a-blind-date date.

"You know what I look like, Mom."

Her grip tightened. "But my purse is there."

Jim picked up her bag then held it out to Alessa. "Could you put this on the chair beside you, please?"

She accepted it with a saccharine smile that didn't reach her eyes.

He dropped into the chair across from her, beside his mother.

"Honestly, darling. I'm sure I've taught you better manners than this. You never handle a woman's purse unless she asks you to."

"You're my mother, not the Queen of England."

"Let's get some food in you. Then maybe you'll be in a better mood."

Doubtful. Whiskey might help, though.

Alessa tried to play footsie under the table. He tucked his feet back as far as he could. Then her foot — her bare foot — slid up his leg until she reached his crotch.

He jumped and slid back his chair.

Her foot hit the floor with a thud, and she grinned into her glass of water.

Mom flagged down their server then requested a basket of bread and a bottle of Barolo. Jim politely declined. Much as he'd love to drown his sorrows, he needed his wits about him.

The waitress returned with the bread, the wine, and three glasses. Was she conspiring with them? Despite his protests, his mother insisted he join her and Alessa for a toast.

"Now, what should we drink to?" Mom asked, glass aloft.

"Freedom of choice?" he muttered.

His mother shot him a hard look. "How about old friends and new chances?"

"I'll drink to that." Alessa touched her glass to his, then his mom's.

He put down his goblet before his mother could tap their glasses together.

"Darling, it's bad luck if you don't clink and drink."

Jim swore he'd seen that on a coaster somewhere. "I'm driving, Mom. How would it look if I got pulled over and had wine on my breath?"

"One glass won't even faze you. Besides, you'd just flash your badge to get out of the ticket. Or any other problem they were flagging you for."

"It doesn't exactly work that way."

"Lighten up, love." Alessa drained her glass. "It's a celebration."

"Oh?" He raised his eyebrows. "And what are we celebrating?"

"Well, darling. Alessa told me you have a new girlfriend. That's worth a tip of the glass, don't you think?"

"I'm pretty sure I told you I was seeing someone. I

don't know why Alessa was talking to you about my love life at all. But if that was why we were here, you wouldn't have toasted to old friends and new chances. You would have told me to bring Chelsea — who you know is only my partner — with me. And you certainly wouldn't have invited *her*." He tipped his head toward Alessa.

"James Patrick McPherson. You apologize this instant."

"For what, Mom? Talking about Alessa like she isn't even here? Which, by the way, she shouldn't be, particularly if you thought we were celebrating a new relationship, which we aren't. And this slight I just made toward Alessa is a far less flagrant offense than the one you made."

"The one I made? What have I done?"

"You blindsided me with an ex-girlfriend at dinner. The difference between our transgressions is like the difference between a misdemeanor and a felony."

"Ex-girlfriend, Jimmy?" Alessa snapped a breadstick in half. "That's hardly fair. We were engaged. You—"

"Darling," Mom interrupted, "spending time with someone you love is hardly a crime."

"Someone I love? I hope you're talking about yourself."

"I raised you better than this. You're embarrassing me. And yourself."

He turned away from her and faced Alessa. "Did you really think this was a good idea? What did you think was going to happen? You'd weasel your way into dinner with us, then we'd put our past in the rearview like a bad dream and move on as though we were never apart?"

"Is there a reason it can't be that simple?"

Jim rubbed his forehead. A raging headache was building behind his eyes.

"The two of you were perfect for each other, darling. You saw it then. Why can't you see it now?"

He looked at his mother then back to Alessa. "I told

you I'd never say anything if you let me go without a fight. Until now, I've kept that promise. But this feels like your gloves are coming off."

"Of course, she's fighting for you, darling. And you're lucky she's willing to take you back after that … mess you found yourself in."

"That 'mess,' as you like to call it, almost destroyed me."

"And Alessa is still standing by you."

All the old feelings of shame and rage roiled through him — feelings he'd do anything not to feel, anything not to reveal. But if that's what he had to do to get rid of her for good, then that's what he'd do. He glowered at Alessa. "As far as I'm concerned, you being here breaks the terms of our deal. You want to tell her, or should I?"

"Tell me what?" Mom looked back and forth between him and his ex.

"Jimmy, love. It doesn't have to be like this."

"You're right. It doesn't."

"Tell me what?" Mom repeated.

"You're the one who came into my restaurant," Alessa said. "At first, I thought you'd changed your mind. But then I saw you with *her*." She spat the last word. Her tone turned to vinegar. "Did you do it to hurt me? A last, spiteful slap in my face?"

"You would know all about hurting people."

"Tell me what?" Mom pounded the table.

The people seated next to them looked over.

Jim gave them a terse smile. "Sorry."

They turned back to their meal, though they kept glancing toward him and his mother.

He turned his back on them and spun to face his mother. "You're getting all bent out of shape, but I'm the one who was wronged here. She's a wolf in sheep's clothing, and if you're not careful, she'll devour us all. But you're too enamored with the facade to see it."

"And who am I in this little analogy of yours?" Mom asked.

The word "dog" was on the tip of his tongue, but instead, he said, "The shepherd."

"Seriously, Jimmy? You're going to compare me to the big bad in a kid's story?"

"I've had fairy tales on my mind lately."

Mom grabbed his arm. "Are you working the Grimm Reaper case?"

"I can't talk about open investigations."

"Darling, I don't want you on that case. It's too dangerous."

"I'll be fine, Mom."

"You're chasing a serial killer!"

The couple at the other table stared again.

Jim shushed her, then he said, "You can't say 'serial killer' in public like that."

"Well, that's what he is. Shouldn't the FBI be on the case?"

She sounded like a noir cop show. Pretty soon, she'd be using words like "ugly mug" and "dame."

"You can't even use that term until three murders have been committed. And there are other factors — time between kills, motive, gratification."

"Gratification?" Alessa's interest perked. "Who determines that?"

Mom looked like she was going to faint.

"It's not a serial killer, Mom. There hasn't been enough of a cooling-off period."

"That hardly makes me feel better."

"It should." It really shouldn't, but she didn't need to know that.

"What if you just didn't find the first bodies yet? He could have been doing this for years and only now is doing it more frequently."

He whipped toward her. "What did you say?"

"You might not know who his first victims were."

"I gotta go." He kissed her cheek, then pushed back his chair. After throwing a handful of bills onto the table, he ran out of the restaurant.

CHELSEA SPENT all day Saturday researching wolves and looking into arrest and citation histories of anyone involved with exotic animals. She had a few leads and considered calling McPherson, but she didn't have anything concrete yet. And she was a bit concerned about what she might be interrupting.

So, she waited.

Sleep had eluded her for much of the night, and she rose far too early for a day off.

Sunday had dawned with a fresh carpet of white on the ground. Diffused sunlight filtered through the dense clouds and reflected off the snow, creating crystalline sparkles as far as the eye could see. She hated to drive over it and mar the pristine groundcover, but soon enough, the city would come to life, and tire tracks and exhaust fumes would blacken the roads.

No point sitting around and waiting for it to happen. She'd catch the early Mass then get on with her day.

Parking was easy at church — not many congregants had braved the icy road conditions. Even afterward, few people had ventured out. PennDOT hadn't salted or plowed yet, and many of the roads were treacherous. The lack of traffic made the drive to her father's quicker than usual.

Truth be told, she wouldn't have minded it taking a bit longer to get there.

Chelsea took a deep breath, steeling herself before her visit. Then she let herself in. The darn door was unlocked again, and it wasn't because he was expecting her — she usually didn't get there until the afternoon. Noise from the television blared from the other side of the wall, and she raised her voice so he'd hear her above the elevated volume. "Dad?"

No answer.

She shook her head and rounded the corner. He sat in front of the TV, eyes glazed over while he stared at the Seals on the screen. Had to be a rerun because it was too early in the day for a live game. If she wasn't mistaken, it was the 1988 New Year's Eve game when their team captain became the only player in hockey history to score five goals in five different ways.

And how sad was it that she recognized which game it was after only a few seconds?

No point in trying to talk to Dad. Not while her arms were full, and he was otherwise engrossed. Chelsea dropped the donuts on the coffee table, then walked straight through to the kitchen to begin putting her purchases away — frozen dinners, coffee, cream, and juice. She'd stopped buying bread and lunch meat when he'd grown too lazy to make sandwiches. Stopped buying him beer even longer ago, once she discovered his prescriptions. He'd complained to her at first, ignoring her reasoning about mixing alcohol and his meds. When she switched tactics and used the no-alcohol-purchases-on-Sundays law as an excuse, he asked her to do the shopping on Saturdays. She didn't.

And after a few weeks, he quit nagging her about it entirely.

Based on the empty bottles in the kitchen, he'd found someone else to buy it for him. A lot of it. Or he'd gone to the liquor store himself.

She'd love to see him get out once in a while. But not if he was buying booze.

At least he hadn't made as big a mess as he had the week before. She brewed a pot of coffee, loaded the dishwasher, then washed the counters. By then, the coffee was ready, so she poured them each a cup.

When she returned to the living room, he'd already eaten his donut. And hers.

Chelsea put his mug down on the side table next to his recliner. Then she perched on the edge of the couch and sipped her drink. Weariness settled on her like a shroud. Too bad she hadn't stopped for an espresso instead. This visit would be a short one. She needed a nap.

"How's work?"

She sputtered, nearly choked on her coffee. Dad never, *never*, started conversations. There were days he didn't answer her when she started them.

"Well?"

"Uh …" Chelsea still had trouble believing he was speaking proactively. "I'm, uh … I'm running down a new lead. Exotic animals."

"Exotic animals? Like wolves?"

"Why'd you jump to wolves?"

"I watch the news."

Did he? She doubted he watched anything that wasn't sports-related. Yet, he'd seen the coverage of her case. "I wasn't aware the news said anything about wolves related to my case. Can't imagine why they would."

"Took you too long to shoo the parasites away. They

got footage of the vic. Her body and face had been blurred out of respect — if you can believe that — but a couple of the channels aired the wolf mask. Pretty sure the story didn't have anything to do with the Three Little Pigs or the Seven Young Goats."

"Goats?"

"You really don't remember your fairy tales, do you?"

"I don't remember one with goats."

"I think it was the fifth story in the book. Might have been the sixth."

"Goats?"

"Look it up when you go home. Doesn't matter. Unless I miss my guess, this is a Little Red story. Started with the cap you got. Don't tell me you didn't realize this. Get your head in the game or ride the bench."

Chelsea squeezed the bridge of her nose. Why did it feel like everyone knew more than she did? Scott had all the forensic knowledge. McPherson had a handle on investigation techniques. Dad was an expert on the lore behind the killer's MO. What did she contribute?

Other than having captured the killer's attention, she was making little to no difference in the case. She might have come to the fairy-tale angle first, but there was no doubt to anyone about it now.

She was the weak link.

And she didn't like it.

Dad shook his head. "Always so fragile. Couldn't even enjoy a childhood story. What makes you think you're going to be able to handle catching this guy if you can't even handle the necessary research?"

"I can handle it, Dad."

"Can you? Because another one is coming, Chels. This isn't over. Your guy's just getting started. And if you don't toughen up, he's going to chew you up and spit you out. Or devour you like the wolf he is."

She jumped to her feet. "I know what's coming, Dad. And I know what I'm doing."

"If that was true, you'd have this guy on the ropes. I sure hope your partner is more prepared than you are."

Chelsea grabbed her coat then stuffed her arms through the sleeves.

A Seal scored on a penalty shot.

"Score!" Dad pumped his fist in the air.

Seemed he was done with the conversation. Well, she was, too. She stormed out, slamming the door behind her.

Small satisfaction, considering he was so engrossed in the television, he probably didn't even notice.

Chapter Twenty-Two

Chelsea didn't manage to nap when she got home, too irritated with her father to rest. So she cracked open his fairy-tale book and found he was right. The goat story was the fifth one. His knowledge of the Brothers Grimm both disturbed and angered her.

Probably one of the many reasons she didn't get a good night's sleep, either.

Monday dawned bleak and cold. She watched the sun rise over the river as she drove to work. It was way earlier than she was due in, but she'd been up for hours. At least she'd miss rush hour traffic.

There was even time to stop at her favorite coffee shop for a macchiato — the largest size they served, with three extra pumps of espresso.

"You sure you want that much?" The barista's eyebrows disappeared under a wisp of bangs. "We already put two pumps in our macchiatos. Three more make five. I don't think that much caffeine is good for your heart, ma'am."

Chelsea scowled at the girl, who couldn't be *that* much

younger than her. "One, I'm not a *ma'am*. I'm a *miss*. But feel free to call me *Detective*." Flashing her badge was pointless, but she did so anyway. "And two, the customer is always right. Add three pumps of espresso. Actually, make it four."

The girl turned to make the beverage, then she served the drink with wide eyes. "Good luck, Detective."

Chelsea gave her a generous tip then sipped her drink as she drove to work.

By the time McPherson strolled in, her drink was finished, and she'd gone through all their files three times. She'd also cleaned her desk, completed some neglected paperwork, made a list of exotic animal offenders in order of geographic proximity to the station, and poured a cup of stationhouse coffee.

McPherson took off his jacket, hung it over the back of his chair, then stared at her before dropping into his seat. One of his eyebrows arched, and his lips quirked. "How was your weekend?"

She tamped down her irritation and bounced her legs up and down instead of yelling at him. He was five minutes late and moving slower by the second. They'd never get on the road at this rate. But picking an argument wouldn't get her anywhere with him, so she just answered his question. "It had its ups and downs, you know? I did a lot of research on wolves. And the exotic animal farms in the area. Did you know that raising exotic animals isn't illegal in Pennsylvania? Thought it was, but it's not. All you need is a permit. There are sixteen permits granted throughout the entire state. Only three within two hours of us. But if you include West Virginia and Ohio, we can expand our list to seven. Also, I—"

"Whoa!" He raised his hands to stop her and chuckled.

"Take a breath. I only caught about half of that, given the whole spiel sounded like one multi-syllabic word."

She giggled. Never expected him to use the word *multi-syllabic*. Or was it a phrase? Did the hyphen make it one word or two?

"Chels!" He snapped his fingers. "I'm talking to you."

She whipped toward him.

He leaned over and peered into their shared wastebasket. "That's a pretty big cup in the trash. Don't suppose it was decaf?"

"Macchiato. Four extra pumps of espresso. Plus this one." She drained her mug, popped up, bounced on the balls of her feet, and clapped her hands together. "Let's go check these out."

"Four pumps? Plus a cup here?"

Was it possible he was moving backward? She pointed her thumbs toward the door and took a big hop in that direction.

"That explains the light speed speech tempo. You know the human body isn't designed to process that much caffeine at once."

"The barista said something similar. I'm fine. If you didn't see my trash or this cup, you wouldn't have known I had any coffee at all."

He scratched his head. "Sorry, Sully. But you couldn't be more wrong. You're lucky your heart hasn't exploded."

"Don't call me that." She jumped back to her desk, dropped onto her chair, then drummed her fingers on her blotter to the same rhythm her heels were tapping. "I'm fine. I'd have to drink a lot more than a large coffee—"

"And six shots of espresso."

"Can we hit the road? We have a case to solve."

"Seriously, are you okay? Your eyes are shadowed and bloodshot, and all your limbs are vibrating."

She leaped to her feet and slung her jacket over her arm. It was too warm in the station to put it on before stepping outside. "I'm driving."

"The hell you are." There was no more humor in his voice. "I'm not convinced you don't need a hospital."

He was as infuriating as her father. Maybe more so. "Fine. But let's *go*. I'll brief you in the car."

Seemed like she waited in the parking lot for half an hour. Maybe more. When he finally joined her by his car, she rounded on him. "Where have you been? I've been out here so long, I think I got frostbite!"

"I can't be more than a minute behind you. We'd have gotten here at the same time, but you ran down the stairs. And you wouldn't be cold if you put on your damn coat."

She looked down at the jacket hooked over her arm, then back at him. "Well, I don't need it in the car, do I? Now let's *go*."

He shook his head and folded himself into the driver's seat.

Chelsea clambered in her side, then turned to him. "Okay. So, I was searching—"

"Put on your seatbelt."

For the love of all that was holy, he was moving slower than maple sap in winter. She secured the safety harness. "Can I speak now?"

"Who's stopping you?"

Maybe he was right. Sure felt like her heart was racing. But it was far more likely a result of irritation than caffeine. "Okay. Like I was saying—"

"Where are we going?"

Chelsea took a deep breath. He was going to be the death of her. She typed an address into the GPS.

"Thanks." McPherson pulled out. "So, did you want to tell me something?"

She wasn't a violent person, but visions of pummeling him raced through her mind. Tempting, but actually walloping the guy while he was driving just didn't seem like a good idea. "I was looking through fairy tales over the weekend. Did you know there's one with a wolf and seven kid goats?"

He glanced at her. "That's what you've been trying to say?"

"Well … yeah."

"I think you need some water. And about three bunches of bananas."

"Bananas?" What was he talking about? She muttered, "You're bananas."

"Water will help flush your system, and the potassium in the bananas will help counteract the caffeine."

"Thanks, Doc, but I don't need anything to counteract the caffeine. I feel fine."

"Sullivan, you're talking a mile a minute, twitching like a tweaker, and not making any sense. I'll give you three options. One, the hospital."

"Absolutely not."

"Two, take a sick day. Go home and sleep this off. Not that you could."

"I'm not sick. Or tired. Sick and tired, maybe, but—"

"Then water and bananas. Because you're driving me nuts."

"You're nuts," she grumbled.

He reached across the seat and put his fingers on her neck.

She slapped his hand away.

"Sullivan."

The warning in his voice gave her pause.

McPherson touched her neck again. "Shit. Your pulse is almost too fast to count. I'm taking you to the ER."

"No!" She put her fingers on her wrist. Her heart rate was a bit elevated. "Maybe adding four shots of espresso to my macchiato wasn't a great idea."

"Plus a coffee after that."

"But we have work to do."

"We're going to the hospital."

"Please, Jim. No. I'm fine, really. Stop at the store. I'll drink all the water and eat all the bananas you want me to. But we need to follow these leads."

He turned toward her. "You have a fear of hospitals?"

"I have a fear of not catching this killer before he strikes again."

The GPS protested when he turned off the programmed route.

"Where are you going?" He wasn't headed toward any of the hospitals in the city. Then again, he wasn't headed toward any of the exotic animal reserves on her list. A hunch had her heart racing faster. "Are you taking me home?"

Did he know where her home was? That didn't seem appropriate.

McPherson shook his head. His jaw ticked, but he didn't speak.

Why was he the one angry? She was the one being bossed around, being benched. Against her will. Just her luck — her dad and her partner were cut from the same cloth. And neither thought she could do her job.

But he turned left when her apartment was right. What was he up to?

A few blocks later, he pulled through the drive-thru at Panera. "Four bottles of water and six bananas, please."

"Six bananas? I can't eat that many—"

His glare cut her off.

She reached into her wallet for cash as he pulled to the

payment window, but he already had his credit card out and passed it to the cashier.

"It's bad enough you're making me eat all this. I can't let you pay for it, too."

He merely pocketed his card then pulled to the next window. A young woman — college-aged, unless Chelsea missed her guess — handed him two bulky bags.

"I was certain this was going to be a car full of chimpanzees."

McPherson gave her a dazzling grin. "I've been known to monkey around sometimes."

Chelsea leaned over. "I've heard people call him an animal."

He shoved the bags into her chest so hard, air whooshed out of her lungs. Then he rolled up his window and pulled away. "Eat your damn fruit."

She peeled a banana and chomped on it.

The GPS stopped recalculating when he turned onto the highway. As they crossed the bridge, she watched the city shrink through the side mirror.

Neither of them spoke until she'd finished half the bananas and two bottles of water. By then, her stomach was cramping. And they were well on their way to the first name on her list.

Chapter Twenty-Three

JIM ORDERED a breakfast burrito while Sullivan went to the restroom. It was their fourth pitstop since leaving the city. All the water on top of her vat of caffeine had taken a toll on her bladder. She hated to see what happened when her digestive tract processed the bananas.

When she came out of the restroom, he was just finishing his breakfast. He held up his empty wrapper before tossing it in the trash. "Want something?"

She shook her head. "I'm full of fruit, thanks."

They walked to the parking lot in silence. While he got situated in the driver's seat, Chelsea balled up the Panera bag she'd used to collect trash then disposed of it in the garbage can closest to the SUV. After she climbed in the passenger side, she turned to him. "I may have been a little … much this morning. I'm sorry."

He shrugged.

"Are you angry because I told that girl you're an animal? She was too young for you, anyway."

Jim shot her a hard stare. "I'm not angry," he lied.

"And I'll decide who's too young for me, thanks. Besides, I wasn't flirting with her."

"Are you kidding? You flirt with everyone."

"No, I don't." He pulled onto the road, tires squealing.

"Fine. Not men. But every woman."

"Still wrong."

"You're right. Every woman, except me."

The vehicle bounced as he veered onto the berm. He slammed on the brakes and swerved back onto the road. "Sorry. Pothole."

Right. So lame, Jim.

He cleared his throat. "You're my partner, Chelsea. I can't flirt with you. It's … it's weird."

"I'm not asking you to. But it's a little disturbing when I see you turning on the charm with old ladies and young girls while you treat me like chopped liver."

"Believe me. I don't think of you as minced meat."

"Right. Sometimes you treat me like a child."

"What?"

"You worry how I'll react to an autopsy—"

"With good reason. You got sick."

"You bought me breakfast."

"I bought you something to counteract the caffeine. Bananas and water were faster than tracking down activated charcoal."

"And how do you know so much about caffeine and its counteractive agents?"

He touched her neck again. "Your pulse has slowed, but you're still not making sense."

"I've done nothing but make sense all day."

Jim snorted.

The GPS directed them down a dirt road winding through the woods.

"Is this right?" He squinted into the trees.

"Now, who's not making sense? The GPS clearly said to turn down this road."

"I'd hardly call this a road."

"Do you think exotic animal refuges should be right along the highway?"

His jaw pulsed his irritation. They passed a little house nestled into the trees.

"Was that it?" she asked.

The GPS indicated they'd reach their destination in one mile.

"Oh."

He shook his head. When the GPS announced their arrival, he parked in front of a fence, turned off the engine, then climbed out of the car without a word.

A bracing wind had caused a crust of thin ice to form over the blanket of snow, and their boots crunched through the brittle coating on their way to the gate. A large sign was posted on it.

GARVIN WILDLIFE SANCTUARY

BEWARE

WILD ANIMALS ON PREMISES

ENTER AT YOUR OWN RISK

Jim barely paused long enough to read the sign before reaching for the latch.

She grabbed his arm. "I think we should reconsider flinging this gate open, willy-nilly."

"Willy-nilly?" He smirked. "Look around, Sullivan. What do you see?"

Her gaze raked over him before she spun away from him to survey the landscape.

He turned and studied their surroundings, too. Sugared pine boughs. Glittering icicles dangling from barren oak limbs. A brilliant splash of red from a cardinal in the trees, his trilling call carried away on the brisk breeze. A lone set of tire tracks — theirs — marring the otherwise pristine winter scene. It was a picture to rival Monet's *The Magpie*.

"Well?" McPherson prompted.

"Why do I feel like you're always assessing my observational skills?"

He sighed. "One set of tires. Ours. That means the owners live here and haven't been out since the last snow. No animal tracks. Seems the indigenous wildlife knows the wolves are here and are staying away. Given there are no wolf tracks between this gate and the door of the structure inside, and there is another fence behind the structure, I'm fairly confident we're safe walking from here to there."

"I hate it when your logic is so … logical."

He grinned, pleased she'd admitted he was probably right. Well, she'd nearly admitted it. Unless there was a pen on the other side of the building or a doggie door in a section of the fence he couldn't see, it was probably safe. Or safe-ish.

Sullivan squared her shoulders, flung open the gate, then strode onto the property.

Jim couldn't help laughing at her false bravado.

"Jerk," she called over her shoulder.

He hurried after her then took the lead, high-stepping through the drifts of snow. The house sagged as though it was sad. Or tired. Each of the three steps to the porch dipped in the middle. The single window facing the front of the house sported a broken screen, the rusty mesh flapping in the wind. The siding — probably once a bright yellow — was a faded shade of sand, and spots of olive green peeked out where the paint had chipped and peeled. He gingerly climbed the stairs, praying they held his weight, then stepped onto the ramshackle porch. When he opened the screen door to knock, it fell off the hinges. He flung it aside, and it clattered to the floor.

She raised her eyebrows

He shrugged, then knocked.

"What should we do about the door?" she whispered.

"We're not doing anything about it. It was clearly already broken."

Sullivan closed her eyes. Took a deep breath. Called him a few names under her breath that made him smirk. She must be feeling better.

The door opened. A man in a plaid robe stood there, curly hair sticking out in all directions. He glanced down at the storm door, then up at Chelsea.

"Sorry." She cleared her throat and pointed at Jim.

He rolled his eyes. "When I grabbed the handle to knock, it fell off the hinges."

The man looked at the door then up at Jim. His brows furrowed, but he didn't pursue the matter. "Who are you? What do you want?"

Jim moved his jacket aside to flash his shield. "I'm Detective McPherson. This is my partner, Detective Sullivan. We'd like to ask you a few questions."

"Ah, come on, man. Why the hassle? My license is paid for. I have the permits, the paperwork. I'll find them if you give me a minute."

Sullivan offered him a weak smile. "Mr. Garvin, we're not here about the validity of your license."

"Oh? Then, why? Oh, my God. Is this about the weed—"

"Mr. Garvin," Jim interrupted. "Before you say something you might regret, perhaps you'd like us to tell you why we've come."

"Landscaping, I mean. Because I'll get the place cleaned up as soon as the weather breaks."

Jim rolled his eyes.

Sullivan stepped closer. "You are aware that recreational marijuana use is not legal in the state of Pennsylvania?"

His eyes grew wide. "Dude. Am I under arrest?"

She glanced over his shoulder, trying to peek inside his house.

Jim shook his head. "Is there a reason we would be here to arrest you?"

"Uh … no?"

Sullivan shot him a hard stare. "Is that a question or a resolute answer?"

"Resolute?" he asked.

Jim stepped between them. "We're getting off-topic. Mr. Garvin, we're here to discuss the wolves you have on-site."

"Oh. Good. I mean, okay. Like I told you, man. They're all legal."

"That's not disputed. We were wondering if any had been injured or had gone missing lately."

"If one of my animals was missing, I'd be legally obligated to report it to the authorities. It's not like losing a dog."

"We're aware of that," Chelsea said. "We also know your license might not get renewed if the state thought you couldn't contain the animals properly."

"We're not with the Wildlife Commission," McPherson said. "We're here investigating a murder."

"A murder? My wolves aren't responsible for that. Wait a minute. You're not trying to blame me, are you?"

Jim sighed. "Mr. Garvin. Bob. Can I call you Bob?"

He nodded.

"Bob, we're not trying to trap you. Not going to pin anything on you. Not even going to tell the Wildlife

Commission anything we learn here today. But we need your help. Lives are on the line. You could be a hero, Bob."

Bob got a faraway look in his eye, and a smile spread across his face.

Jim nudged his partner.

She lay her hand on Garvin's arm. "Bob, will you help us? Please?"

He cleared his throat and pulled the lapels of his robe closer together. "Hypothetically, and I'm not saying this happened, mind you. But hypothetically, if I were to tell you one of my wolves disappeared last Tuesday, would that be the kind of information you'd be looking for?"

"Hypothetically," she said.

"And if, hypothetically, that was the case," Jim added, "I'd ask whether you found evidence of the animal escaping or of someone taking it."

"Ah, dude. I wish I knew. The" — he made air quotes — "hypothetical business of raising wolves isn't too lucrative, you know? Requires me to make my money in other ways, and in the winter, funds are tight. I hypothetically" — another set of air quotes — "canceled my security monitoring company."

"What?" Sullivan asked.

"The cameras are only for show," he explained. "They don't record."

She frowned and passed Bob her card. "Well, if you think of anything else, let us know."

"Hypothetically, right?" Bob nodded.

"Right." She turned around, rolled her eyes at Jim, then walked down the steps.

Before he could follow her, Bob grabbed his arm. "Yo, dude?"

He looked down at the pothead's hand on his arm.

Bob let him go and backed up, hands in the air.

"Yes?" Jim prompted.

"My neighbors up the road?" Bob gestured in the direction of the tiny house they'd passed. "The O'Connors? They might know something."

Sullivan, who'd stopped and turned around, sighed. "Why would your neighbors know anything about your missing wolf?"

"Hypothetically missing." He made air quotes again.

"Bob?" Jim needed him to focus. "Your neighbors?"

"They're old busybodies. I think they sit at their window all day, just looking for something to complain about. And they know *everything*, dude. I can't scratch my ass without the old lady bitching about it. If something weird happened around here, like a hypothetical theft of a wolf in the middle of the night, they'd be your best shot at information."

"Thanks." Jim raised two fingers and offered him a half-hearted salute.

"Dude." Bob nodded, turned around, then closed his door.

Sullivan stomped to the car.

Jim followed, then slipped into the driver's seat. When she'd climbed in, he said, "I guess we're going to the O'Connors."

"They better not call me dude."

He laughed as he headed back down the road.

Chapter Twenty-Four

JIM GRINNED when they reached the O'Connor residence. Stoner Bob might have been clueless about his legal rights, but he was spot-on about his neighbors. The elderly couple was seated at their picture window, looking out toward the road.

Their gazes tracked Jim's vehicle the whole length of the driveway then, if possible, grew even sharper as he and Sullivan walked toward the porch.

Unlike Bob's house, the O'Connor property was well maintained. The floorboards were painted a bright blue. A doormat bidding visitors welcome was decorated with jaybirds in an identical hue. The white siding was as bright as the drifts of snow in the yard. Clear plastic awnings — because they couldn't snoop through duck cloth — flanking the porch were pulled taut as a barrier against the driving wind, and the evergreen bushes surrounding the home were meticulously manicured into perfect orbs.

Sullivan raised her hand to knock, but the door swung open before she had a chance.

The elderly couple had both come to greet them.

Their teamwork was cute. In a disturbing kind of way.

Jim smiled and flashed his badge. "Hello. I'm Detective McPherson. This is my partner, Detective Sullivan."

It rolled off his tongue like a recording. Maybe he was getting used to the idea. He pulled his jacket closed, coving his shield. "Are you the O'Connors?"

The man nodded. "We are."

"Mind if we ask you a few questions?"

"What about?" Mrs. O'Connor asked.

"Your neighbor, Mr. Garvin." Sullivan stifled a yawn. Seemed the bananas and water were kicking in.

Before she could continue, Mr. O'Connor spoke up. "What's that no good, drug-dealing, hippie freak gone and done now?"

"Nothing, sir." Jim's lips trembled as he fought another grin, amused at the colorful description. Old fashioned, sure. But it fit Bob to a T.

Sullivan offered a sympathetic nod, not that their expressions changed because of it. "Seems one of his animals went missing last week. His security cameras didn't catch anything suspicious. We were hoping you might have seen something."

"Of course, his cameras didn't catch anything," Mr. O'Connor said. "Damn things don't work."

"Just courting trouble, he is," Mrs. O'Connor said. "Given the business he's in, he should pay extra for security. Not turn it off."

"You mean, the exotic animal business?" Sullivan asked.

"Pffft." Mrs. O'Connor waved her hand. "If that's what you think, you can't be too good at your job."

Chelsea bristled.

Jim grabbed her arm then gave it a gentle squeeze as he pulled her back a step. "You wouldn't happen to have noticed any unusual traffic last Tuesday night? Maybe a strange vehicle?"

"Strange vehicles come down this road all the time." Mr. O'Connor frowned. "That boy has people comin' and goin' at all hours of the day and night. Up to no good, that one is."

"We'll take that under advisement," Jim said. "In the meantime, if you noticed anything out of the ordinary on Tuesday, we'd appreciate you sharing what you saw."

Mr. O'Connor turned and walked deeper into his house. His wife stayed at the door, staring at them and scowling.

Talk about awkward.

Sullivan stifled another yawn. She was probably going to collapse on her feet, and Jim wondered if he'd have to catch her or would have time to get her back to the car first. Just as he was about to inquire after Mr. O'Connor, the man returned with a thumb drive and handed it over.

"Here's a copy of the security feed from that night."

Sullivan masked a surprised scoff with a fake cough. "You know how to access and copy camera footage?"

Mrs. O'Connor huffed and crossed her arms over her chest. "We might be old, young lady, but we aren't stupid. Because of Garvin's damn-fool antics — pray his poor parents aren't rolling in their graves — we had to increase our own security. And there's no point in having a security system if you don't know how to use it." She slammed the door in their faces.

"Thanks," Sullivan yelled through the closed door. "If we have any further questions, we'll give you a call."

Jim laughed on the way back to the car. "Figured you were the type of girl old folks loved."

"I am."

"Clearly not these two."

"They're not the typical old folks." She frowned and climbed into the car. "Wonder what's on there."

"Let's head back to the station and find out." The engine roared to life, then the vent blasted heat.

Blanketed in warmth and reclining in her seat, her eyelids drooped. She was asleep before they reached the end of the driveway. And Jim had the rest of the drive to wonder about their latest clue.

BACK AT THE STATION, Chelsea yawned and stretched. Her fist grazed McPherson's face, and the stubble he'd grown since his morning's shave scratched her knuckles.

"How many times are you going to punch me, Sullivan?"

"A, when I punch you, you'll know it. And B, if you weren't hovering behind me, it wouldn't be an issue."

"Sorry, we don't have a big screen and theater seats. If I want to watch the footage, I have to be here. And if you weren't crashing from your caffeine binge this morning, you wouldn't be fighting to stay awake now."

His breath was warm in her ear and sent a shiver down her spine. She covered it with another stretch, this one exaggerated and catching him under the chin.

He laughed, but then he took a step back. "Freeze the frame … there."

Chelsea paused the playback. The picture of the driver was grainy, but it was the best they were going to get. A man, early forties. Beard, ball cap. Thick-framed glasses.

McPherson stood, stepped around her, then sat on the corner of her desk, facing her. "Of the three vehicles that night, my money's on this guy."

She had to agree. The first traveler the camera caught

was an old woman. Possible, of course, but hardly likely. Especially since she went back and forth on the road several times. Chelsea's guess was she had been lost.

The second driver was a young kid, late teens or early twenties. Actually, he was probably only a few years younger than Chelsea. He'd be easy enough to track down, but she didn't suspect him. He never traveled back down the road. It was much more likely he was a neighbor heading home after a late shift somewhere.

No, their likely suspect was the guy in the cargo van, a silver Nissan NV200. And she was flooded with relief. Guilt had gnawed at her for considering her father — even in the loosest sense — and seeing a man closer to McPherson's age than Dad's gave her a tiny bit of comfort. Besides, her father didn't own a van. He had a beat-up Impala. And he almost never drove anymore, anyway. So it couldn't be him.

Unless he had a partner.

And just like that, her neck muscles knotted again. Her stomach flopped, leaving her with a queasy feeling.

"Well, what do you think?" McPherson tapped her desk letter. "You want to run down the young neighbor, the old lady, or the guy in the van?"

"I'll start with the van."

"Fine. I'll take the other two. Probably still be done before you. You look like you're going to fall flat on your face."

"I'm fine. Just a little tired."

"You're not sleeping at night, are you? That's what the caffeine was about today."

"I hardly see where that's any of your concern."

He frowned. "When it comes to my partner's ability to do her job, it damn well is my concern. In the last few days, you've been way off your game."

"Last few days? This is our first day back from the weekend. You stalking me now?"

"No, I'm not stalking you. And I don't mean yesterday. I'm talking about workdays. Ever since you got the red cap in the mail. You've got shadows under your eyes, and you're living off espresso shots. I can tell you're not sleeping. I rarely see you eat. This case is getting to you. And if you're compromised, I'm compromised. So yeah, I'm keeping tabs on you. And I don't like what I see."

Chelsea gripped the arms of her chair to keep from jumping up. She was so tired of being treated like a fragile woman or a sub-par cop. McPherson might have a point about the case getting to her, but she'd never give him the satisfaction of admitting it. She could do her job — and do it well — even if things were getting under her skin.

"Just run down your own leads and leave me to run down mine. I can do my job, and I don't need you, my dad, or anyone else looking out for me."

"See? That's our problem. We'll never make a good team if you can't accept that the two of us need to rely on each other." He dismissed her by walking to his desk then hiding behind his laptop. The taps of his fingers on the keys were sharp as gunfire.

Chelsea had a lot she wanted to say but couldn't form the words. Instead, she started investigating her leads and let him work on his.

The picture was too grainy for facial recognition to get a hit. Still, she had to try. And as expected, it turned up nothing. She had a little more luck with the van. A trace of the license plate showed it was registered to a rental company. Maybe they'd get lucky — pull a clearer image of his face from the security footage or obtain a credit card receipt with his identity.

"McPherson? I got something on the van."

He looked at her but didn't say anything.

She tamped down her anger and continued. "It's registered to a rent-a-car company in Monrow. I thought I'd drive over there and see what else I can dig up. Want to come with?" The invitation was the biggest olive branch she was going to offer. And frankly, she was hoping he didn't take it.

He still didn't answer her. But he stood and put on his jacket, then he snatched keys from his desk drawer.

It drove her nuts that he always insisted on driving. Worse still, that he assumed he'd drive to run down *her* lead. But she was exhausted and wouldn't mind resting on the way there. Besides, if she napped, she wouldn't have to talk to him.

The drive to Monrow went pretty much exactly as she expected it to. Chelsea kept her eyes closed, and McPherson kept his mouth shut. It was hard to say if the silence made things better or worse, but there wasn't time to dissect things.

When they reached the rental place, Chelsea marched up to the man behind the counter. She pulled her jacket aside to show the badge clipped to her belt. "I'm Detective Sullivan. This is Detective McPherson. We'd like to ask you a few questions about one of your customers."

"Uhhh… I just work here. You should talk to my manager."

"Is he here?"

"No. It was a slow day, and he has a bad cold. He went home early."

McPherson leaned on the counter. "You're not in any trouble. We're just hoping to get a look at your security footage from last week. Maybe an ID from a credit card receipt."

The kid glanced up at the cameras in the corner. Then

he looked at McPherson. "Is it legal for me to let you see that?"

"Sure. You can show us whatever you want." McPherson grinned at him. "And think what a cool story this will be for you to tell your friends. Especially if it leads to us catching our guy."

A smile broke out on the kid's face. "That would be cool." He chewed his lip and glanced over his shoulder. A door labeled EMPLOYEES ONLY was directly behind him. "I guess I can show you how our system works. You can look through the footage. I can't stay back there with you, though. I'm the only one here, and I have to man the desk."

"Perfect." McPherson started walking around the counter. "Lead the way."

Chelsea followed them, silently seething. This was supposed to be her lead, but as usual, McPherson took over. He could talk until he was blue in the face about team members having each other's backs. Fact of the matter was, he didn't have hers. And she doubted he ever would.

The clerk got them set up at a computer terminal, quickly showed McPherson how to operate the system, then returned to the front desk. That left Chelsea alone with her so-called partner. She stared at the screen while he navigated to last week's footage. It wasn't long until they found their bearded man. He never looked directly at the camera, so they couldn't get a screen capture for facial rec. And he paid cash for the rental, so there'd be no credit card information.

"Damn it." McPherson pounded his fist on the desk. "I knew he'd be too smart to pay with a credit card, but a guy can hope."

"At least we have a timestamp. We can have the clerk pull his rental contract. More likely than not, his address will be fake. But we have to run it down. And if we're lucky, the van will still be on site. We can have forensics go over it."

They walked back out front, and McPherson talked with the clerk. While he was getting the information they wanted, Chelsea looked around. Cameras facing the doors and the counter, yet none of the footage showed his face clearly. This guy was smart. He rented outside of the city. He paid cash. He had all his I's dotted and T's crossed.

If he didn't make a mistake soon, more people would die. And Chelsea couldn't stand to have that on her conscience. If he wasn't going to slip up, then she had to step up.

Had to bring him down. Soon.

McPherson thanked the clerk, nodded at Chelsea, then headed for the door.

She followed him out to the car. When they were both seated, she turned toward him. "So?"

"No point in calling forensics. The van has been out three additional times since this guy returned it. And it's out again. This time, it's a one-way rental. Someone's turning it in South Dakota. We could track it down, but everything will be compromised at this point."

"I think maybe we should, anyway. If there's any DNA evidence in there at all, we'll eventually need it to make our case."

He offered her a few sheets of paper. "Knock yourself out. But any defense attorney worth his salt will argue the evidence was tainted by multiple renters. It will probably be ruled inadmissible."

"I will." She snatched the pages out of his hand. Maybe he didn't see the need, but she knew any piece of evidence — no matter how small or how potentially-compromised — could make the difference when it came time to convict.

McPherson sighed and turned the key. The motor roared to life. "You mind if I stop at Mario's? Since we're all the way down here, might as well get some good cannoli."

"Suit yourself." Mario's did make the best cannoli. Pretty much everything they made was gastronomic perfection. But the thought of a sugary confection — even a high-quality one — made her stomach lurch. She reclined her seat and closed her eyes. By the time they left Monrow, rush-hour traffic on the Parkway would be a nightmare. Made her glad she wasn't driving.

Chapter Twenty-Five

BECAUSE MCPHERSON INSISTED on stopping for pastry, it was late when they got back to the precinct. Late enough that Chelsea could leave for home. Especially since she had gone in so early that day.

The whole way to her apartment, she looked forward to a quick bite to eat and a long, restful sleep. McPherson was right about one thing — she hadn't been sleeping. It would be nice to catch more than eight hours and wake up refreshed. Heck, if she managed to sleep through the night, she might not even need coffee in the morning. Or a vat of concealer to cover the shadows under her eyes.

Chelsea trudged down the hall to her door and was surprised to see a box sitting in front of it. She hadn't ordered anything. Maybe it was for a neighbor. She bent and looked closer at the label. Definitely for her. No return address, but the postage stamp indicated it had been shipped from California.

A wave of excitement rolled through her. Mom must've sent her a present. What a nice surprise.

She hefted the box to carry it inside. It was slightly

heavier than she expected. Chelsea flipped the light switch with her elbow, a lamp washing the apartment in a soft glow. She set the package on her coffee table before hurrying to the kitchen for a knife. Excited, she didn't even bother taking off her coat and gloves. She just sliced through the tape on the box, then flung open the flaps.

A scream ripped from her throat. She leaped away from the table.

Nestled inside the box was a wolf's head. Not a mask, like at the crime scene, but an actual decapitated wolf's head. The fetor of rotting flesh and the coppery tang of blood wafted from the package, and her stomach roiled.

Chelsea ran to the bathroom and vomited until she could do nothing but sag over the toilet, dry-heaving. It was another five minutes before she had the strength to stand. A few minutes more before she could walk back to her living room. This time, she couldn't miss the reek of death and had to approach the box with her nose buried in the crook of her arm.

Once there, she peered into the box again. Something reflected the lamplight, and she gave it a closer look. Metal. Copper? Brass?

She peered down, surprised to find her gloves were still on. At least she hadn't contaminated anything with her prints. After slipping off her Isotoners, she slid her hands into work-issue latex then gingerly shifted the head aside. Gagging, eyes watering, she grasped a bundle wrapped in tissue paper, removed it from the box, then carefully pulled off the paper to find an antique hand mirror with an ornately-sculpted handle and frame. The looking glass was shattered, the cracked shards distorting her reflection into a horrific, Picasso-like image.

The mirror slipped from her fingers then landed on the

sofa. She cringed and hoped it had no gore on it. Then she noticed a note fluttering to the floor.

Chelsea reached for it. Her hand trembled so much, it was difficult to read the message scrawled on it.

Mirror, mirror, held up high.

Who will be the next to die?

My prey can't hide behind fortress walls.

Death in Steel City's hallowed halls.

It took every ounce of restraint she possessed not to crumple it and throw it away. Instead, she took pictures of everything then packed it all up. After she sent a text to McPherson, she carried the box out to her car, then headed back to the station.

As she drove, her thoughts cycled through one disturbing thought after another — the butchered wolf, the threat of another kill.

The fact that the killer now knew where she lived. Unless he had always known …

She again thought of her father. His love for the Brothers Grimm. His knowledge of their original, horrific tales.

That pretty much guaranteed she wouldn't be getting a good night's sleep. Or any sleep at all.

JIM LOOKED at Sullivan's message again as he walked from his car to the precinct doors. She'd sent him one text.

Get to the station. Now.

And despite him texting her back a few times, he'd received nothing further from her. She hadn't answered any of his calls, either. Which both worried him and pissed him off.

He took the stairs two at a time then stormed through the doors into the squad room.

Sullivan was already there, ignoring her damn phone. She was cowering in her chair, which was pushed far from her desk, staring at a large box.

Two detectives on the late shift walked by. They tossed greetings her way while ignoring him. Jim didn't have the energy to care about being snubbed. He was more interested in why his partner was unresponsive — so unlike the unfailingly polite persona she usually adopted. Well, with everyone but him.

But this was about more than Sullivan not smiling or waving. She'd barely managed to blink. That box commanded her undivided attention. And not in a good way.

"Sullivan."

She didn't answer.

It shouldn't have surprised him, as she didn't answer his calls or texts, either. Jim strode to her desk. "Is there a reason you're ignoring me? And what's so damn important I had to come here at this hour?"

She didn't answer. Just pointed at the package.

He looked at her, at the box, then at her again. She didn't look well, so he stooped to look her in the eye. "What's the matter with you? You're white as a ghost, and you're still in your coat and gloves."

Words failed her, so she gestured toward the parcel again.

He sighed, stood, then reached for it.

"Wait! You need gloves."

"Gloves?" At least she was talking again. Jim loomed over the box to get a top-down view of the contents, not that he could, as she'd kept it closed. "What's in there? Evidence? How did you know it was here?"

Chelsea swallowed past a lump in her throat. "I didn't know it was here. It was sent to me. To my apartment."

"Someone sent evidence to your apartment?" He took gloves from his desk drawer, put them on, then opened the cardboard flaps. "Holy fuck. Is that… Is this *the* wolf's head? Garvin's missing wolf?"

She shrugged. "I would imagine so unless we have someone spree-killing wolves, too. Brought it here for the lab to examine, but I thought you should see it first."

"This was sent to you? At your apartment?"

Tears welled in her eyes, and she nodded.

Jim pursed his lips and vented a long, slow stream of breath. He ran his hands through his hair. "Maybe you should recuse yourself from this case."

"Why bother? I'm already on this sicko's radar. He knows where I work, what case I'm working on. He knows where I freaking live. Getting reassigned right now won't change any of that."

"We need to tell Davenport about this. In the meantime, I'm getting a forensics team up here."

"You can tell the captain if you want. We need to keep him in the loop, anyway. But neither you nor he is pulling me off this case."

"Sullivan—"

She held up her hand to stop him. A dark spot on her finger caught her attention, and her eyes widened. If possible, her face grew whiter.

Blood. Wolf's blood.

Her hands trembled as she stripped off the gloves then tossed them in her trashcan.

"Look …" He tried again. Still couldn't manage to complete a thought, though.

"There's more," she whispered.

"What?" Jim peered into the box again.

"There's a hand mirror in there. An old-fashioned one. Ornate frame. Brass. The glass has been shattered. Could have happened in transit, but I doubt it."

He reached for it, extracted it. Studied it. "And what's that supposed to mean?"

She shrugged. "Fits the theme. Snow White's evil queen had a mirror."

"Wasn't it on the wall?"

"Does it matter at this point? Everything has been loosely related, not spot on. Regardless, there's a more direct connection."

"More? What else?"

"He left a riddle. A fairy-tale-like riddle."

McPherson rooted through the box. He didn't have to dig far until he came across the poem. Expensive card stock. Pristine penmanship. After a quick perusal, he looked up at her. "You're right. Mirror, mirror. Obviously Snow White this time."

She nodded again.

"Any idea what it means? Why you?"

Sullivan shook her head. "No clue. I'll think about it. Right now, though, I can't really think straight about anything."

"I'm not surprised." He took his phone from his pocket to take pictures of everything. "Receiving this has to have been traumatic. And that's on top of not being able to sleep lately."

She scoffed. "I sure won't be sleeping now. I have a feeling there's a clock on this. We need to figure it out sooner rather than later, or someone else is going to die."

He heard her unspoken words — before *she* was next to die.

Thank God she didn't give voice to that fear.

"It's going to have to wait until morning, Sullivan. You need to get a good night's sleep. It's not up for debate."

"You must be joking."

"Not even a little. You needed rest before this, and now you've received a pretty big shock. You're liable to fall flat on your face tomorrow if you don't get some sleep tonight. That will make you a danger to yourself, those of us who work with you, and the public we serve."

She looked up at him. "If you're seriously trying to tell me you'd be able to sleep in your apartment after receiving a package like this at your door, then you're lying to me or to yourself. No one in my shoes would want to go home."

"I agree. And I'm not suggesting you do. Far from it. That's the last place you need to be and the last place I feel safe sending you. Stay with me." The suggestion popped out before he even considered how it would sound. He'd have made the offer to any partner. To any coworker. And no one in her position would take it out of context.

No one but Chelsea Sullivan, of course.

"Oh? Are you expecting a three-way with me and your latest chippy? Maybe one of us can make you breakfast while the other shines your shoes before work."

He bit back a sigh. "I don't date 'chippies.' And nobody's waiting at my apartment for me. Even if someone was, this is more important. I would send her home so you could feel comfortable."

"How gallant of you, letting someone keep my side of the bed warm."

Jim crossed his arms and stared at her. "That isn't what I meant. And despite what you might think, I care about your well-being. Which is why you're not going back to your apartment. Not tonight, not ever. I mean, not until we catch this psycho bastard."

"I have no intention of going home tonight."

"At least we can agree on that."

"But I'm going tomorrow. I have things I need to get there."

"We can send someone for them."

"That won't be necessary."

"Then I'm coming with you."

"That won't be necessary, either. I'll be fine once the sun's up."

"Daylight doesn't equal safety, Sullivan. And if you asked Davenport or your dad, they'd agree with me. You shouldn't go back there at all, but if you insist on going, the time of day doesn't matter. But who goes with you does. You aren't going alone. I won't let you."

"You won't *let* me?"

"I'll pull rank if I have to."

"We're both detectives."

"But I have more experience."

"You have more gall."

A headache was brewing behind his eyes. And she was undoubtedly the cause. "I'm your partner, Sullivan, and I've got your back. If you must go, I'm going with you."

Forensics showed up before she could argue further. They took pictures of everything, then they left, taking the box and its contents with them. Before departing, one of the techs promised to send them copies of the photos — though Jim had already taken his own and he'd bet his paycheck Chelsea had done the same — and said he'd put a rush on the tests.

"That's enough for one night," Jim said. "Let's get out of here. Do you want to ride with me, or do you want to follow me to my place?"

"I told you, I'm not staying with you. It would be too weird."

"Well, you're not going to your apartment. And I doubt you have the money to check into the Halcyon."

"There are more affordable hotels."

"If you aren't coming with me, what are your plans?"

"I'll stay with my dad."

He cocked an eyebrow.

"It's the perfect solution. We don't live near each other, so it's unlikely the killer has seen me there. Being a cop is hard-coded in Dad's DNA, so he'll know how to protect me. Even if he didn't, his paternal instinct would kick in, and he'd do anything in his power to keep me safe."

Jim didn't know enough about Sully to know if he was up to the task of protecting anyone, but she hadn't left him with an excuse to veto her plan. And it beat her being alone. "Fine. But I'm following you there. And I'm walking you to the door."

"If you insist on following me, so be it. But you're not seeing me inside."

He merely gestured toward the exit. She might have the final say — for now — on where she stayed, but he'd be damned if he let her keep him from protecting her. And that meant escorting her into her father's apartment and assessing whether the man was up to the task of keeping his daughter safe.

Chapter Twenty-Six

Chelsea didn't talk on the way to her dad's. Neither did McPherson, thank God. The silence during the drive was miserable, yet the trip still ended too fast for her liking.

After he parked, she turned to him. "Thanks for driving me, although I'm not sure how I'm getting to work tomorrow without a car."

"Can your dad take you in?"

"No. He doesn't drive often anymore. And if the roads are bad, I wouldn't want him out on them."

"Not a problem, then. I'll pick you up."

That was the last thing she needed — him showing up at Dad's in the daylight, when the filth would be more noticeable. "I'll text you in the morning. If it's a nice day, I may just walk."

"The station is miles away, Chelsea. I'll pick you up."

She shrugged. "If you insist. Thanks."

"Sure. Whatever you need."

She reached for the door handle.

McPherson turned off the engine and opened his door. "What are you doing?"

"I'm walking you up."

"You don't have to do that."

"Yeah, I do."

"You said you'd give me whatever I needed. Well, I need to do this alone."

"Maybe I should've said, whatever you need within reason. An escort is non-negotiable." He closed his door.

She slammed hers shut. Circled the bumper. Glared at him.

He merely offered his elbow to her.

Chelsea ignored it and strode to the entrance of her dad's apartment building. McPherson followed her through the lobby, up the stairs, then down the hall. She turned around. "There. You walked me to the door. Now you can go."

"My mother raised me to be a gentleman. I'm not leaving until I see you safely inside."

She stomped her foot and blinked back tears. There was nothing she could say to make him leave. All she could do was pray her father wasn't too embarrassed to have a stranger — a *cop* — see his living conditions. He'd lost his house and his wife. Tarnished his reputation, was forced out of his job. All he had left was his legend — and being seen as a withered old man living in squalor would rob him of the little dignity he had left.

"Well? Are you going in or coming to my place?"

She sighed, then stormed inside. He followed her all the way up to her father's apartment. "You can go now."

"Only once I know you're safely inside."

Chelsea glowered at him and knocked on the door.

No answer.

"Isn't it kind of late for your dad to be out? Especially when he doesn't drive?"

"It's not that he doesn't *ever* drive. He just doesn't drive often." Why hadn't she checked to see if Dad's car was in the lot? "Maybe he ran to the store."

McPherson frowned. "Still seems unusual that he's not home when it's so late."

"Dad's an adult. He doesn't have a curfew."

He frowned and knocked, louder and longer than she had.

"He might be asleep."

McPherson pressed his ear to the door. "TV's on."

"He falls asleep in front of the television a lot."

"Do you have a key?"

"Of course. It's in my purse."

He stared at her and blinked.

She rolled her eyes. Of course. Her purse was at home. Right where she dropped it.

McPherson looked down at the frayed welcome mat. "I don't suppose a former cop would keep a key under there."

He wasn't wrong. No current or former cop would keep a house key under a mat. Most civilians wouldn't. But Dad had been careless lately. It wouldn't surprise her if he did have a key under the mat or on top of the doorframe. It also wouldn't surprise her if the door was unlocked.

She tried the knob, which turned without protest, so she pushed open the door about an inch. "Lucky me. Seems he forgot to lock it. Now you've seen me here safely. You can go."

"I saw you to the door, but I don't know about safely. Let's go check and see what's going on with your dad." Jim shoved past her, swinging the door open wide and revealing the shabby room strewn with clutter and trash. He pulled his gun from his holster as he stepped farther into the room.

Chelsea followed close at his heels, praying for a way to explain. To a cop, the place probably looked like it had been ransacked. But she knew her father's penchant for hoarding and avoidance of housework. This wasn't a break-in. It was the norm. She was so steeped in her thoughts that she ran into the back of McPherson, who'd reached the sofa and stopped short.

"Sullivan, call 911."

"That's not necessary. Dad's just—"

"Better yet, call Dispatch. Get a bus here, ASAP." He rounded the couch then dropped to his knees.

She followed, her excuses for her father's living conditions fading as she noted Jim's demeanor.

Then she saw her father and stifled a scream. He was lying on the floor amid a dozen empty beer bottles and a large splatter of vomit. Thank God he was on his side, or he would've choked to death.

McPherson was already checking for a pulse. "Damn it, Sullivan, make the call!"

Chelsea fumbled her phone then called Dispatch. With a trembling voice, she reported their location and the situation, then requested an ambulance. All the while, she couldn't tear her gaze away from her father's unresponsive form. She ended the call as the dispatcher was still speaking and stood behind McPherson, who had begun chest compressions. Tears streamed down her face, splashed on his hands.

He didn't break tempo, didn't look up at her. "Chelsea, go wait by the door. You don't need to see this."

But she couldn't stop watching. Couldn't answer. Couldn't move.

"Sullivan!" He was short of breath, but his voice was sharp. "Step away."

But she couldn't. She had to be with her father, had to see what happened.

And McPherson didn't tell her again. She didn't know

if he knew she wouldn't listen or if he was just exerting himself too much to keep barking orders at her. Nor did she care. She'd grown roots, and he was focused on saving her father.

He stopped chest compressions about five minutes later. "Got a pulse." He sat back on his heels, wiped his brow, and sighed.

Chelsea cried too hard to speak her gratitude.

The EMTs bustled in thirty seconds later and wasted no time putting her father on a gurney.

McPherson glanced at his watch, then reported what he knew. "Found him about seven minutes ago. He'd already vomited. Breathing was shallow. His heart stopped shortly after I checked his pulse. I began chest compressions. Got a rhythm about a minute ago."

"How old is he?" They were already wheeling him down the hall, McPherson jogging after them.

Chelsea brought up the rear, though her feet felt like lead.

"Sullivan!" McPherson jogged back, grabbed her hand, then tugged her down the corridor. "Answer their questions."

She proceeded to recite her father's age and weight and medication protocol.

"He shouldn't be drinking while he's on those meds." The EMT shot her a dirty look.

"I know. He knows. I don't know why he did that. Half the time, he doesn't even take the meds, so I'm sure he wasn't thinking there would be a problem." She was sure he hadn't been thinking at all.

Or had he?

They reached the parking lot. Her father was in the ambulance in about three seconds flat.

Chelsea stood there. Cold, silent. Useless.

Terrified.

"We'll follow you," McPherson said.

One of the EMTs climbed into the back with her dad, and the other ran around to the driver's side. Soon the lights were flashing, and the siren was wailing as the bus pulled away.

McPherson tugged her toward his SUV.

She looked down at their hands, surprised they were still joined.

He helped her into the passenger seat, then ran around the bumper. It didn't take him long to catch up to the ambulance, and soon after that, they'd reached the hospital. McPherson dropped her off at the emergency entrance, promising to park quickly then join her inside.

Chelsea stood helplessly in the lobby, fear churning her stomach and icing her blood as she stared at the gurney speeding down the hallway. After it disappeared behind double doors, she stumbled to the waiting room. Exhaustion caught up to her, and she collapsed into a chair.

Had this been an accidental overdose? Or was this Dad's way out, the last act of a guilty man?

Chapter Twenty-Seven

Chelsea rubbed her chilled hands together and stared at the double doors where her father had disappeared. No matter how hard she willed it, no one came out with a status update.

McPherson strode through the entrance, then hurried to her.

She breathed a small sigh of relief. At least he could keep her company until she heard from the doctors.

He took her hand and squeezed it. "My God. You're freezing. And you're trembling."

Chelsea shrugged.

"Oh, right. You have a thing with hospitals."

She couldn't even muster a denial — especially as it would be a lie. Images long-buried came to the surface. Memories of another night, another fright, just like this one. Same uncomfortable chairs, same muted gray walls. Same smell of antiseptic, air freshener, and death lingering in the air.

Same interminable wait.

The ER doors swung open to let a doctor step through. He approached the waiting area. "Chelsea Sullivan?"

She popped to her feet. "That's me."

"Your father's asking for you. I can take you back to see him."

"Thank you."

The doctor pressed a button on the wall, then the doors opened. When he passed through, Chelsea dashed after him. She followed him down the hall, her rubber-soled boots squeaking on the polished linoleum until they reached a treatment bay surrounded by a curtain. "He's in there. You can go in now."

"Thank you." She slid the curtain back then stepped inside. "Dad? Are you all right?"

His eyes fluttered open. "Hey, Chels."

Tears streamed down her face. She perched on the side of his bed and grasped his hand. "What were you think-ing? You could have died."

Dad shook his head. "I'm fine. Don't even know why you're here. Was surprised when the nurses told me you were out front. I only asked the doctor to call you back because I knew you'd be worried. Needlessly."

"Needlessly worried? You're kidding, right? We found you on the floor in a pile of vomit. You could've choked to death. Your heart stopped! And don't even get me started on mixing your medication with liquor."

"You sound like your—" He clamped his mouth shut. His jaw ticked a staccato beat, and his heart rate monitor matched it.

"Mom? You think I sound like Mom? Given the situa-tion, can you blame me?"

"I'm not discussing this. Not discussing her."

"Nice, Dad. Just ignore everything you don't want to

discuss like it'll go away if you don't address it. Well, guess what. It doesn't."

"That's funny, considering I apparently ignored your mother, then she went away."

Chelsea closed her eyes and sighed. "I thought we weren't talking about Mom."

"We're not."

She swallowed past the ever-growing lump in her throat. "You had me scared."

"Toughen up, kiddo. I'm fine. It'll take more than a couple of drinks to put me down."

Despite her efforts, a soft sob escaped her.

He sighed. "Why don't you tell me why you dropped by the apartment to begin with?"

"You're lucky I was there."

"Duly noted. Now stop changing the subject."

She was changing the subject? Pot, meet kettle.

"Chelsea, why were you there?"

Her pulse pounded behind her eyes. She closed them, rubbed them. Didn't alleviate the pain in the slightest.

He tapped her hand. "What aren't you telling me?"

"We're making progress on the case. But I hit a … wrinkle."

"Go on."

Chelsea mostly stuck to the truth, though her motivation changed from seeking protection from him to seeking answers. She had to know how involved he was. "I received a package from the killer. He left a riddle I can't solve. I thought maybe you could help me."

"What do you mean, you received a package?"

The concern in his voice and on his face instantly exonerated him. She cleared her throat. "That's kind of the other reason I stopped by to see you. I was hoping I could stay with you for a few days."

He pushed himself up in the bed. "Are you telling me that sick son of a bitch has your home address?"

"Apparently." She looked down at her hands, clenched tightly in her lap. Her knuckles turned white.

"Does your partner know? Davenport? They need to get a protective detail on you. Plain-clothed cops, unmarked cars. Twenty-four hours, round-the-clock."

"Yes, Dad. My partner knows. I haven't had a chance to tell the captain yet, but I will."

"Give me my damn phone. I'll call him myself."

"No. I'll take care of it. For all I know, McPherson's on the phone with him now. Or already called."

"How do you not know whether your partner called the captain yet?"

"He's been with me since I turned in the evidence. We planned on calling the captain after I got settled at your place. He's out in the waiting room. Since he has nothing to do but sit there, he's probably already called Davenport."

"He's been— Was he at my place with you?"

"Yeah." She grabbed his hand and squeezed it. "He's the one who found you."

Dad's face turned red, and he started muttering under his breath.

"Don't be that way, Dad. He saved your life."

"What?" The red in his face drained away, leaving his skin a ghastly white.

"McPherson was there to take care of me, but he ended up saving you. Don't you get it? Your heart stopped, remember? If it wasn't for him, I would've lost you."

"If you had been alone, you would've saved me."

She shook her head. "I-I froze. I'm sorry, Dad. But seeing you that way … I couldn't handle it."

"Dammit, Chelsea. If you can't keep your head about

you in an emergency situation, you have no right being a cop."

She jumped off his bed. "And you have no right lecturing me. If it wasn't for you, I wouldn't have issues like this."

"Me? What'd I do?"

"You almost died. Twice now. I can't keep coming to the hospital for you, watching you lie in a bed like this."

"Keep coming? You act like I make a habit of this."

"Once was more than enough. Twice is all I can take. You can't do this to me again."

He closed his eyes and leaned back against his pillow. "I don't want people in my house. Especially cops."

"If you kept the place clean, it wouldn't be an issue."

"Don't tell me how to live in my own home, young lady."

"Given I'm the only one who cleans your apartment, I think I have the right."

His nostrils flared, and the heart monitor speeded up again. But when he spoke, his voice was low. Menacing. "Chelsea Bridget Sullivan, you watch your tone with me."

She rolled her eyes, took a deep breath. Talking back had never been tolerated. Heck, she'd only tried it once when she was young and had learned pretty quick not to do it again. But someone needed to set him straight on a few things. And she was the only one in a position to do so.

But seeing him lying there attached to a monitor by various tubes and wires, pale and weak despite his ire, she didn't have it in her to argue further. So, she said nothing.

"Tell me about the riddle."

Chelsea hated how he changed the subject when he didn't like what was said. Also hated how she allowed him to do it. If he wasn't in the hospital, if he didn't look so frail and breakable, she wouldn't allow it. Not this time.

But he was, and he did, and she would. That was their dynamic — he was the demanding father, and she was the dutiful daughter. Besides, with respect to the case, he might be of help to her. "He sent me a note, a broken hand mirror, and … "

"And, what?"

"And a wolf's head."

"Another mask? Like at the last crime scene?"

She shook her head. Had to force the words out. "No. An actual head." Her voice was barely above a whisper, and it gave out at the end.

He let out a stream of curses that would make a sailor blush.

"How about you take a crack at the riddle?" She recited it to him.

His fingers drummed on the side rail of his bed while he thought. Then he looked at her. "The mirror and the opening of the riddle. That's from Snow White."

"Yeah. I recognized it. But what's the rest mean?"

"Fortress walls? Hallowed halls? I'm not sure. Yet. But I'll get it."

"Okay. Well, maybe, for tonight, you should just rest." She leaned over and tried to fluff his pillow.

"I'm not an invalid."

"I know. But you've been through a lot in the last few hours."

"And yet I'm strong as ever. You're the one who fell apart, not me."

Her pulse thudded in her ears. Her vision tinged red. "How could you fall apart, Dad? You'd already fallen to the ground and passed out cold. And that was before your heart stopped."

This time his face didn't turn red. It was more of a violent shade of purple. "The doc wants to keep me overnight for observation. You have a key to my place. Use it. And lock the damn door behind you. Good night, Chelsea."

"Dad?"

But he rolled over, effectively dismissing her.

She blew him a kiss he couldn't see and probably wouldn't want, then she walked back to the waiting room.

McPherson stood when he saw her then rushed to her side. "How's he doing?"

"He'll live. If I don't kill him, that is."

"That good, huh?"

Chelsea shrugged. "He's ornery, which is one of his two typical emotional states. So I guess he's feeling okay."

"And I guess that means you're not."

"He's just so darn frustrating. Pretty much like all the men in my life. You'd think I'd be used to it."

McPherson squared his shoulders. "I'll let that comment slide since you've been under so much stress tonight."

"You're right. I'm sorry." She sighed. "I'm tired, and my nerves are shot. That's why I have no filter."

"The fact that you find it necessary to want a filter when you talk to me is a problem. We're partners, remember? No secrets."

"I can't do this right now. Will you take me to my dad's? I want to clean his place before he's discharged tomorrow."

"Let's go."

He drove back to her dad's apartment, parked, then exited the car.

She scrambled out after him. "Where are you going?"

"Upstairs. I don't remember either of us locking his door, so you have no idea what you're walking into.

Besides, the whole reason I took you here in the first place was because you shouldn't be alone."

"It's late. I'm tired. I still have a bunch of vomit to scrub out of his carpet. I don't have the energy to argue with you about this."

"Good. Don't. You wouldn't win, anyway."

Resigned, she sighed and entered the apartment building. McPherson followed her up to her dad's unit. He was right — neither of them had thought to turn the lock on the knob. Which actually was a good thing, as she didn't have his key with her.

"Wait here while I clear the place." He pulled out his gun as he crossed the threshold.

But she followed him in.

He whispered over his shoulder, "I told you to wait in the hall."

"And I clearly didn't listen." She didn't bother whispering. Or drawing her weapon. No one would be crazy enough to hide in Dad's apartment. It was filthy and currently reeked of vomit. "You don't need to check all the rooms."

"I'm going to, anyway."

"Of course you are," she muttered. "Do what you have to. I'm going to get started."

McPherson conducted a quick sweep of all the rooms while she got a bucket and rags. At this late hour, she didn't even bother worrying about him seeing the condition of the apartment.

And points in his favor, he didn't comment on it.

More points, he joined her in front of her dad's recliner and helped clean up the mess.

When they were finished, she put everything away then looked around the kitchen. Maybe it was time to consider a Visiting Angels kind of program for her father. Or maybe she could get a two-bedroom apartment and make him stay with her. At least then she could keep a closer watch on him and make sure his messes were cleaned daily.

McPherson leaned in the doorway, thumbs tucked into his front pockets. "I really don't think it's safe for you to stay here alone. We have no idea if the killer knows where your father lives. And without him here, you have no backup."

"I'm too worked up to sleep, anyway. Just take me back to the station."

"Talk about a one-eighty. Half an hour ago, you were exhausted."

In all honesty, she still was. She was tired of dealing with all of her dad's issues, tired of walking on eggshells around her partner, and tired of everything about their case. But those were also the exact things flying through her mind at light speed, keeping her awake.

He tipped his head toward the door. "Why don't you come back to my place?"

"Dawn's only a couple hours away, and I won't be able to sleep. Just take me to work."

"Are you sure?"

She nodded.

"Let's lock up, then."

He followed her into the hall.

Chelsea made sure to turn the lock before pulling the door closed behind her.

McPherson tested the knob, and after confirming the apartment was secure, gestured for her to walk down the hallway. "Your chariot awaits, milady."

As she was at a loss for words, she just headed toward the car.

Chapter Twenty-Eight

AT THE STATION, Jim suggested Sullivan lie down on the sofa in Davenport's office, and to his surprise, she agreed. It might have been presumptuous of him, but she needed to rest, and that was the only couch he knew of in the building. The only other option he could think of was a locker room bench, and that was hardly a comfortable alternative.

He'd texted the captain when Sullivan was with her father at the ER. Maybe — probably — he should have called, but there was nothing Davenport could have done in the middle of the night, so Jim figured a text would suffice. If he answered, it meant he was probably already awake. And if he didn't, there was no reason to disturb his sleep.

Davenport hadn't answered. Now two hours closer to the start of the morning shift, rather than risk a second text waking the captain, Jim chose the better-to-ask-forgiveness-than-permission approach and made the executive decision to settle Chelsea on the worn but welcoming sofa in the boss's office.

Jim closed the door with a soft snick, then he turned to head back to his desk. Blocking his way were the jackasses he'd had the misfortune of meeting in the locker room on his first day. "Moe. Larry. Curly. Or was it Shemp?"

He actually knew their names. Made a point to learn them after their last encounter. The one on his left was Jeremy Berger, a local high school football hero who couldn't cut it in college. The one on the right was Ethan Miller. Jim had worked with his sister Frannie in Zone Two. They came from a family of cops, but rumor suggested Ethan was forced to follow in his father's footsteps and had no love for the job. But it was the one in the middle who was the big problem — Oliver Thompson, the trio's spokesperson. His family knew the mayor somehow, so the kid was practically Teflon. Plus, the little bastard sailed through the academy. Was good enough at his job but managed to piss people off everywhere he went. Thought good grades and good looks entitled him to skip a few rungs on the ladder and didn't like it when he was forced to pay his dues.

Right now, he was pissing Jim off in a big way.

Thompson jabbed him in the chest with his finger. "Too early for the captain to be in. What were you doing in there?"

"Last I checked, detectives don't answer to uniforms." He knocked the guy's hand away. "And even if we did, I sure as hell wouldn't answer to you."

The two silent stooges grabbed Jim's arms then dragged him toward the locker rooms, following their fearless ringleader. The station was practically dead at that hour. His only backup was falling asleep in Davenport's office, and he'd take a beating before bothering her.

Not that he'd need backup.

Given the three morons he was dealing with, a beating

wasn't likely. Miller and Berger were the type who thought there was safety in numbers, who had fun intimidating others but seldom followed through. Only if Thompson egged them on would they act. And maybe not even then.

It came down to Thompson and whether he was willing to get his hands dirty. Odds were, he was all bluster and no bite.

Jim, on the other hand, never minded getting his hands dirty, and he had the reputation to back it up. It meant he rarely had to throw down anymore. Everyone knew if provoked, he handled business.

And these three idiots had provoked him.

Maybe his reputation didn't extend past the boundaries of Zone Two. Then again, the rumors had, so why shouldn't the rest of it?

That told him one important thing — these three were morons. And he couldn't discount anything when it came to morons.

He didn't fight — much — as they pulled him through the corridor, knowing there were cameras in the bullpen and hallways but not in the locker rooms. That's where he'd make his move.

"We told you we didn't want your kind here," Thompson said.

"Yeah," Berger agreed.

Apparently, that was the best he could muster. Miller didn't even say that much. He might have squeezed Jim's arm a little harder for a second, but it happened so fast, it was hard to know for sure.

"I mean, maybe the two of you are ideal partners." Thompson pushed open the door leading to the stairwell. "You being a dirty cop and her daddy being one. Her apple probably doesn't fall far from the family tree."

That comment took Jim from annoyed to angry. "You

can think whatever you want about me. Spread the rumor far and wide. But leave Sullivan out of it."

"Aw, what's the matter?" Thompson sneered at him as he opened the door to the locker room. "You two partners in more than one sense of the word? Partners in crime? Partners in the sack?"

The second the door closed behind them, Jim lunged. He broke free of Berger and Miller, lowered his shoulder, then plowed into Thompson. Took the little prick to the ground. Landed two solid strikes to the little bastard's face before his pals pulled him off. This time, their grips on his arms were a lot tighter.

It would take a hot minute to break free of their grasp. And their buddy could get a few licks in while he struggled.

Only made him thrash harder.

Thompson scrambled to his feet, blood dripping from his nose. He pulled his service weapon from its holster.

"Hey, wait now." Miller's fingers relaxed.

Before Jim could pull free, Berger yanked both his arms behind his back. "Not such hot shit now, are you, McPherson?"

His breath was hot on Jim's neck, but the gun in his face had his blood running cold.

"You never said anything about *shooting* him," Miller whispered as he backed away.

"I asked you a question, dumbass," Thompson said, ignoring Miller and advancing on Jim. "Where's all your bluster and bravado now?"

It wasn't the first time he had a gun trained on him. It wasn't even the first time it was a cop holding the weapon. But it was the first time his hands were restrained when it happened. That changed things. He bucked, trying to break free.

Berger countered by tightening his grip and stepping even closer.

Leaning back, Jim lifted his feet. While Berger staggered under the strain of bearing his weight, Thompson advanced on him.

Miller, eyes wide, held out his hands but did little else to stop the attack.

Jim thrust his feet forward. His right foot planted on Thompson's chest, but his left hit his hand. As he kicked, the gun went off, the report of the shot echoing off the cement walls and metal lockers.

Berger released him.

Jim wheeled around, making sure no one was hit.

Berger's eyes were wide, but he was unscathed.

Thompson, face pale, dropped his weapon and shook his head. His mouth moved, but either no sound came out, or Jim's ears were ringing too much to hear.

Other than possibly being in shock, Thompson was fine. So, Jim turned toward Miller. An angry red line marred his cheek, and he wobbled on his feet. His hand trembled as he touched his face. Blood stained his fingers when he lowered his arm.

The door burst open, banged off the wall. Norm and Charlie surged through the door, guns at the ready.

Thompson and Berger raised their hands and backed away. Miller stood where he was, staring at the red smear on his hand.

Only Jim didn't react.

The two veteran detectives quickly took in the scene, then holstered their weapons.

Charlie ran his hand through thinning hair.

Norm shook his head and glared at Jim. "Tell me that piece isn't yours, McPherson."

"I have more sense than to pull my weapon on a fellow officer."

Charlie's eyebrows arched.

"Inside the fucking precinct."

Norm scowled. "It's no secret you had an altercation with these three on your first day. In this very room."

"And now one of them looks like you used him as a punching bag. And the other is shot."

"Grazed," Jim corrected.

"That makes it better?" Charlie asked.

"Well, he's not dead, so yeah."

"Of all days to come in early," Norm muttered.

"If we didn't, this could have been a lot worse," his partner countered. Then he looked at Jim. "We have enough to do without all the paperwork this is going to require. Not to mention the IA investigation."

"Well, before you get more pissed off at me, you might want to put your considerable years of experience to good use. Only one of us has an empty holster here." He turned so they could see he still had possession of his gun.

Their heads turned in sync toward Thompson.

"Fuck," Norm muttered. "What the hell were you thinking, rookie?"

"Hey," Thompson said, "there's only one person here who's shot his partner, and it's not me."

"It hadn't been you," Charlie said. "Can't say that now."

"When the mayor hears you're trying to railroad me—"

"Yeah, we know. You're gonna pull some strings; make this go away. Meanwhile, we're the ones who're gonna have to explain this shit to Davenport."

"Davenport." Jim slapped his forehead. "He in yet?"

"No," Norm said. "Why?"

"I have Sullivan sleeping in his office." He headed toward the door. "I wanted to catch him when he comes in, give him a head's up."

Charlie flung his hands up. "I'm never coming in early again."

"Why would you do that?" Norm asked.

"The case we caught?"

"The Grimm Reaper?" Charlie nodded. "What about it?"

"He's targeting her. She's received mail from him both at the station and at home. The last bit was a wolf's head. Not a mask, the actual fucking head hacked off a wolf. I took her to her father's to spend the night, but we ended up taking him to the hospital." They didn't need those details, so he skipped them. "She's exhausted. And a bit of a mess. Understandably."

"Sully's in the hospital?" Charlie asked.

"And Chelsea's a target?" Norm added.

"Yeah. Anyway, Davenport's office is the only place I know of with a couch here. She needed sleep, so I made her lie down in there. If that's crossing a line, it's my fault. But I want to tell him to his face before he walks in on her."

"Sure, of course." Norm gestured to the door. "Go wait for him. We'll deal with this … nonsense for you."

"If you need something, let us know," Charlie said. "Chelsea's family. We told Sully we'd keep an eye on her."

Jim shook his head. "She wouldn't like that."

"And we would never tell her," Norm said. "You better not, either."

"Mum's the word." He gave Miller one last appraisal — the kid would be fine — sneered at Thompson and Berger, then pushed past the veterans on his way out.

Norm grabbed his arm before he made it through the door. "Press is calling the Grimm Reaper a serial killer."

"I know."

"Timeline's pretty fast for that. There's almost no cooling off period between kills."

"I know. It's bugging me, too."

"Did you consider he had earlier victims? Maybe ones no one found yet?"

Jim thought back to the dinner he had with his mother. "I have been kicking that around a bit, but nothing's popped yet."

"Or maybe he's refined his method," Charlie said, "and the earlier vics don't exactly match his current MO?"

"Feels like I've been playing defense since this started. Never gave that a thought. Thanks."

"You need us, you let us know." Norm stepped out of his way.

Charlie nodded. "Anything, anytime."

"Will do." Jim exited the room then started down the stairs. Before the door closed, he heard Thompson begging the detectives not to tell Davenport or IA. It was the first laugh he'd had in a long time.

Chapter Twenty-Nine

Chelsea felt too weird in Davenport's office, so she went back to her desk. McPherson couldn't have left her alone for more than a minute before she decided she couldn't stay there, but the bullpen was empty when she walked to her desk. Fifteen minutes later, she was still the only one in the room.

Maybe he'd gone home for some shuteye, even though he said he wouldn't leave her.

Typical. Couldn't count on anyone.

Her situation was untenable. Without sleep, she'd be a liability, not an asset. But she couldn't sleep here. Hopefully, they could have an easy, in-office day, and she'd get to catch up on pillow time later.

Might as well get a start on things now. She gathered everything she had on the case, got a cup of coffee, then got to work.

McPherson joined her a few minutes later, still in the same clothes. So, he hadn't gone home. Props for him. He'd bought a can of soda from the vending machine, and her stomach lurched. It was way too early for that. But he didn't open it. Instead, he laid it on top of his hand.

Either he was really weird, or she was really tired. Or both.

Probably both.

But she didn't question him about it. She just went back to work.

Chelsea had no idea how long she'd sat at her desk, poring through files, forensic reports, and witness accounts, but her eyelids were beginning to droop. All the statements contradicted her theories, and all the photos blended with her nightmares.

"I need good coffee, not station sludge," McPherson said. "Want to come with me?"

"No. I feel like I'm missing a crucial detail. Just going to keep looking over all this stuff."

"I can bring you something."

She shrugged. Caffeine was the only way she would get through the rest of the day, but it might also keep her up tonight. Before she made a decision, she yawned.

"I'll surprise you. Do not leave the precinct while I'm gone." When she didn't answer, he said, "You hear me?"

"Yeah. Sure. I'll be here."

He stared at her for a while as he slipped on his jacket, then he pulled his phone from his pocket. As he left, his thumbs tapped furiously on the screen.

She didn't really want coffee. What she really wanted was to sleep. Fat chance of that happening, though. Davenport's office just felt wrong, and besides, he was there now. Dad's apartment was empty, so that would bug her more than soothe her. And no way was she closing her eyes at home. Maybe she could curl up on a bench in the locker room and catch a nap for a couple of hours. She didn't promise McPherson she'd stay at her desk. Just the building.

She headed for the locker room. Before she got there, she realized she wasn't alone in the hallway. Chelsea took a deep breath before turning around. "Why are you following me?"

Norm, one of the veteran detectives she'd originally hoped to be paired with, stood behind her. "I'm not following you. I just happened to be heading this way."

"Toward the women's locker room?"

He chuckled. "All right. You got me."

"So?"

"We're not supposed to let you out of our sight."

"By whose orders?"

"It was more like popular consent."

She crossed her arms over her chest and scowled at him. Popular consent. That meant McPherson rallied the troops. "My partner text you before he left?"

He offered a small smile. "You might not go to Happy Hour with us, but you're still one of us. Hell, most of us would watch out for you just because of your dad. He used to bring you to the station when you were little, and we were still uniforms. Do you remember?"

Chelsea nodded, and her expression softened. Fond memories, but they brought her little comfort now. She didn't need to be watched over. She needed to be one of the boys — something she doubted she'd ever be.

"We're not going to let anything happen to you."

"I'm in police headquarters. What could possibly happen?"

He shrugged.

Chelsea flung her hands in the air and returned to her desk, Norm in tow.

McPherson had returned. He grinned at her when she

took her seat. "Brought you a latte. Decaf. I've seen you on hi-test. It's not pretty."

She glared at him. But she took a sip. And tried not to let her pleasure show on her face. Even without caffeine, it was so much better than precinct coffee.

Captain Davenport opened his door. "Jim? A moment?"

McPherson jumped up then strode across the room.

She rose, too, but Norm blocked her way. By accident or by bad luck, she wasn't sure, but by the time she got past him and reached the captain's office, he knew the whole story.

Wouldn't surprise her if McPherson had called him when he was on the coffee run.

"I want you off this case, Chelsea. We'll put you in a safe house until it's over."

"No. Absolutely not."

"This isn't up for debate."

She put her hands on her hips and stomped her foot. "You wouldn't pull McPherson off. Or Norm or Charlie. Or any of the other men in the department. I'm no different."

"It is different."

"Because I'm a woman? Because I'm Sully's daughter?"

"No." Not that he sounded remotely believable. "Because this is your first case. You don't have the experience to deal with this kind of … psychological torture."

"And I'll never get the experience if you pull me off."

"I'm watching out for her, Captain."

Chelsea gaped at McPherson. So did Davenport.

"I've got her back. She's right. This is her job. We'll give you hourly updates if you want, but let her see this through."

His loyalty surprised her. It also pleased her.

Not that she'd tell him that.

Of course, now that she realized the whole department was babysitting her, she felt a little less gratified.

Davenport stared at McPherson for a long moment. Something unspoken passed between them. Then he turned toward her. "Fine. But no going off on your own. I want regular updates. And feel free to loop in some of the other guys if you need them."

Chelsea could barely suppress her smile.

"We will," McPherson said.

The urge to grin evaporated as they returned to their desks. Why did her partner think he was in charge of her? And why did Davenport let him call the shots? The whole stupid department had more influence than she did. She'd always be the odd man out. Or woman.

"Looks like someone brought donuts," McPherson said. "Want one?"

She shook her head, too frustrated to speak.

While her anger at her colleagues grew, her anger at her father dissipated, replaced by a terrible nagging feeling. She tried to suppress her thoughts, but the unease plagued her.

This was the one instance where the evidence and her theories weren't miles apart.

Dad was a fairy-tale expert, a Brothers Grimm connoisseur. He was angry at the world — at the police department, at Mom, sometimes even at her. Certainly had been at the hospital.

The queasy churning in her stomach intensified. Could it be? Would he —

No. She couldn't even consider it. No way would he do something so heinous.

Except, maybe he would. Ever since he took early

retirement at the insistence of the department, he'd been bitter. Ever since his divorce, he'd been prone to fits of rage. Bouts of depression, too. That's why he was on the SSRIs.

And ever since she'd caught this case, she'd thought it. Didn't want to give voice to it, but it was in the back of her brain — a niggling itch that too many details fit.

Did she even know him? Not the hard-nosed cop or the strict-but-caring father, but the man he'd become? Now, with the drinking and the pills? She had no guarantee he was thinking straight. And if he was emotionally compromised and not in his right mind? Who knew what he'd be capable of?

Dad always told her his childhood was difficult, his parents distant and cold. Even cruel sometimes. Particularly his mother. Had those emotional scars finally split open? Had the problems with his marriage and career pushed him over the edge?

Cormac Sullivan was obsessed with fairy tales. He knew how cops work and how to foil their efforts. He had mental and emotional problems.

And he knew where she lived.

Her stomach roiled, and she grabbed her wastepaper basket. She dry heaved over it, cramps forcing her to gag even though she had no food in her belly to purge. After a full minute of retching, she sat up and looked around.

Thank God no one had seen her. Or if they had, they didn't draw attention to the fact.

She put the can back under her desk and stared at her laptop. The words blurred into nonsensical symbols.

McPherson returned and handed her a cup. "I got you a maple glazed. Best in the box."

"I don't like maple."

"Everyone likes maple."

She shrugged.

"Look, it's not the breakfast — or lunch — of champions, but you need to eat something. The sugar will give you a brief surge of energy, and when you start to crash, you'll finally get some much-needed rest. You have enough hours in today. Time to clock out."

She glanced at her watch and was surprised by the time. "We're not off duty for a couple more hours."

"You're forgetting, we came in early. The other guys can cover."

Chelsea stifled a yawn. "Believe me, I didn't forget. But we're not off duty yet. It's not right."

"I already cleared it with Davenport. Besides, you're looking pretty rough."

She glanced down at her wrinkled clothes, ran her fingers through her tangled hair. Didn't even want to think about her makeup — or lack thereof. When she looked up, she saw Scott walking in, smiling at her. Chelsea glared at her partner as she waved at the ME. She steeled herself for the words she was about to force from her mouth, but they were the only ones he was likely to hear. "Fuck off, McPherson."

His eyes widened. "Now I know you're tired."

Scott's smile faltered as he waved back, but he continued to approach.

"How so?"

"You never drop an F-bomb. Hell, you never swear at all. Words like 'heck' and 'darn' are strong for you. It's time you clock out."

In for a penny, in for a pound. "I'll go home when I'm good and damn ready."

"Now you're just forcing it. Don't embarrass yourself."

She stammered, sputtered.

"Most importantly," he continued, "you can't go home."

Scott reached her desk, but his affable expression was gone. His tone was almost hostile. "Thought I'd see if you'd had lunch."

As invitations went, she'd had better. Couldn't think of many worse, actually. What could she possibly have done to anger him in the five seconds between the door and her desk? "I'm actually about to clock out. Had a rough night last night."

"I'm sure."

She cocked an eyebrow. What was that supposed to mean?

"Raincheck, then?" He turned before she could reply.

"What on earth …"

"Personable guy," McPherson said.

She sighed.

"Come on. Time to get you to bed."

Scott glared at her before slamming the door on his way out of the bullpen.

Chelsea stared after him, then she glowered at Jim. "Pardon me?"

"You know what I mean. You're running on fumes."

"So are you."

"You already told Dr. Death you were clocking out. Don't want to be a liar, do you?"

"I hate you." But she didn't. And there was no heat to her words. It was just easier to pick a fight than to give voice to her true concerns.

Now Jim sighed. He bent down so only she could hear him. "Chelsea, I know you're scared. It's not a sign of weakness. A crazy man has his sights set on you. Any of us would be freaked out."

"I never said I was freaked out."

"No, you didn't. I did. You're afraid to admit anything to me. So, I'll make the first move. The situation has *me* wigged out. I can only imagine how you must feel. I know we're not close — yet — and you've made it clear you're not impressed with my social life. But I promise you'll be both safe and respected with me. Let me help you."

"I don't know, McPherson … "

"Well, I do. Get your stuff."

"Why don't we go back to my apartment instead? I'll pack a bag, then check into a hotel."

"A hotel will cost money. What I'm offering is free. And unlike your home, this is a secure building with doormen and security guards. You'll be perfectly safe. And I'll be able to relax knowing it. We both need that peace of mind. And a solid eight hours of sleep. Minimum."

She chewed her lip and looked up at him.

"I'll take your silence as agreement. Now, let's go."

Chelsea sighed. "I can't."

"Why not?"

"Don't you see? Someone's after me. If I go to your place, I put a target on your back."

"I'm your partner. A cop. A target's already on my back."

If she had any other option, she'd take it. But she didn't. And she was tired. Maybe, if she was in a secure building and with someone else — someone armed — she might actually get some sleep. So she slipped on her jacket, wrapped her scarf around her neck, tucked her hands into her pockets, then followed him out to his car.

As soon as she climbed inside, her phone rang. Chelsea glanced at the screen. Dad — the last person she was in the mood to talk to. She didn't want a lecture, and she definitely couldn't keep her suspicion out of her voice.

What if he needed a ride, though? They could be discharging him.

If that was the case, the hospital could call her. Otherwise, she didn't want to deal with him right now. Pocketing the device, she let the call go to voicemail. Whatever he wanted to say, it would have to wait until she was ready to deal with it.

She spent the rest of the ride agonizing over her suspicions and praying she was wrong.

Chapter Thirty

It was weird walking into her apartment. The last time she'd been there, she'd left in a hurry. Her purse was still on the floor where she dropped it. And even though the box was gone, she could picture it — clear as day — on the table. A chill snaked up her spine, and she shuddered.

"Do you need help packing?"

"Like I'd let you root through my drawers."

He chuckled, and his smile lit his eyes.

"Make yourself at home. Help yourself to anything in the kitchen. I shouldn't be too long." She left him to entertain himself and walked into her bedroom. After grabbing a bag from her closet, she filled it with work clothes, pajamas, socks and underwear, and her favorite pillow. Then she went into the bathroom and packed a toiletry kit. How long would she be living at his house?

Nope. Not *living* with. *Staying* with. Big difference. And it better not be for very long.

Chelsea decided to not to take much with her. If necessary, she'd do laundry and buy any hygiene products or cosmetics she needed. Better than showing up looking like she was moving in. She wheeled her bag back to the living room. "I'm ready."

"That's it? One bag? One not-so-large bag?"

"I can't imagine I'd need more than what I have. I don't expect to need a place to stay more than a night or two."

"I hope you're right, and we catch him that fast. But in case we don't, wouldn't you like a few more things than what you have?"

"Catch him or not, this is a short-term arrangement."

"Huh-uh. You're not coming back here until this is over."

"I'm not debating this with you right now. Or ever. If I realize I'm missing something I need, I'll buy a replacement. Or come back for it."

"You're not coming back."

"I'm not going to be your prisoner. When I'm ready to be here alone again, I'm coming back. Case closed."

"You're right. You're not coming back until the case is closed."

"That's not what I meant."

McPherson shrugged. He took the handle of her suitcase from her. "Anything else?"

She snatched it back. "It's my bag. I'll carry it."

"Hey, my mama raised me right. I'll carry your bag." He took the handle from her. "Now, answer my question. Do you need anything else?"

"Oh!" She darted into her room, grabbed her phone charger, then hurried back. She held it up to show him. "Can't forget this." Then she tucked it into her purse.

"Got your laptop?"

"Good idea." She returned to her bedroom, grabbed it, then stuffed it into a briefcase along with a notebook and pen. Back in the living room, she said, "Now, that's everything."

"Are you sure? Do you have any notes from the case or anything that you want to bring with you?"

Maybe she should bring the Brothers Grimm book with her. She went to the bookcase, took it off the bottom shelf, then stuffed it into the briefcase, too. "This time, I'm sure. I'm ready."

"Nothing else?"

She felt like a child as she shook her head.

"Positive? Looks to me like you live off ice cream. Do you want to pack a cooler full before we leave?" He tipped his head toward the kitchen and laughed.

"Ha-ha. Everyone has a vice."

"Most women drink wine. Or shop."

"I don't drink. And I have enough shoes."

"Fair enough. Speaking of shoes, did you pack the ones you want?"

Darn it. She held up a finger, dashed into her room, and selected a few pairs from her closet. After stuffing them into a drawstring gym bag, she returned to the living room. "Okay. This time I'm really, really done."

He chuckled as he took the drawstring bag from her, then wheeled her suitcase out the front door.

She shouldered her purse and briefcase. After following him into the hall, she locked up.

McPherson twisted the handle to double-check the latch, just like she knew he would.

Then they headed for his car.

Chapter Thirty-One

Jim tried to hide his smile at the look of wonder on Sullivan's face. He could see she was impressed with the building. And also a little troubled. But he was only concerned with her safety now, and as promised, security here was much better than at her place. The doorman was gracious, the guards alert yet polite. And anyone who made it past their watchful eyes still had to get through two locked doors and ride a pass-key elevator before they got to his unit, the door to which had three different locks.

After a few quick turns of the key, he welcomed her into the apartment with a dramatic bow and an exaggerated sweep of his hand. "Make yourself at home."

Directly across from the door was a wall of windows boasting a gorgeous view of the rivers and mountains beyond it. The two cars of the incline were passing each other on their ways up and down their respective tracks, the little red trolleys a duo of bright beacons against the snow-covered mountainside.

Chelsea walked through the living room to watch the

show. She stood there, staring out the window, for a full minute.

"They won't disappear if you look away," he said. "They go up and down all day, from five-thirty in the morning till almost one at night."

When she turned to face him, her cheeks were a rosy pink. "I'm sorry. It's just such a pretty view. From my apartment, I pretty much just see more buildings."

"I've been to your apartment. You're selling your view short. Steel City is one of the prettiest urban areas in the country, maybe the world. Hard to find a view to complain about."

"I'll agree with you on that. We do live in a pretty city." The unintentional rhyme made her chuckle.

He headed for the kitchen. "Can I get you a drink?"

"Water, please." She stood with her back to the windows and looked around the open-concept apartment. The living room sprawled in front of her, and the dining and kitchen areas stretched out to her right. Two doors to the left of her would take her to the bedroom and a bathroom.

When her gaze lingered there, he knew what she was thinking. He was about to reassure her of their sleeping arrangement, but she spoke first.

"Your home is lovely."

He crossed the room then handed her a glass. "Thanks. I wish I could take credit, but unfortunately, it's not mine."

Her face paled. "Please tell me you did not take me to one of your girlfriends' apartments."

"Well, at least you've gone from calling them chippies to calling them my girlfriends, not that they're either. And no, none of the women I date casually owns this place. A very special woman does."

"Oh?" Her tone was frostier than the ice water he'd given her.

He fought not to smirk at her expression. "Yeah. Well, her and the love of her life."

"What kind of kinky crap are you into?"

McPherson laughed. "You should see the look on your face. Priceless. I'm talking about my mom and dad. This is their place."

She sighed, and her shoulders sagged. "Your parents? Do you … do you still live with them?"

"I'm a serial dater in my early-thirties."

"Mid-thirties."

"It's a matter of perspective. In any case, don't you think me living with my folks would be inappropriate? On many levels?"

"I don't understand. If this isn't your apartment, why are we here?"

"For starters, no one would think to look for you at your partner's parents' home. Even if the killer staked out my place in hopes of finding you there, you'd be safe here, far from anywhere he'd look. More to the point, my parents keep this apartment for nights when my dad works late, or they have social functions in the city. I'm welcome to stay here anytime they're not using it, which, as you can see, they're not. And before you say it, this is not an imposition."

"I'm sure they didn't expect you to bring guests to sleep over."

"I didn't bring guests, plural. I brought you, singular. And my parents wouldn't mind. In fact, they'd insist on it."

"They *would*?"

"What I meant was, they wouldn't mind helping a police officer in trouble. I know they'd appreciate someone offering me a place if I needed it. But they're out of state and don't even know. And if they weren't, they'd be at their house, not here, so, like I said, this really is no imposition. Make yourself at home."

Sullivan stepped away from the windows then walked into the living room. She sunk into an oversized chair with a matching ottoman.

It was Jim's favorite seat in the apartment. The chenille fabric was soft to the touch, and the cushions were so comfortable, they practically conformed to every curve.

She closed her eyes and leaned her head back.

"You can stay in the bedroom. I'll put your things in there." He started walking toward one of the doors she'd spied earlier.

"Oh, no. I wouldn't want to take your bed from you, and I certainly don't feel comfortable staying in your parents' bedroom."

"How many times do I have to tell you? My mama raised me right. You'll take the bedroom."

"Don't be ridiculous. I'm a lot smaller than you, and I weigh a lot less. I'll be more than happy on the couch."

"I'm bringing your luggage into the bedroom."

"If you do, I'll just drag it right back out."

He shot her an intense stare.

She returned it with equal determination. "Honestly, Jim. If you want to be a good host and help me feel at home here, you won't fight me on this. I really will feel more comfortable on the couch."

"Jim?"

"That is your name."

"One you don't use."

She sighed. "Would you please put my bags down and relax? You're making me nervous."

"Are you sure?"

"I'm about to leave."

Jim left her bags between the bedroom and bathroom doors then joined her in the living room. He dropped onto a recliner then propped up his feet. "Ah. I'm more tired than I thought. Don't feel like cooking. How about we order a pizza?"

"You cook?"

"I'm no Bobby Flay, but I get by."

She giggled. "You know who Bobby Flay is?"

"Why wouldn't I? He has about seven hundred different shows on TV."

"That's why I laughed. You don't look the type to watch the Food Network."

"I don't. I channel surf. His name comes up a lot."

"Right," Chelsea smirked and nodded.

"Forget I mentioned it."

"What? The cooking or the pizza?"

He pretended to think for a moment, tapping his chin and looking toward the ceiling. "I'd say both, but I'm starving. So just forget about the cooking stuff. Do you have a favorite pizza place? I don't know of any who deliver ice cream."

"Me, either. Wish I did. And for the record, you can't shame me about my ice cream addiction. So don't bother trying."

"I wasn't trying to shame you. It's just that I've never seen so much ice cream in one place before. I mean, other than at a creamery."

"I know you think I'm fussy. Prudish. I don't drink. I don't swear."

"You did today."

"Often. I don't swear often. I know all this stuff is

unusual for a cop. But if you understood what I've seen, what I've dealt with, it would make more sense to you."

He pushed his footrest down then leaned forward to rest his elbows on his knees. His gaze was intense. "Is this about your dad?"

Her eyes widened, and she sucked in a sharp breath. When she spoke, she sounded breathless. "What would make you say that?"

"I was there, Chelsea. I saw the bottles, the vomit. Saw your reaction to it all. How long has he had a problem?"

Tears welled in her eyes.

"Sorry. I overstepped."

She shook her head.

He sat back, reclined again. "I understand, you know. Parents can be tricky. All of us can, truth be told. The faces we show the public are never the faces we show those closest to us."

She stared at him.

It was too much. He was walking a tightrope and about to fall off onto the side of TMI about himself. "One of my favorite pizza places is right down the street. You like pepperoni and sausage?"

"I usually get mushrooms and olives. Sometimes artichoke hearts. Or spinach and feta."

"You're not a vegetarian."

"No. But that's how I like my pizza."

His eyebrows furrowed. "What do you do for protein?"

"There's protein in cheese."

"Cheese is not a good source of protein. Meat is. Like a nice juicy steak or, I don't know, pepperoni and sausage on a pizza."

"That just makes the pizza greasy."

"Grease is what makes pizza good."

"Agree to disagree. How about we go halfsies?"

He shook his head. "I'm starving. I'm not limiting myself to a fraction of a pie. I'll order two."

"How much pizza can one man eat?"

"I guess you're about to find out. Besides, it's great cold for breakfast."

She wrinkled her nose. "If we're ordering two, can I get olive oil instead of tomato sauce on mine?"

"And you wonder why you don't blend in with the rest of the cops." Jim reached into his pocket for his phone, then started scrolling through his contacts.

"You saved the pizzeria's phone number in your favorites list?"

After punching a number, he held the phone to his ear. "When you call as often as I do, it only makes sense."

"If you call them that often, I'd think you'd know their number by heart. Then again, with your Food Network addiction, maybe you don't order out as often as you'd like me to believe."

A smile spread across his face. Chelsea was loosening up, bantering a bit. Either she was too tired to keep up her walls, or she was starting to relax around him. He hoped it was the latter.

While he placed their order, she rooted through her purse then came away with her phone and charger. She plugged it in near the sofa, a frown on her face.

Jim ended the call. "Problem?"

"Stupid battery is drained. Guess I went too long without a charge. Can't even get the screen to flicker."

McPherson pocketed his own phone. "It'll charge by the time we've had dinner. Pizza will be here in about forty minutes. Probably less."

She stifled a yawn. "Good. I'm starving."

"But you're more tired."

"I think it's a tie." But she closed her eyes.

Two minutes later, Jim picked her up. On his way to the bedroom, he second-guessed his decision. It felt all kinds of wrong to take the bed and leave her on the sofa, but he knew she'd flip out if she woke in the bedroom, and he couldn't risk her going back to her apartment.

With a sigh, he lay her on his sofa. After covering her with a blanket, he put his phone on silent. When the front desk called with the pizza delivery, he didn't want his ring tone to wake her.

CHELSEA'S BODY ACHED, and she stretched to get rid of the kinks in her joints. She blinked, then looked around. Bolted upright. This wasn't her bedroom! Where the heck was she?

Her heart slammed against her ribcage as she jumped to her feet.

Dawn was breaking, the soft light of a pending sunrise filtering through crisp, cellulose window shades that spanned an entire wall.

She took a deep breath and dropped back to the sofa. McPherson's. She was at his place. Or rather, his parents' apartment.

Chelsea grabbed her phone from the end table to check the time. The screen flashed a notification of a missed voicemail. Her body bristled, a defense against the tirade she was about to hear. Dad. She'd forgotten all about the call she'd ignored from him. Probably hadn't been a good idea to do so, as putting him off would only make him more bitter.

Steeling herself for the inevitable impending lecture,

she played the message. Once, twice. The third time. He didn't sound angry. Then again, she couldn't really tell how he sounded. The words were garbled as the reception cut in and out. There were more dead spots than clear spots, and the few words that managed to come through were staticky. Chelsea played the recording one last time. If she strained really hard and made a few creative leaps, she could make out the words *riddle*, *killer*, and *castle*.

Dad had figured out the clue.

Or he'd been the one who sent it, to begin with.

A chill crept up her spine.

She had to give him the benefit of the doubt, so she repeated the thought — Dad had *figured out* the clue.

The word *castle* evoked images in her mind, places in town she loved. Places that could easily fit within the framework of fairy tales. There was Cultura Temple on SCU's campus, with all its nationality rooms and foreign artifacts. The Gothic architecture on Fifth Avenue. The old mansions on Millionaires' Row. Milhouse Castle. Several library branches. Even the courthouse.

What had he discovered? Which building was it?

Chelsea dialed her dad's number, but he didn't answer. Was he punishing her for ignoring him yesterday? Typical. Petty. And totally inappropriate, given the stakes. Sighing, she looked up the number for the hospital, and when the receptionist answered, she asked for her father's room.

"One moment, please." After a few moments, she said, "Would he be under another name?"

"No. It's the only name my dad has. Cormac Sullivan." She spelled both names. "Came via ambulance last night. No, two nights ago." Her sleep schedule was so messed up, she'd lost track of time. "They were holding him for observation."

"Please hold."

The music set her teeth on edge. It made every second stretch to five. By the time the woman came back on, Chelsea felt like she'd lost a year of her life. "I'm sorry, miss. Your father checked himself out of the ER. He was never admitted."

"Thank you." She inhaled deeply then exhaled slowly. It was a good thing he'd lived because she couldn't kill him if he was already dead.

No time to deal with his nonsense now, though. He'd turned her onto another lead, and with the Grimm Reaper case, every second counted.

She dashed across the room and pounded on McPherson's bedroom door. "Get up! We have a clue!"

He flung open his door, already dressed for the day. His hair was damp from the shower, and the slightly too-long ends licked his collar, getting it wet. He smelled like mint and sandalwood, a compelling mix of toothpaste and after-shave, and he swiped at a spot of blood near the cleft of his chin. "I know. I was just about to wake you."

"You know? How do you know? Did my dad call you, too?"

He shook his head. "No. Davenport."

She looked down at her phone. Other than her dad's, she hadn't missed any calls. "Davenport? I didn't get a message from him."

"He told you he wanted you to take a step back from this case."

"And we all agreed I wasn't backing off."

"I remember. Which is why I was about to wake you."

"Well? What did he say? Did he figure out the clue?"

"No. Why? Did you?"

"My dad left a message. I called him back, but he's not answering. Anyway, he said something that sparked an idea. I think I can narrow down the location of the next murder."

McPherson shook his head. "Don't bother. We already have it."

"You do? How, if no one's figured out the clue yet."

He frowned, his expression grim. "Because we've got another body."

Chapter Thirty-Two

THE COUNTY'S community college had four campuses. The western campus primarily focused on fine arts and its theater, a historical landmark, was a castle-like building of gothic architecture design.

It all made sense now.

Fortress walls — a castle.

Hallowed halls — a college.

Traffic was still light, as rush hour hadn't officially begun yet. But pedestrians lined the sidewalk, blocking the entrance to the building. Even though it was early, it seemed the whole campus was aware of what had happened and had come to get a glimpse of the crime.

Chelsea wished they'd all go away. Those who managed to see anything would regret it. And would have to live with the images for the rest of their lives.

She and McPherson pushed their way through the crowd, ducked under the crime scene tape, then rushed inside. The activity was centered on the second floor of the building, so they climbed the stairs.

In the main hallway, they found another girl whose life

ended too soon and in too grisly a way. Like the others, she was found naked, hands clasped at her stomach. This one, however, was found beside an apple. The fruit was a beautiful specimen. Large, red, glossy. Not a blemish on it, save for the one bite that had been taken from it, revealing the juicy interior. It had been taken a while ago — the flesh had oxidized and was now brown. One of the forensic techs snapped a picture of it, then he dropped it into an evidence bag.

She turned her attention to the vic. The girl wasn't blonde. Some detectives would say the hair color and the apple broke the killer's MO, but Chelsea knew better. This wasn't about blonde college girls. This was about fairy tales. In this case, one specific fairy tale — Snow White. Snow White had dark hair, and so did this victim.

Scott was already on scene. He looked up when Chelsea and McPherson walked over, and a grim smile crossed his face. "Good morning, Chelsea. Or perhaps 'greetings' is more appropriate."

"You're right. This is not a good morning. Not for her, anyway."

"Got an ID yet?" McPherson's voice was gruff, his words short and to the point.

The ME shook his head. "You have to ask one of the officers. I just got here."

"Time of death?" he continued. "Anything unusual?"

Scott scoffed. "Unusual? Haven't all the murders been unusual? Say what you want about the guy, but you've got to give him credit for his extraordinary methodology."

"Yeah," McPherson said. "He's a real artist."

Scott scowled and turned back to the body, muttering under his breath.

Chelsea thought it sounded like "cretin."

She stooped down to get a look at the vic's face. The

girl's complexion was flawless, her features exceptional. Truly the epitome of a fairy-tale princess.

"Pure as the driven snow, huh?" Scott shook his head.

She nodded. "It's so sad. All these young lives, cut short. All this potential wasted."

McPherson was talking to one of the officers. When they parted, he tapped her shoulder. "Vic's name is Gretchen Moore. She's a student here, not at Alcoa or SCU. Looks like the killer's hunting grounds have expanded."

"Speaking of hunting grounds," Scott said, "you'll probably find this interesting."

"Find what interesting?" Chelsea asked as she rose.

"MCU has already bagged and tagged them, but they haven't taken them to the lab yet if you want a quick look."

"Look at what?" McPherson pressed.

Scott pointed at a brownish blotch on the floor. "Found organs here."

The blood drained from Chelsea's face. "Organs? You mean, human organs? Like kidneys or hearts?"

"Yes, that kind of organ. More precisely, lungs and liver. I need to do a proper analysis of them to determine their origin."

"Lungs and liver?" McPherson asked. "What's that have to do with Snow White?"

"You don't know your childhood tales, Detective?" Scott said. "In the story, the Evil Queen conscripted a huntsman to kill Snow White then return to her with the girl's liver and lungs as proof of her death. But he couldn't do it and disobeyed his queen. After sparing Snow's life, he returned to the castle with boar's organs, instead."

"Right, right," McPherson said. "That's jogging my memory. But wasn't it a stag's heart?"

"No," Chelsea said. "Boar's lungs and liver."

"Wait," McPherson said. "These princesses. They were all saved by true love's kiss, right? Have you been checking their mouths for DNA?"

"I have," Scott said. "Nothing."

"Little Red wasn't a princess," Chelsea said. "And no prince saved her. Certainly not with a kiss. For that matter, in the original version, Snow White was saved by love, but not by a kiss."

"Oh?" Scott said.

"The dwarves put her in a glass coffin when they couldn't revive her. A prince came along, found her, and asked the dwarves to let him take her with him."

"Ew. Perv." McPherson wrinkled his nose.

She rolled her eyes. "I don't think he was a necrophile. I'd like to think he just wanted to give her a proper burial. Anyway, when the prince picked up the coffin, the bite of apple was dislodged from her lips, and she woke."

"Damn it." McPherson ran his hand through his hair. "I thought we might have had a breakthrough."

Scott looked up at her. "I didn't know that. How do you know so much about fairy tales, Chelsea?"

"My dad. He's a bit of an expert. Used to read them to me all the time when I was little. When I moved out, he gave me the book. It's a first edition, very old. Probably worth a lot of money. Might be the nicest gift he ever gave me, not that I wanted it."

"Why wouldn't you want a first edition Brothers Grimm book?" Scott asked.

She shrugged. "I never liked the stories. Too gruesome for a kid. I used to tell him so. All the time. But he made me listen to them."

"I'm sorry. That must have been hard for you. But I'm sure he meant well."

"Right. And he means well, now, too, I suppose. When

I was young, he told me the monsters in the stories weren't real, and if I was going to fear anything, it should be the monsters in real life. I'm pretty sure he gave me the book as a reminder of that."

"But you aren't a kid anymore."

The leer Scott gave her was purely predatory, his smile a wolfish grin. She felt his gaze rake over her body as sure as she'd feel his hands. Her face flamed under his attention, and she opened her coat and flapped the lapels to fan her burning cheeks. "Yes, well … No. No, I'm not a child. Dad still wants me to see the world his way, though. And the stories in that book are his way of making his point. They're the original versions, a lot more violent than the Disney versions we get today. Dad knows them all by heart. Tried to make sure I did, too, though I've blocked some of the more gruesome details from memory."

"Sounds like his experience could be beneficial to your investigation. Have you spoken to him about the case?"

Chelsea nodded. "I have. A little. When he's not lecturing me, we've discussed it. In fact, it was something he said that led me here."

"Yeah," McPherson said, "that was helpful. But it was a little too late. By the time you played his message this morning, we had already been called to the scene."

One of Scott's eyebrows arched. "What time did you start work today?"

Chelsea's cheeks were still burning from earlier. Now they practically flamed. Her face must have turned violently red at the implication. Before she could correct his erroneous assumption, McPherson answered.

"We walked out the door at the crack of dawn today."

Scott's face fell, and he wouldn't meet her gaze. He hurriedly stood then brushed off his knee. "I need to get this body back to the morgue. If nothing has come in since

I left, I'll be conducting the autopsy in about an hour. No reason for you to be there. Barring any unforeseen delays, I'll have my preliminary findings to you this afternoon."

"Okay, well—"

But he was already walking away.

Chelsea considered going after him, but he was issuing orders to the techs for body transportation. So she rounded on McPherson. "Why would you do that?"

"Do what?"

But the look of mock innocence didn't sway her.

"You let him believe we slept together. That we've been sleeping together."

"All I did was tell him how we got the information. Any inferences he makes are on him. Why do you care, anyway? You and Dr. Death taking your romance to the next level?"

"My love life is none of your business."

"Ah. Things aren't going well. I get it."

"I didn't say that. And if they weren't going well, your comments would have made things worse. I thought you had my back."

"Have you considered this is how I have your back, Sullivan? I don't think the guy is right for you. If I led him to think you weren't available, it's because I'm trying to protect you."

"I hardly need protecting from Scott. He's a perfect gentleman. Kind, considerate, cultured."

"What? All the things I'm not? Thanks."

"I … Are you … Do you mean you're… I wasn't comparing him to you."

He crossed his arms, and his jaw ticked. Then he sighed. "I didn't mean it that way. I just meant … well, I took it as an insult, not a comparison."

She cleared her throat. "This is hardly an appropriate

place for a discussion like this. Not that there's ever a good one. It's unprofessional."

"We're partners, Sullivan. No secrets, remember?"

Yeah, Chelsea remembered. But she had certain thoughts, certain feelings, that she'd never be able to share with him.

Chapter Thirty-Three

IT WAS A LONG, tedious day. They had to take and sift through dozens of witness statements. All were pointless — no one saw anything. Just a lot of onlookers after the fact.

For the first time, Scott let her down. He did not complete the autopsy that day, so there was no preliminary report to review. More to the point, he wasn't even in the office the entire afternoon, so she couldn't inquire about when the autopsy would be done, nor could she explain McPherson's comments to him.

It wasn't as though they were dating. A single evening out and a few conversations didn't qualify as a relationship. Still, she felt she owed him an explanation. Especially if she wanted to see him again, which she did. Maybe.

Truth be told, she didn't have romantic feelings for him. Wasn't sure she ever did, but she certainly didn't now.

Still, Scott deserved better. He was a good man. And good for her, at least as a friend. She definitely needed to clear things up with him. Hopefully, he'd be in tomorrow so they could talk.

In the meantime, she and McPherson spent the entire

day going over everything. Top to bottom, left to right. They left no stone unturned.

They also had no new leads. Hadn't received the forensics report from the wolf's head, either. Another hair had been found. The DNA results weren't in yet, but she knew it would match the others. But with no viable suspects, they had nothing to compare it to.

All in all, it had been a crappy day. What she really wanted was a pint of ice cream and a fuzzy blanket. But she couldn't go home. Not yet. So she allowed McPherson to take her back to his parents' apartment.

He walked into the kitchen, calling over his shoulder, "I know you don't drink, but would you mind if I had a glass of wine?"

"Of course not. This is your home. Do what's necessary to relax." She perched on one of the stools at the island.

"Great." He grabbed a bottle from the wine rack and an opener from a drawer. "While I feed one of my vices, why don't you feed one of yours?"

She wrinkled her forehead as she tried to figure out what he meant.

McPherson turned around, then opened the freezer. When he spun back toward her, he had a carton of ice cream in his hands. He set it down in front of her.

"Ice cream? Thank you." It wasn't her preferred brand or flavor, but the gesture warmed her heart. "When did you have time?"

"I'd like to take credit, but I can't. It was the housekeeper's day to come by. I asked her if she'd pick up some groceries on her way."

"Well, thank you. Thanks to both of you."

He took a bowl from the cabinet and a spoon and a

scoop from the drawer, then he placed them on the island. "Do you eat seafood?"

"Yes. I love seafood. Why?"

"Spicy food okay?"

"Sure. Wherever you want to order from, tonight is my treat."

"That won't be necessary."

"I insist. It's the least I can do. I didn't even chip in for my half of last night's dinner."

He scoffed. "You didn't eat, either."

"Doesn't matter. I ordered."

"Well, you're not paying tonight."

"Don't make me argue with you, McPherson. Or I'll just call somewhere and place an order myself."

"That would be a waste."

"It's my way of saying thanks."

"You can show your appreciation by enjoying your dinner."

"I can't enjoy it if you pay for it again. Let me take my turn."

"Chelsea" He shook his head and laughed at her. "I'm cooking."

"What?"

"I'm cooking dinner. Provided you like grilled shrimp and arrabbiata sauce over fettuccini. Or I can make something else if you'd rather."

"No. That sounds delicious." She smiled — his inner Bobby Flay was showing. "Thank you. How can I help?"

"That's okay. I've got it covered. It won't take long."

"Can I at least make a salad? Set the table? Something?"

"If you want to make a salad, great. Thanks."

They set to work making the meal. McPherson put on classical music, and they both settled into a comfortable rhythm with each other. Conversation was light and simple, and so was the workload. She washed the produce, cut it, then filled a bowl. As she was mixing the dressing, mouth-watering scents of garlic and tomatoes wafted from a sauté pan. Soon, they were seated side-by-side at the island, indulging themselves.

She speared her fourth shrimp, then held her fork so he could see it. "This is delicious."

"We make a good team, don't we?"

Chelsea popped the morsel into her mouth. The conversation lulled while they ate, and the satisfied smile fled from her face. Her mind raced from one soul-crushing thought to another, sucking her enjoyment from the meal. Today's murder was her fault. If she had only answered her father's phone call the night before, that poor girl might still be alive. But, no. She had been so busy running from her imaginary monsters, she'd let a real one wreak havoc on the town.

"You've grown quiet. Is everything okay?"

She put down her fork. "I could've stopped it."

"Stopped it?"

"Gretchen Moore. Her murder. If only I had answered my father's phone call, we would've had a lead. We could've stopped him before he killed her. This is all my fault."

"That's not true." He took her hand, squeezed it. Laced their fingers together and didn't let go. "Even if you knew the exact location, you didn't know she had been abducted. You couldn't have put a stop to it once things were set in motion."

"I was thinking about it. I don't think she was abducted. Brianna Lawson, our first vic, was found in her home. She wasn't abducted. Our second, Mariah Jones, was found in the woods. There was no evidence of her body being transported there. I think he found her there or lured her there and killed her at the site. The same with Gretchen Moore. It would be impossible to carry a naked woman through the streets of the city and not be noticed. Or even to drag a clothed corpse into the building and then strip her. I think the murder occurred right in the school."

"People would've noticed a murder happening in the main hallway of a campus building."

"Would they? You're far less likely to be noticed inside than outside, even if the inside location is a well-traveled hallway of a college. It was late at night. Foot traffic had to be virtually nil. But I don't think she was killed in the corridor. I think she was killed in a classroom then placed where we found her."

"Crimes of opportunity?"

"I don't think so. These girls were targeted. Carefully selected. But the times and locations of their deaths were chosen so the killer didn't have to move the bodies. At least, not far."

He released her hand and leaned on the counter. "But that means they all knew the killer. And we haven't found any commonality between the three victims to suggest they knew any of the same people."

"They may not have known the killer. Maybe it's someone in a position of authority. Or someone a college girl would inherently trust. Someone like a preacher or a teacher. A doctor, a cop." Or an ex-cop? God, she hated to think it. Was it possible?

"I'd feel better if we could find a common link between the three," McPherson said. "Four, if we count you. Maybe more."

Chelsea's blood ran cold. "I'm not a college student. And I'm not a victim."

"Not yet. And I'd like to keep it that way. Which is why I want to find that link, that common thread. I'm inclined to think this all comes back to the fairy tales and not the girls themselves."

"No. It has to be about the girls. They're all young, all beautiful. They fit a specific demographic."

He shook his head. "I don't know, Chels. I think the killer is looking for girls who fit the descriptions of the characters. The question is, why fairy tales?"

"And I think the opposite. I think the girls come first, then the characters. Something about these women reminds him of those stories, and he's then compelled to act them out."

"Well, one is definitely the cause and the other the result. Maybe if we can figure out which is which, we'll have a better understanding of the killer and can finally bring him in."

"We've hit the magic number now. Are we ready to make it official and call him a serial killer? Or because of the timeline, are we calling him a spree killer?"

"I wanted to talk to you about that," he said. "Timing does make it look like a spree killing. Signature says serial. But what if we missed something?"

"Like what?"

"Like earlier victims. Maybe not even in the city. If our guy started months ago instead of days ago, and if he changed his MO a bit as he developed into his current methodology, it definitely isn't a spree killer. And it proves he's methodical, which we kind of know, anyway. His killings are well-planned, well-executed. It stands to reason he didn't start that way."

"But nothing popped when we searched for vics killed this way."

"We need to widen the search. Broaden our parameters for the details. Or maybe we just haven't found the earlier vics yet."

"I hate to even consider the ramifications of that."

McPherson shrugged. "We have to. Regardless, Davenport is thinking about calling the Feds."

"Davenport? When'd you talk to him? And why wasn't I on the call?"

"He insisted on regular reports, remember? If you want to stay on the case, we have to tell him everything. And since you haven't contacted him once since leaving his office, I've been touching base."

She looked down at her plate, chastised. Embarrassed. He really was a good partner. "I should have done it."

"Doesn't matter who does it, Chelsea. Just that it gets done."

Without discussing it, they both stood and started clearing the dishes. It didn't take long before everything was washed, dried, and put away. The whole time, Chelsea pondered the killer's motivations. Did the girls make him want to reenact the fairy tales? Or did the fairy tales compel him to seek girls who looked like the characters?

Dad would know. Too bad he was being spiteful and refusing to answer her call.

McPherson made her a cup of tea, then poured himself another glass of Cabernet. After taking their drinks into the living room, the conversation picked up right where it had left off.

"What do you think started this?" she asked.

"His fascination with fairy tales?"

"No. Well, yes, that. But I meant the killings themselves. Something had to be a trigger."

"Could be anything. We're talking about psychopaths and sociopaths — people who can't feel empathy. They enjoy inflicting pain on their targets, often as a way to punish a person who hurt them. Their victims are surrogates for the real tormentors."

"But they always have that tormentor. What sets them off, prompts the killings?"

"It varies. Could be one too many insults or rejections. Could be the death of a loved one. Sometimes it's an unrelated trauma. Until we know who our killer is, we probably won't know his true motive."

"Too bad. If we knew his motive, we might be able to figure out who he is."

"First thing tomorrow, we'll go over all the evidence again. In the meantime, maybe we should look through your book." He gestured toward her computer bag with his wine glass. "There might be something in there we haven't considered, haven't seen. It might be worth another call to your dad, too."

"I tried him a few times today. Once this evening, too. He's screening his calls. Did I tell you he checked himself out of the hospital?"

"No, but I knew."

"You did? How?"

"I called to check on him."

She didn't even know what to say to that. "Thanks."

"I was concerned. No big deal."

"Well, maybe you should try calling him. He might take your call, but he won't take mine. I think he's angry because I didn't answer yesterday." Guilt gnawed at her gut, and she set aside her tea, her stomach too queasy for even a sip of the mild beverage.

"I see it on your face, Chelsea. I know you're wallowing in guilt over it. You need to stop. It wasn't your fault."

"I let my frustration with my father color my judgment."

"If you don't mind me asking, what happened in the ER?"

"Pretty much what you'd expect. I made accusations. He made excuses. When I pushed the subject, he turned the tables and started lecturing me. It's nothing new. It's been this way since I was a kid. He got worse after he left the force. Was practically unbearable after the divorce. Yet somehow, I feel guilty about it all."

"Ah, guilt. An emotion I understand all too well. Parents have a way of getting under our skin, Chelsea. You're not the only one."

"Oh? If you don't mind me asking, was your dad insufferable and overbearing, too?"

He scoffed, the bitter bark of derision telling her more than his words ever could. "If you're asking if my dad bullied me, then no. It didn't make him any less abusive, though."

"I wouldn't call my father abusive. I think maybe I gave you the wrong idea."

"You took the same classes I did, Chelsea. You know there are all kinds of abuse — sexual, physical, mental, emotional. Your dad terrorized you with those stories. That's emotional abuse."

"He didn't mean to, though. He was trying to toughen me up, trying to prepare me."

"I'm not sure abuse has anything to do with intent. Not entirely, anyway."

Might be right about that. On some level. "Your dad? Did he hurt you?"

McPherson shook his head. "Let's just say the apple doesn't fall far from the tree. Though for different reasons."

Her skin chilled, and she wrapped her hands around her cup. That was one of the main reasons she became a cop — to prove that idiom wrong. "I'm sorry. I don't understand."

He drained his glass. "Don't get me wrong. I love my dad. But he wasn't always the upstanding family man he is today. That took a lot of years of suffering and many more years of counseling."

She was more confused than ever, but she didn't prompt him. He needed to choose to share, not be goaded into it. So she waited, hoping he would decide to unburden himself of his painful memories. So many seconds ticked by, it looked like he wasn't going to.

But then he did.

"To put it as politely as possible, my dad was a womanizer. I'm not sure if he started cheating before I was born, but he certainly made no secret about it afterward. Mom was home taking care of me, and he was out taking care of … his baser urges. It broke her heart, and when I was old enough to realize what was happening, it broke mine. Nearly broke our family."

"What changed?"

"He got a woman pregnant. That was mom's hard line. She said sharing him with another woman was bad enough, but she wasn't going to make me share him, too."

Chelsea set down her cup and pulled a blanket over her shoulders. She couldn't imagine having a step-sibling that she didn't speak to. Didn't *know*. Couldn't imagine her father turning his back on a child of his — but maybe parents saw things differently when they didn't actually father their children.

Then again, it was more likely a matter of morality. And she couldn't imagine her father cheating on her mother, either.

"What happened after that?"

McPherson shrugged. "Mom gave him an ultimatum — us or them. The woman had a miscarriage before Dad made up his mind. Probably made his choice easier on him, although it made it harder on me. I didn't trust him for the longest time. The only reason I ever came around was because my mother begged me to. She and Dad went to counseling for years. Worked hard in therapy and out. She said God gave her the grace to forgive him. She must have a damn good relationship with the Guy Upstairs. I didn't have it in me, but she told me she had enough faith for both of us and damned if she wasn't right. I eventually got over the feeling of betrayal. Or if not over it, I at least found a way to move past it. I don't let it define our relationship anymore. Don't let it define him. He's been faithful to Mom, to our family, ever since. My relationship with him is stronger than ever, and so is their relationship with each other. But like I said, it took a long time. And while they were repairing their trust and love, the parent-child dynamic took a back seat. At the time, because I wasn't getting what I needed from them, I started seeking it elsewhere."

"That's why you date so much?"

He shrugged. "It was easy to find comfort in the arms of a willing participant, as long as she didn't want a commitment from me. Dad got married then played the field. I play the field because I don't want to get married. Big distinction in my book, though it probably looks pretty similar on the outside looking in. But that's who I am. I don't want to commit to someone knowing how wrong it can go."

A look crossed his face. She couldn't read it, but she sensed hurt and anger. And it seemed to go deeper than the pain his father had caused. But she didn't ask, and this time, he didn't volunteer.

"Anyway, it's pretty hard for me to trust someone in a relationship when I see how badly it can end up."

"Yeah, but now you also see how wonderful it can be."

His gaze locked on hers, and he stared at her for a long while. "I suppose if I ever find the right person, things will change. Until then …" He shrugged.

"Do you think we're like our parents? Destined to repeat the same patterns over and over?"

"God, I hope not. I might date a lot of women, but if I ever settle down, I'll never cheat. That's breaking at least part of the mold, right?"

Chelsea nodded slowly, only vaguely listening to him. Was her father really capable of these heinous murders? And if so, did she also have a predisposition to such violence and depravity? It was the same old nature-versus-nurture debate she'd been having with herself since she learned she was adopted. More so since Dad's fall from grace. And now the answer mattered more than ever. She didn't want to be like Cormac Sullivan. Probably not the man he used to be. Definitely not the man he was now.

Was he guilty of what IA said? Was he guilty of these latest crimes?

She reached for her tea, needing some action — any action — to settle her nerves. Her hands trembled, and the china cup rattled against the saucer.

"What's bothering you?"

But she couldn't meet his gaze, let alone give voice to her fears.

Chapter Thirty-Four

Evening after Gretchen Moore was found
Woodland clearing
Emerson Park in Steel City, Pennsylvania

HE COULDN'T GO BACK to the community college's fine arts theater, as his presence would surely be noted. So, he returned to Emerson Park with the hope that visiting the location of one of his masterpieces would soothe his soul and quiet the constant barrage of fulmination in his head.

The police tape was still up around Mariah Jones's crime scene, the yellow tails where it was tied together fluttering in the crisp breeze. Above him, the naked limbs of maple trees formed a skeletal canopy, the dark bark appearing black in silhouette beneath the blood-red sunset.

It was his favorite time of day.

Mother always preferred the promise of dawn because it offered endless potential, though he shuddered to think what possibilities she yearned for.

He, on the other hand, had always favored the gloaming. If he'd made it to eventide without punishment, it was a good day. And if he hadn't, he still had dreams beckoning him to a world without beatings, humiliations, and fears. Dreams where he splashed in the river, with the sunlight warming his skin and the water simultaneously cooling it. Dreams where friends hoisted him on their shoulders as the hero who saved the day. Dreams where he celebrated his victories in the impassioned embrace of an adoring woman.

But that's all they were. All they ever could be. Just dreams. Nighttime fantasies of a life he'd never have.

Still, seldom did he have nightmares. His subconscious couldn't conceive of horrors worse than those he lived.

When Mother died, he lost his idyllic dreamscape. Gone were the recreation and reverence and conjugal relations his mental self experienced when his physical self could not. It seemed what one world was missing, the other provided. With Mother now powerless in the earthly realm, she ruthlessly commanded his oneiric dominion.

An overwhelming wave of pain crashed over him, surged through him. He caught himself against the tree, the bark digging into his tender palm as he struggled to breathe past the lump in his throat.

He missed her. Desperately.

She'd been his moral compass, and without her guidance, he was lost.

But he was kidding himself. Or lying to himself. Mother still had authority over his waking hours, too. There was no retreat from her castigation, no haven from her censure. He could not hide any immoral transgressions or conceal any impure desires. She was with him day and night, night and day — judging his every thought, criticizing his every emotion.

Inciting his every move.

Mother inspired action. Insisted on it. When she saw evil, she demanded its perpetrators be smote with righteous fury and unwavering resolve.

Evildoers like Mariah Jones, whose public face of a nursing home volunteer masked her actual identity of a massage parlor whore.

Evildoers like Brianna Lawson, whose daytime persona of an activist for special needs children couldn't hide her nighttime alter-ego as a drunken harlot.

Evildoers like Gretchen Moore, whose innocence on the stage was a mockery compared to her promiscuity in the wings.

Evildoers like Allison Parker, whose pretense of helping preschool children was a charade hiding her true, salacious intent to lure their fathers into her bed.

Evildoers like Chelsea Sullivan, whose guise of a pure and virtuous police officer was tainted by her crass language and debauched associations with her lecherous partner.

Mother's diatribe was a never-ending call to action in his brain. She pointed out all their flaws. Preached to him of their obscene behaviors. Pronounced him judge and jury of their transgressions and proclaimed it his moral obligation to right their vulgar wrongs.

If he could only get her to stop talking. If he could only find respite once more in his dreams.

But Mother was with him always now. Day, night, dawn, twilight.

He no longer had a favorite time of day. Every moment was Mother. Mother. Mother.

Mother.

After pushing away from the tree, he wiped off his hands and looked down at the snow-covered earth where he'd displayed Mariah Jones not long ago. The sun had melted into the horizon, causing the trees to cast long gnarled stripes of shade across the crystalline blanket beneath him, their undulating shadows reminiscent of snakes.

"The serpent tempted Eve," Mother said.

"I've already used an apple in one of my scenes."

"The Brothers Grimm wrote three Tales of Snakes. I believe the first would suffice."

"My apologies, but I don't remember that one."

She sighed. "Why am I not surprised? It's the one where the devoted and diligent mother in the story rescued the daughter and killed the snake, only to have the funeral bird cry and the redbreast create the girl's burial garland."

Now he remembered, though if he recalled correctly, the mother in the story was the cause of her grief, not the serpent.

Regardless, the moral of the story was the same.

The girl was going to die.

Chapter Thirty-Five

"HEY. WHAT'S THE MATTER?" Jim was concerned by Chelsea's sudden silence. Maybe he'd gotten too personal, too fast. But if that was the case, her reaction was extreme. It had to be something else. "Talk to me."

Her hands shook violently. She put down her cup, probably so she didn't spill her tea, but the effort nearly made her drop it.

He crossed the room then sat on the sofa, next to her chair. Resting his elbows on his knees and leaning toward her, he said, "Hey. It's okay. Whatever it is, we can deal with it."

She shook her head.

Jim took her hand and rubbed it between his. "You're like ice."

Chelsea sucked in a shuddering breath. She whispered, "I'm scared."

"That's nothing to be ashamed of. You've caught the attention of a serial killer. I'm scared for you. But I promise I'm going to keep you safe."

Again, she shook her head. "That's not what I meant."

"I don't understand."

She closed her eyes, took a few deep breaths, then looked at him. "Sure, it's disturbing knowing this guy is fixated on me. But that's not the worst part."

"What is, then?"

Her mouth opened, but no words came out.

"Chelsea, I'm your partner. You can tell me anything."

"I'm afraid it's my dad." The sentence was blurted and ran together into one long, multisyllabic word.

"You're afraid what is your dad?"

"The killer. The Grimm Reaper." Her voice cracked on a sob. "I've been thinking about it for a while now, and as much as I'd like to believe it isn't him, it all adds up. He's got the knowledge. And the anger. He's in a really bad place, and he's not taking his medication consistently. I never would have thought he was capable of such violence, but now … I just don't know."

"It can't be him. He's been sick."

"He could have a partner."

"Chelsea, your father wouldn't target *you*."

She took a shuddering breath. "Dad's not the same, Jim. I may not be able to fit all the pieces together yet, but the picture is really starting to look like him."

He squeezed her hand. "Look. I heard about his forced retirement. I also know his record and reputation. If it's any consolation, I think the charges were bogus. IA gets stuff wrong all the time. If they were so sure, they wouldn't have let him take his retirement and pension. They'd have thrown the book at him."

"I always believed he was innocent, too. Or tried to. Deep down, I had to believe it. He's flawed, but he's a good man. But maybe it doesn't matter now. Whether he is or isn't, he's still bitter. The only cop he says good things about is his former partner. Not even *me*. If anything, he's more critical of me than supportive. And he hates everyone else. What if this is his way of getting back at the force?"

"Who was his partner?"

She sniffled and blinked back tears. "Grimes. Ralph Grimes."

"So let's talk to him. See what he has to say."

"We can't. He retired last year and moved to — Oh, my God." The blood drained from her face.

"What?"

Her voice was almost too quiet to hear. "He moved to California."

"Okay. So?"

"So the first package I received. The one with the little red cap? It was shipped from California. I distinctly remember because I initially remember thinking it was from my mom."

Jim patted her leg. "Here's what we're going to do. We're going to put a tail on your dad. I know you said he doesn't go anywhere, but if he does, we'll know. And if we see something suspicious, maybe Davenport will let us go to Cali and talk to Grimes. If not, we can Skype or something, so we can question him and read his expressions. We'll figure this out. I promise."

"You don't think I'm a terrible person for suspecting him?"

"No. Not at all. A good detective follows all the evidence, no matter where it leads."

"This is more of a hunch. No, a simmering fear."

"Look at it this way. We're going to keep an eye on him so we can clear his name, not prove him guilty."

"God, I'd love to be able to do that. It's more than he ever got when he was active duty."

"Believe me. I get it. Now, no more worrying. Get some

sleep. We'll get on this tomorrow." He pushed to his feet and started to walk toward his room.

"Jim?"

He looked back at her.

"If you don't mind me asking, did you have a problem with IA?"

"Why do you ask?"

"Because you left the downtown zone for the university beat, and you seem much more accepting of my father's claim of innocence than most other cops. Only a few of his closest friends — Davenport, Charlie, Norm — kept an open mind. And I'm not even sure if they believe him. They're just less willing to believe the story than anyone else. Except you. All that makes me wonder why."

"Your dad had a stellar record before the investigation. And the best IA could say was they had suspicions and couldn't clear him. That's why so many cops hate Internal Affairs. They ruin you, no matter what. Whatever happened to innocent until proven guilty?"

"You didn't answer my question. Why did you transfer?"

"You're pretty intuitive, Sullivan. You know that? That's why you're a good cop." Maybe too good. She was like a kid after sweets, and he wanted to avoid the entire candy store.

"I get it. You don't want to talk about it."

He sighed, and he returned to his recliner. "No, I don't. But I owe you an explanation. Especially since I keep telling you we need total transparency."

"I won't judge you. What could be worse than suspecting your father of being a serial killer?"

Jim took a deep breath. "I'd rather suspect a loved one than be a suspect myself."

Chelsea shook her head. "I don't know. It's killing me to suspect my dad. I think I'd rather the heat be on me."

"No, you wouldn't. Trust me. We can investigate your dad. Hopefully, clear him. Then neither he nor anyone else will know what you thought. But when your whole precinct, maybe the whole Steel City PD, suspects you of wrongdoing? There's no fixing that."

"What did IA suspect?"

He got up. Paced. Ran his hand through his hair. "Initially? Stealing from the evidence lockup."

"Initially? There's more?"

"So fucking much more."

"How did … What … Why would they think that?"

"We had a period of about six months where seized evidence was disappearing. A lot of it was from our cases. Money. Drugs. Weapons. Not a lot. Just enough here and there to pad someone's wallet. The quantities missing were so small, it took a while before anyone even noticed. If it had stayed small, maybe no one ever would have noticed. But the quantities got bigger. Perps started to walk. Then suspicion landed on me. Not *us*. Not me *and* my partner. Just me."

"Why?"

"Because on top of the thefts being associated with our cases, I got a new car."

"Lots of people get new cars."

"You've seen my work car, Chelsea. It's a luxury SUV, which is bad enough. But you haven't seen the sports car I take out in good weather. It's not really something a cop could easily afford."

"What kind is it?"

"A Maserati."

Her eyes widened. "Some of those cost more than a house."

"A small house. But yes, I'm aware."

"Okay. How did you afford it?"

"I didn't. It was from my dad. Trying to buy my affections, I guess."

"That's easy enough to prove."

"You'd think so. Look around." He gestured around the room. "Clearly, my parents have money. But IA had no other suspects. They implied I was dirty and gave my parents the money so it couldn't be traced to me."

"That's absurd. I'm sure your parents have pay stubs, investment records."

"Of course. Didn't matter. IA decided it was me, so they didn't look at anyone else. But they couldn't pin things on me, so I kept my job. At that point, it didn't matter. The damage was done. My department didn't care. No one knew the details of the investigation, which meant no one knew we had the financial documentation to prove everything was above board. After IA gave up on me, they gave up on the case. And everyone treated me differently afterward. Even my partner. In fact, he went from my best friend to my loudest accuser."

"You're kidding?"

"No. So much for having my back, right?"

"I'm so sorry."

He shrugged. "That's when I decided to do IA's job for them and figure out who the dirty cop was."

"And did you?"

"Oh, yeah."

"I can't believe I never heard any of this. Who was it?"

Jim scoffed. "It was Dom. My partner."

"What?"

"I asked for a few days off to get my affairs in order. Acted like I saw the writing on the wall and was going to quit before I got canned. Or worse. My captain gave me a week. I could tell he hoped I didn't come back. And while I was off, I followed Dom. Caught him handing evidence over to … to who doesn't matter. It was a pretty big local drug dealer. In exchange for cash. I should have recorded it and turned him in. Instead, I confronted him."

"What happened?"

"Worst possible outcome. We fought. There was a shoot-out. The dealer had a whole crew with him. I got knocked out. When I came to, some of them were dead. The rest had fled. Two civilians got caught in the crossfire and died. Dom was bleeding out. He gave a deathbed confession to the EMTs. Died before they got him in the bus."

"That's awful." She pulled the blanket tighter. "At least he confessed."

"Yeah, for what little it was worth. He was shot with my gun."

"You shot him?"

"No. I was knocked out for a time, remember."

"I'm so sorry."

"Me, too. The civilians were killed with my gun, too. It was a mess. Just had Dom's word for what went down. There were no witnesses to corroborate his story. He told the EMTs one of the crew knocked me out, took my gun, and shot the place up, trying to pin everything on me. IA decided my partner and I were a team — Why else would I have been there? — and Dom was trying to protect me. Once again, they didn't have proof. But I only had my word. Which, at that point, didn't amount to much."

"You didn't lose your job, though."

"I lost my best friend!" He closed his eyes. "I lost my reputation, my credibility. Two civilians lost their lives."

"That wasn't your fault."

He sighed. "No. Not directly. Worse, most of the

department believes IA. And I can't prove I'm innocent. Won't ever be able to. Only thing that saved me was a GSR test. Came up clean. I never fired a shot that day. And still, most people think I'm guilty. I'm just lucky Davenport knew me and believed my version of the story."

"He didn't believe the accusations about my dad, either. Or at least he gave him the benefit of the doubt since IA couldn't prove their allegations."

"Davenport's a good man. That's why I trust him. I didn't want a partner when I transferred. Begged him not to make me work with someone else. Not after what happened. But he said he knew what was best for me and the department. I still protested, but he insisted. And I'm glad he did. You're a great partner, Chelsea."

Her face flamed, and she looked down at her lap. "Thanks, Jim. I think you are, too."

"I'll always have your back."

"I know that now. And I've got yours."

An awkward silence fell between them, broken only when he cleared his throat and stood. "Well, we have a big day tomorrow. Try to get some sleep."

"I will. Goodnight, Jim."

"Goodnight." He walked into his room then closed the door behind him.

After everything they'd shared, sleep probably wouldn't come easy. He was glad they finally trusted each other enough to share some of their deepest secrets, but telling his stories — even the abridged versions — had left him raw.

And even though he'd played devil's advocate for her benefit, he had to admit she might be onto something.

Cormac Sullivan wasn't just their prime suspect. He was their only viable suspect.

Chapter Thirty-Six

THE ME FINALLY DELIVERED FORENSIC reports from their second vic. Jim and Sullivan poured over data regarding the wolf mask, the wolf's head delivered in the mail, the tox screens, and all the DNA evidence collected at the crime scene. They only had preliminary information from the Gretchen Moore murder, but they could start comparing Brianna Lawson's case to Mariah Jones's in greater detail.

Jim took heart in the fact that none of the girls suffered a sexual violation. At least they'd been spared that. It was small comfort, considering they were stripped, killed, and posed as part of some twisted fantasy. But he'd take any bright spot he could find, no matter how small.

"Why no outside element for the third vic?" he asked.

"What?"

"Rapunzel had an open window. Little Red was found outside. Why no outdoor element for Snow White?"

She shrugged. "Maybe because she had 'Snow' in her name?"

It was as good a guess as any. Better than the big fat nothing he'd come up with.

Sullivan continued poring through the reports. "They were all injected with a drug called Succinylcholine."

"SUX? That's a paralytic. It renders the body incapable of movement. Including the diaphragm and lungs."

"I know. It doesn't make sense, though. Brianna Lawson died from asphyxiation, but it wasn't the drug that suffocated her. She was strangled by the braid. The drug just rendered her unable to resist or defend herself. The same is true of Mariah Jones. She bled out from the neck wounds, but she had to be paralyzed in order for the fake bites to be administered. Gretchen Moore also had the compound in her system. But she had cyanide, too."

"That makes sense. Snow White fell into her sleep because of a poisoned apple." He leafed through the reports. "And cyanide was found in the apple."

"But not enough to kill her. Not in one bite."

McPherson frowned and continued reading the report. "Here." He pointed to the middle of the page. "She had two needle marks. One in her neck — the SUX, like the other girls. But there was one between her toes. She wasn't a drug user, so that means the killer injected her with a second needle. The cyanide."

"Why go to the trouble? He poisoned the apple, so the myth was complete."

"Unless she didn't die from biting the apple. Maybe the amount in the apple wasn't enough. It was only one bite."

"Might not have been a bite of poisoned apple at all. Maybe he poisoned it after. Or maybe she wasn't even the one who bit it."

He looked at the report. "Stomach contents didn't show any apple."

"We should analyze the apple for saliva. Or maybe bite marks. If we can get dental records —"

"The apple will have rotted by now. The bite marks won't match."

"There's still DNA."

"MCU swabbed the apple at the scene. DNA matches the hair. But we have nothing to compare the samples to."

"Darn it. Every time I think we have something, it's another dead end." Chelsea scanned a few more pages. "The Snow White scene — lung and liver, both from a boar. Just like in the story."

"We knew they would be. He's been too careful about the details."

She flung her files onto her desk. "Yet somehow it doesn't soften the blow any."

"Are you sure you want to see this through? Given the situation, no one would think any less of you if you took a step back."

"And I thought you were glad I was your partner."

He frowned. "That's not what I mean, and you know it. I'm worried about you, Chels."

"I appreciate it. But this is my job, and I'm not letting him scare me away from it."

"All right. So what next? Are you up for more interviews?"

Before she could answer, one of the uniforms came through. "Mail's in." He dropped a small envelope on her desk and started to walk away.

Sullivan glanced at the label. Blood drained from her face as she looked up at Jim. "No return address, but the postage is from in-state. In town."

"Same handwriting?"

She nodded.

Jim grabbed gloves as he got up, then he walked around the desk to stand behind her.

As she reached toward the envelop, fingers trembling, he squeezed her shoulder. "Don't touch that. Not without gloves, anyway. That's evidence."

"Yeah. I know." She stretched past the envelope to a decorative box on the corner of her desk. After taking a pair of gloves from it, she slipped them on.

But Jim had lost patience and picked up the envelope. It was light, felt empty. But he knew better.

Sullivan stood and snatched it from him. "It came to me." She carefully opened the flap, but before removing the contents, she looked up at him. "Hey, this time it's an envelope instead of a box. We might be able to get DNA off of the glue."

"The techs will check for that. Now open it up. What's inside?" He leaned over her shoulder as she peeked inside, but all he saw was a slip of paper.

She turned the envelope over, then a needle fell onto her desk along with the page.

Jim expected another fairy-tale reference but couldn't connect the dots. "So?" He tipped his head toward the needle. "What's it mean?"

"Sleeping Beauty, unless I miss my guess."

"I don't know much about that one. Just that she slept until the prince kissed her and woke her up."

"Her name was Aurora. When she was born, she had seven fairy godmothers who intended to bestow blessings upon her. The first six gave her gifts of beauty, wit, grace, dance, song, and goodness. Before the seventh could give her blessing, Maleficent appeared, jealous because she wasn't invited. They didn't intend to slight her, but she'd been away for so long, they thought she was dead. Of course, she didn't give them a chance to explain. She offered a malicious blessing, or rather, a curse — Aurora would prick her finger on the spindle of a spinning wheel before her sixteenth birthday, then she would die. The final fairy used her gift to change the curse from death to a deep sleep.”

“Those Grimm brothers were sick folks.”

“They didn't make up the stories. They just gathered a bunch of folktales and printed them in one large collection.”

“Regardless, it's messed up.”

“Can't argue with you there.”

Jim jutted his chin toward the paper. “Give it a look. What's it say?”

After she unfolded the note, they read it together.

A blessing of beauty. The maiden is fair.
A blessing of song. But maiden, beware.
By needle-prick does your fate arrive.
There is no way you will survive.

“Well,” she said, “we just learned something.”

“Don't I fucking know it.”

“Did you catch it, too?”

His brow furrowed. “Why are you grinning?”

“Because he's using a modernized version of the story. The one with Flora, Fauna, and Merriwether.”

“Who?”

“In later versions of the story, there were only three good fairies. The note only mentions the first two gifts — beauty and song, which were Flora's and Fauna's — so we can safely assume he's using a later work.”

“And how does that help us?”

“Because … Huh. Well, I don't know exactly. But it's something.”

"That's what you got from the note?"

"Yeah. What did you see?"

"Shit." Jim kicked her chair. It slid across the floor then crashed into Norm's desk.

The old detective looked up. "Problem?"

Sullivan crossed the aisle then started pushing her chair back to her workstation. "Sorry."

The stoic detective just turned back to his work.

After she tucked the seat under her desk, she turned to Jim. "What was that all about?"

"I can't believe how naive you are."

"Excuse me? Now you're the fairy-tale expert?"

He ran his hand through his hair and started pacing in small circles. "He said 'you' in the note. This isn't about some random vic. He went from involving you as a detective to involving you as … "

"As his target. I'm next on his list. We already knew that."

"No. We suspected it. And even so, he chose another vic before you. But this is blatantly calling you out. We're putting you into protective custody."

"No, we're not."

"Damn it, Chelsea. Don't make me pull rank on you."

"Pull rank? Did you really just say that, *partner*? We've discussed this already. You're not my boss. We're both detectives."

"I have more experience. Learn from me. You're in danger."

"Then use me. I'll be bait."

He stopped in front of his workstation. This time he kicked his own chair, but it slammed off his desk instead of sliding across the floor.

She sighed. "Look, I appreciate the concern. I do. But

honestly? We don't *know* he's set his sights on me. It could be a poetic 'you' or a word designed to scare us."

"Or it could be that you're the next victim."

"I'm calling MCU. We'll have them process this stuff."

"Great. I'm going to talk to Davenport. Maybe he can talk some sense into you." Jim stormed away.

He'd be damned if he'd lose another partner on his watch.

Chapter Thirty-Seven

As McPherson walked away, Chelsea called the lab. They promised to collect the evidence immediately then start processing it immediately.

Before a tech came, she stared at the postage again. The date — it was when Dad was in the hospital. He couldn't have sent it!

Not unless he had an accomplice.

That was ridiculous. He was basically a hermit. And he hated everyone. Except for Grimes, who was in California.

Well, he had been in California. Chelsea had no idea where he was now. If he and Dad were working together, he could have flown back.

She needed to talk to her father. Needed to know. So she pulled her phone from her pocket and called him. Again, no answer.

Screw that.

As Chelsea jotted a quick note for McPherson, the tech showed up. After turning over the envelope, letter, and needle, she headed for the squad room. Since she didn't have a car, she left to find someone to drive her to her dad's house.

Luck finally smiled on her. Rafferty was the first person she saw. They'd gone to the Academy together, and while they occasionally flirted with each other, they had never been anything more than friends. Good friends. His back was to her, but he wasn't with his partner. And he didn't look like he was about to go on patrol.

"Hey, stranger."

After he turned, a huge smile crossed his face and lit his eyes. "Hey there, *Detective* Sullivan. How the hell are you?"

"So formal, Neil. Has it been so long that you forgot my name?"

In three long strides, he reached her, wrapped her in his arms, then picked her up in a breath-stealing hug. Once he put her down, he stepped back and studied her. "It has been too long, Chels. Got your big promotion, then forgot all about us peons on patrol."

"Better be careful, or I'm going to start calling you POP."

He cocked an eyebrow.

"POP? Peon On Patrol?"

Neil groaned and rolled his eyes. "So, what brings you all the way down to the squad room?"

"I need a favor."

"And you think calling me POP is the way to make that happen?"

"I'll bake you a batch of cookies."

"Oatmeal?"

"If that's what you want."

"Your recipe. The one with peanuts and raisins."

"Sure."

"Two batches?"

"I need a ride, Neil. Not a kidney."

He shrugged. "Can't blame a guy for trying. Besides, I think black market organs go for more than a pile of baked goods."

"You saying my cookies aren't worth a quarter mill?"

"I plead the fifth."

She laughed, then he joined her.

And they both knew she'd bake a double batch for him.

"To your chariot, milady." After Neil gestured to the door, they walked to the motor pool. "So, where are we headed?"

"Short trip. Just over to my dad's place."

They made small talk on the way. He asked about her new job, and she answered in generalities. It wasn't that she couldn't talk about the case with a fellow officer. It was that she didn't want Neil to worry if he knew which case she was on.

And how dangerous it had become.

They reached Dad's apartment in less than five minutes. Chelsea climbed out of the car. Before she shut the door, she leaned down to talk to him. "Thanks, Neil."

"No problem. Want me to wait for you?"

"That's okay. I'll probably be here a while."

"If you're sure." He shrugged and put the car in gear. "Don't be a stranger."

Chelsea shut the door and waved him off. She appreciated his concern, but it was unnecessary. She was just going to see her dad.

Well, she hoped it was unnecessary. If Dad was the killer, or working with him, she could be walking into a world of hurt.

Then again, would he be avoiding her if he wanted to

kill her? That didn't make sense. No, it was far more likely he was punishing her.

She hoped.

A quick scan of the parking lot showed his car in his reserved spot. It looked like it hadn't been moved in days. No tire tracks or footprints in the snow and the windows hadn't been scraped.

She walked inside, jogged up the stairs to his apartment, then knocked on the door. What a surprise — no answer. Then she tried the handle.

Darn it all, anyway. Why did he refuse to lock the stupid thing?

Chelsea slipped inside. He hadn't opened the blinds that morning, and the apartment was dark. The only light came from the television, which was blaring.

He wasn't in his chair.

It made no sense. He was always there.

The usual clutter littered the table and floor. She dodged the mess to walk around the back of his chair, then headed for the bedroom.

"Dad!"

No answer. Maybe he was napping.

She stopped beside the end table long enough to grab the remote. When she turned off the television, the silence was jarring.

Thud.

Her head snapped up. Did she really hear that, or was it a trick of her ears from the sudden quiet? Chelsea stood perfectly still, listening. Her heart raced. She heard nothing else, but as she waited, she grew convinced she hadn't imagined the noise. The sound came from down the hall.

Maybe Dad was in the bathroom. She didn't want to invade his privacy, but she was starting to get a sick feeling in her stomach. Perhaps he'd been drinking again and had fallen. Or he could have had an accident and was in and out of consciousness, unable to get to a phone.

Chelsea ran to the bathroom. The door was cracked open. She peeked inside.

Not there.

The only place left to check was his bedroom. Icy panic flooded through her. If he was in there and wasn't answering her, it likely wasn't out of spite. It was because he couldn't. Which meant a medical emergency. He could have had a stroke, a heart attack.

Might have OD'd again.

Any number of things.

She raced down the hall, flung open his bedroom door without knocking. He lay on his bed, curled on his side. Asleep? Passed out? Certainly in no condition to have made the noise she'd heard earlier.

"Dad?" He didn't move, so she pitched her voice louder. "Dad!"

Not so much as a flinch.

Chelsea walked over to shake his shoulder. His skin was cool, his breathing shallow. She flipped him onto his back.

Eyelids didn't even flutter.

She checked for a pulse. It was faint, but he had one. It was just like the other night, but this time no vomit, no booze bottles. She didn't see his medication in the room or even a glass of water, so she had no information to give the EMTs other than his current condition, which wasn't good.

Chelsea called dispatch to expedite the bus, all the while keeping her eye on the slight rise and fall of his chest. As soon as she ended the call, it stopped. No inhale, no exhale.

Tears streamed down her face as she started CPR.

When the EMTs arrived, they took charge. This time, she rode in the ambulance, watching her father for any sign of improvement. There was none. But no one gave up working on him.

At the hospital, a medical team met the EMTs. They didn't miss a single chest compression as they transferred care from medics to doctors.

She was ignored by all parties as Dad was rushed through the ER doors. No one told her anything. Not that there was anything to be said at the moment. He'd stopped breathing. His heart had stopped beating. Nothing had changed since she'd started CPR in his bedroom.

Chelsea was once again forced to wait for news of his condition. Only this time, she was all alone.

Chapter Thirty-Eight

CHELSEA GLARED at the clock on the wall, convinced the hands moved backward. The longer she waited without news of her father's condition, the more convinced she was that he had died. Or was dying. Or would eventually die from whatever the problem was.

She had begged him, pleaded with him, to take care of himself. He knew hospitals drove her crazy. And it was all his fault. She developed her irrational aversion to medical facilities of all sorts the first time he tried to kill himself — the intentional overdose when his divorce was final. Mom was already across the country, and Chelsea had been forced to deal with it alone. That's when she first nearly lost him. She hadn't been in a hospital since then. Not until the accidental overdose the other day.

And now, she was forced to go through it all again. This time, without even her partner to calm her fears.

She gagged on the cloying sweetness of the air freshener, on the acidic tang of the bleach and disinfectants. She cringed at every squeak of a shoe sole, every crackle of the PA system. Her back hurt from the uncomfortable chair, so she rose. Stretched her legs. Paced.

None of it made the time pass faster.

The ER doors swung open, then a doctor stepped into the waiting room. "Chelsea Sullivan?"

Just like the other night.

A chill raced up her spine, and her body trembled. When she spoke, there was a tremor in the lone word she managed to whisper. "Yes."

He crossed the room, then gestured to the chairs in the corner. "Have a seat, Ms. Sullivan. We need to talk."

Here they came. The words she always dreaded hearing. No matter how she steeled herself, she wasn't prepared. Perching on the edge of the chair, Chelsea affected her best stoic expression. Meanwhile, her insides roiled. She feared the inevitable and railed at the unfairness of it all.

"Your father is resting."

What? Resting? She shook her head. That didn't make sense.

"I know he was in bad shape when he got here. His heart had stopped, and from what I understand, a similar thing happened to him recently. Miss Sullivan, he should not be mixing alcohol and medicine. If he can't be trusted when he's on his own, perhaps he shouldn't be."

"I agree. And we had a discussion about him mixing alcohol and his medicine. But I don't think that's what happened here."

"He presented with all the signs of toxicity."

"That doesn't make sense. Last time, I found bottles and pills all around him. But this time, there was nothing in his apartment. I'd gotten rid of all the alcohol myself. And he hadn't left the house — his car hadn't been moved."

"Could he have walked somewhere? Called a cab? FASTr?"

Like Dad would ever pay someone to drive him somewhere when he could drive himself for free. "No."

"Are you certain?"

"He'd never call a service if he had access to a car. I'm telling you, he hasn't left the apartment since he came home from the hospital. And after I called for the ambulance, I looked around. There's no evidence of any alcohol anywhere. No bottles, no cans. So he didn't have it delivered, either."

"Well, I'll know more when his tox screen comes back. I don't know what it was yet, but I know he took something. If you could find out what, I could start a targeted treatment protocol. But until and unless we know what he took, there's little we can do. And time is of the essence."

"I'll go back to his place and look again. But I don't expect to find anything."

"Anything you can tell me will be of help. Check trash cans, hiding places. Even if you doubt something could be hidden somewhere, look anyway."

"I'll try." She knew there was nothing in the apartment, but she wanted to move the conversation along. "Can I see him now?"

"For a moment. We're about to take him to the ICU."

Seeing him quickly was better than not at all. Chelsea prepared herself, then she followed the doctor back to the ER bay.

JIM SAT AT HIS DESK, scrolling through open cases. But he could hardly concentrate. He was seven shades of mad. While he was in Davenport's office — for all the good that did him — Chelsea had snuck off to her father's apartment. Now, she wasn't answering her phone, and Sully wasn't answering his. Worse, neither of them was at his apartment, if they ever were. He'd driven there. The door was locked, no one answered, and there were no signs of activity inside.

Now, all he could think about was Sully's knowledge of fairy tales. His fascination with the case. Him possibly being the killer.

And him being alone with Chelsea.

He slammed his cup on his desk. Coffee sloshed over the rim. Muttering a particularly colorful string of expletives, he mopped his mess with a notepad. What the paper didn't absorb, he dabbed with his sleeve. Good thing he wore black today.

Just as he was about to click to the next file, something caught his eye. He studied the details of the case more closely and compared them to the three known Grimm Reaper victims. Allison Parker was killed in a neighboring county. She was in her early thirties, not her early twenties. She was found naked, but she hadn't been posed.

The clincher was where she was found and what was around her. Parker had collapsed in her kitchen — or it was made to look like she'd fallen there — in front of her oven, the door of which was open. One counter held a cooling rack full of cookies. Another held a loaf of bread. The heel had been cut off and was found clutched in her hand. She'd squeezed it until it crumbled.

Bread crumbs.

Sweets.

Oven.

Hansel and Gretel.

The ME had ruled the case as "possibly" natural causes. Said it could have been an aneurysm, but she'd have needed to conduct an autopsy to be certain. Unfortunately, the body had disappeared from the morgue before she'd had a chance, and no one ever found out how. They were lucky Parker had no family to sue them.

Jim didn't need the body to know the woman hadn't died from natural causes. She was an earlier victim of the Grimm Reaper. Possibly his first victim. It was certainly early enough that he hadn't honed his process. And maybe he'd been sloppy enough to have left behind a clue.

God, he hoped the evidence was all documented and accounted for. He called the detective in charge to ask for all the case files, all his notes. Anything else he had, no matter how seemingly inconsequential.

This might be just the break they needed to solve the case.

Chapter Thirty-Nine

Dad might be opposed to using a FASTr, but it didn't bother Chelsea. She called the service, and a few minutes later, her ride showed up. In no time at all, she was back at her father's apartment. She had to get the building manager to let her in, so she lost about five minutes. Which, in the grand scheme of things, wasn't so bad. But she was itching to get inside, so it felt like an eternity.

Soon enough, she was inside, searching for anything that might have had a negative interaction with Dad's medicine.

As expected, she found nothing.

She hadn't emphatically defended her father to the ER doctor because she couldn't be entirely sure she was right. When Cormac Sullivan wanted something, he found a way to get it. It had actually surprised her that he hadn't purchased more alcohol, if for no other reason than to spite her. But she'd been all through his apartment looking for him and hadn't seen any signs of whiskey, beer, wine, or any kind of alcohol. There'd been nothing. Not a single bottle or can. And he wasn't the type to hide the evidence in the trash, so he wouldn't be caught. If he was drinking, he wouldn't have cared if Chelsea saw the bottles. Might have even flaunted them just to make her angry.

So if it wasn't an overdose and wasn't natural causes, what the heck was it?

She began a methodical search of his apartment, this time looking for anything out of the ordinary in addition to drugs or liquor. Twenty minutes passed by. Thirty.

Then she saw it.

A copy of the original Brothers Grimm fairy-tale book.

It wasn't a first-edition like her copy. This one was soft-cover and well-worn. Probably purchased at a secondhand bookstore. Or he'd owned it for a long time.

The thought disturbed her, more than she'd like to admit.

What did he have it for? He had no young children, no grandchildren. This copy wasn't a first edition, wasn't a family heirloom. It should hold no sentimental value.

Then why?

Unless he *was* the serial killer. It was the only thing that made sense.

Maybe he had second thoughts about chasing her, taunting her, tormenting her.

Maybe he decided he didn't want to kill her but realized she'd never give up the hunt.

Maybe this was his way of telling her he respected her investigative abilities, knew she was onto him, and would bring him down.

She could see her father killing himself before going to jail.

But the postmarks. They didn't fit. One was from California —Dad could've asked his old partner to send it. But the second was local, and he'd been in the hospital on the day it was sent.

What was she missing?

Unless Grimes was in on it and had flown back to Steel City? She made a mental note to check on his whereabouts as soon as she got back to the station.

Her scalp tingled, and her heart dropped. The killer used SUX in all of his crimes. Maybe dad wasn't the killer.

Maybe he was a victim.

But SUX worked quickly. Dad was breathing when she found him. Shallowly, but he was breathing.

Only for a short time, though.

The thud.

Her blood chilled.

There had been a noise before she found him. She'd thought it had been him, falling or dropping something. But what if it wasn't? What if it had been the killer hiding from her?

What if he was still there?

He wouldn't be. What would be the point?

Unless he was waiting for her.

Chelsea drew her gun and approached the closet in the bedroom. She was going to check it earlier, but the last time she opened the door, an avalanche of clothes fell out. Dad wouldn't have hidden alcohol in there — he never would have found it again — so she'd put off looking in there.

But what if bottles weren't what had been inside?

She flung open the door, weapon drawn. The usual heap of clothes was there. But it sported a deep depression on the top, as though someone had been sitting on it.

A chill skittered up her spine.

The killer had been in the apartment with her. Had probably only drugged Dad moments before she had arrived.

And the sicko had locked the door when he left, knowing she'd eventually realize she hadn't locked up and someone had been there.

He was taunting her.

She called the hospital to tell them what to test for, then she called Jim.

They'd just cleared her father's name unless he did have a partner who double-crossed him. But instead of feeling better about the case, she felt worse.

Her father was nearly killed by the Grimm Reaper. And she was undoubtedly next.

CHELSEA PERCHED on the edge of her dad's bed, wincing while McPherson yelled at her. There really wasn't time for his lecture, but she knew he'd been scared for her and needed to get it out of his system. When he finally paused to take a breath, she jumped in.

"I know you're angry. And in some respects, you probably have a right to be."

"Some respects?" His eyebrows arched. "Probably?"

"But you were trying to get me off this case, and if anyone should be involved, it's me. While you were busy conspiring with Davenport, I found a clue."

"Found a clue? You nearly found yourself dead."

"No, I nearly found my father dead. If I hadn't gotten here when I did, he would've been."

He blew a long breath through pursed lips. "And I'm grateful for that. I really am. But like you said, you found a clue. One that indicates the killer was here at the same time as you. Do you understand the danger you were in? With no backup?"

"Rafferty drove me here."

"But you didn't fucking let him in! You were alone. At risk. You're lucky this SOB didn't attack you while you were here."

"That wouldn't make sense. That doesn't fit in with his fantasy."

"His fantasy is living out a twisted version of fairy tales. This time, with you as Sleeping Beauty. He wants to put you to sleep, Sullivan. For good. And you offered yourself up on a silver platter."

"You've already admitted you didn't know much about Sleeping Beauty. Let me clue you in on a few things. The princess's name? Aurora? That means dawn. And guess what — my name is associated with dawn because of the song 'Chelsea Morning.' Also, after Maleficent's curse, a good fairy put the rest of the realm to sleep, including the king and queen. That's why the killer poisoned my dad."

"After. You said the king was put to sleep *after* the princess."

"I know. But I think he's doing it out of order to taunt me. It's part of his game. He never follows the stories perfectly."

"Fuck, Chelsea. Don't you see? That's why I'm so mad at you. You put yourself in harm's way. And you're next. You've just admitted it."

"I know. And that's what's going to help us catch him."

Chapter Forty

JIM HADN'T TOLD Chelsea about the earlier victim he'd discovered. He'd been too angry. Now that he was calming down, he wanted to talk to her about it. Wanted to go through all the evidence with her. But first, Davenport needed to vent his frustration with her.

Couldn't blame the guy. His partner had a knack for driving everyone to drink.

Chelsea sat on the edge of her seat, suffering through the captain's lecture while Jim paced. At least she had the good sense to look chastened, though it didn't quite look genuine.

Not that Davenport seemed to notice. He was on a roll.

"I know you're new at this, Chelsea. But you're not new at being a cop. You know better than to go to a crime scene without backup."

She sighed. "I didn't know I was going to a crime scene. The first time, I was going to visit my father. And the second time, the hospital sent me. I was looking for something that might save Dad's life. If I had any indication the killer was there, I would have called the whole force. I want this guy more than anyone."

Davenport slapped the arm of his chair. "And that's the problem. You're too emotionally involved, too compromised."

Jim couldn't agree more.

"I respectfully disagree, Captain. It's my passion for the case that's going to get it solved."

"No, it's your stubbornness and naïveté that's going to get you killed."

"I have a plan, and it'll work. You've got to give me a chance to try." She looked at Jim. "Tell him it'll work."

"Oh, no. This is your harebrained idea. If it's so good, he won't need convincing."

Davenport leaned back in his chair and studied her.

"Come on, Captain." Jim stopped pacing, pressed his hands on Davenport's desk, then leaned over it. "You're not really considering this, are you?"

"Sit down, Jim."

A knock sounded, and all three of them turned toward the door. Norm poked his head in. "I know this isn't my case, but one of the techs dropped off a report, and he didn't want it getting overlooked."

Chelsea jumped to her feet and stretched out her hand for the paper. "What did they find? What didn't they want us to miss?"

Norm held the paper out of her reach as he walked past her to Davenport's desk. He passed the report to the captain, then he turned and touched her arm. "Your dad wouldn't want you in the middle of this."

She shrugged off his arm. "My dad would expect me to do my job."

He shook his head and sighed. "Not once you went from hunter to hunted."

"Thanks, Norm." Davenport lifted the paper. "Ask the techs to check everyone's phones. Might as well sweep the building, too."

"They're already on it." He walked to the door. "Said it should take about an hour. Asked me to get yours."

Davenport passed his cell over. Then he nodded at Chelsea and Jim. "Hand them over."

Chelsea was almost vibrating with a need to see the report, but she complied.

Jim took his from his pocket then tossed it to Norm. "Any idea how long it'll be? I'm waiting on some important information."

"Not sure."

"Have them check these three first," Davenport said. "And their desks."

"You got it." Norm left.

Chelsea looked at Jim. "What information?" Then she turned to the captain. "And what's wrong with the phones?"

"Techs just finished processing the evidence from all three vics. All their cell phones had been cloned. They're sending units to see if their apartments had been bugged."

"Cloned phones?" Jim said. "Do they know who did it? Or how?"

"Not yet." He passed the report across his desk.

Jim scanned it, but there was little to go on.

Chelsea leaned over his shoulder to read it, then she elbowed him. "And what information?"

"Evidence from an old case in Aldrin County. Found a woman in her house in Mission Station. It loosely fits the Grimm Reaper's MO, so I think it might be his first kill. Or there could be others even earlier. If I'm right, we found our serial killer's first victim. And something has made him escalate recently."

"That changes things." She faced Davenport. "It's more important now than ever that we catch this guy. You've got to let me try my plan."

He studied her, looked at Jim, then met her gaze and sighed. "All right, Chelsea. I'm inclined to agree with you. This guy has been ahead of us at every turn, and your plan might be the only one that will stop him."

Jim jumped to his feet. "Captain."

Chelsea leaped out of her seat, too.

Davenport held up his hand. "I understand your objections. But you'll be there. You've got her back, right?"

"Of course. But—"

She bounced on her toes and grinned at him.

Jim shot her a dirty look. "Fine. But I'm running the op. What I say goes, and I want a lot of safeguards in place."

Davenport nodded. "I agree."

That wiped the smile from her face.

"When you figure out the details, let me know what you've got. Dismissed."

Jim shot him a look then left.

Chelsea had rushed out ahead of him and was already at her desk. One of the forensics guys was there, waiting for her. He gave her a phone.

She took it, studied it, then looked at the tech. "This isn't mine."

"Yours was cloned. Here's a replacement, totally clean."

"It was cloned? How?"

The tech shrugged.

Jim nodded at him over Chelsea's head. "Do you have mine, Tyler?"

He rooted through the box he'd set on her desk then pulled out a phone. "Yours was clean. But remember, a lot of your correspondence was still compromised. Any phone call, text, or email between you and Detective Sullivan was visible to the cloner. Your desks are okay."

"Thanks." McPherson took his phone and put it in his pocket.

Tyler nodded.

"Can you give me Detective Sullivan's old phone, too?"

"Why? It's compromised."

"Just give me the phone."

"I don't have it. Talk to Devani in the lab." He picked up the box and walked away.

McPherson grabbed his desk phone.

While he was talking to Devani, Chelsea made a call. He heard her ask for a doctor in the ICU, but he couldn't hear what they discussed. They ended their calls at the same time.

"By the smile on your face, I assume it was good news," Jim said.

She nodded. "Barring any unforeseen problems, Dad's going to be okay."

"That's great news, Chels."

"Thanks." She took a deep breath. "So, are you getting the phone?"

"Not yet. Soon, she said."

"Why do you want it?"

"One problem at a time." He grabbed a pen from his cup holder and drummed it on his desk. "You know you don't have to do this, right?"

Chelsea lowered herself slowly into her chair. Her gaze was frosty, her voice laced with agitation. "Jim, we've been through this. The captain approved it. I'm not arguing anymore. What. Is. The. Plan?"

He tapped the pen louder, faster. "I still think it's a bad idea, but if you insist on being bait, then you'll be bait. We need to dangle you somewhere the killer can't pass up."

"My apartment. It's the obvious choice."

"I don't like it. Too many exit points."

"I have one door, Jim."

"Yeah, and one window with fire escape access. Plus, your building has a front door and a basement entrance. Too risky."

"Then what's your brilliant idea?"

He stopped banging the pen then threw it across the desk. "You know, if you were a little more concerned with your safety, I wouldn't have to be."

"So much for partners always having each other's backs." She crossed her arms.

"Oh, I've got your back. It's the rest of you I'm worried about. One of us has to be."

"You act like I'm not concerned about my safety."

"Are you? Any rational person would be. But instead of being cautious, you're putting yourself in the line of fire. It's reckless, dangerous. And not just for you. All of us watching you will be in jeopardy, too. But you don't care about that. All you care about is your first collar."

"How dare you?" She leaned forward and slapped the surface of her desk. "My dad was a cop. A darn good one. If anyone in this department can respect the well-being of fellow officers, it's me. Yeah, we'll all be in danger. But that's the job. And we all knew the risks going in."

"That's just it, Sullivan. We accept the risk because we manage it. But a sting like this? Especially with a rookie? Too many variables, too many unknowns. And the fact that it doesn't concern you only proves my point. You're too green to handle a job like this."

"Stop calling me a rookie!"

Jim had to give her that, at least. He kept saying it even

though it wasn't true, and on some level, he knew he was just doing it to push her buttons.

But, on another level, he genuinely was concerned. "You're right. I'm sorry. You're not a rookie in the technical sense. But you *are* a rookie detective. And this is a big case for anybody, let alone for a first case."

"I put in my years as a beat cop. I earned my detective's shield. I'm ready for this."

He stared at her for a long time. Finally, he stood and looked down at her. "We're not doing it at your apartment. Your dad's in the hospital, and the killer knows you'll be there to visit him. We'll do it there."

"Are you crazy? Talk about multiple exits. And civilians! My apartment is a much better choice."

"The hospital is perfect. We'll have your dad moved to an undisclosed room and put guards on him. I'll be in a bed, pretending to be Sully. You will visit him — me — alone. This is why I wanted your compromised phone. To discuss you taking time off to go to the hospital. That will draw the killer in, and then we'll get him."

"You don't look anything like my dad."

"That's the plan, Sullivan. Take it or leave it."

Chelsea clenched her teeth and glared at him.

"It'll never work. You're a generation younger than him. Ruggedly handsome where he's just rugged. Your hair is dark and thick, Dad's is gray and thinning. Your skin's tan and taut, his is pale and wrinkled. He's got dark, puffy circles under his eyes. You couldn't pass as my father in front of a blind man."

"You think I'm ruggedly handsome?"

She rolled her eyes. "I have an idea."

"Do tell." He winked.

"You're incorrigible."

"Thank you."

"It wasn't a compliment."

Jim smiled, though he didn't really feel like it. He'd tried to lighten the mood. And had succeeded. A bit. But it didn't take the edge off.

"Look, the killer will never believe you're my dad. Not when you look" — she waved her hands at him — "like this."

"I can't do anything about how I look."

"You can't. But I know someone who can."

Chapter Forty-One

Chelsea tried to ignore McPherson's grumbling the whole way down to the morgue. He must have been really angry because he didn't even try to charm Janice. Just waited, tapping his foot, until she announced their arrival and got Scott's permission to send them to go back.

"Chelsea, how nice to see you." Scott offered her a big smile. At least he seemed to be over whatever had made him angry the last time she'd seen him. Then the warmth faded from his face as he nodded at McPherson. "Detective."

McPherson grunted his reply.

Scott turned his attention back to her. "How can I help you today?"

"I'm glad you asked. We need your theater skills."

"I'm sorry. You need my what?"

"Your theater skills. Specifically, your makeup talents."

McPherson sighed.

Scott's brow furrowed. "What do you want, exactly?"

"I want you to make Jim look like an old man. Specifically, my old man."

He shook his head. "I don't understand."

"We have a plan to catch the killer."

"By making Detective McPherson look old?"

"The Grimm Reaper is now targeting me, and he's using Sleeping Beauty lore to do it."

"How do you know?"

"He sent me another letter. And he tried to kill my dad."

Scott jumped to his feet, rounded his desk, and pulled her into an embrace. "Oh, Chelsea. I'm so sorry. I've been so busy, I haven't had time to check-in. I should have been there for you."

"That's okay," McPherson said. "I was there for her."

Chelsea bristled. He was doing it again.

Scott released her, glanced at McPherson, then met Chelsea's gaze as he leaned against his desk. "You said 'tried' to kill your father. I assume that means he was unsuccessful."

"I got him to the hospital in the nick of time."

"Thank God."

She nodded. "Dad will be all right. But I want to use this to our advantage. If you can make Jim look like my father, I'll sit by his bedside. When the killer comes to finish the job, we'll get him. And Dad will be safe in a different room. Maybe not even in the hospital at all."

"Wait a minute. Your father doesn't fit the MO. He's not a young, attractive woman."

"It's not about women. It's about the story. In 'Sleeping Beauty,' Maleficent's curse put Aurora's family to sleep, too. The whole realm, actually."

Scott rubbed the back of his neck. He walked around his desk and took his seat, then he looked up at her. "Wait. All the citizens of her land were cursed, too?"

"I thought you knew fairy tales."

"Apparently, I don't know this one as well as I thought."

"It doesn't matter. This is about my dad. Or about Jim looking like my dad."

"No, I don't think so." Scott shook his head. "If what you say is true, the whole precinct is in danger. That's Aurora's — or your — realm."

"Huh-uh," McPherson said. "The killer injects his victims with SUX. No way he can inject a whole building of cops without getting caught."

"He's going to go after my dad again. I know it. That's why I need your help."

Scott stared at McPherson, tilting his head to view his face from different angles. "Yeah. I should be able to make you look old and weak without a problem."

McPherson's nostrils flared.

Chelsea grabbed his arm and squeezed it, then she tugged him until he sat in the visitor's chair. "I'm not worried about his body. It will be covered with the blankets. But his hair's too thick, too dark."

"I'm not fucking shaving my head."

"I could give him a bald cap."

"Dad isn't bald. He's actually got a lot of hair for a man his age. But it's graying. And thinner than Jim's."

Scott tapped his chin and continued staring at McPherson's face. "Chelsea, do you have a photo of your father?"

She took the phone from her pocket to pull up her photos, only to realize she didn't have *her* phone and shouldn't access her personal accounts from her burner, just in case. "No, actually, I don't. I'll bring you one tomorrow."

"How about you email it to me tonight? I'll start working on a sculpture of it at home, and I'll pour the mold for the mask so it's ready to go tomorrow. Actually, I should take a mold of Detective McPherson's head first. That will make certain my sculpted mask is a proper fit."

"We don't need it to be perfect," Jim said. "He's not going to see me up close until it's too late."

"I take my work seriously. A project like this, done right, will take a couple of days."

She shook her head. "We don't have a couple of days, Scott."

He sighed. "I don't like it, but I suppose I can do the sculpt on a generic form. It will take me longer to fit it, though. And then there's the wig."

Jim scowled. "I think adding a little powder to my hair will suffice."

Scott shook his head. "Suit yourself. But I don't want my name associated with this project. It'll ruin my reputation as a makeup artist. And I make no guarantees you'll look like the subject."

McPherson squeezed the bridge of his nose. "This is getting way too complicated. I just need a few creases on my face and a little gray in my hair."

"I wanted to do this tonight," Chelsea said. "Can't you just put some kind of putty on his nose to change the shape?"

"Even appliances take time. I need that photo — actually, photos from different angles would be best — and at least twenty-four hours."

Every second that ticked by could be the difference between catching the killer or him catching her. She hated to wait, but the plan didn't work without Scott.

"All right. Tomorrow morning, at the latest."

"I've got you covered, Chelsea. A little glue, a little blending, and I'll turn the detective into an old man."

"He's not *old*. He's sixty."

"Just get me the photos as soon as you can."

"Thanks, Scott." She smiled at him.

He returned it, then looked at McPherson. His brow furrowed, and the corners of his mouth turned down.

Jim muttered under his breath as he stormed out of the room.

Chapter Forty-Two

Chelsea sat beside McPherson at the kitchen island, picking at her dinner. He said he'd made chicken piccata because it was fast. She suspected it was just as likely he wanted to drink the remainder of the bottle of wine.

"You've hardly touched your food. Don't you like it?"

"It's delicious." Even though her stomach churned and her body thrummed with nervous energy, she tried to look calm and took a large bite. She hadn't lied — the chicken was succulent, tender. The capers gave it a briny tang, and the lemon juice provided a fresh brightness.

Didn't make it easy to swallow, though.

"Then what's the problem?"

She put her fork down and sighed. "I wanted to put things in motion tonight. I want this all to be over."

"Me, too."

"Maybe we could go to the hospital, visit my dad. We might get lucky and catch the killer breaking in."

"Absolutely not. He's got a twenty-four-hour detail. That'll have to be enough until we get there."

Chelsea toyed with her napkin. "What if tomorrow is too late?"

"We've got a good unit on your dad. I picked them myself, and Davenport agreed. Sully'll be fine."

"That's not what I mean. I know the guys will keep him safe. I'm just worried the killer will see the officers tonight without them noticing him. Then he won't come back."

"The guys are in scrubs. No one will give them a second glance."

"But what if—"

"Chelsea, stop." McPherson took his plate to the trash can then scraped it clean. He hadn't eaten much, either. "We aren't going tonight. We shouldn't be going at all."

"I'm not arguing about this again. You got your way. We're waiting until tomorrow."

"No, I didn't get my way. If I did, you'd be off the case and on your way to California to see your mother."

"That's hardly a way to keep me safe. We know the killer either has a connection in California or travels there sometimes. I'd be in more danger without backup. And there's no reason to endanger my mom and step-father."

"There's no reason to endanger you, either." He scrubbed his dish so hard, she feared it would crack. "There has to be another way."

"There is. Let's do the sting at my dad's. That way, we won't have to worry about civilian casualties. At least, not as many. And there are more hiding places for us."

"But it'll be easier to spot us."

"It's worth the risk."

Jim jammed the plate on the drying rack. "Whatever, Sullivan. I'm going to bed. Apparently, I have a big day tomorrow." He stormed to the bedroom then slammed the door behind him.

After Chelsea finished cleaning up the kitchen, she turned off the lights. Too keyed up to sleep, she sat and stared out the windows at the river. Dots of white twinkled on the water's surface, a pale reflection of the lights shining on the mountain beyond. The incline cars inched up and down the cliff, slowly ticking off time in ninety-second increments.

Morning would never get there at this rate. Or her heart would burst out of her chest before then.

She took a deep, calming breath then started the next count to ninety. Only about six hundred more passes until they put their plan into action. And she'd probably count every last one of them.

When the incline shut down for the night, she had counted two hundred trips up or down the hill. With nothing left to look at, she closed the blinds then lay down.

She continued counting to ninety — the numbers a soothing mantra in the otherwise still night — until she finally fell into a restless sleep.

Chapter Forty-Three

THE SIGNATURE BLEND of chemicals and bodily fluids that pervaded every inch of the morgue even reached Fletcher's office. The good news was Jim could no longer smell a hint of it. The bad news was he could barely smell anything with the prosthetics on his face. Just the occasional whiff of adhesive that held the mask on. And that was hardly better than the reek of disinfectant and death.

His face itched. He stared into a mirror. This was so much more elaborate than he'd wanted. Or was necessary. He reached up to scratch his nose — for about the fiftieth time — and once again, Fletcher slapped his hand away.

Chelsea stared at him in disbelief. "You look remarkably like Dad. Taller, of course. And broader. But to a stranger, you'd easily pass for him. Especially when you're tucked under blankets and viewed from a hallway."

Fletcher fussed over details Jim couldn't distinguish.

She touched his arm. "It's fine. He looks great."

"If you had let me take a mold of his head, I could have made it perfect. I could do it now and have the piece ready for tomorrow morning."

"No." She and Jim answered in unison.

"Okay!" Fletcher started putting his supplies away. "Do you need anything else?"

"This is more than enough." Chelsea turned her head to smile at him, but she couldn't tear her gaze away from her partner. "It's remarkable."

"It's not remotely my best work. If my theater group saw this, they'd replace me."

"Don't be ridiculous." This time, she did look at Fletcher.

He met her gaze with a smile. Or a grimace. Or something that moved his lips in a generally upward direction.

Jim couldn't have cared less. They weren't looking at him, so he seized the opportunity to scratch his nose.

"Thank you, Scott. This could be the difference in the case."

"I certainly hope so. I'm not comfortable with your partner using you as bait."

"I'm not fucking using her," Jim growled.

"No? Could have fooled me."

"Guys, please," she said.

"This is her crazy idea." Jim put down the mirror. "And for the record, I think it's a bad one."

Fletcher raised his eyebrows and looked at her. "You mean they didn't have to talk you into this?"

"No. I volunteered."

"Chelsea, if I had known how reckless this plan was, I wouldn't have agreed to help."

"Just because it's my plan doesn't mean it's reckless. It's not. It's a good plan. Solid. It'll work."

He scowled. "It's fraught with potential problems."

"Jim has my back."

Fletcher's scowl deepened. Jim didn't know if he was

happy to annoy the guy or if he was bothered by the two of them agreeing on something.

Probably a little bit of both.

Chelsea continued trying to convince the pompous ass, shutting Jim out of the conversation, which was fine with him. "Scott, don't worry. In addition to Jim, we have undercover units at the hospital. Eyes everywhere. I'll be fine. You just wait. When we get back this afternoon, we'll have the killer in custody."

Fletcher shook his head and turned to Jim. "I hope you know what you're doing."

Chelsea stepped between them. "That's enough. I have one father. I don't need two more." She put her hand on Fletcher's chest then pushed him out of her way. "Thank you for your help. And your concern. We'll let you know how it goes." Then she grabbed Jim by the wrist and pulled him toward the door.

"I can walk on my own."

Her burner cell rang. She looked down, stopped in the doorway, then dropped his hand. "It's the doctor, returning my call. I left this number for him yesterday. Took him long enough to call back."

"Answer it," Jim said.

But she already had and covered her other ear as she talked.

Jim and Fletcher stared at each other. Chelsea turned away from them, shaking her head.

"I guess I should thank you," Jim mumbled.

"Don't hurt yourself, Detective."

Jim sighed. After what had happened in the locker room, he couldn't afford a fight with someone else affiliated with the department. But man, he'd give anything to knock that smug bastard down a peg or twelve.

Chelsea ended the call then pocketed the phone.

"Well?" he asked.

"Dad's doing much better. He's awake, alert. Ornery as ever, so he must be feeling better. Nagging every nurse he sees to let him leave. Per our request, they've cleared one section of the fourth floor and are moving him there."

"Only a section?"

"They're pretty full. It was the best they could do. The name 'Russell Sheppard' will be on his door, so no one will know it's him. Dr. Abernathy and the head nurse are seeing to it personally and haven't told anyone else. Other than the administration, that is."

"Did they tell the unit we have on him, too?"

"They did. One of the officers went to check out the new room. The other is accompanying my dad as they move him."

"I want them to check in when your dad is settled." He took his phone from his pocket then sent a text.

"If you'd like," Fletcher said, "I can check on him while you're undercover."

"I'd appreciate that. Thanks."

"No," Jim said. "You're not on the cleared list of visitors, and I don't have time to get you added."

"I see." Fletcher crossed his arms.

"Thanks, anyway." Chelsea smiled at him. "Hopefully, this will all be over soon, and Dad can get out of there and go home."

"Great," Jim said. "Now, can we go?"

"Lead the way."

Jim couldn't get out of there fast enough. He strode to the door.

She waved goodbye to Fletcher, then preceded him into the corridor.

They made small talk in the car on the way to the hospital. He was far from cheerful but tried to keep the sharp bite from his tone. She had enough to deal with without his attitude.

When she lapsed into silence, he reached over and squeezed her hand. "I'm sorry about last night. I was just … I'm worried. But we've dotted all our I's, crossed all our T's. You'll be okay."

"I never doubted it."

And that's what he was afraid of. She had no doubts at all. Just reckless abandon. But he kept that to himself, too.

When they got to the hospital, Jim turned to her. "You remember what to do?"

"Of course."

"All the details?"

"Yes."

He took a deep breath. "All right. If you change your mind at any time, for any reason, just let me know."

"I will. But I won't."

He shook his head. "Give your dad my best. I'll see you soon."

"Soon." Chelsea headed for the elevator while Jim left to get into position.

CHELSEA KNEW she and Jim had to part ways to put their plan into action, but she felt oddly vulnerable when they did. No time to let doubts consume her, though. She'd had the chance and had been insistent on putting this plan into place. She'd talked the talk. Now she had to walk the walk. Literally.

So, she continued down the hallway alone.

When she reached her father's room, she tapped lightly on the door. "Hey, Dad."

"Chelsea." He brightened and scooted up in his bed. "Come in."

"How are you feeling?" She perched on the edge of his mattress and squeezed his fingers.

"Good, good." Dad looked down at his hand in her grasp. "I understand you saved my life."

A lump formed in her throat, so she nodded, though she wasn't sure he saw her answer.

"I owe you my thanks. I owe you my life."

She leaned down, hugged him. Allowed a sob to break free. He felt small in her arms, and she wondered if McPherson's hulking form would be a convincing body double.

Dad patted her back. "Shh. It's okay." He stroked her hair. "I'm fine. You'll see. It'll all work out."

Chelsea righted herself, then wiped the tears from her eyes. He was right. It would work out. And she'd see to that as soon as she left him. "I have to go back to work, Dad. But I'll come see you later."

"Don't come here. I'm going home."

"You're not well enough to go home yet."

"Well, I'm not staying here."

"Gotta go." She smiled and blew him a kiss. It was nice to see him back to his old self — even if his old self was impossible to deal with.

"I mean it, Chelsea. I'm leaving."

Little did he know he wasn't. The guards were already in the hall, and they'd never let him past the threshold without her authorization.

With one last wave, she walked out his door.

It was time to put her plan into action.

❧

FOR JIM, the hardest part of an undercover op wasn't the bust. It was waiting for the action to start in the first place. He didn't know what the hell Chelsea was doing, but he was getting restless.

No "getting" involved. He was restless. Lying motionless in bed wasn't as easy as it looked.

His phone rang. He glanced at the caller ID. Sullivan's burner. At least she'd used the right phone. He swiped his finger across the screen. "McPherson."

"Hey. It's me. I just left Dad's room. He's doing well."

"That's great news."

"Thanks. Listen …" She took a deep breath. "I know we had a plan, but I'm reconsidering. My dad's chomping at the bit to go home, and I'm afraid he's going to leave on his own if I don't take him."

"I didn't like your plan, anyway."

Chelsea sighed. "I know. But I'm not ready to give up on it. I just need to delay it. I want to take Dad home, get him situated. Once I'm sure he's okay, we can revisit this. Give me a couple days. Three, max."

"Forget it, Sullivan. I'm pulling the plug."

"You can't."

"Fuck yes, I can. Davenport put me in charge, remember? I've already done a shit-ton of prep for this doomed op. I'm not doing it again."

"Then we'll do it now. I'll tell Dad I'll bring him home tomorrow."

"No. You asked for a few days off. You've got them. By the time you're ready to come back, I'll have a new plan. Or better still, we'll already have this guy."

"Jim—"

"No. It's over, Sullivan. You're off the case."

"You can't do that."

"I just did."

"You're insufferable."

"Insufferable? I've been on my best behavior, but nothing's good enough for you. I cook for you, give you a place to stay. Changed my whole social calendar to accommodate you and your delicate sensibilities."

"Yeah? Well, I probably saved you a raging case of crabs."

"No, I've been dealing with a raging crab — you."

"That's it. I'm moving out. I'm going to stay with my dad for a few days, then I'm going home."

"Captain doesn't want you on your own."

"I'm not on my own. I'll be with a former cop. One I trust a hell of a lot more than you."

"Whatever. Make sure you're out before dinner. If I'm not babysitting you anymore, I plan on making up for lost time. Enter at your own risk. Unless a threesome interests you."

"You're disgusting."

"You're a prude."

She huffed.

"Go get your things. I won't be home for a while. On your way out, leave the key on the table in the entryway. And don't let the door hit you on the way out."

"Fine." She ended the call.

Jim stripped off the hospital gown, pulled on his sweatshirt. Slipped the hood over his head. Took a quick peek in the bathroom mirror — weird to see how he was going to look as an old man.

Satisfied with his appearance, he strode out of the room.

Chapter Forty-Four

"You mind waiting for me?" Chelsea asked the FASTr driver. "I won't be long."

"It's your dime."

She went up to the McPherson family's apartment, gathered the few things she had, then returned to the waiting car. "Now I need to go to the hospital."

"We were just there."

"And we're going back."

He sighed and put the car in gear. "Like I said, your dime."

Chelsea tried to look natural as she casually looked out the window. If they'd picked up a tail, she didn't notice. Again she took the phones out of her pocket, and after choosing the correct one, called the hospital. "Please have my father wheeled down to the lobby. I'll be there in seven minutes to take him home. Thank you."

"Seven," the driver said. "That's awfully specific."

"I clocked our time from the hospital, so it's an educated guess."

"I see. So, your dad sick or injured?"

"Injured, I guess."

"You guess?"

"Long story."

"Just wanted to be sure he wasn't contagious. I've got a big weekend lined up."

Why did people think random strangers cared about their plans? "Good for you."

He sighed. "Not much for small talk, are you?"

"I've got a lot on my mind."

"I bet you do. What with your sort-of-injured dad, and all."

Chelsea looked for a tail again. They were getting close to rush hour, and traffic was picking up. It would soon be difficult to notice a particular vehicle in the congestion. She wouldn't be able to relax until she was at her father's.

Who was she kidding? She wouldn't relax then, either.

When they pulled up to the main entrance of the hospital, she got out of the car and approached the doors. An orderly came out, pushing her father in a wheelchair. A tall nurse walked beside him, carrying a sack full of Dad's effects.

Chelsea nodded to them both. "Thanks for your help."

"Here you go." The nurse handed her the bag but didn't make eye contact. He was busy scanning their surroundings.

"I'll get him situated." The orderly helped Dad out of the chair and into the back of the car while Chelsea climbed in on the other side.

"All set?" the driver asked.

"Yes." She gave him Dad's address, then they were off. While he navigated traffic, she reached for her father's hand.

He gave hers a firm squeeze in reply but didn't speak.

When they reached the apartment, she paid the driver, gave him a generous tip, then asked for a receipt.

He took her bags from the trunk. "You going to be able to get him and all this inside by yourself?"

"I'll manage. Thanks."

The driver shrugged, wished her luck, then left.

Dad reached for her bags.

She grabbed his arm. "No. You can't. You're supposed to be recovering, remember?"

He rolled his eyes as he started to shuffle toward the door.

When she'd packed for McPherson's, she purposely didn't take a lot. But now, carrying her things plus the bag from the hospital, she appreciated Jim for carrying her luggage the last time.

Chelsea struggled to get everything inside but somehow managed. Her head was on a swivel, but she didn't see anyone. She whispered through gritted teeth, "Are you sure they're here?"

He gave a discreet nod.

"I don't see anyone."

That earned her a sigh and an almost imperceptible shake of his head.

She took a deep breath. Her nerves were shot. It all felt real now, and as much as she wanted people to think she was ready and able, she was terrified.

If any of the undercovers had missed something …

If the killer had gotten in before they'd set up …

If she kept nervously babbling and revealed the plan …

McPherson was right. Her initial plan had been risky. Reckless. Foolhardy.

His was better, though not by much.

Before they clocked out yesterday, the department had

done a sweep of every place Chelsea might be — her apartment, Jim's, his parents', her dad's unit, and his room at the hospital. They'd checked the station again, too. Her place was being surveilled, as was her dad's hospital room and his home. They found bugs in his lobby, the stairwell, and every room in his apartment. And they'd left them all intact.

It wasn't safe to speak. Rather, it wasn't safe to speak off-script.

She took a shuddering breath.

He squeezed her hand, and it buoyed her resolve.

Chelsea pitched her voice a little louder than usual to make sure the listening devices picked her up. "Almost there, Dad. Then we'll get you to bed."

He looked at her and rolled his eyes again, then he grumbled something unintelligible to stay in character.

By the time they got to the door, her arms ached from lugging the bags, and her heart thudded in her chest — equal parts exertion and fear. She unlocked the door, then the two of them stepped inside.

The apartment was in the same squalid condition she'd left it in when she found her father. Thinking crime techs had been there, sweeping for listening devices and judging her father was painful and embarrassing. Dad would hate knowing it. But he always said, "Anything for the greater good."

Of course, it was that attitude that got him in trouble with Internal Affairs.

She set her luggage down then rooted in her bag for a notebook and pen. "Come on, Dad. Let's get you to bed."

Once they were in the bedroom, she scrawled a note. *Where are the units?*

He took the pen from her and jotted his reply.

Two across the hall. Two in an unmarked in the lot. We have eyes on the front and back doors from other buildings.

She nodded. It would be better if someone was in the bathroom or closet, but the slightest noise might give them away, so this was the best they could do. Besides, she had McPherson. He was all the backup she'd need.

He offered her a tight smile as he climbed into her dad's bed. It was kind of disturbing. The makeup had transformed him into an older man — like her father, but not. It was proof that he'd be dashing well into his golden years.

No, he didn't really look like her dad, but he had been aged about twenty-five years, and that would be good enough. Regardless of who he looked like — or didn't — the makeup job was amazing. She *knew* there was a young man under it, but it was next to impossible to tell. And with the dim lighting, the killer would be fooled into thinking it was, in fact, her father. At least until he got close. And by then, it would be too late, and he'd be snared in their trap.

As long as she didn't blow it.

McPherson tipped his head toward the door.

Time to play her part. Chelsea cleared her throat. "I'm going to clean up, then I'll bring you some soup."

McPherson winced and shook his head.

Okay, so she was a little too loud and annunciated a little too much. Scott would be horrified at her acting abilities. She'd never be a thespian.

But she could do this.

The script they'd devised called for her to do "daughterly" things. That was a role she knew well. Chelsea began tidying, sorting. Cleaning and scrubbing. Dirty clothes were thrown in the laundry, and dirty plates were stacked in the dishwasher. When the kitchen surfaces had been scoured until they gleamed, she put a pan on the stovetop then opened a can of soup.

She hoped McPherson liked Bean and Bacon. It was all Dad had left in the cupboard.

Scratch that. She hoped the killer would come now. They could dine tonight on steak, lobster — whatever Jim wanted. It would be a celebration fit for kings.

But no one showed.

Jim glared at her when she gave him the soup, but he began spooning it up. His expression was priceless.

She stifled a laugh and began making mundane small talk. "If you get a good night's rest, we'll see about sitting in the living room tomorrow. At least for a little while. There's probably a Seals game on."

He grunted and slurped the thick broth. When he was finished, she took the bowl from him and left the room. She cleaned up, checked on him again. Said goodnight, then watched a rerun of *Bones*. When the murder mystery had her nerves frayed, she put on Food Network. Bobby Flay was on. It made her think of Jim, which almost made her smile.

Almost. It was impossible to smile with so much at stake.

Where was this guy? He had to know they were there, they were vulnerable. Why wasn't he attacking?

Despite her nerves, her eyelids began to droop. She'd barely slept the night before, and it was catching up to her. Chelsea rose, stretched, walked into her dad's bedroom.

McPherson lay there, staring at the ceiling and drumming his fingers on the mattress.

She scribbled another note.

Getting tired. Going to make coffee. Want some?

He shook his head.

She grabbed the pen again.

Do you think he'll show?

Again, he shook his head.

Chelsea frowned. This could drag on for days. And she was already stir crazy.

Need anything?

This time, he reached for the notebook.

Get some sleep. You're driving me crazy.

She waved goodnight then retreated to the living room. The couch would be more comfortable, but she sank into the recliner then propped up her feet. It was like a hug from her father.

And with that image, she succumbed to sleep.

CHELSEA WOKE to a sunbeam laser-focused on her eye. She jerked her head aside and squinted into the light. Dust motes floated in the bright stream.

Dad's apartment. The plan!

She jumped to her feet then dashed to the bedroom. McPherson leaned against the headboard, his gaze flittering around the sparse room. He looked at her when she entered and raised his eyebrows.

"Morning, Dad. How'd you sleep?"

He grunted.

Chelsea was pretty sure that wasn't an in-character reply. The tone of disgust was all Jim.

"How about some scrambled eggs and dry toast?"

Jim grabbed the notebook and pen.

How about we chalk this up to a giant bust and go out for breakfast?

As much as she'd love an omelet and a cinnamon roll, it wasn't the time. She took the pen from him.

One more day. I know he'll come today.

He rolled his eyes and shrugged.

Chelsea went to the kitchen and started breakfast, convinced the killer would come by day's end.

JIM DIDN'T THINK he'd ever been so miserable spending two days in bed with a beautiful woman at his beck and call.

Sullivan had been so sure the plan would work. But she'd been wrong. The killer never showed. And despite her asking for one more day, he'd been all too eager to end the sting.

He stood in the parking lot, barking orders at the uniformed officers who had participated in their failed op. She stood off to the side, a forlorn look on her face, dragging her toe across small mounds of snow and watching them melt under the heat of her boot.

Jim had never seen her look so miserable.

When he was done giving everyone their new instructions, he turned to her. "We tried it your way. I'm sorry it didn't work. I really am. But I can only stay in this disguise for so long, and I've well exceeded my limit. We need to try something else."

"One more day. Just one. I know we'd get him."

"Get in the car."

He hopped into the driver's side. She shuffled her feet but finally climbed into the passenger's seat.

Jim pulled out of the lot, drove down the road, then turned onto a private drive that led to a now-vacant home of a former university big wig. He stopped in front of the house then put the car in park.

"Just one more day," she begged. "It's not too late."

"God, no. No more." He ripped the mask off his face

to the sound of her frustrated sigh. After he got the main prosthesis off, he pulled down the visor then stared into the mirror, picking at the remnants of glue on his cheeks and forehead.

"I guess you've decided, then." She huffed and crossed her arms.

"Damn right, I did." He shoved the mask toward her face. "Smell this."

She recoiled.

"All this shit is hot, and it fucking stinks. I'm done."

"Then I'll wait there myself. Or back at my place. Maybe if the killer knows I'm alone, he'll come."

"Absolutely not. We're both going home, cleaning up. Getting some rest. Everyone has orders to regroup tomorrow at the station. Maybe the captain will have an idea."

"I'm not going home. I'm not tired, and I'm not convinced it's safe there. They found bugs at my place, too. Remember?"

"Of course, you're not going to *your* home. You're coming with me to my home. Well, to my parents' place."

She shook her head. "It's been two days since I checked on my dad. This whole time, I couldn't call the hospital because he was supposed to be with me. If we're not continuing the operation, then I'm going to see him."

"Davenport would have told us if there had been a problem."

"I need to see him."

"Fine. I'll come with you."

"That's okay. It's perfectly safe. We've got a unit on him. And it's broad daylight. I'll be fine."

He grasped her shoulders then turned her, so they sat face-to-face. "Chelsea, there's a good chance the killer didn't come because he didn't believe what he was hearing.

Do you understand the implications? That means he's got a close eye on you. And you're in danger everywhere."

She pulled back, wrinkling her nose. "No offense, Jim. But it's not just the mask that smells. You need a shower."

"Well, you were able to bathe at your dad's. In my defense, I wasn't allowed to move for two days."

"Then how'd you work up such a sweat?"

"Frustration with my partner."

She scowled at him. "Regardless, I'm going to visit my dad. I need some time with him. I'll see you tomorrow at work."

He flung his hands in the air. "And where do you plan on spending the night?"

"I'm staying at the hospital as long as they'll let me. When visiting hours are over, I'll grab a hotel room nearby."

"Don't be ridiculous. I'll drop you at the hospital. After I go home and shower, I'll come back for you."

"I won't be done with my visit by then."

"No rush. Visit as long as you'd like. I'll feel better knowing there's someone else watching you."

"That sounds creepy."

"You know what I mean. Now, come on. I do need a shower. I feel disgusting."

They made small talk on the way to the hospital — nothing about the case — and before he knew it, they'd arrived.

"Thanks for the ride. I'll see you later."

"I'll be back soon." But he was speaking to a closed door.

~

CHELSEA WAVED to him from the hospital door. Neither of them moved, then he beeped the horn.

Okay. He was waiting for her to go inside. It was frustrating. Considerate and smart, but frustrating.

She entered the hospital, then rode the elevator to the fourth floor. Chelsea had never seen a ward so empty. No one was at the nurses' station. No one was in the halls. Neither of the undercover officers was outside Dad's door. She headed down the corridor toward the room where "Russell Sheppard" was resting. Her spine tingled.

God, how she hated hospitals. The deserted floor only added to her dread. She knew that wing had been evacuated in order to protect her father, but her footsteps echoed, reverberating back to her, each *click, click, click* of her shoes on the floor reminiscent of a death knell.

Halfway to her father's room, someone called out. "Excuse me. You're not supposed to be here." The man spoke with an English accent. His voice was a balm to her frazzled nerves even though he was trying to shoo her away.

Chelsea moved her jacket aside to show the shield clipped to her belt. "I'm Detective Sullivan. I'm here to check on my father."

"Oh, sorry. I didn't realize." He walked toward her. "I'm Dr. Phillips. I've been taking care of your father."

"Dr. Phillips? I thought he was seeing Dr. Abernathy."

"We're partners."

She stared at him. There was something familiar about him. Something in the eyes, or maybe his profile. Must have seen him in the ER.

"Unfortunately, Dr. Abernathy had a family emergency. I'm filling in for him."

She knew all about family emergencies. "Oh. That's

too bad. About his family, I mean. I hope everything's all right."

"I'm given to understand everything is working out well."

"That's good." Chelsea wanted to be polite, but her thoughts were on her father. "If you'd excuse me. I'd like to see my dad."

"Of course. If you have any questions, I'll be in the other wing, making rounds."

"One thing … do you know where his security detail is?"

"They were there the last time I was in the corridor. Maybe they stepped into his room?"

"I'm sure that's what it is." But she wasn't. "Thanks." Chelsea turned and started down the hall. Something pricked the back of her neck, and she looked behind her. Dr. Phillips stood there, syringe in his hand. "What …"

"Good night, Chelsea."

Her vision blurred, grayed. Then her world faded to black.

Chapter Forty-Five

JIM WASN'T sure a shower had ever felt so good. He could have stayed under the spray for an hour, but he had a feeling Sullivan was going to do something stupid, and he wanted to get back to her before she did.

If he couldn't stop her, at least he could be there to back her up. And since he didn't know what stupid thing she was about to do, his only recourse was to be there before it happened. Or at least during.

Towel slung around his waist, water dripping from his hair, he stood in his bedroom — his, not the bedroom at his parents' place, since it was much closer to the hospital — and checked his phone. No message from Sullivan, of course, but there were two others. One was a voicemail from Naylor, the detective who'd worked the Allison Parker case. The other was a colorful text from Davenport. Neither he nor his partner had checked in, and the captain was equal parts worried and pissed off. He also wanted answers about an anonymous report he'd received regarding a beatdown of three beat cops in the locker room.

Fucking Thompson probably ratted him out.

At least there was no mention of the bullet graze, not that *that* was his fault.

Probably should call the station first, but if he could report something positive when he checked in, it would go a long way toward easing tensions. So, he dialed Detective Naylor.

"McPherson, I'm glad you called. I didn't really want to leave this information in a message."

"Sorry I missed you earlier. You have something for me?"

"Yeah. Listen, our ME is a good person, but she's overworked and understaffed."

"Ours, too." He thought about Fletcher and tried to keep the contempt out of his voice. "They all are."

"I know. I just … I don't want you thinking less of her because of it. Or filing some kind of report or—"

"Naylor, you guys are doing us a favor. We all want to catch this guy. I have no reason to throw your ME under the bus."

"Okay. Good."

"So, what do you have?"

"I told you the body was stolen. Meredith — that's our ME — still had some tissue samples. But with no body and no family and no pressure from anyone, the case got set aside in favor of more pressing matters."

"It was a murder case. What's more pressing than that?"

"All the other murder cases. We had five more at the time, all with bodies and families and—"

"I'm sorry. I understand." Sort of.

"Well, anyway, when you called about Parker, I talked to Merry. Told her what you were dealing with. She ran the samples she had, and they tested positive for SMC."

"What's SMC? And how does it relate to my case?"

"Hang on." The sound of rustling papers came through the phone. "SMC stands for succinylmono-choline." He sounded the word out slowly. "It's a metabolite associated with SUX."

SUX? That was another promising link to the Grimm Reaper. "What's a metabolite?"

"Has something to do with how the drug breaks down in the body. SUX doesn't stay long, so it's really hard to test for. If I understand correctly, it turns into SMC and some other stuff, which last longer. So, there's a good chance my vic and yours were dosed with the same thing. Yours were just found closer to the time of death."

"Do you know how long SUX stays in the system?"

Nothing but silence greeted him.

"Naylor? You there?"

"Yeah. Listen, I think you need to talk to a forensic pathologist."

"I will. But tell me what you know."

He sighed. "It can be gone in minutes."

Then how could the reports show SUX in the blood of all their vics?

"I'm sure it's just someone extrapolating, McPherson. Telling you it had to have been SUX because the vics were found with SMC in their blood."

"You're not supposed to speculate on the reports. You can draw conclusions for the jury, but the evidence needs to be accurate."

"I know."

"It's not like our crime lab to make that kind of mistake."

"Well, you should check the name on the report."

"I will. Someone needs a serious talking to."

"It's not just that."

"What?"

Naylor sighed. "Merry gave me the visitor logs for the night Parker's body went missing. Everyone was interviewed, of course, and everyone had alibis, reasons to be there, and no obvious reasons for tampering with evidence or stealing a body."

"But?"

"But … I hate to tell you this, but one of the names on the list is going to be very familiar to you."

CHELSEA'S EYELIDS FLUTTERED OPEN. Her head was foggy, her limbs heavy. Felt like she'd been hit by a Mack truck. She glanced around the room.

Where was she?

Wherever she was, it was freezing. Unless coldness was a side effect of whatever she'd been dosed with.

She tried to sit up but found herself unable to move. Thrashing and bucking got her nowhere. Despite having control over her body, which was proof she wasn't drugged or paralyzed — small consolation — she was restrained.

Her wrists and ankles were bound, each tied to a tall spindle on an elaborate four-poster bed. The mattress was soft, the sheets luxurious. A brocade comforter woven with metallic threads was folded near the footboard, but no matter how much she wanted to huddle under it, she had no way of doing so.

The walls in the cramped, windowless room had been painted a lustrous gold, and on them hung large pieces of art, their placements meticulously measured — each frame hung at exactly the same height, and all were equally distributed around the room.

Chelsea would have rubbed her eyes to clear her vision

if her hands were free. The flame of every candle — and there were dozens of them giving off overpowering scents of cinnamon and pine and freshly baked pie — was surrounded by a glaring halo. She blinked rapidly then squinted. Soon she was able to make out minute details. Her blood chilled as it pumped through her veins.

Fairy tales. Each frame housed an intricate painting of a fairy tale scene. Cinderella, Beauty and the Beast. Rapunzel, Little Red, Snow White.

Sleeping Beauty.

Her heart raced, and she yanked harder at her bindings. They didn't give at all. She was stuck there, at least until the killer came for her.

Chelsea took a few deep breaths, trying to center herself. If she couldn't keep her wits about her, she'd never get free. What did she know so far? She had been drugged, but not with SUX. Or it had been a small dose and had already worn off. She still had her clothes on, so she hadn't been sexually assaulted, not that the Grimm Reaper raped his victims. And because she was still dressed, he likely wasn't ready to kill her yet. Her abductor was the doctor from the hospital — Dr. Phillips.

Phillips. Why didn't she realize that sooner? Phillip was the name of the prince in "Sleeping Beauty." Another clue, just like all the packages and notes. But she hadn't figured it out. Not in time, anyway.

The doctor had looked familiar. She assumed it was from seeing him at the hospital, but maybe it wasn't. Maybe she had come across him at a crime scene.

Chelsea searched her memory for any inkling of him. Was he someone they had interviewed? Someone in the crowd?

The hair on the back of her neck stood. She knew where she'd seen him. The cargo van in the O'Connor security tape. His features had been hard to make out, but she was sure of it now that she had a real person to compare to the image on the video.

Relief washed through her. At least she was now absolutely certain her father wasn't the killer.

Dad!

Had the killer gotten to him, too?

"Hello?" she called. "Hello!"

The knob turned, then the door opened with the smallest squeak of the hinges. Dr. Phillips entered and approached the bed. "Finally, you're awake."

She stared up at him. "My dad. Is he …"

"Your father is fine."

Relief enveloped her. She closed her eyes and vented a slow, deep breath. A droning sound bothered her ears, set her teeth on edge. It escalated and got louder until she swore she felt it vibrating around her. Then it slowly faded away.

"Where is he? My dad?"

"Don't worry about him. He was a means to an end. A clue, nothing more. His life or death is immaterial to me."

"It's not to me."

"He's still at the hospital. With his guards."

"I didn't see any of them."

"I'm sure someone will find them. Eventually."

"What did you do?"

"Stop asking about him," he snapped. "He's fine."

"Who are you? Why are you doing this?"

"Who am I? You mean you still haven't figured it out?"

She shook her head.

"Not even a guess?"

"Do I know you?"

"Oh, yes. Quite well."

Someone she knew. Someone who recently experienced a trauma — the trigger that spawned the killing spree. Someone clever and with considerable means to pull off his crimes.

He shook his head. "And I thought you were a better detective than this. Or maybe I'm just that good."

"What?"

He reached up and clawed at his face.

Makeup. A prosthetic mask, just like the one Jim had worn. Just like—

Oh, God.

Her stomach roiled, and she closed her eyes.

Chapter Forty-Six

"Come, sweet Aurora. Open your eyes and feast upon the visage of your Prince Phillip."

Part of her wanted to keep her eyes shut forever, to stay locked in her mind where she couldn't get hurt no matter how dark her thoughts were. But the other part, the detective part, needed to face her attacker. She opened her eyes and met his gaze. "Why, Scott?"

"Why?" His voice changed again, not the rich timbre of the thespian nor the sophistication of the British doctor. Not even the warm sound of the ME she'd grown fond of. His tone took on an effeminate quality — soft, creepy. Kind of like a menacing Mr. Rogers. He even had on the cardigan and sneakers. "I should think it obvious. You're my Sleeping Beauty."

She scoffed. "Sleeping Beauty? In case you haven't noticed, I'm wide awake. And unlike Aurora, I fight back."

"Don't be that way, darling." He ran his knuckles over her cheek, down to her jawline, then across her collarbone. "Sleeping Beauty is delicate, fragile. Docile."

"Then you picked the wrong girl. I'm anything but."

"You're wrong, my dear. I've been watching you for weeks. In fact, I daresay I know you better than you know yourself."

If her heart hammered any harder, it would burst right out of her chest. She rode the adrenaline spike and lashed out. "What's the matter, Scott? Did the girls find your fascination with fairy tales weird? They kept shooting you down, so you got them in another way?"

"If you're trying to get a rise out of me, you won't."

"A rise? I doubt you're capable of that. None of your victims were sexually assaulted."

His face darkened. He loomed over her, bent down to peer into her eyes. His breath was hot on her cheeks. "None of my projects has been about sex. And I don't intend for this one to be, either. You're to be my masterpiece."

As he admonished her, spittle shot from his mouth and landed on her face. She cringed and tried to turn away from him, but he grasped her chin and roughly turned her head so she was facing him.

"Keep playing your psychological games, Aurora. It only makes my work sweeter."

Okay. New tactic. "Is this about your family? About your mom and dad?"

He straightened and stepped away from her. When he spoke, his voice had an edge. "Ah, yes. Now we're getting somewhere. Go on. Weave your psychological profile of me, Detective."

"What you told me was true, wasn't it? This is all about little Scotty having a rough childhood. What is it? Your only fond memory is of being read fairy tales when you were a boy?"

He sneered. "See? I told you. You're a better detective than you give yourself credit for."

"Did your father torment you with the stories, too?"

"My father? Ha. That's rich. My father was nothing more than a pathetic cuckold, sniveling at my mother's feet. She, on the other hand, was the one with all the power."

Chelsea tried to play the role of the demure female he wanted, hoping it bought her time — and maybe enough goodwill — to get free. She spoke softly to him. "What happened, Phillip?"

"What happened? Where to begin?" He sat on the edge of her bed, reached for a lock of her hair, then let it trail between his fingers. "Silky."

Dad had no conditioner, and his shampoo had left her hair dry and brittle and smelling like the forest. But who was she to argue with her captor? "Thank you. So, you were telling me about your family?"

"You asked me once if I had siblings. I don't. But I did. I was a twin."

"I'm sorry. What happened to him?"

"Her. We were fraternal twins, though we looked nearly identical. Mother preferred her to me. Preferred girls in general, I believe. She dressed us alike. Frilly dresses, with lace and ruffles. Patent leather Mary Jane shoes with eyelet-trimmed bobby socks. We were pretty. I dare say I was a smidge prettier than Susanna."

Dear God, please don't let my horror show on my face.

"Would it surprise you to learn she clothed me in dresses until I left for college? That I was forced to wear my hair long and curled and tied up with a bow?"

She blinked back tears. Swallowed bile.

"I was homeschooled until college. That's the first I was allowed to be her son. I cut my hair short, trimmed my nails low. It was the first time I ever wore pants. I found they weren't as comfortable as I'd hoped."

"I'm sorry," she whispered.

"Do you know the story of Hansel and Gretel, Aurora? The real version?"

Chelsea sucked in a breath, fearing the story he was about to tell and praying he'd spare her the details. "I do."

"It was a time of great famine."

He was going to tell her. "You don't have to, Scott."

His head whipped up. His heated glare burned into her. "It's. Phillip."

She reached for him, though she couldn't move her arm. "Yes. Of course. Phillip. I'm sorry."

"You're sorry. You're sorry. Sorry, sorry, sorry. Where have I heard that before? Oh, right. Nowhere. Never. Not addressed to me. Mother told Susanna, but never me." He rose. Paced. Ran his hand through his hair. "Where was I? Ah … the story. A time of great famine. The mother abandoned her children in the woods."

It was a stepmother. Not that it mattered.

"The kids found their way back home following a trail of pebbles. People think it was breadcrumbs, but it was pebbles."

It was ashes. But she nodded her agreement.

"When they got there, the mother killed the boy and made the girl cook him for their supper. It wasn't a wicked crone in the woods. It was the *mother*."

Stepmother.

"And she killed her own son, so she, her husband, and her daughter didn't starve."

This far was bad enough. But what came next used to make Chelsea's stomach roil every time her father read it to her.

"The girl obeyed, of course, because good little children honor and obey their mothers. But she couldn't destroy her brother's tender heart. So, she hid it in a hole in her back yard, covered with thatch."

It was in a tree.

"That night, she was too sick to partake of the meal, but her parents dined like royalty. When they had finished, she took her brother's bones and buried them with his heart."

She'd put the bones in the same tree.

"The next day, a myna bird popped out of the hole and accused the boy's mother of murdering him and feeding him to the family."

It was a cuckoo. Chelsea remembered that detail vividly because there was a cuckoo clock in the hallway, and it always freaked her out to hear it. She didn't learn until she was older that cuckoos can't mimic human speech.

"The mother threw a rock at the bird. But he caught it, threw it back, and killed her with it."

It was a lump of salt that she threw up into the tree at the cuckoo. And the bird didn't catch it and throw it back. She missed hitting it, and gravity did the rest.

"I told you this story, Aurora, so you would understand."

"And I do. You don't have to say more."

"No? I don't have to tell you that my mother confused me with my sister and killed the wrong child? She made my father butcher Susanna like a suckling pig, made me roast her over a spit in the back yard? I don't have to tell you that she made me and my father dine on Susanna for a week? That as I sat at the table, choking on my sister's flesh, my mother celebrated the demise of her wretched son. She gnawed every morsel of meat off what she thought were my seven-year-old bones with a satisfied smile on her face, then licked her fingers clean? You don't want to hear any of that? Maybe

I should skip all those details and go right to my punishment when she realized she'd killed the wrong child. Would you like to hear that? It makes for a chilling bedtime story."

Chelsea's stomach churned. Her abject fear and desperate fury were replaced with a deep-seated sympathy for the little boy who had been damaged and tortured at so young an age. She looked up at him. "Scott, I am so, so sorry."

"It's Hansel!" He cleared his throat. Straightened his hair, his clothes. Took a deep breath. "It's Phillip."

"You deserved better. But what happened all those years ago doesn't need to color what you do now. You deserve a happily ever after. You don't have to do this."

"Oh, but I do, Aurora. This world is imperfect, impure. Finding any innocence is a rare treat, an occasion to celebrate. But after the initial wonder of such a precious discovery, it's my duty, my moral imperative, to preserve it. At all costs."

"You want to preserve me by killing me?"

"It's the only way. I must grant you safe passage from this realm before the evils of society corrupt you. You're already being negatively influenced by your lecherous partner. I have to save you from the evils of the world. Set you free before you succumb to earthly temptations. Release you from the filth and depravity of this mortal coil."

The guy was completely mental. "There's a flaw in your reasoning. I'm not innocent, not perfect. You're trying to preserve a condition that's fictional."

"You're wrong, Princess Aurora. You are a beacon of purity. But you're on the brink of corruption, and I must save you. In the short time I've known you, I've learned so much about you. About your duty to family, your commitment to society. Morning through night is spent in service to your subjects. You have no vices — you don't swear, smoke, drink. Or you didn't, until recently. Until Jim McPherson tainted you just by his mere proximity. You are in danger of further, lasting corruption, and I must preserve you before you capitulate. It's too late. You've been living in sin. But I can absolve you."

"You mean because I'm staying with Jim? I'm not living in sin. I'm in hiding. From you! If you hadn't been after me, hadn't sent me those clues, I wouldn't have been forced from my home. The world isn't ruining me. You are!"

"It's police work. Politics. Only a matter of time. I asked you on one date, and you accepted right away. No hesitation, no courtship. You're on the verge, Princess. The machinations of the evildoers are everywhere, and I must protect you from them."

"It's the twenty-first century, Scott."

"Phillip!"

"I'm not a damsel in distress, and I certainly don't need a prince to rescue me." She tugged at her bindings, then cried in frustration at their rigidity.

He laughed. "Rest now, Sleeping Beauty. Your time is nearly nigh."

She jerked and writhed, pulled on her restraints until they dug painfully into her flesh. "You sick fuck! Let me the hell out of here!"

"Tsk-tsk. Such language is unbecoming a lady of your stature. I must teach you a lesson."

"Untie me, and we'll see who teaches who what."

"Whom. Really, Aurora. You're better than this."

"Let me go!"

"You must atone before you can move on. Mother demands purity."

"Your mother is dead! She can't demand anything of you anymore."

"Mother is always with me." He raised a syringe and squirted some liquid out of it. The liquid arch splashed on her arm. Light glinted off the needle, the uplifting sparkle a mocking contrast to the ominous chemical inside.

She thrashed again and strained against her bindings.

Scott merely shook his head. "Do you realize we've known each other sixteen days, Aurora? A magical number, sixteen." He injected the compound into her arm. After he removed the needle, he stabbed it into the fleshy part of her fingertip.

Chelsea stared at the drop of blood that pooled there, her vision blurring until all she could see was a crimson smear on the sheet.

Scott spoke again, his voice distorted and sounding far away. "And before the sun sets on their sixteenth day together, he shall prick her finger, then she will die."

The SOB had this quote wrong, too.

She tried to tell him, but her tongue was thick, her thoughts sluggish. Then, once again, her world went dark.

Chapter Forty-Seven

Jim DIALED his captain on speakerphone as he stepped into boxers.

"Where the hell have you been?"

"I dropped Sullivan off at the hospital on my way home. I needed a shower. Never would have left her if I'd spoken to Naylor first."

"No one's answering at the hospital."

"What?"

"Sullivan's phone goes straight to voicemail."

"Maybe she had to turn it off because of hospital machines or something."

"The unit on Sully isn't answering, either. I sent Norm and Charlie to check on things. You have any idea what's going on down there?"

Jim's foot tangled in his pant leg, and he nearly took a header into his dresser. Managed to catch his balance, but only after stubbing his toe on the steamer trunk at the foot of his bed. He rattled off a string of curse words.

"And what the fuck's going on with you?"

"Sorry. Tripped. I'm headed to the hospital now. Sullivan's in danger. Naylor — the detective I've been talking to across the river? He put a few missing pieces together for me. Allison Parker is an earlier Grimm Reaper victim. And we're pretty sure Scott Fletcher took her body from the ME's office."

"Our ME?"

"Yeah." He pulled his shirt on over his head. "I'll catch you up later. I need to get to the hospital. Can you send someone downstairs to pick up Fletcher for questioning?"

"Already on it. Get in here. Now."

"But Chelsea—"

"Isn't at the hospital. Units aren't there, either. Norm just texted. He and Charlie are staying behind to watch Sully."

"I'll be there in five." Jim sat on his bed to pull on socks.

"And we need to talk about the locker room incident."

"More important things to do now, Captain. I'm on my way. And don't let anyone near Fletcher. He's mine."

"WHAT DO you mean no one knows where Fletcher is?" Jim paced Davenport's office. He desperately needed to break something, punch someone.

Where was that little shit, Thompson? Wouldn't mind going a few rounds with him if Fletcher wasn't available.

"He called off sick yesterday. Didn't even call in today. Sent some unis over to his place. No one was there. Not even any signs that he'd been there recently."

"Anyone check with that theater troupe he does make-up for?"

"Yes, Jim. I've done this a time or two before."

"Sorry."

"They haven't heard from him, either. But we did get this security footage from the hospital." He tapped a few keys on his laptop then turned it so Jim could see the screen.

A man in scrubs and a lab coat was talking to Sullivan outside her dad's room. She didn't look frightened. Probably Sully's doctor. Or a doctor on that floor.

"Someone approach her after they talk?"

"Just watch. Carefully."

Jim bent down to study the image better. "He looks familiar."

Sullivan started walking away from him. His hand came up just as she stepped out of view of the camera.

"Rewind that. What was in his hand?"

"Pretty sure it's a syringe."

"Is that Fletcher?" He leaned in closer. "Oh, my God. That's the guy in the vehicle on the wolf guy's neighbors' security cam."

"There's a sentence you don't hear every day."

"That's proof it's Fletcher! He made himself up to look like that."

"No, it's circumstantial evidence that the grainy footage you have from the old couple matches the slightly less grainy footage we have from the hospital. You and I both know it's Fletcher, but we don't even have enough for a warrant yet."

"But what about his name on the ME's visitor log the night Allison Parker's body went missing?"

"Jim, I don't even know if we have enough to prove the Parker case is the first of the Grimm Reaper killings."

"Come on, Captain. It has to be. Well, an earlier one, anyway. I was thinking it was his first, but there's no way to know for sure. There could be bodies out there we haven't found yet from before Parker. Bodies we may never find."

"It's not enough. We need a smoking gun."

"He doesn't use a fucking gun!"

"You know what I mean."

"We've got plenty. An early vic—"

"Possible vic."

"With a similar fairy tale MO. Fletcher's name on the visitor's log the night that body disappeared. He had access and means to transport a body."

"He did."

"We have a series of bodies here, also staged to look like fairy tales. We have him on camera near the guy with the missing wolf—"

"We don't know it's him."

"Come on, Cap. The guy's a make-up master. He made me look like I was sixty. It would be nothing for him to change his appearance. And he used the exact same make-up for the doctor at the hospital as he did on the old couple's camera."

"But we can't prove that person was Fletcher."

"What about the lab results? Naylor told me SUX doesn't stay in the body long. Our ME should have known that, explained the difference between SUX and SMC. He didn't because he knew if this ever went to trial, a defense attorney could have that thrown out. Or at least cast serious doubts on its validity. Plus, as a doctor, he has access to SUX."

"Fletcher doesn't work with living patients. He'd have no reason to obtain SUX."

"You seriously don't think he could get access to it? The hospital is probably full of the stuff. And he's in and out of there all the time."

"All circumstantial!" Davenport sighed. "Jim, we have to think rationally and do this by the book. Or he could walk."

"We'd have to bring him in for him to walk away."

"You and I both *know* it's Fletcher. But we can't *prove* it. Not yet."

"But Sullivan can," Jim said. "We have to assume he abducted her."

"We can assume someone has. Unless you have a better reason for her to be MIA?"

"Of course not."

"Then we have a missing cop, assumed abducted by a serial killer. Which means I can alert every department in the state to be on the lookout for … "

"For Fletcher."

"No. Can't do that. I'll have to release the image of the doctor who took her."

"He looks nothing like Fletcher in that make-up."

Davenport sighed. "Does it even fucking matter? This guy can look like anybody. We could send his real photo and the one from the hospital. For all I know, he could turn himself into a woman and walk right through this door, and we'd never know. How can anyone be expected to spot a chameleon?"

"Release what you have. I need to find Sullivan. Every second she's with him … " But he couldn't finish the thought.

"How long has the Grimm Reaper been keeping his vics before … " He closed his eyes, took a deep breath, then looked at Jim. "Before killing them?"

"Fletcher wrote those reports. Can't trust anything in them."

"But if you could?"

He shrugged. "Twenty-four hours. One a day longer, one a little less. But he likes Chelsea."

"And does that mean he'll end it quickly for her or draw it out?"

"I have no fucking idea. We need to find her. Now."

"So, any idea where he might have her?"

"We need to go over every detail of every version of Sleeping Beauty. Sullivan has a first edition Brothers Grimm book, but I don't think Fletcher's working out of the same one. He has an old version, but not as old as hers. So there's no way of knowing what details he might seize on or which edition he's working from."

"Get to work on that," Davenport said. "I'm going to pull up everything we've got on Fletcher."

Jim headed back to his desk. Fucking fairy tales. Some knight in shining armor he was turning out to be. He had no idea where the princess was, so how was he supposed to slay the beast who'd taken her?

Chapter Forty-Eight

T**HIS** T**IME**, when Chelsea woke, the room was dark. It was also colder, if possible, and smelled faintly of burning rubber, rotten eggs, and lingering candle scents. Scott had turned out all the lights and closed the door, cloaking her in a stygian shroud.

The unknown was so much worse. The ceiling that had earlier seemed low enough to touch now receded into infinity. The warm, lustrous walls also faded into nothingness, making the room seem as vast as space itself. And equally cold and lonely.

She strained her ears, listening for a clue to her situation. Had she been moved? Was she alone?

A soft snore beside her cut through the silence. Oh, God. Was he in bed with her? Had he …?

Chelsea shifted her weight. Sleeves tangled around her arms, pant legs bunched at her ankles. She was still clothed. At least she had that going for her. That, and she wasn't dead.

Why wasn't she dead?

He'd spoken the quote from the story. Mangled it to

serve his purposes, but he'd said the words. And pricked her finger. By all accounts, she should have been injected with SUX, stripped naked, then displayed …

No point in dwelling on that thought.

Where the heck was she, anyway?

In the Grimm version of the story, Aurora and her family slept in the castle. The good fairy made bushes grow around it to keep out intruders. At least, until Prince Phillip came to rescue her.

Where in Steel City was a castle surrounded by overgrown shrubbery? Nowhere.

Had he taken her from the city?

She had to get out of there. He was in the room, so if she could get free, she could trap him inside then run. As far as plans went, it wasn't a good one. But it was all she had.

Chelsea started pulling at the bindings. She couldn't tug and jerk them — the movement of the mattress would alert him to her activities. It would be a long, slow process. Torturous. Still, it was her only hope.

She worked methodically. The binding on her right hand had the most give, so she focused on it even though she kept working on the left, too. Her skin burned where the rope rubbed. Something warm and wet trickled down her arm — blood.

The love song from *Phantom of the Opera* began playing, startling her. She whipped her head toward the song and saw a small burst of blue light.

A few bars later, the music stopped. A soft scratch sounded, then came the warm flicker of flame on a matchstick. Scott began lighting candles around the small room, and despite herself, Chelsea craved the little bit of warmth they provided.

As he walked around her, she pressed her arm against

the mattress so he couldn't see what she'd done. She was surprised to find he hadn't shared the bed with her but had instead slept on a cot he'd set up next to her.

Made sense — he was obsessed with preserving his perception of her innocence.

Scott looked at his phone then set it on his cot. "Six on the dot. Time to rise and shine."

Six in the morning. McPherson had to be combing the streets for her. She needed to stall. Engage Scott in conversation. Give the police time to track her whereabouts.

He stretched, yawned, looked down at her. "Did you sleep well?"

"Why didn't you kill me?"

An oily smile snaked across his face. "Are you in a hurry to die?"

"No. But you pricked my finger. I thought …"

"I see. Well, it might interest you to know that I injected you shortly after midnight. That started the clock. Twenty-four hours with you before I have to finish your tale."

"Why prick me then if we're not at the end?"

"The princess slumbers for a long while."

"No." She shook her head while searching for something to say that would prolong the conversation. "I don't think so. That doesn't fit your pattern."

His expression hardened. "I was tired. And you, my feisty princess, aren't to be trusted on your own."

She sighed.

And just like that, he was affable again. "Would you like something to eat?"

"No, thanks. I don't have much of an appetite."

"Nonsense. I have a larder full of delights. I'll be back shortly. I need to go yonder to prepare your feast." He patted her foot on his way out of the room. When he opened the door, a gust of cold air blew in. All the candles flickered, and a few died out.

A larder? He was delusional. And completely mercurial. Maybe he was bipolar. Or had one of any number of psychological conditions.

Of course, he had a host of mental disorders. What little she knew of his family life made them practically inevitable.

Her heart sank. He was disturbed. Certifiable. And if he really believed in the story, she'd never convince him to let her go.

Yonder. He said he had to go yonder to prepare her feast. That meant she was alone. An outbuilding of some sort? A garage? A shed? It wasn't much to work with, but every clue helped.

She continued straining to get free, wincing and hissing as the ropes rubbed her flesh raw. But a little pain wouldn't stop her. Her only chance was to slip free, and she was making progress. There was more play in bindings. Time ticked on, though she had no sense of its passing. Could have been one minute, could have been an hour.

Then his footsteps sounded, soft taps with a gritty, grating undertone. Kind of like cinders on asphalt. Definitely no carpeting out there. Another clue.

When he opened the door, she craned her neck to get a glimpse of what lay beyond her opulent prison. But he closed it again before she could see anything.

Scott carried a tray to the bed then set it on her pelvis. One dish, covered with a silver dome. Chelsea had no idea what he'd made, but the smells wafting to her made her stomach growl. Still, after the bastardized version of Hansel and Gretel he'd told, he'd have to pry her jaw open and force feed her to make her take a single bite.

He sat beside her and began doing something with the food. The tray wiggled on her abdomen and pressed on her bladder. It took all her effort not to relieve herself in the bed.

"I'm sorry I can't release you. But I can't trust you won't run. Never fear, though. I am happy to feed you."

"I don't want anything."

"Don't be silly. Of course, you do. Besides, you need to keep up your strength."

"What for?"

He inhaled sharply, then vented slowly. "Mind your tone."

"No."

The silverware banged as he slammed it down. He stood, picked up the tray, then deposited it on his cot.

At least her bladder felt better. A little.

When he turned, he'd composed himself. His words were measured, his tone controlled. "Very well. If you don't wish to dine, why don't we sing?"

"How about Awolnation's 'Jailbreak'?"

He scowled. "Sarcasm is not befitting someone of your station. I'm trying to make your last day special, Aurora. I think a little gratitude is in order."

"Fuck off."

Scott strode to the door. "You obviously need some time to yourself. Make wise use of it. It's your last chance to make peace with your fate." He left, slamming the door behind him.

A few more candles blew out.

Chelsea struggled with the ropes, fought with all her might to get free. He'd left the silverware. If she got loose, she'd have a fork, maybe a knife, at her disposal.

She didn't know how much time she had but suspected it wasn't a lot. Scott had a fantasy he wanted to act out, and the clock had started ticking when he'd last stuck her with a needle.

Faster, faster … just a little more.

Her skin burned, screamed. But she didn't slow. Blood seeped from the self-inflicted wounds, lubricating her wrists.

Finally, her right hand popped free. She fumbled with the left binding, then the ropes at her feet. When she stood, she nearly collapsed. Her feet had fallen asleep, and the pins-and-needles feeling shot up her legs.

Chelsea ignored the sensation and hobbled over to the tray. Jackpot — fork and knife. Clutching one in each hand, she crept across the room.

Her slick hand slipped on the doorknob, then she tried it with the other. Locked. Of course.

She turned her head to press her ear to the door. While she listened for any noise outside the room, her gaze landed on cot.

He'd forgotten his phone!

Chelsea ran to it, dropped the silverware, snatched up the device. Her hand was bloody, the slippery fluid nearly causing the phone to slip through her fingers. As soon as she gained control of it, she tried to open it.

Crap. Password-protected.

She couldn't call McPherson, so she dialed 911.

"This is 911. How may I help you?" The dispatcher's voice cut in and out. It was hard to parse the message, harder still to hear.

Chelsea fumbled with the volume as she walked around the room, trying to do better than a single bar of service.

"I'm Detective Chelsea Sullivan of the Steel City Police Department," she said quietly. "I need you to put a trace on this line right now and connect me with Detective Jim McPherson in Zone Four."

"Hello?

She repeated herself word for word, but slower and slightly louder.

"Ma'am, it is a crime to make prank calls to 911." The connection was cutting in and out, but the message was clear enough.

"This is not a prank!" Chelsea didn't feel safe speaking above a whisper, but she tried to sound as harsh and authoritative as possible.

Another rumble sounded, faint then growing louder. At the peak of the noise, the floor vibrated beneath her. She spoke over the din, reciting her badge number and again requesting a trace on the call. As the rumble and racket diminished, she said, "I've been abducted and am being held against my will. I don't know where I am, but my life is in jeopardy. I need backup. Immed—"

The door flung open then banged against the wall. Scott snatched the device from her hand then tried to end the call with a quick stab on the screen.

She shrieked and turned to run. Plowed into him, taking them both to the ground. The phone was knocked free of his grip. It bounced under the bed.

Scott groped for his cell with one hand while holding onto her ankle with the other.

Chelsea screamed as she fought to kick free of his hold. "Scott Fletcher has me! Scott Fletcher!"

JIM PUSHED HARDER on his already-floored gas pedal. Forty-five miles and three counties in just over thirty minutes. Had to be some kind of record.

Which didn't mean a damn thing if he was too late.

Davenport had sent units to the hospital and Fletcher's

home, but Jim didn't think it would be that simple. Sleeping Beauty was kept in a castle surrounded by overgrowth. The morgue certainly didn't fit the bill, and Fletcher's mansion on Millionaire's Row didn't, either. It was a lot bigger than a house, though it was by no means a castle. And though it was covered in ivy, it was still very much in the city and not a forest.

On a hunch, Jim had decided to try Fletcher's childhood home. It had taken a considerable amount of digging into his early life to find the information, but when he did, it all made sense.

Fletcher's mother had died recently, not long before the murders began. Scott, her only living descendant, had inherited everything.

Including a small house in the woods in Mission Station — Aldrin County.

It wasn't a castle in the traditional sense of the word. But every man's home is his castle, and this one was in a fucking forest.

Every fiber of his body knew Sullivan was in Mission Station. He didn't doubt that.

What he doubted was that he'd get there in time.

He called Naylor as he was closing in on Fletcher's childhood homestead. "Hey, listen. I kind of need a favor."

"Last thing I did for you got me in trouble with my ME."

"My partner's life is on the line."

Naylor sighed. "What can I do for you?"

"I'm a bit out of my jurisdiction here. Mind meeting me? Maybe bringing a uniform or two you trust?" Jim parked a few doors down from the old Fletcher residence. A light was on in the home, but there were no signs of activity.

"Where are you?"

He gave Naylor the address and a brief rundown of the situation as he crept up the road. "I'm approaching the house now."

"Wait for backup. I'm already headed to my car."

"Can't. My partner might be in there. If you don't find us inside, check the rest of the property, any outbuildings. Maybe the tree line. This place is in the sticks. If she's been screaming for help, no one heard her."

"McPherson! I can be there in five minutes."

"Then you'll catch up soon." Jim ended the call. Put his phone on silent, so any incoming communications didn't give away his position. He took his service weapon from his holster then peeked in the side window.

Though a table lamp was lit, there was no indication anyone was home.

The rapid, rhythmic *click-clack, click-clack* of a train pulled his attention from the house to the back of the property. Tracks ran parallel to the river, but to his knowledge, there was no longer any rail service on this line, which went all the way into the city. Admittedly, he was no expert, but he found it odd. He walked around to the back of the property. There were footprints in the snow. Several sets.

He shone his flashlight on them. Not several sets. One set — male, average size. In two directions. At least two trips. No female prints, but if Fletcher took Sullivan out here, it was when she was knocked out, and he would have had to carry her.

The flash of red and blue indicated Naylor was near. Still, he didn't have time to wait. He turned toward the back door of the house.

But as the noise from the retreating train died down, Jim swore he heard Chelsea's voice.

Swore she was screaming Fletcher's name.

Swore the sound was coming from one of the coke ovens across the tracks.

Which was exactly where the footprints headed. And where a loud bellow emanated before evaporating in the wind.

So Jim dashed in that direction.

Chapter Forty-Nine

CHELSEA'S FLIGHT or fight response cranked all the way to crush, kill, destroy.

"What have you done?" Scott bellowed. His nails dug into the friction burn around her ankle.

As she struggled to pull free from his grip, she cocked her other leg back. Her foot exploded forward, connecting with his nose.

An inhuman howl escaped him. He released his hold on her to clutch his face. Blood dripped from his fingers.

She popped up, darted for the door.

He plowed into her, tackled her to the ground.

The air whooshed out of her lungs. Breath eluded her. Her eyes watered. Tears stung the fresh scrape on her cheek. She gasped, choked. Sputtered.

Scott ground her face deeper into the floor. He shifted his weight, jabbed his elbow into her spine.

She shrieked.

Then, as fast as he'd pinned her, he let her go. "Look what you made me do! Your complexion, marred! Our special day, ruined!"

Chelsea didn't give a flying fig about her complexion. She jumped to her feet then lunged for the cot.

Scott tripped her, and she crashed to the ground. He rolled, stretched under the bed. Came up with the phone, held it aloft. "A-ha! It was off the whole time! They'll never find you!"

Her heart sank. The operator didn't believe her, and he'd managed to hit the "end" button before the fight before she'd screamed his name. It was going to go down as a prank call. Everything she'd done to get free, to get help — it was all for nothing.

He walked toward her. "It's over, Aurora. I win."

No. She couldn't let him win. Wouldn't. She panted for breath. Groped behind her for the discarded flatware or anything else she could use as a weapon. "That's not my name. And this isn't how my story ends."

Scott swiped at the blood pouring from his twisted nose. Bruises were already forming under his eyes. He gingerly pressed his fingers to his face. "I think you broke it. You. My demure princess. I knew you'd been corrupted!"

Chelsea's fingers wrapped around the handle of the knife. "I'm not a princess!" Wailing a banshee's war cry, she plunged the blade into his chest.

Instead of embedding in his flesh, the flatware bent. She relaxed her hand and watched the useless utensils tumble to the floor.

"I told you, this is our special day. The finale of your story. And it will end as I choose, before midnight." He unzipped his cardigan and opened it, kind of like a flasher exposing himself.

Chelsea hung her head. It was no ordinary cardigan. It was one of those intelligent garments that had pouches for phones, tablets, wallets, keys … even water bottles. And in one of the pockets, the one she'd connected with, was a book.

Scott reached for it, pulled it free. Showed her the cover.

101 Fairy Tales.

The book wasn't as old as her father's, which might explain why the details he knew about the stories weren't the same as the ones she knew. But there was no doubt in her mind the pages of the Sleeping Beauty story were well-read.

He walked to the bed, patted the mattress. "Come. Lie down. I'll read to you before you slumber."

Chelsea glanced at the door. He stood between her and her exit. And his ankles weren't bloody and swollen.

"Tsk tsk tsk." He shook his head.

She had no escape.

"Come on. We have time for one story."

If he was reading, he wasn't killing. If she had to, she'd convince him to orate the entire book.

Scott patted the mattress again.

She limped to the bed, then climbed onto it.

"Do I need to restrain you? I'd like to think we can spend these last few minutes trusting each other."

"You don't have to."

"You'll be good?"

What was she? An infant? "Yes. I'll behave."

"Wonderful." He sat beside her, opened the book so she could see it. Flipped to the page that Aurora's story began on. Scott cleared his throat. "'The Sleeping Beauty in the Woods.'"

"Wait."

He looked at her, brows drawn. "What?"

"I already know this story."

"I should think so. It's yours."

"Read me one I don't know."

"Don't you know all of them? You told me your father read them to you."

"I've blocked out so much of that time. Read me another story. A different one. Your favorite."

"This is my favorite."

"Fine. Then read me your second favorite."

He studied her for a long while. Finally, he said, "'The Story of the Youth Who Went Forth to Learn What Fear Was' is one I'm fond of. Do you know it?"

She did, but she wasn't about to admit it. "No. Would you read it to me?"

"Very well." He leafed through the book, found the story, and began reading it in his theater voice, the timbre rich and melodic.

She tried to plot another escape, her gaze darting around the room, looking for any possible weapon. There was nothing.

Scott rambled on about the boy who didn't know fear. He was brave and bold and dared to accept a frightening challenge to win the hand of a princess. After lasting three nights against various horrors, he wed the king's daughter, but he never learned fear.

If her life wasn't forfeit, she'd feel sorry for Scott. Of course, that was his favorite story. As a child, he was probably frightened by everything. Only made sense that he'd relate to that tale.

That hardly made him a sympathetic character now.

"The End."

Already?

Scott closed the cover.

She'd never seen such an ominous sight.

"And now, it's time." He turned to put the book on the cot beside the bed.

Chelsea lunged at him, punched him in his broken nose.

He yelled and grabbed his face.

She raked her nails down his hand, then pushed him off the side of the bed.

Scott howled when he hit the floor with a thud.

Chelsea bolted for the door. Her fingers, slick from his blood, slipped on the knob. Arms wrapped around her from behind.

He lifted her, flung her into the corner. Pain exploded in her shoulder as she crashed into the wall, in her temple, when her head smacked the floor.

Ears rang. Vision blurred. The coppery tang of blood bloomed on her tongue.

Scott stalked toward her, each footstep portending her doom.

One chance. She only had one chance. Chelsea lurched to her feet. The room tilted, spun. Listed to the side.

She fought for her footing and launched at him. No longer able to see, to hear, she pummeled anything within her reach, her arms raining a wild flurry of blows on something. Anything. Someone.

Him.

Chelsea swung again and again until her arms were numb, and her knuckles cried for her to stop.

But she didn't.

She clobbered and walloped and battered with blind, righteous fury.

When her arms were pinned, and she was lifted, so her feet were off the ground, she kicked. Thrashed. Butted her head back.

"Chelsea! Chelsea! Shh. Shh. I've got you. Settle down. I've got you. It's over."

That voice. She knew that voice. Not any of Scott's various affectations. It was a deep, soothing voice. It meant protection, safety. Security.

Her body stilled. The arms around her and body behind her radiated warmth and strength. She took a deep breath. Sandalwood. Mint. "Jim?"

"Right here. You're safe. It's over." He put her down, released his hold.

She tried to turn around, but her legs couldn't hold her up. He swept her off her feet.

Chelsea knew it was him. Knew his smell, his sound. She allowed him to carry her until a blast of cold air hit her face, assaulted her lungs. Her eyelids fluttered open.

Jim.

She sobbed and wrapped her arms tighter around him.

He crooned in her ear and held her close, allowing her to melt down in his embrace as he took her to freedom.

<h1 style="text-align:center">Chapter Fifty</h1>

WHAT A DIFFERENCE A DAY MADE. After doctors checked Chelsea out at the hospital, they wanted to keep her for observation. A suggestion she flatly refused. And because Jim had refused to leave her side, she had a ride home.

She had missed her bed. And slept better than she had in days.

Now, they both sat in the bullpen, surrounded by their fellow detectives and a few uniforms from downstairs. Chelsea stared at Jim's computer screen. He'd navigated to a local news site. A picture of the coke ovens in Mission Station filled the screen.

He smiled at her, then he looked at the group of detectives clustered around their workstation. "Quiet down."

She fought to keep the smile from her face as Jim read the news story aloud. She managed to keep her pleasure from showing, but she couldn't keep her cheeks from burning.

"'Fletcher's reign of terror was brought to an end by Detective Chelsea Sullivan, who was kidnapped, tortured, and held hostage by him in a windowless room constructed inside one of the unused coke ovens in Mission Station. Then she turned the tables. After obtaining his phone and placing a 911 call, Sullivan single-handedly subdued the Grimm Reaper until her partner, Detective Jim McPherson, arrived with help from the local PD. Fletcher is recovering in the hospital under armed guard and will be arraigned once released.'" He looked up at her. "Looks like we've got a genuine hero in our midst."

The squad burst into applause. Norm started a chorus of "For She's a Jolly Good Fellow."

Chelsea was unable to keep the smile from her face.

When the song ended, Davenport said, "Don't you all have work to do?"

They returned to work, some giving her nods or pats on the back before walking away.

"You two, with me." Davenport walked to his office, and Chelsea and Jim followed. "Close the door." Once they were seated, he said, "Damn fine work, Sullivan."

"Thank you, sir."

"You, too, McPherson."

"It was all her."

Could her cheeks burn hotter? "It was a team effort, Captain."

"A team I put together. I knew you two were a good match."

The answer was yes. Yes, her face could flame hotter. She was surprised she hadn't spontaneously combusted yet.

Chelsea cleared her throat. "We looked into Mason's involvement. He was the one who sent you the package from California, but there's nothing to indicate he was complicit with Fletcher's scheme. He was just doing his boss a favor."

"Strange fucking favor," Jim said.

"True." Davenport nodded. "But Fletcher is a strange

fucking guy. I mean, stealing and killing a wolf to make fake jaws from its teeth? Why not just sic the real wolf on the girl?"

"Because it would have marred her," Chelsea said. "He was furious with me for getting a brush burn on my cheek. He thought of his victims as art, and a real wolf would have ruined his work."

"Sick fuck," Jim said.

"DNA is back," the captain said. "Every corpse was found with a hair, and each strand was a match to Fletcher. Dumbass left us a way to pin every murder on him."

"Makes sense." She shrugged. "He couldn't sign his masterpieces with a signature. That was the only way he could tag the work."

"Is he going to get off with an insanity plea?" Jim asked.

"I don't know," Davenport said. "He's one twisted SOB. Delusional. Still, I think there's a case to be made that he knew what he was doing when he was doing it."

"He called me Aurora."

"What?" Jim and Davenport said in unison.

"At some point, after he'd taken me, he stopped calling me Chelsea. I don't think he knew me as me any longer. Not entirely, anyway. He knew my supposed indiscretions, but I was no longer Chelsea Sullivan to him. Maybe he didn't know himself, either. His voice changed, and he referred to himself as Phillip. Slipped once and called himself Hansel."

"Like the brother of Gretel?" Jim asked.

"I still haven't told you everything he told me when he had me. His childhood …" She shuddered. "If he does plead insanity, I would understand."

"Well, his mental state is for the courts to decide,"

Davenport said. "In the meantime, I want you to take a few days off, Sullivan."

"The doctor cleared me. I'm fine."

"Take the time. I'm sure your dad could use the help."

"But—"

"It's not up for debate. The chief wants you two doing press on this. That means you have to look your best. At the moment, you don't. So, go. Heal. Come back refreshed."

"But—"

"You're dismissed."

In the bullpen, she looked at Jim and wrinkled her nose. "Press?"

"It's all part of the job." He followed her back to their desks. "Seriously, Chels. You did great work."

"Thank you."

"But it wouldn't hurt to rest."

She rolled her eyes. "I am fine, you know."

"I know. But I'd rather my partner not be the walking dead. You've got so many bandages, you look like a mummy."

"*The Walking Dead* is about zombies."

"I'm not talking about the show." He ran his hand through his hair. "You had me scared out of my mind."

Chelsea patted his cheek. "Like you said when you found me, it's okay." She pulled on her coat and grabbed her bag. "But if I have to take time off, I'm going to spend it with my dad. When I come back, I'll be bandage-free. In the meantime, try to stay out of trouble."

"No promises."

"You can handle the press without me if you'd like."

"No chance. You're the star."

She stuck her tongue out at him.

He laughed and waved goodbye.

Chelsea walked down to the lower level, then headed for the back parking lot. As she passed the stairs to the morgue, a shudder ran through her. But she didn't slow her stride.

Before heading to her dad's, she stopped at the library and made her way to the customer service desk. "Could you tell me who I should speak to about donating a first edition children's book to your collection?"

"One moment." The librarian placed an in-house call. She spoke to someone in hushed tones, then she hung up. "Maeve will be right with you."

"Thanks." Chelsea waited off to the side until a thin, white-haired woman in a tailored pantsuit approached.

"Hello. I'm Maeve Donnelly. You inquired about donating to our collection?"

"Yes." Chelsea reached into her bag and produced the book. "It's been in my family for a while. My father assures me it's a first edition."

Maeve held out her hands. "May I?" After Chelsea passed her the book, she walked to the customer service desk to examine the offering. She studied the binding, leafed through the pages, ran her finger over some of the drawings. Even bent down and sniffed it. Then she turned to the copyright page. "Miss …"

"Sullivan. Call me Chelsea."

"Chelsea, this book is worth a lot of money. Are you sure you want to part with it?"

Was she ever. "I'm sure."

"And you don't want to loan it to us. You want to gift it?"

"That's correct. I'm done with fairy tales."

"But it's a family heirloom."

"Trust me. I won't miss this book. It's yours."

"Well, thank you. If you give me a moment, I'll get you

a receipt for your records."

"No, thanks."

"But, for tax purposes, you'll need a record of your donation."

No way would she take any remuneration for that book — not even on her taxes. She'd burn the darn thing before making any money off it. "Goodbye, Miss Donnelly."

As Chelsea drove to her father's house, she started to worry. Maybe Dad wouldn't be okay with her giving the book away.

When she reached his apartment, she turned the knob. Locked. She looked under the mat. No key. Good for him. He was finally acting like a cop.

Former cop.

As she rooted in her bag for the key, the door opened.

"Chelsea." Dad stepped into the hall and wrapped her in a hug.

She melted into his embrace, content to listen to his heart beat.

"Come in. I was just fixing myself a snack. We'll have a bite to eat and catch up."

When she entered, the scent of sauce wafted to her from the kitchen. "What are you snacking on? Lasagna?"

He chuckled. "Pizza. I was feeling peckish. Come to the kitchen. I'll get you a plate."

Eating in the kitchen? From a plate? Who was this man, and what had he done with her father?

She followed him through the apartment. It was even cleaner than she'd left it. He'd gotten rid of all the clutter in the living room, and the soft scent of lemon furniture polish lingered in the air. In the kitchen, the table was, in fact, clear of newspapers and mail, and the top had been buffed to a soft sheen. "Place looks great, Dad."

He put a pizza-filled plate in front of each of their

chairs, then he pulled hers out for her.

After he took his seat, she grabbed his hand. "Hey. Is everything okay?"

"I could ask you the same thing, Chels. You really put yourself at risk."

"It's part of the job."

"One your mother hated. I didn't understand what I put her through. Not until I almost lost you."

She squeezed his fingers.

"I'm sorry, Chelsea. I've made a lot of mistakes. But I've turned over a new leaf. I'm taking my medicine, not drinking. I know it's going to be hard, but I'm really going to try."

"And I'll be here, every step of the way. Cheering you on, helping you. Whatever you need."

He lifted her hand to his lips and kissed her knuckles. "You scared me."

"That seems to be the general consensus."

"Your partner, too? McPherson, is it?"

She nodded. "The whole department."

"If everyone was concerned, that should have told you something. You shouldn't be so rash."

"I come by it honestly."

Dad smiled.

"And you can hardly blame me for being abducted."

He shook his head. "Eat up."

As she took her first bite, she looked around the immaculate kitchen. Dad had cut out every article that had run on the Grimm Reaper. The one with her picture instead of Fletcher's was in the center of the collection.

Dad put down his slice then wiped his fingers and hands on a napkin. "Davenport said the train on the 911 call helped the cops locate you."

"It did, I suppose. They probably would have been

there sooner, but the dispatcher initially thought I was making a prank call."

"You know there's been no trains running since 2016."

"What are you saying? The tracks are haunted? I heard them, Dad. I *felt* them rumble past."

He laughed. "No. The company running it used to have scenic tours from June to October, but they closed down because they couldn't afford the expense. Owner thought if they could make it an all-year event, they could turn a profit. Been testing the winter readiness of the trains and the tracks. You couldn't have been luckier."

"Well, Jim had it figured out, anyway, so it didn't really matter."

"I think I'd like to meet this fellow."

"Sure." She took another bite of pizza and burned the roof of her mouth.

"Rail tours are almost certainly going to resume now that there's a murder scene on the route. Maybe we could all go."

She looked up at him, jaw already hanging open because of the scalding cheese.

Dad burst into laughter. "You should see your face! Priceless."

"You're not funny."

"Yes, I am." He took another bite. "I still want to meet this guy, though."

They made small talk as they munched on their pizza — for frozen, it was pretty good. When they were through, he insisted on doing the dishes himself.

"At least let me dry."

"I'll wash and dry. You can wrap the leftovers."

"Okay." Chelsea took foil from the drawer. "Dad, I need to tell you something."

"Go ahead."

She tore a sheet from the box, the ripping sound cutting harshly through the calm of the kitchen. "I got rid of your book."

He stopped scrubbing, turned, and looked at her.

Chelsea rushed on before he could say anything. "I'm sorry. I know it was important to you. But after what happened, I didn't want the reminder in my house. Or even in yours. I didn't want it anywhere near me. I gave it to the library. I'm really—"

"Hey!"

She stopped. Blinked. Waited for the tirade.

Dad held his soapy hands up like a surgeon and pressed a kiss on her forehead. "I'm not happy you donated it."

Chelsea swallowed, the action painful because of the lump in her throat.

"You should have burned the damn thing."

She let the tears fall. "You're not upset?"

"I have you. That's all that matters. Not some dumb book." He dried his hands. "Now, want to see if we can find a hockey game?"

"It's eleven o'clock in the morning."

"There's probably a rerun on the hockey channel. And we play DC tonight. We could make a day of it."

"I do hate Washington."

"That's my girl." He took two sodas from the refrigerator, grabbed a bag of chips from the counter, then walked into the living room.

Chelsea followed. She settled into the corner of the sofa. If she could talk him into ice cream later, it would be a perfect day.

The End

When he was a child, they erased all record of him from the world. Now he's returning the favor.

Jim McPherson grew up with the proverbial silver spoon in his mouth, but he gave it all up for the simple life of a police detective. He thought he'd get some distance from his former jet-set friends, but a serial killer is targeting that exact demographic, and he fears his parents might be on the list.

Pick up your copy of Twice Upon A Lie Today.

About the Author

Nolon King writes fast-paced psychological thrillers set in the glitzy world of entertainment's power players with a bold, insightful voice. He's not afraid to explore the darker side of human nature through stories featuring families torn apart by secrets and lies.

Nolon loves to write about big questions and moral quandaries. How far would you go to cover up an honest mistake? Would you destroy your career to protect your family? How much of your soul would you sell to get the life of your dreams? Would you cheat on your husband to keep your children safe? Would you give in to a stalker's demands to save your marriage?

9 781629 551456